The Skye
in June

ISBN: 1-4196-8966-5
ISBN-13: 9781419689666
Library of Congress Control Number: 2008901064

Visit www.juneahern.com or www.booksurge.com
to order additional copies.

The Skye
in June

J. Ahern

Praise for J. Ahern's "The Skye in June"

From Scotland to San Francisco Ahern's story mixes mystery with humor in her captivating tale of secrets and sisterhood in her first novel, "The Skye in June."

— Daniel Hallford, author of *Upper Noe* and *Pelican Bay*
    danielhallford.com

We need more June Ahern's in this world... smart, irreverent, sassy and deeply dedicated to her wisdom and the natural encouragement of intuition in all children. Her fictional novel portrays her understanding of the psychic world woven around a magical mystery.

— Litany Burns, Clairvoyant/Medium and author of *The Sixth Sense of Children* and *Develop Your Psychic Powers*
    intuitivenation.com

No matter what June writes, her work is colorful, entertaining and insightful. She has a gift for holding the reader's attention. I've enjoyed her writing in all its forms—books, columns, studies—since 1988 and it only gets better.

— Suzette Martinez Standring, author of *The Art of Column Writing: Insider Secrets from Art Buchwald, Dave Barry, Arianna Huffington, Pete Hamill and Other Great Columnists*
    readsuzette.com

Cover art by Cynthia Spurgin

Author photograph Jerry Briesach

Dedication

Jerry, thank you for your unwavering love and support.

Acknowledgments

I would like to thank the following people who helped make this book possible.

A special grateful acknowledgment to Gayvin Powers, my creative colleague, for her editing assistance, guidance and help with manifesting my story into a book. Along the way we both learned so very much and laughed often.

Stacy Horn, my editor for her dedication and patience. My Red Pen Queens who generously read and reread with pens poised; Maria Callaghan and Ellen Pearson, who also kept my Scottish information accurate to the times, Mary Stallings, Terry Gutherie, Veronica Bryan and Deb Zonies, Alice Mollet and Jamie Craddock. Marie Callaghan for her memories of Eureka Valley. Suzette Martinez Standrig for her wisdom and nudge to publish. Doug Zeghibe and his support of my "girl power" story. My son, Daniel, for his seal of approval that the book isn't just for "chicks." My sisters, Ellen, Marie Ann, Patricia, Frances and Teresa——for if it were not for our myriad sisterhood adventures this colorful tale of Catholic schoolgirls might not have been written.

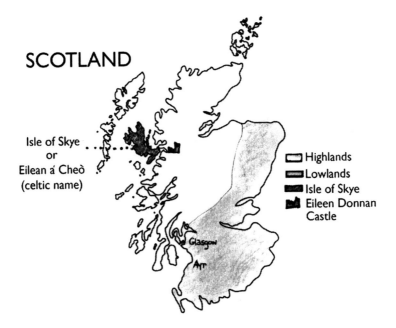

SCOTLAND

Isle of Skye
or
Eilean a' Cheò
(celtic name)

☐ Highlands
▨ Lowlands
■ Isle of Skye
◤ Eileen Donnan
Castle

Glasgow

Ayr

Table of Contents

Chapter One:
Glasgow, Scotland

May 31, 1950

THE RAIN DRIZZLING down the windows of the black taxi shrouded the riders inside. The driver maneuvered his way around the bombed-out rubble and newly constructed tenement buildings in post-war Glasgow. Cathy MacDonald, the sole passenger, leaned her small blonde head against the misted window. She was bound for St. Andrew's Infirmary to deliver yet another bairn.[1]

Cathy's fingers dug into her seat as she readjusted her bulky body. No position seemed to bring relief to her discomfort. She let her head fall forward onto the back of the driver's seat. "Does he have to hit every stone in the road?" she muttered, under her breath as the taxi bumped along.

"Don't you worry, Missus. I'll get you there in time." The rough sandpaper voice of the taxi driver startled her, and she wondered if he had heard her question.

"Your man's Jimmy MacDonald, right?" he inquired.

His talking only irritated her, but not wanting to appear unfriendly she tried to focus on what he had asked. Her response came as a muffled sound that could have been an answer or a retreat from the question. She caught him peeking a glance at her in the

---

[1] Bairn – Scottish for child.

rearview mirror. She braced herself for the next question, knowing what it would be.

"You Mr. B's daughter?" The driver, along with so many others in Glasgow, deeply respected Willie Buchanan, or Mr. B, as he had been known for as far back as anyone could remember. Mr. B had earned a reputation for being a fair man. Years ago he had rallied a group of well-off citizens to provide funds to support youth soccer teams for the town's underprivileged children. He had insisted that the money be shared equally between Catholic and Protestant teams—an unusual act, since prejudice between the two religious groups was still very intense in Scotland. Although some people protested, most citizens supported his efforts.

The taxi swerved sharply to avoid a pile of building rubble. Cathy moaned in protest, which made the driver wish her husband was there to help with the situation.

"Where's Jimmy?" he asked.

"Working," she replied, her voice barely a whisper.

She fell away from the driver's seat and closed her eyes. She took a deep breath in and then blew out sharply as jolting cramps came one after another. *If Jimmy hadn't been so worried about getting to his second job, he could've been with me. He'd tell the driver to slow down*, Cathy thought. She didn't want this ride to be over too quickly. She wasn't ready to walk up the four broad stone steps to St. Andrew's Infirmary to lie on a bed under a stark white sheet waiting. Not wanting to sound demanding, she stopped short of asking the driver to slow down. Instead she moved her hands over her belly and whispered hoarsely, "Wait, wee one. Just a bit longer."

It was eight o'clock at night by the time they arrived at St. Andrew's. Cathy opened the door and paused a moment to breathe in the cool air before struggling to get out. She stood there, swaying, momentarily mesmerized by the silhouette of the full moon in the sky. It would not illuminate the night for a few more hours, when spring's late twilight would drop into darkness. Rain clouds moved above, blanketing the full moon. To Cathy, the light and dark of the Scottish sky was like the passing of time. Gently caressing her belly, she thought of the time when she had stood on a hilltop surrounded by the celestial beauty of the Scottish Highlands. The gibbous moon had hung high in the northern skies as she drew down its power to herself and made a wish for the future. She shuddered as she remembered how a force of energy had surged through her body when she uttered the wish. Exhilarated by the rush of energy, she had mistakenly thought her desire had been granted. Now, in sadness, Cathy looked away before seeing that the clouds were once again revealing the moon.

The driver offered to take Cathy's arm to help her up the steps. "No," she said adamantly, assuring him that she had been on the same journey to the Infirmary enough times before. But he insisted on being of some help to her.

"I don't want your man to think that I didn't take care of his missus," he said jokingly.

She pointed to her small cloth bag. The driver grabbed it and ran up the steps, leaving it at the door. He tipped his cap as he rushed back down to his car. Relieved of his duty, he quickly sped off to find his next fare.

She hesitated for a moment before walking up the steps to St. Andrew's. She reflected on her last five visits to deliver her babies there. She hoped that this birth would be easier. Her legs shook as the life within her pressed downward, reminding her of her reason for being there. She seized hold of the cool metal railing to pull herself up the steps while she supported her huge belly with the other hand. Her well-shaped calves were of little help to her tiny frame burdened by the weight of pregnancy. Painfully, she moved down the corridor of the Infirmary while keeping her moans to a minimum so as not to draw undue attention.

Two nurses met her in the maternity ward. One was a bleached-blonde who Cathy didn't recognize. But she did remember Head Nurse Nell Gunn, the tall, thin nurse who was as stiff as her crisp white uniform, which was always starched to smooth perfection. Nurse Gunn had taken care of Cathy during her past few deliveries. They greeted each other politely as though meeting after a church service.

Nurse Gunn introduced her colleague. "Nurse Lockhart will get you settled in, Mrs. MacDonald. I'll telephone your doctor that you're here."

"Here, let me take your bag," the blonde nurse said cheerily, picking up the cloth bag and escorting Cathy to a birthing room directly across from the nurses' station. She helped her change and get into bed and then gently laid a white sheet over her.

"I'll be right outside if you need me, dear," Nurse Lockhart said. She left the door partially open behind her.

Cathy was all too glad to be left alone. She lay panting, staring at the soft hallway light shining through the half-closed door.

After a while she heard footsteps rapidly clicking on the polished floor outside her room. Head Nurse Gunn entered the birthing room.

"Dr. MacFadden should be here presently. He said the baby was quite overdue and had been expected at the first of May. That means that this *wean's*[2] almost a month late. Is that right, dear?" asked Nurse Gunn.

Cathy only moaned.

"Don't worry Mrs. MacDonald, we'll take good care of you," the nurse said as she rearranged Cathy's sheets before leaving her alone.

Cathy could hear the nurses chatting about personal issues and professional matters. She found their conversation helpful to lessen her discomfort between contractions. In and out of the world

---

[2]   Wean – Scottish for a small baby. In Glasgow, wean commonly refers to children of any age.

around her, between lapses of silence, the time passed with the low murmur of the nurses' voices.

She turned her head to the window and saw that the darkness had finally arrived. Laboriously, she pulled herself up out of the bed and shuffled to the window. The strong beams of the moon's light sprayed across her face as she peeked through the curtains.

Cathy heard Head Nurse Gunn's voice through the partially opened door. "Och, that poor woman. None of her births were easy on her. And that man of hers. God help her having to put up with him."

When the nurse's voice dipped into a whisper Cathy was sure Nurse Gunn was telling Nurse Lockhart about the death of her first born. She also imagined the nurses gossiping about the last time she was at St. Andrew's and how Jimmy had showed up drunk to meet his new wean.

The life within her journeyed further down the channel and Cathy cried, "Oh, oh! Please, no now."

Nurse Gunn appeared at Cathy's side and helped her back to bed.

"Alright, Mrs. MacDonald, let's check and see how we're doing." She laid a file on the bedside table and pulled down the sheet covering Cathy.

Gasping in pain and frustration, Cathy protested the examination. "It's no time. Leave me alone. Please."

She saw the nurse squinting up at the large clock on the wall above the birthing bed. Her pale face bunched up like a shriveled dry apple. "This wean will no wait much longer. I'd say we'll be seeing a new wee MacDonald any minute now."

Firm, measured footsteps coming down the hospital corridor interrupted Nurse Gunn's examination. Nurse Lockhart popped her head into the birthing room to announce Dr. MacFadden's arrival. She scooted into the room just in front of him. The doctor, a tall, six-foot-four Highlander, was a stylishly handsome man. His presence silenced both nurses.

Nurse Lockhart raised her pencil-thin eyebrows at the doctor's sexiness while the thin, dour Nurse Gunn stood ramrod straight awaiting his instructions.

The three stood around Cathy's bed.

"Hello, Mrs. MacDonald. I am glad you came back to visit. But so soon?" the doctor said pleasantly, putting a friendly hand on the pregnant woman's shoulder. He then picked up Cathy's chart from the bedside table and loosening his tie, read in silence. His eyes furrowed deeper.

Cathy watched his face closely. He had been the attending physician at all of her girls' births. She trusted him completely. He knew her greatest hopes and fears.

After her last delivery Dr. MacFadden had tried to convince Cathy not to have any more babies because of the difficulties she had had with each of the births.

He looked at his watch and said, "Labor pains every minute for the past three hours? Well, ladies, let's help Mrs. MacDonald get that baby out before the witching hour is upon us."

Chapter Two:
Battle of Wills

June 1, 1950

B Y EARLY MORNING, the hushed murmur from women lying in hospital beds holding their newborns gave the ward a peaceful, happy feel. Cathy had only a few hours of sleep after delivering her baby in the first hour of the new month. She looked tired but pretty, with a crocheted white bed jacket across her shoulders and her hair pinned back on each side.

"Good morning, Mrs. MacDonald," a cheery voice sang out.

"Oh!" Cathy jumped. Startled by the closeness of the nurse, she hurriedly stuffed a tin-framed photo into her handbag and snapped it shut.

"Mother, here's your bonny wee lassie," said Nurse Hamilton, leaning forward with a small pink bundle to nestle into Cathy's arms. Nurse Hamilton, a tall florid-faced Highlander who had been at St. Andrew's Infirmary for many years, was one of Cathy's favorite nurses.

Cathy immediately moved the blanket back. Tenderly, she traced the roundness of her new daughter's pink face. "We made it, my wee pet," she whispered.

"I heard this birth was the hardest one on you yet. How are you feeling now?"

As she turned to answer, she found Nurse Hamilton gazing lovingly at the picture of Our Lady, the Blessed Virgin Mother, holding Baby Jesus, which hung above the doorway of the maternity ward. She knew the nurse had strong religious beliefs and had seen her saying the Rosary at the bedsides of ailing mothers.

"The Blessed Virgin Mother must have a plan for you and that wean," the nurse said, crossing herself before exclaiming, "Oh, look, a wee tuft of fiery red hair. Lovely, isn't it?"

They looked at a red curl popping out from the pink blanket followed by inquisitive blue eyes that stared up at Cathy. *Surely this baby daughter will capture Jimmy's heart,* Cathy thought. Jimmy had said unkind things to her for not giving him a son, as though his wife gave birth only to girls just to spite him.

A tear dropped from Cathy's eyes onto the baby's face as she ran a finger through the soft tuft of newborn hair.

"You're no crying, are you? Och, it'll be alright, dear. You're just a wee bit tired," said Nurse Hamilton. She separated the curtains and opened a window, allowing fresh air into the room. Cathy breathed in. It was truly a beautiful day in Glasgow.

"She's the spitting image of you. Except for the red hair. Your other weans were all wee blondies, were they no?" Nurse Hamilton asked.

The mother murmured an agreement.

"What will you name this one?" the nurse asked as she moved around the bed to tuck in the sheets tightly.

Cathy sleepily gazed out the window and answered, "June."

"*June?*" the nurse said. She looked inquisitively at Cathy. "That's a wee bit different, eh? Is that because you had her in June, dear?"

"Aye. Perhaps that's so." She hoped the nurse wouldn't ask any more questions. As nice as she was, Nurse Hamilton was also a devout Catholic. Cathy knew that June was not the kind of name given to a Catholic baby. It was traditional to name a child in honor of a saint.

Nurse Hamilton was not a narrow-minded person. She knew there were many girls in the world named June, although she had never heard the name given to a Catholic baby in her fifteen years at St. Andrew's Infirmary. Her mind went through the list of saints' names and she didn't find *June* anywhere. She asked no more questions, not wanting to appear too nosey.

Still, her curiosity continued as she rolled a cart of dirty linens toward the nurses' station.

"Let's have that, dear," greeted the hospital's laundry woman, a round, pudding-faced person.

Knowing that the woman was also a faithful Catholic, Nurse Hamilton inquired, "Have you ever heard of a Catholic bairn born here being named June?"

"June? No in this hospital. Who named their wean that?"

"Mrs. MacDonald," answered the nurse in a hushed voice. She felt guilty for gossiping.

The laundry woman's lips opened in a round, surprised circle. She knew that the MacDonalds were religious people. "Wee Cathy MacDonald? That woman is more tired out from having weans than I thought. Can't you suggest a good Catholic name?"

Nurse Hamilton merely shrugged her shoulders and tightened her lips, wanting to end the discussion before it was overheard.

"Well then, I think it's time to stop breeding when you run out of Saints' names," the laundry woman said. She shook her big head and chuckled. "Oh, wait 'til her man shows up. All them girls. Must be like a right convent at their house."

She waddled down the corridor pushing her cart and singing out, "Saint June!"

༄ ༄ ༄

The new mothers in the six-bed ward were served pots of steaming black tea with creamy milk and sugar. Cathy felt a wave of contentment flow through her tired body as she enjoyed a cup of tea. Intuitively, she sensed that this child would bring her what she longed for—peace of mind. Although only thirty years old, she knew that June would be her last child.

It's best not to dwell on that, Cathy thought as she gently placed the sleeping newborn in the bassinet next to her bed. Refreshing her tea, she peeked over the rim of her cup at the young mother next to her. "What did you name him?" she asked.

With a teacup at her lips, the full-faced young woman widened her large, dark-brown eyes at Cathy. Putting down her cup, she said, "How'd you know I had a boy?"

"The blue blanket Nurse wrapped him in."

"Oh, aye, of course! Look at him. He's lovely. Like a wee Clootie dumpling wrapped in a hankie."

Cathy laughed heartily at the young mother's description of her baby. Babies wrapped in blankets did indeed resemble the Scottish boiled pudding wrapped in a towel. Politely, she inquired further, "Is he your first?"

"Och, no. My third."

Surprised by the answer, Cathy mumbled, "Oh my!" The woman didn't look much out of her teens, although she already had that gravel tone of voice heard in heavy smokers.

"And he's got a big *baw-face*[3] just like his two brothers," the young woman said, extending a hand to Cathy. "I'm Jenny. Your new wean is no your first either, eh?"

"Goodness no! I've got four girls at home and now this wee one." Cathy added quietly, "One passed away right after birth."

"Oh my, I am so sorry." The young woman smiled sympathetically at the woman with the sad blue eyes and pale, flawless skin.

Cathy looked away from Jenny's pity. Then she turned back and with a sly, half smile she gestured to the young woman to hand over her teacup. "Would you like me to read your tea leaves?"

"You can do that?" Jenny asked in surprise.

"Well, I never have before, but a *tinker*[4] once read mine. It can't be that hard."

"What'd she say ta ya?"

---

3   Baw-face – Scottish description for a large, round face.
4   Tinker – A gypsy.

"She said that I'd have a lot of bairns. She got that part right. And she said I'd cross a bridge of gold to live in a faraway place. Maybe I'll be happy there." Cathy put down her cup. "Let's have a look, Jen, and see how many more weans you'll have."

Taking the last gulp of tea, Jenny handed over her teacup and plunked down her plump bum next to Cathy on the bed. She peered over the older woman's shoulder, intently watching and quietly waiting for news of her upcoming good fortune. Cathy took the cup in both hands. She moved it from left to right, looking at it from different angles. The women tilted their heads to the right as Cathy angled the cup in that direction.

Jenny held her breath in anticipation until she could wait no longer. "Tell me you see gold in my purse and me in a big house. Oh, and one more wean. I want a wee lassie the next time."

Pointing out a collection of leaves clinging to the side of the cup Cathy said, "See that boat there? Aye, well, that's bringing you good news from abroad."

"Is that right? My sister just left for Australia for a new job! And my ma's hoping she'll find a man, too! What else do you see?"

Looking back into the cup Cathy prophesied, "I see your husband will get a promotion at work and then you'll move to a new flat next year."

She handed the teacup back to Jenny and smiled. "There you go."

"Oh! I am a lucky woman!"

The women laughed and began to chat about babies.

At that moment, Jimmy MacDonald, a stocky, working-class man, strolled into the ward. His sour look dampened the women's laughter. The women froze in place for only a brief second before Jenny stepped away from Cathy's bedside.

He walked quickly over to his wife's bed. He pulled up a straight-back wooden chair and sat down with a thud. His long, sharp nose narrowly separated his squinty, hazel eyes, which he set directly on Cathy. He rubbed a hand over his face as though to wipe away the tiredness from it. In his deep, throaty voice he inquired, "How are you doing?"

She covered herself with a sheet, pulling it up around her milk-swollen breasts. "Alright. Did my mother tell you I had a girl?"

"Aye. Said she telephoned the hospital before coming by the flat this morning."

"Take a wee peek at the baby. She's lovely." Cathy nodded her head toward the bassinet.

Jimmy rose slightly to lean over it. The baby's eyes fluttered then suddenly opened wide. He pulled away. "Looks like your mother, staring at me with those watery blue eyes."

Although she understood that he must be tired from work, she was in no mood to listen to his grouchiness. Staring him squarely in the eye, she retorted, "I was thinking she looked like *your* mother."

Jimmy leaned in closer, clutching the blanket in his thick calloused fingers. "Don't you speak ill of the dead. You hear me, woman?"

Cathy thought Jimmy's rough Glaswegian voice was embarrassingly loud. She quickly glanced around the ward to see if the other women could hear them quarrelling. They were busy with their own babies and paid no heed to the MacDonalds. She bit back her angry words, not wanting to add to the tension between her husband and herself.

He took a deep breath and said more quietly, "Shouldn't be taking time off work, but I just wanted to see you." He gave her a weak smile

She didn't smile back.

"Your mother's already getting on my nerves telling me how to take care of my girls," he complained.

"Tsk. She's just trying to be helpful, Jimmy."

"When are you coming home?" he bleated.

"Dr. MacFadden thinks I need to stay a wee bit longer."

"What's he know about what we need?" he snarled. "Me and the lassies need you at home. That's where you belong, woman."

Cathy was afraid she'd say the wrong thing and upset him, which was easy to do. So she said nothing.

He said, "Speaking of my mother... I've been thinking about this for a while. Just in case you didn't give me a son, I'm naming the baby Elizabeth, in her memory."

She had no choice but to tell him the truth. "I've named her already," she said hurriedly. "It's June. And I've made up my mind on that."

Jimmy leaned away from his wife with an incredulous look on his face.

"What do you mean *you've* made up your mind? Och, stop your blethering about you've made up *your* mind! What's wrong with you?"

With her mouth set in determination, Cathy thought how cruel he could be at times. *It's my wean. I gave birth to her,* she argued inwardly. She looked directly into her husband's eyes. His haggard face caused her to reconsider continuing the quarrel. It was true that he was more bad-tempered than ever since taking a second job. Still his hard work had afforded them a larger, more expensive new flat with a separate bedroom for the girls, an inside bathroom with a large bathtub, and even a parlor, Cathy's favorite room. It was much nicer than their previous cold-water flat with a kitchen, one small room and a toilet in the outside hallway that was shared with two other families. Her faced softened and she leaned back on the pillow, sighing.

"Look, *hen*[5], that's a heathen name," he said. "She's no a pagan baby. I've picked a name. A good Catholic name—a saint's name. You know she's got to be named for a saint. All our girls are named after good Catholic holy women—Anne, Margaret, Mary and Helen."

A fiery anger filled Cathy's stomach, spreading upward past her heart and lungs. "Jimmy! Just this once I've decided something. Just once. I've said that I've made up my mind and that's that! If you don't like it . . ." she hesitated before continuing in a tight voice, ". . . you can bloody . . ."

---

[5] Hen – A Scottish term of endearment for a female.

He clenched his fists in his rough, dark-brown work jacket as though preparing to launch them. He'd been in many a fight, and even the bravest men backed away from him. This was *his wife,* and he meant to get his way.

"Jesus woman! Don't get cheeky with me! I've spoken! Her name will be *Elizabeth!*"

They stared at each other. Unable to withstand his wife's steely glare, Jimmy was the first to look away. Cathy knew she had won.

                          ◌◌◌ ◌◌◌ ◌◌◌

Nurse Hamilton swaddled baby June in a soft yellow blanket as Cathy packed her small cloth bag. Jimmy stood outside the ward with his hands in his pockets, waiting for his wife and new daughter to join him. The nurse walked Cathy into the hallway, handed her the baby, and bade them all farewell.

As the MacDonalds walked away, they saw Dr. MacFadden sauntering down the hallway of the maternity floor. The doctor adjusted his glasses as he came closer to them.

"Hello there, Mr. MacDonald." He extended his hand to Jimmy. "You're no leaving us already are you, Mrs. MacDonald?" the good doctor said with a nice smile.

"She's better off at home where she's needed." Jimmy's answer sounded gruff to Cathy. When she had told her husband that the doctor thought she needed extra bed rest and ordered her to stay a week, instead of the usual five days allotted new mothers, Jimmy had said no. Cathy knew that her husband wasn't too fond of "the big *chucker*[6]," as he called Dr. MacFadden, who was from the Isle of Skye in the Highlands of Scotland.

The doctor motioned Jimmy to step over to a quieter place away from the busy corridor. Jimmy told Cathy to wait before he followed the doctor down the hallway.

---

[6]   Chucker – Pronounced "chookter." A yokel from the countryside or a farm.

Dr. MacFadden leaned his shoulder onto the once-white wall. Unlike the faded white wall, the doctor, with his powerful build, youthful complexion and dark, wavy hair, didn't show his true age of forty-five years. While Jimmy, in his worn clothing and thinning hair, looked older than his forty-one years. He straightened himself to match the doctor's towering presence. It was useless. He was still a full head shorter than Dr. MacFadden. Jimmy leaned back and crossed his arms. "Is there a problem?" he asked.

"Aye, sorry to say but there is, Mr. MacDonald. This birth was exceptionally difficult on your wife. I'm recommending that this be her last baby. It will be very dangerous for her health if she were to birth again. Something is not right with her and. . ."

"Aye, something is wrong with her, alright," Jimmy interrupted him. "As for what happens with more children, I can't say. God decides that. No you or me."

The doctor rose to his full height, accentuating every inch of their differences. Impatiently, he said, "Mr. MacDonald, if your wife gives birth again, she'll be seeing God before you know it."

"We'll talk to our priest," Jimmy responded with his arms crossed tightly on his chest.

"Man, did you no hear me right? We're talking about your wife. If it were my wife. . ."

"But she's no, is she?" Jimmy argued. "I'll make the decisions for us."

"Good. Then I recommend condoms."

"Doctor! You being a Catholic, you ought to know better than to talk about that!"

"My God man, it's 1950! We're living in modern times. Give your children a chance for a better life."

"Just because I'm no educated like you don't mean I can't take care of my family. I work hard. My family has what they need."

Without waiting for a response, Jimmy quickly walked away while angrily rummaging through his pockets for a cigarette. He hustled his wife and newborn down the hall.

∾ ∾ ∾

Cathy stood in the hospital entrance with baby June in her arms. As she waited for Jimmy to hail a taxi, she closed her eyes for a moment to enjoy the sun on her face. The streets were busy with double-decker buses slowing down just enough to let passengers jump on and off. She was glad that Jimmy was generous enough to call a taxi and not make her take a bus.

When the baby stirred in her arms, she opened the blanket to find June's eyes watching her. A wave of comfort filled her heart as she nuzzled her baby's face, and took in the fresh scent of her newborn.

Her serenity was disturbed by the gravel voice that spoke in her ear. "Thought you were to stay longer."

She turned around and saw Jenny. Her shoulder shrug was enough explanation for the other woman.

"Oh, aye. A mammy's always needed at home. Well, dear, cheerio and good luck," Jenny said. As she started down the stairs, she yelled loudly back to Cathy, "Thanks for doing the fortune-telling for me."

Jimmy bellowed to his wife to hurry up as a taxi pulled over to the curb. He barred her way as she stepped up to the open door of the taxi. "What does she mean you're telling fortunes?" he asked.

Flustered by the accusation that she was doing something forbidden by their religion, "She's just kiddin'. Come on, let's get home," she said, brushing off the incident.

He firmly took hold of her arm and said, "I don't know about you and what's going on. Something's no right."

Cathy shook off his hold and pushed past him into the open door of the taxi.

Chapter Three:
The Gypsy Fortune Teller

A TINY OLD GYPSY woman draped in faded but once brightly colored clothes walked through the mist and up the stone stairwell of a tenement house at 12 Dumbarton Road in Partick, a working class neighborhood in Glasgow. The sounds of the bells on her bracelets preceded her as she walked up to the first of the four landings in the building. Her craggy face peeked out of her cowl. Her boney knuckles rapped on the first door. She pressed an ear to it in hopes for sounds of life.

The sound of young children's laughter grew closer from behind the door.

Cathy MacDonald opened the door to find the gypsy. The old woman stood still, except for her eyes, which slowly peered up at the younger woman. A tiny smile crept over the gypsy's face. "Read your fortune, missus?"

Mary and Maggie, Cathy's two middle children, stared at the old gypsy woman with wide-eyes. Maggie loudly announced the gypsy, "Granny! Come see the witch!" Mary jumped up and down. "Witch! Witch!" she chanted. Baby June perched on Cathy's hip began to babble along with her excited sisters.

Exasperated, Cathy's eyes didn't meet the old woman's, as she sighed and said, "No, I don't think so." She started to close the door.

The gypsy moved quickly, placing a hand flat on the door to stop it from shutting. "I can see you long for a lost love." She peered into Cathy's face. "Am I no right, missus?"

Startled Cathy locked eyes with the gypsy. She opened the door a little. The two girls stood motionless on either side of her, mesmerized by the tinkling of the gypsy's bracelets. "Come on, gie's[7] your hand. I'll tell you more for just a shilling."

Digging into her faded, flowered apron, Cathy pulled out a couple of coins. The old gypsy looked down at them, and then flashed her questioning eyes up to Cathy.

Granny B popped her head out from the kitchen and looked down the hallway toward the front door. "Tell that tinker to go away. You're too busy for that malarkey!" she yelled.

Quickly, the tiny old woman grabbed the coins out of Cathy's hands and stashed them in her tattered clothing. "That's fine enough, lady. Now, let's see your palm."

Cathy looked nervously over her shoulder and down the hallway. The two girls tried to see what was happening, but she eased them out of the way to conceal what the gypsy would say. Balancing the baby on her hip, she held out her free palm. The old gypsy gently cradled it in her surprisingly soft hands and moved her fingers across Cathy's palm as though to smooth out the crisscrossing lines.

Suddenly, baby June reached out to the old woman's face, touching a deep crease. The ragged gypsy reciprocated, and patted a curl of the baby's flaming red hair. "Aye, this wee lassie, I can see she's a special wean. The seventh child of seven, is she no? That's good luck. She can see what others can't. She's *fey*[8]," the gypsy declared, nodding her head knowingly.

"And you, dear," the gypsy's dark-brown eyes looked up to the sky-blue eyes of the young woman. "You're going to move far away from here," she said as she sighed loudly. "Sorry to say but you'll no find the happiness you seek there."

Cathy moaned lightly. The old woman, seeing sadness cross the younger woman's face, added soothingly, "Sometimes we think that

[7] Gie's – Scottish slang for "give us"
[8] Fey – Clairvoyant.

we've lost something only to find that it was still there all along. You *ken*[9]?"

She didn't understand what the gypsy was talking about. She sharply pulled back her hand and put it on the door behind her. "But this wee one," the old gypsy nodded to June. "She'll bring you the love you're after."

Granny B's voice interrupted them. Cathy placed a finger over her lips to quiet the gypsy.

The door suddenly swung open. "Away with you," said Granny B, angrily waving a dishrag at the gypsy. "An' you, get in here," she said as she pulled Cathy into the flat.

"Them tinkers. The whole lot nothing but troublin' thieves. You didn't give her any money, did you?" Granny B asked.

Cathy walked silently past her into the kitchen. "You're so gullible, girl," chided Granny B. "You're lucky she didn't steal one of your weans right out from under your nose."

"Oh, Mammy. They can't even feed their own weans let alone mine. Anyway, I felt sorry for the old woman. Her hands were like ice." She put June on the floor and handed her a rattle to play with.

"Well, maybe you're right. This is the worse chill we've had in February for ages," Granny B conceded.

Annie, the eldest MacDonald child at six years old, stood on a chair next to the stove and stirred a pot of thick Scotch broth soup while Maggie and Mary took turns licking a big wooden spoon dripping with sweet batter.

Granny B turned her attention to the two sisters who were now fighting over the spoon. "See, you two! You put that down! Annie, hand Granny that thingamajig," she said, pointing to a large rolling pin dusted with flour. The quarreling girls ran screeching out of the kitchen when their grandmother raised the rolling pin above her head in a threatening manner.

---

[9]   Ken – To know. To understand.

"Them twins. A right handful, they are," Granny B muttered. She often referred to Maggie and Mary as "the twins" or "the Irish Twins," a term for children born less than a year apart.

A small whimpering sound came from the crib next to the fireplace. It was Helen who, at twenty-months, was not round and rosy like the other MacDonald girls. Cathy thought of her as more like a pale elfin child, but without the mischievousness. Helen was a quiet toddler, a sweet child who still preferred to lie in her crib or be held.

Cathy bent down to her daughter and noticed that the toddler was tugging on her ear, which was a painful red. The wheezing from Helen's lungs had gotten louder all day. *This damp cold weather will be the death of us yet,* Cathy thought as she picked up her sickly little girl.

"Tsk. Poor wee soul. Sick again?" Granny B asked worriedly. Her home remedies hadn't worked their usual magic. The women had discussed taking Helen back to see Dr. MacFadden, but Jimmy discouraged it, saying it was a waste of time. "She'll grow out of it," he had said.

Easing her tired body into a rocking chair, Cathy tried to soothe the crying child. June watched Helen intently as her sister sat on their mother's lap. She held up her hands and started to babble, signaling to her mother that she wanted to be picked up. The tired mother gave a small gasp as she scooped up the baby, placing her next to Helen. The girls straddled their mother, and all three rocked back and forth. The toddler looked at her baby sister with heavy eyes. June placed her tiny hand delicately over her sister's red ear. The sick toddler soon quieted as she sank deeply against her mother's body. Cathy saw the redness in her ear fade to a pale pink. *June's touch always seems to help Helen,* she thought.

In a rare and blessed moment of silence, Cathy took a prolonged inhale and closed her eyes. After a few moments she looked over at her mother who was preparing supper. "Mammy, didn't you tell me that you had a wean born dead?"

"Aye. Sad. Just like your wee Baby Kit." Granny B continued her baking preparations and said no more about the infant Kit who had been her namesake. The baby had lived for only a few days. "Both of us have suffered the deaths of our first born. God giveth, and God taketh away. Tsk. Aye, it's a *sair fecht*[10]."

"It is indeed. So that makes me the seventh child, right?" An awkward stillness filled the kitchen. The only sound was the big black kettle on the stove that had started to boil. Granny B ignored her daughter until Cathy said, "You never talk about it, Mammy."

The older woman stared at her daughter with hands on her hips. "Leave the past alone, lassie. Nothing can be done about it. Why you asking? Did that tinker say something?"

Cathy shrugged and said nothing.

The conversation was interrupted by a big bang coming from the other room. "Och, for God's sake! Will you see what those wee devils have destroyed now! Here, I'll take Elizabeth. Come on to your Granny." Granny B reached to take June.

Cathy's face darkened as she laid Helen on the big overstuffed chair and held June tightly to her chest. "Oh Mammy! You and Jimmy! You're only confusing her. Her name is *June*, Mammy. No Saint Elizabeth or Mary Queen of Heaven or any other bloody holy name. It's June and that's that."

The kettle began steaming as Granny B rushed to quiet its whistling. She picked it up off the stove, and placed it harder than usual on the counter, spewing water all over.

"Well, Elizabeth is her baptismal name. Thank God for that," she muttered as she crossed herself.

---

[10] Sair fecht – Scottish for a sore fight; something disappointing.

Chapter Four:
The Orange Walk

July 12, 1953

THE STONE LANDING outside the MacDonald's flat quickly picked up the heat that came with the weather change and although it had drizzled the day before, producing a refreshing low fog, the heat of the July afternoon now permeated the atmosphere. The MacDonalds' flat soon became hot and stuffy.

Jimmy and Granda B had stepped out onto the landing to get out of the way so Granny B could prepare the meal.

"Things are going to be hot today," Granda B mused as he carefully lowered his whiskey glass from his lips, enjoying the last drop of Johnnie Walker Red—his favorite whiskey.

The revelry of laughter, singing and the banging of drums from the nearby parade belied the upcoming clash of Glasgow's citizens. If history were its gauge, the day would most assuredly grow in violence that would last well into the next day.

Granda B's tawny brown eyes flickered over to Jimmy, his son-in-law. The old man watched Jimmy's strong muscular body tense up with each drumbeat that, like an anxious heartbeat, grew louder and louder. While the two men were very different in looks—the elder was tall, white-haired and slender, whereas Jimmy was short and stocky with dark brown hair—they were very much alike in their strong beliefs on family and religion. Both were proud men. They had a right to be, they thought. They had managed to keep a decent job in a town where Catholics often found good work opportunities difficult to come by. Jimmy had done so well in his day job that recently he had finally given up his second one. That was until last week when he was let go from his job.

Granda B's low, calm voice cut short his son-in-law's thoughts. "Aye, it is a shame, son. I told you that my cousin would take you on at his electrical shop."

"Och, Dad, it's no just that. It's the whole thing of being let go just like I was," he said snapping his fingers loudly and grimacing with anger. "All because some bloody *Proddy*[11] comes along every time and takes our jobs away. It keeps me from getting ahead."

Granda B had the same distaste for the Protestants in Scotland, having lived with their prejudices against Catholics much longer than Jimmy. But he knew not to agree with his son-in-law. Jimmy would anger at the drop of a hat and the whiskey might encourage him to do something that would bring trouble to the family.

Still, Jimmy's words caused Granda B to think back on that day, many years ago when his youngest son, Francis, had died. Granda B's stomach started to burn as it always did when he remembered that horrible time. Against his father's orders, Francis had gone with some friends to watch the *Orange Walk*[12], a parade of Glasgow Protestants celebrating their religion. A brick tossed from the crowd of Protestants had struck his beloved son, killing him instantly. Months later, Granda B told his wife that Francis' spirit had visited him during Mass. The spirit had instructed him to help unite the two religions. Soon afterward, Granda B began his crusade by founding and raising funds for the Francis Buchanan Glasgow Youth Soccer League, an organization for children from both religions. Although

---

[11] Proddy – Offensive slang for a Protestant.

[12] Orange Walk – Orange is the color of the Protestants; green is the color of the Catholics. The colors can still incite discord, although that is now mostly in Northern Ireland. The Orange Walk celebrated a 17th century victory over Catholic rule and religion.

the program had brought him some comfort, his grief and anger over his son's untimely death never stopped.

Speaking with the wisdom of time, the old man said to Jimmy, "It's a bit better with them now than in my days. Just be patient, son, you'll get another job."

The men were interrupted by the voices of two young girls, one crying and one yelling, coming up the stairwell.

"*You're* the stupid cow!" Annie yelled at her unseen target as she stomped up the stairs onto the landing with her crying sister in tow.

Mary's golden speckled-brown eyes, usually bright with mirth, now brimmed over with tears.

"What you *greetin*[13] about?" Jimmy asked her.

"Them boys throwed stones at us," Mary said, rubbing her freckled arm with a red mark on it.

"They hurt her. I'm going to tell Granny," said Annie, angrily. Her usually light blue-gray eyes were as dark and steely as a Scottish winter sky.

Granda B bent down to Mary. "Oh lassie!" he sighed. "Never you mind them bad boys, pet. Granda'll take you to Granny. She'll give you a wee *sweetie*[14]," he said as he brushed back his favorite granddaughter's wavy blonde hair. Mary sniffed, but managed a big smile for her grandfather.

"My girls can't even walk to school without one of those Proddys causing trouble. Annie, tell Granda what happened the other day," Jimmy said.

Annie scowled. "A big boy asked, 'Where you goin'?' I said to school at St. Michael's. He says, 'I hate papists.' An' he hit me in the face. I didn't cry, though. I kicked him and ran away."

"Go on, hen, show your Granda what happened to you," Jimmy said. She moved her hair aside and tilted her head upward to show Granda B a bruised cheekbone.

---

[13]   Greetin' – Scottish for crying.
[14]   Sweetie – Scottish for a treat; candy.

"Jesus, Mary, Joseph!" Granda B said. "Right you are, lassie, no to cry 'cause of them. You're a brave one, Annie, you are."

Annie nodded solemnly. She knew that crying was not encouraged in her Scottish household, whereas bravely defending yourself had a place of honor.

She continued her ranting against the boys downstairs. "And they said we was stupid *papist*[15] cows. Them boys are ugly, bad Proddys. Right, Daddy?"

Before her father could answer, a male voice yelled loudly from downstairs. "Billy! Hurry up, man!"

"Hold your bloody horses!" came the loud response from the flat upstairs. Billy, a young man in his early twenties, skid down onto the MacDonald's landing. He stopped short when he saw Jimmy and Granda B standing, glaring at him. Billy had known both men for most of his life, but in that moment, he eyed them as though he had happened upon the enemy camp. His bowler hat and orange sash across his chest was the uniform of his team—the Protestants. The young man quickly ducked his head so as not to look at the two, although he did manage to mumble a greeting. Granda B cocked his head and acknowledged the greeting with an "Aye."

Billy continued thumping down the stairs, staying close to the stone wall to put as much space as possible between him and the two men. He had gone only a few steps past the landing when Granda B said loud enough for his comment to echo, "That *bauchle*[16] is lucky I'm no longer a young man. He'd be eating that orange sash." He turned to tickle Mary's plump belly as she laughed. "Let's go see your Granny," he said.

The door opposite the MacDonald's opened. Mrs. MacSwan, a short, round woman in her mid-sixties, came out, arranging an orange sash on her shoulder. Satisfied with her uniform, she looked

---

[15]   Papist – Offensive slang for Roman Catholics.

[16]   Baunchle – Scottish slang for a person quite short in stature, often heavy set, and with an awkward gait.

up to see her neighbors staring at her. Her warm, light-brown eyes and ruddy face gave her a merry look.

"Oh! Hello there gentlemen and young ladies," she sang out in a cheery voice.

The men nodded slightly to her.

"Hello, Mrs. MacSwan," Annie said, smiling broadly. She liked her kindly neighbor and the homemade treats she baked.

The spry elderly lady didn't miss a step on her mission to join the growing noise of the parade. "Cheery-bye! Off I go," she called out behind her.

With the day's purpose in mind, both men shook their heads at the irony of the woman's friendliness. Mrs. MacSwan was off to the Orange March, the Protestant rally march celebrating an old victory over the Catholics.

The MacDonald's front door was cracked open wide enough for the delicious smell of baking steak pie to waft through to the landing. The enticing scent—a reminder that good times were still available to the family—drew the four back into the flat.

Granny B was cooking the big Sunday dinner, a family tradition that everyone looked forward to. Cathy sat in the overstuffed chair with three-year-old June on her lap. Mother and daughter looked alike: petite bodies, small noses and large eyes. The most noticeable difference was Cathy's light blonde hair, which paled in comparison to June's bright red ringlets.

Maggie, who sat on the floor next to the chair listening to the story, was tall and strawberry blonde with green eyes. Helen lay in her parent's alcove bed in the big kitchen, sleeping soundly after a night of difficult breathing. "She has a cold," the MacDonalds agreed.

In a soft, lyrical voice, Cathy was telling her daughters a favorite story. It was the same story her mother had told her when she was a little girl. "Green lady, green lady, come down for your tea. Your tea is all ready and waiting for thee."

Granda B interrupted the story when he came into the kitchen, holding Mary. He put her down and she quickly ran over to her mother. "What's wrong, hen?" Cathy asked, cupping her daughter's tear-stained face in her hands.

As Cathy comforted Mary, June slid off her mother's lap and walked over to Helen. She stood on her toes to get a better view of her sister lying on the top cover, apparently asleep. No matter how she struggled to climb up into the bed to be with her, she slid back down again. Everyone else in the room was focused on Jimmy's story about how Annie bravely stood up to a Proddy.

At the end of the story, Granda B kept his promise. "Granny, give Mary a wee sweetie to help her feel better."

As she reached up to the cupboard, Granny's hand froze in midair at the startling sound of June's wail, "Mammy, Mammy! Ell-ell!" which was how June pronounced Helen's name.

Gruffly, Jimmy said, "Shhh, June, don't wake her up. Get away from there."

"I'll see to it," Granny said handing a package of biscuits to Annie. "June knows when Helen's no doing well."

Granny tried to shoo June away and said, "Och, will you no wheesht[17]!"

Smoothing back Helen's dark-brown hair, Granny B's eyebrows furrowed when she saw her granddaughter flushed with fever. Helen's health was a constant worry to Granny B. She thought of how puny her four-year old granddaughter was in comparison to her other rosy-faced grandchildren. Even June, a year younger than Helen, was already a bit taller than her ailing sister.

She tilted her gray head and put her ear close to Helen's mouth. "Mother of God!" she cried out. "I think the wean's no breathing!"

Cathy quickly joined her mother. Leaning close to Helen's face she heard only a very slight breath. "Oh Mammy, shouldn't we get her to the hospital?"

"Och girl, you can't think of going out there now," Granda B said as he sat down at the kitchen table.

---

[17]   Wheesht – Scottish for "be quiet and stop talking."

The sound outside grew to a loud drumming. Suddenly, the crashing sound of breaking glass interrupted them. "Shit," Jimmy said as he ran out of the room and toward the noise.

His three older girls stood near a broken window. A brick lay near it. Annie picked it up and was ready to throw it back outside. The Irish Twins jumped up and down cheering her on.

Maggie and Mary shouted shrilly, "Throw it back at them!"

The noisy drumming and loud singing was now right outside the window. Adrenalin rushed through Jimmy, his heart beating wildly from the growing tension. He didn't want things to get out of his control. Quickly, he grabbed Annie by the back of her blouse to keep her from throwing the brick.

"Get back to the kitchen!" he yelled.

He led the girls toward the kitchen and away from the broken window.

"Jimmy, Helen's needing a doctor. Now!" Granny B said forcefully.

The group jumped, startled at her loud pronouncement.

"Are you daft, woman?" Did you no hear that crash in there? There's nothing but trouble out there for us," Granda B said, opposing her command.

Helen started to gasp loudly. Jimmy looked over at his wife cradling their sick daughter. With troubled eyes she begged softly, "Please."

"Aye, alright." Turning to his father-in-law, he announced firmly, "The women are right about this, Dad. We have no choice."

Silence spread across the room as the seriousness of Helen's condition sank in. June's shrieking cries broke the silence as Helen's body thrust back and became rigid. The indecision was broken.

Granda B picked up his cap and jacket. "Right you are then. Give me the wean. Jimmy, you stay put."

"No, Dad. I'll take her myself. The rest of you just wait." Jimmy said.

"I'm going too. She needs her mother." Cathy began to wrap the sick girl in a large woolen shawl.

"You'll need me to help, Jimmy. We'll go to the corner shop and phone for a taxi. Granny'll stay with the girls," Granda B said.

June started to wail and her grandmother picked her up in hopes of stopping the disturbing noise. "Och, it's no that bad, henny. See. Helen's sleeping nicely now."

The wailing girl couldn't be comforted. Stretching out her hands to her sick sister, she screamed like a *banshee*[18], "Ell-ell!"

The high afternoon sun directed its brilliance onto Jimmy's face as he emerged from the dimness of the building. He put one arm up to his eyes to deflect the sun while the other arm tightened around the blanketed girl. He paused, uncertain of the best way to get around the crowd. Cathy, frantic to keep moving, bumped right into him. Granda B, bringing up the rear, moved the family forward with purpose.

The marching band passing by brought forth loud singing of a tune well known to the Protestants on the street, which was meant to offend the Catholics. The anxious trio knew they were in a dangerous situation and worried about being stopped. But it wasn't easy to move past the exit of the building. It was blocked by a group of young men watching the parade, cheering and yelling as it passed by.

Jimmy tried to push his way through the group by throwing out his arm in a sweeping motion. "Come now. Out the way," he yelled.

A young, dark-haired man, who appeared to be drunk, took quick offense at being pushed aside. "Hey, Mac, where you think you're going?"

Jimmy answered him in an uncharacteristically quiet manner, "Look man, we've a sick wean here. Will you no get out of our way?"

---

[18] Banshee – A woman in Gaelic folklore whose wailing warns a family that one of them will soon die.

The troublemaker grinned foolishly for a second, then drew his lips into a sneer. A fighter himself, Jimmy knew what could follow a look like that. In a preemptive first strike, Jimmy shoved the hooligan, sending him stumbling backwards. The group of young men, in anticipation of the escalating brawl, tightened the circle around Jimmy's family.

Granda B stepped out from behind Cathy to tower above them all. He addressed the dark-haired young man, "Come on now, Andy." And to the others he simply said, "All of you—move aside. Let the woman come through." The group parted.

Jimmy stood silently, awed by how his father-in-law seemed to know so many people in Glasgow. Still apprehensive, Jimmy handed Helen to Cathy in order to free both hands in case of further trouble. A broad-shouldered young man pushed Jimmy from behind. The shove felt more like a punch and forced him to stumble forward into the group of Protestants.

An older man put a hand up to the tall bully, stopping his next move. "Easy now, lad."

But the young Protestant did not back off. His beet-red Scottish face showed his eagerness for a confrontation—a good fight for the cause. He raised his fists and spat out from his snarled lips, "Bloody papists pigs."

A small, round ball of a woman holding an orange banner on a wood stick slapped the aggressor's arm. Her strong hit was precise and stinging "for such a wee lady," according to revelers at the pub later that day.

"Glenn Sweeny! Don't you dare hurt that wean," the round woman said. "Hands down, now!" She turned to Cathy, "Come along, Mrs. MacDonald."

Everyone stopped, as if frozen in time. The young man's fists dropped as he stepped back and carried out Mrs. MacSwan's instructions. Her many years as a schoolteacher had perfected her ability to stare down the hooligans.

The group stopped bothering Jimmy's family and turned away to watch the parade. The three scurried quickly down the street, sticking close to the safety of the buildings and away from the crowd.

The sign hanging lopsided on the door of the corner store stopped them in their tracks. It said in bold capital letters, "CLOSED FOR ORANGE WALK."

"That can't be. It bloody well can't be," Jimmy mumbled.

At first he knocked loudly on the door and then began to pound frantically on it. His voice got louder. "Open up! It's Jimmy MacDonald. We need your phone. It's an emergency. Open up!"

Cupping his eyes to peer into the darkened shop, he could see a telephone but could hear no sounds inside. No one would open up for him.

"Son, it's no use. Let's get going," Granda B said taking a hold of his son-in-law's arm.

"Where, Daddy?" Cathy anxiously looked up at her father.

He helplessly looked out at the sea of raucous people passing by, waving colorful orange banners held high.

Suddenly Helen's limp body jerked backward and then slowly went limp. Cathy pushed the shawl aside and looked down at her daughter's ashen face. Helen's eyes were wide open in a vacant stare.

"No. No. Please, Mother of God. Not my wee lassie," she sobbed, shaking her head in denial. "Helen!" she screamed over and over, desperately calling her daughter back into her world.

Jimmy stepped forward to catch his still daughter as his wife collapsed to the pavement. She refused to give Helen up.

The drumming had grown faint as the parade moved farther down the road.

Chapter Five:
Family Sorrow

THE WEATHER SHIFTED to damp gray in the days following Helen's death. The fog rose off the River Clyde and lay like a wet blanket over the MacDonald's building. Inside the flat, Cathy and her mother sat in the cold parlor waiting to leave for the Funeral Mass.

The grieving young mother's face was stark white against her high-collared black dress. She didn't want to go to the funeral.

Granny B had combed back her daughter's hair, securing it from falling across her eyes, and put a chain with a golden cross around her neck to show that they were a proud Catholic clan. She spoke gently to Cathy as they prepared to leave.

"You know, hen, I have also suffered the great loss of children," her mother said. "It's the worse thing a parent ever has to face. But you must be brave for your living children. They are what counts now."

Cathy eyed her, and silently wished she could return to bed and not have to be so brave.

❧ ❧ ❧

The wide stone steps of the church were dotted with family, friends and neighbors chatting in hushed voices. The talking ceased when the motorcar arrived with the grieving family. Somberly, Jimmy walked in front with the older girls close around him. He had decided that June was too young to go. Mrs. MacSwan offered to care for the youngster, and Cathy agreed, knowing that June would be too distraught at seeing her sister in a coffin. The little girl's sobs had hardly stopped since that fateful day. Only Annie's cuddling could console her.

Granda B held firmly onto Cathy's arm as they walked down the aisle of St. Michael's Church toward the small wooden coffin in front of the altar. Granny B had to talk her husband into walking with his daughter. At first he said he was too ill to go to the funeral. His stomach had been paining him terribly all morning. She knew what was paining him the most. He was reliving the deaths of Francis and Stevie, their eldest son who died serving in World War II.

The packed church soon became hot and stuffy. Cathy sat crammed between her father and husband. She didn't hear what the priest was saying. To her it seemed as though his voice droned on about God's will and how Helen was now happily in Heaven with the angels. Her arms ached to hold her daughter one more time. But she knew that time would never come again.

Later, back at the MacDonald's flat, the low hum of people paying their respects filled the sorrowful home. Mourners wandered around with drinks and cigarettes in hand. Long stretches of smoke hovered close to the ceiling, making the gloomy day seem even darker.

Cathy sat motionless in the parlor with her hands folded in her lap. She was visually shivering. The small fireplace didn't offer much warmth. Over the past few days her petite frame seemed to have shrunk in size, as though drawing away from the confusion surrounding her.

After a few hours Peter, one of Cathy's three remaining brothers, began to gently usher the guests out of the door.

Granny B put her arm around her daughter's trembling shoulders. "Hen, come on in the kitchen. It's warmer there."

When they entered they were met with Peter's loud voice talking to the other men in the family.

Granny B took charge of the noisy kitchen and told her son to lower his voice and for Janet, Peter's wife, to take the children out to play. Flicking her cigarette ash into the sink, Janet hesitated. "Mum, I'm so very tired," she said pouting with her bright red lips. "Been up all night with Wee Gordie's coughing, and after what happened to Helen. You know."

"Och, away with you," said Granny B catching a glimpse of Wee Gordie, her grandson, running past the kitchen, chasing Mary and Maggie. He had kinky dark hair, round green eyes and apple red cheeks that gave him the look of an impish elf. He was a picture of health. "Can you no think of anyone but yourself?"

Patsy, another daughter-in-law, quickly stepped in to soothe the brewing argument and offered a solution. "Don't worry. Ned and me will take the bairns outside." She took charge of the situation by herding the MacDonald girls out of the kitchen and calling out to their many cousins from around the flat. Granny B was glad that her shy son, Ned, had found such a responsible wife.

Bernie, Granny and Granda B's eldest living son, hung back, hoping not to be asked to help with his children. He had brought his five to the funeral by himself because his wife was about to deliver yet another child. Granny didn't miss her absence as the two women didn't get along and were prone to quarreling.

Under Patsy's supervision, the children quietly walked out of the flat in single file line. June broke free from the line and ran zigzag past her aunt into the kitchen, ducking anyone who put out a hand to restrain her. She ran straight to her mother and stood solemnly in front of her. With vibrant blue eyes boring directly into her mother's swollen eyes, she said demandingly, "Don't go away Mammy."

Aunt Patsy swooped up the little girl. "Think you can get away from me, eh?" she said as she carried her out of the room.

In a low, encouraging voice, Granda B said, "Drink a wee bit, hen. It'll help you relax." He picked up a glass of whiskey and moved it toward Cathy's mouth. Smelling the whiskey, she turned her head away and wrapped her arms around her middle.

A sudden angry voice jolted everyone away from their thoughts. "My wee girl would be here if I could just have gotten her to the hospital," Jimmy shouted. "She'd be here with us, where she belongs. No in some damn grave."

"It's no your fault, man, it's them. Can you believe some of them Orange men having the nerve to come by today?" Bernie said, dourly.

"Aye, I could hardly stomach it," complained Peter, tossing back his drink. "We're second class citizens right in our own hometown."

"Och, you lads don't know how bad it used to be in Glasgow," Granda B chimed in. The men's voices became louder and angrier at each disparaging comment made against the Protestants.

Cathy's loud sobs surprised the men. Jimmy went to his wife's side. Uncertain how to comfort her, he dropped to his knees in front of her and said, "I'm sorry. I never realized how sick Helen was. I let you down, didn't I? Oh, Cathy, please."

Laying a hand on Jimmy's shoulder, Granda B said gently, "Son, maybe God had a different plan from what you know. He kens what's best."

In a surprisingly strong retort, Cathy challenged her father. "Dad, how can you say that? If God knew what was best for me He never would have taken another one of my weans. Have I no suffered enough?"

No one answered her. Peter finally broke the silence, "Jimmy, I think you and Cathy should think of leaving. Start over. Maybe go to Canada or Australia. Me and Janet have been talking about it ourselves. You can get a good job in the building trades there."

"How can they go, eh?" Granny B said shaking her head in disagreement, "They've no money to leave. No son, they'll no be going, especially at a time like this."

Bernie struck a match to light a cigarette. "Aye, Glasgow's a tough town for us Catholics. If it hadn't been for that parade your wee..."

Suddenly, a chilling high-pitched wail filled the kitchen, causing everyone to jump.

"No more! I can't take it!" Cathy cried out. "My weans, one by one, gone! I'm cursed. Oh Mother of God! I've sinned, Mammy! God is punishing me." She rocked back and forth so violently that Jimmy fell backward onto the floor, stunned by his wife's hysteria.

Bewildered, Bernie sputtered, "What's she blethering about? Who cursed her?"

Patsy appeared in the doorway. "Och! Wheesht, all of you. My *heid's a loupin*[19] with you men goin' on," she said as she walked over to Cathy.

Granny B, shocked by her daughter's outburst, recovered quickly. "Aye, she's right. All this talk about leaving Glasgow. Willie, take the boys down to the pub," she said nodding in the direction of the front door. "Go!"

Granda B extended his hand to Jimmy to help him up off the floor. "Right, you are. Let's go boys," he said as he moved the men along. He was glad to get out of the stuffy kitchen filled with sadness and anger.

The door had just closed when Cathy, arms clenched across her abdomen, moaned deeper and louder than she had when giving birth to her children. A pain so intense seared through her that it pitched her off the chair and she fell onto the floor. She lay curled in a fetal position gasping in pain. Blood pooled around her. Granny B quickly bent down to her daughter.

Patsy grabbed some dishtowels and lifted Cathy's dress to soak up some of the flowing blood. "There, there, Cathy. Lay still now," she said. To Granny B she whispered, "I think she's losing another one. Don't let her move. I'll call for an ambulance."

She bumped into the MacDonald sisters at the front door.

"Can't go in there now," Patsy said, pushing the girls back.

Annie cried, "June said Mammy was going with Helen to Heaven. Is she dying, too?"

---

19   Heid's a loupin' – Scottish for a severe headache; my heid's a loupin' means my head hurts.

The children swarmed around Patsy with frightened questioning eyes. Patsy fidgeted with a button on her cardigan while she tried to think of what to say to keep the children calm.

Just then, Mrs. MacSwan popped out of her door. "Hullo! I'm looking for children to eat the sweets I've just baked. Anyone interested?" she asked winking at Patsy.

Patsy gulped in relief when the children's heads turned toward Mrs. MacSwan. Happy for the offer, Margaret and Mary ran over to her flat. Annie and June stayed behind staring at their aunt.

"I want my Mammy," June said, lips quivering.

"She's sleeping. You don't want to bother her," Patsy replied back.

"She's no sleeping," said June defiantly.

"The truth is your Mammy's very sick and I'm going to get the doctor. So, you go, pet, with your big sister to Mrs. MacSwan's."

The two MacDonald girls stood looking somber-eyed at their aunt, trying to figure out if she was fibbing.

Finally, Annie took hold of June's hand and tugged her toward Mrs. MacSwan's flat. She said, "The picture in your head wasn't right. Mammy's no dying."

⁓   ⁓   ⁓

The men knew something was very wrong when Patsy banged into the pub. She quickly explained the bad news to Jimmy and the others. They tossed back the remains of their drinks and rushed out of the pub and back to the flat.

Jimmy and Peter followed the ambulance to the hospital in a taxi. A hospital clerk led the men to a waiting room. Moments later Dr. MacFadden rushed past them, not noticing the two waiting men smoking nervously.

After a while Dr. MacFadden and a clerk entered the room. The doctor explained the complications surrounding the miscarriage and said that Cathy needed immediate surgery. It took only a moment for the doctor to realize that the two men weren't coherent enough to understand the gravity of the situation. They reeked of alcoholic fumes and had blurred speech. Further explanation was useless. The doctor indicated to the clerk that Mr. MacDonald should sign the appropriate form for surgery. He then turned away and went back to work.

The waiting room had two large curtained windows, a few uncomfortable chairs and a low wooden table scarred with cigarette burns. The men propped their feet up on the table and waited. The room became cold and drafty as the night wore on, which made things worse for the two grieving men.

It wasn't until early the next morning when Dr. MacFadden entered the room looking for Jimmy. He found both men slouched in chairs, asleep. Shaking Jimmy's shoulder, he said, "Did you not listen to me when I told you that if you got your wife pregnant again it could be the death of her?"

In a stupor of sleep, Jimmy mumbled, "My wife's dead?"

The doctor towered over Jimmy who sat slumped in his chair. His furious tone made Jimmy feel small.

"I told you about condoms, did I not?" the doctor said angrily. "Are you that selfish that you can't think of anything but your own pleasures?"

Jimmy was suddenly jolted wide-awake. "It's no my fault she lost it. And never you mind about what my wife and I do in our bedroom. You dirty minded. . ."

Enraged, he jumped up too quickly and bumped right into the doctor. "I can see you're no faithful to your religion," he said accusingly.

Dr. MacFadden shook his head wearily, sighing as he rubbed his tired eyes. "I had to perform a hysterectomy on your wife, Mr. MacDonald. You'll never have to worry about her getting pregnant again."

The news sank slowly into Jimmy's consciousness. As he watched MacFadden stride off, it occurred to him that he'd never have a son.

Chapter Six:
Leaving for a New Life

March 16, 1954

THE AIRPORT TERMINAL'S windows shuddered from the vibration of the planes as they roared into and out of Scotland. But Cathy and Granny B, sitting close to each other, didn't notice. The older woman, still wearing dark mourning clothes, held her daughter's hand. "I'll miss you and the girls so much," she said sadly.

"It's already settled. Jimmy will have a secure job with no worry about some Proddy taking it away." Cathy replied as she watched Maggie and Mary chase each other back and forth, giggling. Mary was hugging a doll. It was a special doll. Three days earlier Granda B had given it to her for her seventh birthday. She lovingly carried it with her everywhere. Annie was taking June for another walk down the corridor, trying to keep her amused.

Granny B looked at her in desperation. "It just that I'm afraid, hen, that you'll no come back home to me again. I'm no getting any younger, you know."

Resolutely, Cathy looked into her mother's eyes. "Well, Mam, you made sure you got me home before."

The old woman looked away. Her fingers fumbled over one another and settled on her wedding ring. "You've no forgiven me, have you?" Granny B asked. "There isn't a day goes by that I don't say a prayer to Our Lady for peace between us."

In an effort to avoid any more talk with her mother, Cathy strained her head to look toward her husband who was waiting at the ticket counter. She could see Jimmy was reading the list he made earlier that day of the tasks to complete and information that was needed for their move. They made sure nothing was forgotten by marking off the items on the list as they were completed.

Jimmy held tight to the list because it also contained the telephone number of his friend Sandy Jordon in America. He had been a good pal to Jimmy since they were children, and the two wrote to each other after Sandy had emigrated a few years ago. He had encouraged Jimmy to join him, promising a good job. The very day Jimmy had confirmed his family would move, Sandy secured a job for his pal alongside him at the shipyards. Jimmy had told Cathy that moving to the United States was the best chance they had for a new start. "Life will be better there," he assured her.

Looking away from her husband, Cathy said a silent prayer that her husband would never learn of her secret about Dr. MacFadden making a substantial contribution to help the family have that new start. She knew he would never have taken the doctor's money. A few weeks after her emergency visit to the hospital, Jimmy forbade her to ever talk to Doctor MacFadden again, since he felt that the doctor had too much influence over his wife. Paralyzed by grief, she didn't question his command, but secretly confided in her mother where the money had come from. As a precaution, she asked her mother to say the money was a gift from her and Granda B. Granny B agreed to keep the secret, which wasn't a problem since Granda B had already promised to give them some money to help with their move.

Her thoughts were interrupted when she saw her husband walking toward them, smiling and waving tickets. He started to collect the luggage and handed his three oldest daughters their small carry-on bags. "Okay girls! Come on now. We're off!" he said cheerfully.

He took hold of Granda B's hand. He wanted so badly to express how much the old man had meant to him. That he meant more to him than his own father did.

"You've been like a father to me," he said sincerely. "I can't thank you enough for everything."

"I only wish I could have done more," Granda B said sadly. He respected his son-in-law for being a hard worker and good provider. He kept hold of Jimmy's hand a bit longer. Tears formed in his eyes.

"I promise you, I'll pay you back," Jimmy said.

"Och, you'll do no such thing," Granda B said, dismissing the idea.

"We'll write when we're settled. Then I'll bring you both out for a grand holiday in America."

"Oh, aye. We'll be sure to do that! Good luck, son." Granda B forced himself to smile.

Jimmy turned to the three older girls and didn't see his father-in-law grimace with pain as he touched his stomach. Like the pied piper, Jimmy led Annie, Maggie and Mary outside under a glorious full moon to board the plane. The girls hesitantly followed him. They were torn between the excitement of going on an airplane for the first time and the fear of leaving their home and grandparents.

Granny B held onto her daughter. Cathy stood stoically, feeling only numbness in her heart. She had cried so many tears over the years that her eyes couldn't shed any more.

Finally she gently pulled away from her mother. Staring at Granny B's lined face she said, "Mammy, I know that you did what you thought was best for the family and, for that, I hold nothing against you." She glanced over at her forlorn father as he stood staring out a large window at the plane she would soon be getting on. "Tell Daddy cheerio for me," she said, her lips trembling slightly.

She picked up her bag with one hand and took June's hand with the other. Turning away from her mother she followed her family to the plane—without once looking back.

Chapter Seven:
Reaching the Shores of America

THE AIRPLANE'S RUMBLING engines churned loudly during take off. Cathy sat between Mary and June. As the plane left the ground, Cathy felt Mary squeeze her hand hard. June pressed her face against the window. Her breath coated the Plexiglas as the shores of Scotland faded and could no longer be seen.

Jimmy and Cathy had decided that a night flight would be best. Their hope was that everyone would sleep during the first leg of the long journey. But sleep was elusive. The power of the plane's vibration as it ascended into the sky left them all feeling lightheaded and queasy.

Maggie was the first to cry out for help. "Daddy, I'm going to be sick!"

Neither parent was prepared to deal with four pitifully sick children. Hearing their cries, a stewardess rushed forward with brown paper bags.

The cough June had before leaving Glasgow worsened into spasms. A doctor had said it was the whooping cough. The medicine he gave them didn't help and June continued to cough. Cathy and Jimmy fretted. They knew that if their daughter's cough caught the attention of the American immigration officers, the family could be detained until she was declared healthy enough to enter the United States. Or, worse yet, they could be sent back to Scotland.

The night was very long and seemed even longer with the loud rumbling of the propeller plane. Jimmy and Cathy prayed for daylight, while the girls moaned and whined, asking "Are we there yet?"

Cathy couldn't rest with June sleeping fitfully on her lap, her little legs twitching and giving small kicks. Once she jerked awake, shouting, "Mammy, don't leave me!" Cathy rocked her as she did during the weeks following Helen's death when June had shouted the same concern in her sleep. Later, the sleeping girl awakened her once more when she grabbed the bodice of her mother's dress and cried frantically, "I can't breathe."

June's restlessness started to get the best of Cathy's patience. She looked back to see if Jimmy was awake, but he wasn't in his seat. She debated whether to ask him if he'd take a turn with June. But in the past he had often protested about caring for her, saying that June was such a handful with her constant chattering. Finally, in tired desperation, she struggled out of her seat, telling the girl to hold still.

Cathy wobbled down the aisle of the plane to find Jimmy. She found him standing at the back, smoking and talking with another passenger. She stood next to him, listening for a moment as the men reminisced about why they were leaving and the uncertainties of what lay ahead. Quietly she made her request.

At first he was irritated but he wanted to make the journey easy for his wife, so he went back to his seat and picked up June. Hoping to keep her quiet, he opened one of the children's books that they had brought along. A picture of a sailboat cruising through the water caught her eye. Pointing to it, she asked her Daddy, "Did I fall off this boat?"

"No," he answered, sharply.

When he started to turn the page, she put her hand on the picture. "Where are the people on the boat?" she asked.

"Will you just listen to the story?" he said, slapping her leg.

She quickly stopped talking. He continued reading until her small chest heaved a deep sigh, signaling the beginning of sleep. With his daughter cradled and asleep in the crook of his arms, Jimmy soon fell asleep, too. Eventually, one by one, sleep came to each member of the family.

∽ ∽ ∽

At the New York airport immigration inspection line, their hope of being welcomed into their new country was dashed as their worst fear was realized. The beefy immigration officer had laid out on a table every article in the MacDonald's suitcases. It embarrassed Cathy, and made Jimmy angry. They felt vulnerable. June's face was flushed red as she hacked and shook while coughing.

"Hi-yeh, how you feel-un?" the officer asked, drawing out the syllables in hopes of being understood by the new arrivals.

June didn't understand his strange language. She hid behind her mother. Cathy was glad when her daughter pressed her face into her coat, which muffled the coughs.

"She's caught a wee cold coming over. That plane was terribly chilly," the nervous mother answered the officer with a slight laugh. She hoped to sound nonchalant about the coughing.

The officer pressed his lips tight, saying, "Hmm."

June peeked out from behind her mother. The family stood frozen in place as they waited for the decision. The customs officer looked at the redheaded girl and then at Jimmy, Cathy and the other girls, who huddled together and stared back at him. As immigrants, their entry or denial into America was at the mercy of this man, who could quarantine them if he deemed that June might be carrying a contagious virus.

The officer looked intently at the bright, blue-eyed little girl. Suddenly, June gave him a big grin, widening her apple-red cheeks. In an unprofessional moment, the officer put his feelings into his job,

"Okay. Put your things back in," he said gruffly. He then stamped their passports and turned his attention to the next passengers waiting for inspection.

Cathy felt Jimmy's hands shake as he took her elbow, moving her forward. She could see sweat on his brow. At a safe distance, he whispered in her ear, "Our Lady heard your prayers."

She fingered the rosary beads in her pocket.

൭ ൭ ൭

The long journey and the time change had an overpowering effect on the family. They were disoriented, and didn't know whether they felt tired or awake. They waited for their next flight lounging on uncomfortable chairs. Jimmy bought tea that was weak and barely warm. The girls were thrilled with the new experience of Coca-Cola, an American drink. June climbed onto Cathy's lap, offering her a sip of the soda. Together they gazed out the long, tall windows, and were mesmerized by the brightness of the full moon in the dark sky.

"Mammy, look, the moon lady's face," June said.

"Man in the moon, it's called," Cathy said softly, not wanting to awaken the other children who were lying across each other asleep on the seats.

"Did you see that he followed us all the way?" June asked.

"I did, hen."

"It's a lucky sign. That's what Annie said."

"A good omen, it is, for our new life," Cathy agreed.

൭ ൭ ൭

The moon was only a grayish outline in the chilly dawn sky when the family left the airport lounge and boarded their airplane that would take them to their final destination. Shortly after takeoff, June developed a piercing earache.

Cathy was prepared. On the previous flight a stewardess had given her little square packets wrapped in colorful paper and said, "Bubble gum. It'll help if your girls' get earaches from the pressure of the plane."

While Cathy unwrapped the gum for June, Annie wobbled up the aisle to see if she could help comfort her little sister. Her mother told her to bring the other girls so they too could have a square of gum.

After chewing the gum to soften it, Mary was the first to discover she could blow bubbles. She blew and blew, making a spectacular big, pink, round bubble before it exploded with a "bang!" to the amusement of her sisters.

The girls entertained themselves blowing bubbles, some small and some big. Annie was the first to notice the extra bonus: Inside the small colorful gum wrapper was a funny cartoon about a boy named Joe Bazooka. The girls delighted in their first experience with the sugary American treat.

The drone of the plane, combined with the long hours of travel finally caught up with the MacDonalds. After a while, with their spirits lifted, they pulled up the blankets and fell easily to sleep.

༄ ༄ ༄

Jimmy's voice woke the family. "Girls, quick look," he said pointing out his window. Sun spilled through clouds that encircled the top peaks of a grand bridge. There it was. . . The Golden Gate Bridge! They were almost at their new home in San Francisco.

The girls rushed over to join their father at the window. Jimmy started singing the song he taught them on the bus ride to the Glasgow Airport, "San Francisco, open your Golden Gates."

Cathy joined the others looking at the spectacular view. She stared, captivated by the sight of the bridge.

Chapter Eight:
Eureka! San Francisco

AFTER THEIR LONG twenty-four hour journey, the MacDonald family restlessly awaited Sandy Jordon's arrival to drive them to their new home in San Francisco.

"Don't worry. He'll be here soon," Jimmy told his exhausted family after he hung up the phone. He moved a few steps away and lit up his last remaining cigarette.

Slumped down on a large, battered suitcase, Annie and Mary leaned against each other and discussed what kind of candy they'd find in San Francisco. Annie listed her favorite sweets, then Mary hers.

"I'm going to get a whole bag of that Bazooka bubble gum and that candy the plane lady gave me, Peppermint Patty," Mary said, nodding with finality.

"Soon you'll be Peppermint Fatty eating all that stuff!" Maggie said teasingly.

"Shut up, stupid cow" Mary yelled, springing up and ready for a fistfight.

"Girls!" their father boomed at them.

Maggie sat with June on the sidewalk with a pad of paper and crayons strewn across a suitcase. June chose the crayons and instructed her older sister on which colors to use on each figure in the imaginary family they were drawing.

"No, Maggie, put this color here," June said pointing outside the lines.

"No. You've got to stay in the lines," her sister said. "That's the right way."

June frowned at her, frustrated that her sister wouldn't do what she instructed.

Jimmy took another drag on his cigarette and snuck a sideways glance at his wife. Her face was drawn and pale. She was rubbing her temples, trying to ease her headache.

An hour after they arrived, a big blue car drove up to the curb in front of where the MacDonalds waited. Sandy jumped out.

"Jimmy! Cathy! Girls! Hello!" he grinned with outstretched arms.

Elated to see him, everyone jumped up to greet their host. Jimmy grabbed his friend's hand.

"Oh, man, is it good to see you," he said, pumping Sandy's hand up and down enthusiastically.

At forty-eight, Sandy looked just as boyish as ever, except that he was rounder and his face a deeper shade of red. "It's a bloody long trip, isn't' it?" he asked.

The family muttered an agreement. They were more intent on getting the luggage into the car and getting on their way than in having a conversation.

"Here, girls, give me those bags." Sandy opened a large, empty trunk at the back of his car.

Cathy hurriedly helped the girls put their small carry-on bags into the car's trunk. "Goodness sakes, Sandy!" she exclaimed. "Look at the size of this *boot*[20]. It's big enough to house a bunch of tinkers."

"Everything's big in America," said Sandy with his infectious jolly laugh. Soon the mood of the tired travelers lightened.

"Well it's a lovely car, Sandy." She handed him the last of the smaller bags.

"It's a Chevrolet Bel Air," he beamed. "I bought it new. It's my pride and joy, next to my missus, of course."

---

[20]   Boot – Car trunk.

Sandy had come to America in 1946, right after the war. Within a year, he wrote home that he had married an American woman. His family in Glasgow, thinking that he'd never marry, had told Jimmy and Cathy they were thankful for the good news.

As Sandy stuffed the last of the suitcases into the trunk, Mary brought over her own traveling bag. "Mr. Jordon, can I put this in?" she asked.

"Call me Uncle Sandy."

"Are you my uncle?" she asked curiously.

"I am now. We're each other's family here."

She looked intently, studying him. "Are you a Catholic?"

He patted her head, "Of course. I'm your daddy's friend. Why wouldn't I be a Catholic?"

"Will we have a Granda here too?" Mary asked.

"We've already got a Granda *and* a Granny," said Annie as she heaved a heavy bag into the trunk, not waiting for Sandy to help.

"Mammy, will Granda B come here to live with us?" Mary wanted her mother to confirm the new situation with their new relatives in America.

"Of course not," said Maggie, rolling her eyes. "We're too far away for them to come. We'll never see them again."

Mary frowned at her sister's remark. "Liar. That's not true, is it Mammy?"

With her head deep in the trunk of the car, Cathy paid no heed to the girls' voices as she looked through a suitcase for some cardigans. Even with the sun shining, the weather in California was colder than she'd thought it would be.

"It's true, Mary. We'll never see them. Just like you won't see Helen anymore," said June, sitting on the car's bumper, swinging her legs back and forth and chewing bubble gum.

With her hands full of different colored cardigans, Cathy heard June's words about Helen. Her face paled, tears gushed forth, and, although she cupped cardigans over her mouth, sobs broke through her lips. Jimmy rushed past the girls to help Cathy into the comfortable leather seat in the back of the car.

"Girls, get in the car. Now," Jimmy ordered. "We'll be off in a minute. June! Off that fender." He moved toward the front of the car where Sandy was bent over the open hood, anxious to show off the engine.

Maliciously, Maggie hissed at Mary, "Stupid cow. Shut up about Granda and Granny." And to June she said, "You made Mammy cry. Troublemaker."

Annie took control before a shouting match erupted. She walked past Maggie and bumped her shoulder hard. "Shut your mouth," she said.

Sulking, Mary did as told, and shoved June aside as she climbed in. June followed her, slapping at Mary's backside. Maggie moved aside, and with an exaggerated bow, waved Annie into the car. "You first, Queen Anne. I'll sit by the window."

Annie wanted to keep peace for the sake of her mother. "I'll let you do that, Margaret, just this once," she said sweetly to Maggie. She knew that her sister hated to be called by her proper name.

The men closed the hood and got into the front seat. Remarking on the size of the engine, Jimmy said jokingly, "That's a huge piece of machinery. Hope you can handle all that horsepower!"

"Aye, man, I can handle it!" Sandy revved up the engine and then let the roar calm down to a purr. The men nodded their approval of the sound. Sandy started the car and drove towards San Francisco.

The girls settled into the back seat with their mother. Cathy turned her head to look out the window. She remained quiet, not answering the girls' questions. Soon the chattering voices died down and the three oldest girls were lulled to sleep by the car's hum.

June peeked out the corner of her eye and saw her mother wiping tears off her cheeks. The little girl felt sure her mother was thinking of Helen. The next time June peeked out she saw her mother's eyes slowly closing.

Too excited to doze off herself, she stood up and put her elbows on the front seat and listened to the men.

Sandy said he and his wife had just bought a new house in a part of San Francisco called the Sunset. "It's got three bedrooms and two bathrooms."

"Two bathrooms? What do you need that for?" Jimmy asked jokingly. There's only the three of you."

"You'll have a house in no time. And I know a man who's selling a car. I'll fix you up with him. It's great here in America."

"A car? Don't they use buses here?" Jimmy looked at the cars zooming past them on the freeway.

The men began to talk about football. Sandy told Jimmy that in America football was played differently, and that the Americans called Scottish football soccer. For a Glaswegian man, soccer was a passionate subject. Arguments about the two rival teams, the Protestant Rangers and the Catholic Celtics could easily lead to fist fights. Sandy said there were many football teams in the States, and that religion wasn't associated with them. He went on to say that American football was reserved for "pansies" that needed gear. "They're afraid they'll get hurt, poor, wee lassies," he added.

June enjoyed herself looking at all the new scenery passing by and listening to the men talk. She liked seeing her father relaxed. Everything seemed better when he laughed. He told Sandy the story about when Peter's wife, Janet, gave birth. The doctor, who was also a Ranger's player, had rushed from his game to deliver the baby without taking time to change from his soccer uniform. When he arrived at Janet's bedside she screamed at him to get away from her. She didn't want any Protestant touching her body, let alone her baby!

With tears of laughter running down his face, Sandy choked out between laughs, "Och, away with you. You're full of it, man!'

"I am not! I'm telling you the truth," Jimmy could hardly talk for laughing. "They had to call in a Catholic doctor. But I never did find out if he was a Celtic fan."

The humming of the car and deep laughter of the men finally lulled June to sleep with her head resting on the front seat. When the car stopped, the girls woke up and rubbed the sleep from their eyes. Outside they saw a parade of cars following a bus.

Jimmy opened a door. "Here we are. Home," he said happily.

Eagerly, the girls scrambled from the car to stand in front of a three-story building. Their mother jumped awake at the sound of the girls' chattering and stumbled out of the car. Surprised by a car whizzing past, she flattened herself against Sandy's Chevrolet and watched the continual stream of traffic rushing past.

"Careful there!" warned Sandy, holding the largest suitcase under one muscular arm and a smaller one under the other.

"It's an awfully busy street," said Cathy. Not that it bothered her, since the MacDonalds had lived on the Dumbarton Road thoroughfare, in Glasgow. But she had envisioned that they'd live on a wide street with palatial houses and gardens. She thought of the many movies like "Meet Me in St. Louis," which was one of her favorite images of what life in America would be like. Lining both sides of this busy street were tall apartment buildings with stores underneath. Nothing like the buildings the films had shown.

"Well, it's a main street. Called Market," said Sandy as a streetcar rattled past.

Jimmy walked over to stand next to her. Smiling, he said, "See up there? That'll be our home." The couple leaned their heads back and looked up the tall building to the top windows.

"It's big, clean and affordable," Sandy said as he unlocked the front door of the building. "In the flat below yours is a Polish couple. Came over after the war," he explained as he went in the door. "Up we go!" he called back to the MacDonalds.

With arms full of suitcases, the men disappeared into the building. The rest of the group followed them.

Inside June saw a steep wooden staircase that turned slightly as it continued upward. Annie beat her sisters up the stairs and reached the top floor first. She looked over the banister and shouted down to her mother, "Mammy, there's thirty steps! I counted!"

The girls ran around the flat in excitement. Their feet banged loudly on the bare wood floors as they called out to each other, "Come see this." Cathy put her hand to her forehead and yelled at the girls to stop running.

They hastily explored the rooms. Sandy told them that the room next to the kitchen, the pale pink room lined with wainscot, would be their bedroom. Their mother said the large double bed with a red and black tufted headboard was where the three youngest girls would sleep, while a single bed next to the window was for Annie. Both Maggie and Mary claimed their side of the bed and decided that June would sleep in the middle.

The kitchen was smaller than the one in Scotland, and didn't have an alcove bed for Jimmy and Cathy. The girls continued exploring and found some of their parents' suitcases in a separate room down the hallway from theirs. It had a double bed with a light wood headboard and a long low matching dressing table with a big mirror attached. The girls stood in front of it, striking poses and making faces.

The sisters ran back down the hall to their bedroom to begin unpacking. June drifted out of the room to explore more of her new home. In the empty living room she found Cathy standing still in the light of the sun shining through the tall bay windows. She crept slowly into the room to stand at the window with her mother. She leaned into her mother's legs and put her arms around them.

"So this is San Francisco," Cathy whispered in awe at the view. She had heard that San Francisco was one of the most beautiful cities in the world. Never had she dreamed that one day she would make it her home. Above the rooftops of the tall buildings were two rolling hills alongside each other. Just peeking over the top of them came a low fog moving towards her at a snail's pace.

"They're called Twin Peaks," said Sandy, interrupting Cathy's visual meditation.

He came up behind Cathy and June and pointed to the two hills. "My house is beyond them, over by the ocean. It's about three or so miles from here," he explained. "It's wonderful to be able to walk down to the beach. You know we Scots need to be by the sea. But, funny thing is, I still think of Scotland as home. You know what I mean?"

June glanced at Sandy and saw a faraway look in his eyes. She thought she heard her mother say, "Will I still think of Scotland as home in years to come?" But when she looked up, her mother's lips were closed in a small sad smile. The three stayed looking out the windows in silence. Jimmy came in to join them, watching the fog continue its slow roll down the peaks, spreading across rooftops like a plush carpet. Soon it would cover the entire Eureka Valley, the area of San Francisco the MacDonalds now called home.

Chapter Nine:
Making the Home Sacred

THE MEN HUFFED and puffed as they maneuvered a large, deep green horsehair couch up the stairs to the flat. Cathy waited at the top listening to Jimmy wonder aloud how much she might have spent on the heavy furniture. Between grunts and groans, Sandy remarked, "Jesus, Jimmy, this is the heaviest couch I've ever moved."

Cathy had gotten right to business exploring the Salvation Army, St. Vincent de Paul and every other thrift furniture store she could find. She made her selections after examining and debating over each piece. She chose durable furniture that was in decent shape that fit into her budget. By the end of each day, she and the girls would come back to the flat exhausted but excited about their finds. They carried all they could, and left the rest for a later pick-up.

The girls enjoyed unpacking the big trunk shipped from Scotland. In it was kitchenware, photos and knickknacks. There were shouts of delight as the newspaper and cloth wrappings were removed, revealing the treasures underneath. The girls went from room to room, discussing the location that best suited each item.

By Saturday night, the flat acquired a lived-in look and the hollow echo reverberating off the hardwood floors lessened. The next day the family attended their first Mass at their new parish church. Later on Sunday they enjoyed an early dinner, a savory steak pie with gravy and buttery mashed potatoes. Cathy's most praise-worthy dish showed that they had a reason to celebrate.

After dinner, the girls, with full bellies and happy attitudes, prepared for their first day of school. The older sisters laid out their clothes and supplies while June, too young for school, was also busy. She had told her sisters that they should make a special place for remembering Helen. She found an empty cardboard box and transformed it into a pretty table by covering it with one of Cathy's large colorful scarves. She then arranged small stones on the box, carefully moving them until they were aligned in a perfect circle. She wished that the stones were more like the huge ones in her dream, where she sat in the center of the stone circle they had formed.

The girls petitioned Cathy for a photo of Helen to place on the table June created. The family albums were presented to their mother.

Cathy sat in the kitchen trying to decide which photo to give to the girls. Each photo was too dear to part with, but, after all, it was for the girls. She gently touched one of Helen at two years old, happily sitting on a fat Shetland pony at Ayr. "That was a happy day," Cathy recalled. Every summer, Granda and Granny B would take the family to the seashore vacation town of Ayr for a week. She took the photo from the album and gave it to June.

"Oh, thank you, Mammy. It's a beautiful picture," June said as she reverently held the picture in her open palms. "Helen will be happy she's in our room. You can come visit her in there, too."

June took the photo and tenderly placed it within the stone circle. When the table was ready, she joyfully announced, "Here's Helen."

Annie came forward with a small statue of Our Lady—a gift to her from Granny B—and placed it next to the photo.

Maggie put one of her drawings next to the stone circle. "This is Baby Kit." The drawing was of a baby with saucer-shaped blue eyes, two pink dots for cheeks and yellow hair with a red dotted bow in it. "That's how she'd look if she'd didn't die," Maggie said. The girls agreed with a nod.

It was almost time to share their creation with their parents. Mary said, "Wait!" as she ran out of the room for a moment. She came back with small pink flowers that she had plucked that day from the garden downstairs. The flowers completed the altar.

"Maggie, where's the other drawing you said you'd do for me?" June asked.

"Here!" she said holding up a large piece of paper. On it was a picture of a beautiful angel dressed in a long, flowing pale-green robe with wings extending the width of the paper. The angel floated in a soft blue sky over a field of bright yellow flowers. A halo in a darker shade of yellow encircled her bright red hair and deep navy eyes that stared out.

Cathy playfully snuck up behind the girls who were "oohing" over the drawing. "Oh Maggie! You're very talented," she exclaimed.

Jimmy walked by the bedroom, holding a hammer, nails and a large framed picture of Our Lady, the Virgin Mary. He had heard his wife's voice coming from the girls' bedroom "Where'd you want this hung?" he asked Cathy.

"Come and see this," she said, holding up the drawing.

"That's unbelievable!" he said, pleased with what he saw.

"Maggie drawed it for me. I told her how my angel looked," June was also proud of her sister's talents. She pointed out the picture of Baby Kit, saying that they were still all together.

"They're lovely pictures," Jimmy said kindly.

Maggie glowed from the attention. She loved drawing and coloring, almost as much as dancing and singing.

"This is a good place for you girls to say your night prayers at, eh?" Jimmy said.

"But the angel one's too big to put on our altar," said Mary, pointing to the small box.

Jimmy took the drawing and, with a quick tap to a nail, secured it on the wall above the small table.

"It's like she's watching over Helen and Baby Kit," Cathy said quietly.

Standing back, Jimmy looked at the table and said suddenly, "I know what we need." He left the bedroom and came back with a dark wood frame that had held a black-and-white photo of his stern looking parents. He easily slid the photo of Helen into the frame. It was perfect. He also brought in a tapered white candle in one of the bronze candlesticks that had belonged to his mother. Lastly, he handed them a crucifix.

June looked at the cross with Jesus hanging on it. She had always thought that it was sad to see Jesus being hurt, and she didn't want it in her room.

"Daddy, this is for girls in here, and Jesus is a boy," she said.

Cathy hoped Jimmy wouldn't get angry with June for rejecting the cross. But, surprisingly, he just shrugged his shoulders and said, "Aye, alright."

He lit the candle and gave it to June. With both hands, she ceremoniously placed it behind the circle of stones and under her angel drawing. It was getting late and the room had grown dark during the creation of the altar. The family sat quietly in the small, sacred space illuminated by candlelight.

Chapter Ten:
Holy Savior School

THE MACDONALDS ARRIVED in San Francisco with much promise of a new beginning, and a note from their parish priest that secured the three older girls an immediate acceptance into a Catholic school. The family's reputation was firmly established by the first day at Holy Savior, the neighborhood parochial school.

The March winds had died down and the day was warming up. The heavy, woolen sweater itched Maggie's arms as she, along with her mother and sisters, walked along Diamond Street toward the first day at school. Annie had helped her mother iron the school uniforms to perfection. She was proud that Maggie, Mary and she looked clean and tidy in their white blouses and pleated navy-blue skirts. But Cathy wasn't as satisfied. Even though she had stayed up late sewing the night before, the hem on Mary's skirt was hanging on one side. She searched her handbag for a safety pin, called Mary to her side, and knelt down to pin up the skirt. It didn't help that her daughter was bouncing from one foot to the other while humming a little ditty that Granda B had taught her.

The days will come and the days will pass when Orange men[21] will go to Mass.

And the Fenian[22] boys will kick their ass right up and down the chapel path.

---

[21] Orange men – Scottish or Irish Protestants.

[22] Fenian – Refers to Scottish and Irish Catholic revolutionaries seeking independence from Britain in the 1850s. They were unsuccessful.

Cathy tried to stifle a laugh, but it burst forth anyway when she looked at Mary's twinkling dark eyes and joyous face. Impulsively, she gave her daughter a quick bear hug and said, as seriously as she could, "In America they don't fight over religion. Let's not sing that. Okay?" She stood back up, "Let's go." Cathy hoped her seven year-old would do better in this school. The Scottish schools hadn't been easy for Mary, with her rambunctious ways and slowness to grasp her letters and numbers.

On the walk to school, Maggie held her head high and sashayed down the street. Of all her children, Cathy knew Maggie would do well no matter what school she attended. She had always been a popular and good student. On the way, Maggie wondered aloud to her sisters about which boy's initials would be the first written on her new school PeeChee folder. When Mary reminded her that Daddy told her to stop this boy crazy thing, Maggie boasted that a lot of boys were crazy for her, and that maybe she'd invite a special one to her upcoming eighth birthday just two weeks away.

Cathy wanted them to enter the schoolyard together as a family, but Annie had walked ahead and was already at the gate. At nine years old, Annie was independent. She did what she thought best, often without consulting her mother. *She's like Granny,* Cathy thought about her eldest.

She tugged at June's hand to rush her along to where Annie and Maggie stood waiting for Mary. No longer skipping, Mary trudged up to them.

"I don't want to go to this school. Please can we go back to see Granda?" Mary said in a wavering voice.

Taking the frightened girl's hand, Cathy told her gently, "We're too far from him now, pet. You'll make new friends here."

The bell sounded.

"Mammy, you and June go now. We're not babies," Annie said in a matter-of-fact tone as she took Mary's hand, pulling her into the yard. Cathy started to protest, but let them go.

Students began streaming around Cathy and June, bumping into them as they hurried inside the yard. Two girls stopped to look at the little girl. One touched June's ringlets, pointing them out to a girl with rusty orange hair and pale colorless skin dotted with blotchy red brown freckles.

"Dee-Dee, look how cute she is!" the girl said.

Dee-Dee smiled down at June. She then looked back up at Cathy and said, "I wish my hair was more like hers. I hate mine!"

Cathy didn't see anything wrong with the orange frizzed cap on top of the girl's head. She'd seen many variations of red hair in Scotland. Of course, her daughter's Titan-red had always attracted compliments.

June felt a special kinship with Dee-Dee. She touched her skirt and said, "Your Granda loves your hair."

Dee-Dee gasped. Her face drained and her freckles stood out bolder on her sallow skin.

"Did she know your grandfather?" her friend asked.

"How could she? He's been dead for three years," Dee-Dee said with annoyance and fled into the yard.

Hearing her daughter's comment, Cathy told June, "See, you hurt that girl's feelings. You're not being a nice girl."

June began to say something about the girl's grandfather, but her mother shushed her. Frustrated by her mother's reaction, June leaned further into the chain link fence and watched the children entering the schoolyard.

Cathy waited by the fence, peering into the yard to see how her other daughters were faring. She saw the Mother Superior, the principal of the school, a tall, thin nun that she had met a few days before, directing her girls by pointing in the direction of two assembling lines, one for girls and one for boys.

Annie stoically walked to the back of the girls' line clutching her new blue binder against her chest. Cathy wished she'd smile so she wouldn't look so serious.

"Annie misses Granny," June said.

"Och, stop blethering about grandas and grannys," Cathy mumbled, keeping her eyes on the girls.

Maggie went towards the front of the line, slowly walking past the nun and shooting her a dazzling smile. She stepped in between a gangly freckled-face girl and a short blonde. The freckled girl made a face and elbowed her out of the line. With a sad face, Maggie walked solemnly back to the tall nun. Standing in front of the principal, she whispered something and pointed at the insulting parties without looking at them. The tall nun had to bend low to hear the new pupil. Upon hearing the complaint, the principal snapped up broom-straight with nostrils flared wide. She narrowed her eyes at the offenders and took the new student's hand, placing her in the very front of the line. Maggie gave Mother Superior a gracious smile.

"Maggie won, huh?" June said excitedly.

Cathy didn't answer her as she moved along the fence until she had a better view of Mary, who had disappeared between the two lines. Mary walked slowly, head hanging between her hunched shoulders. Her mother imagined Mary's face was blushing a hot, embarrassed red. Without paying attention, Mary swayed over to the boys' row and bumped into a big boy who immediately pushed her backward. Startled, she almost fell, but regained her footing. She dropped her newly bought school supplies and swung a fist upward with all her might, catching the big bully squarely on the jaw. He stumbled into his jeering friends who quickly propelled him back into the chubby girl.

"A fat girl beat you up!" they laughed.

June gasped. "Them are Proddy boys, huh Mammy?"

No response was needed for June to begin scurrying around to pick up small pebbles on the sidewalk.

"We're gonna have to beat them bad boys up," she murmured to herself.

Before Cathy could run to interfere and before the bully and Mary got to round two, a leprechaun-sized nun with a beaked nose and black habit billowing behind her rushed to the dueling students. Swiftly, she dug her talons into Mary's shoulders with a fierce grab that caused her to screech from pain. She pushed her into the girls' line and reprimanded the other students with a wagging finger. Cathy would learn later that day that the little nun was Sister St. Pius, Maggie's third grade teacher. The nun was known for not having to use many words to keep the students in line. Her looks alone could defeat the most rebellious students and the children knew better than to question her authority.

Silence fell across the schoolyard. Cathy wondered if the Mother Superior tolerated the fearless little nun's method of quelling the pandemonium. She was sure that there were some students who needed it, but wished it hadn't happened to Mary on her first day of school.

Mother Superior's head turned minutely toward a round nun standing to the side of her. The round nun shook her head ever so slightly. From that interaction, Cathy had hope that the Mother Superior would take pity on Mary and not punish her further for fighting with the boy.

The two lines began to move toward the school doors. June gaily waved good-bye to the passing students, some of whom snuck a tiny wave to the little girl. Cathy took hold of June's hand and led her across the street toward the church.

∞ ∞ ∞

Mother and daughter stopped at a small garden at the side of the church. A bronze fence gave the garden a sense of privacy. In it was a statue of the Our Lady, the Blessed Virgin surrounded by spring flowers in early bloom, which added to the beautiful serenity of the small sacred space.

In quiet respect, mother and daughter entered the garden. The sunny day created an aura of peacefulness and the only sound was the soft murmur of children saying a morning prayer at the school across the street. Cathy knelt on the lovely wooden prie-dieu in front of the statue.

June looked up to the serene face of the Our Lady, whose palms were opened outward in a welcoming gesture. The little girl felt a beckoning from the statue's gentle smile. Her mother indicated to her to kneel. Slipping her hand into her cardigan pocket, Cathy took out crystal blue rosary beads and began to pray. Copying her mother, the girl bent her little head, although she was more interested in the small white and yellow daisies next to her. Peeking up at her mother, she gingerly extended her hand to pull out a flower, tugging it gently until it surrendered to her. She raised the flower as an offering to her mother who was deep in prayer. Nudging her mother, she whispered, "Mammy. Mammy!"

The faint sound of June's voice broke Cathy's concentration. Gradually, she opened her eyes to see a yellow daisy in front of them. She accepted the gift. June then yanked on her mother's sleeve and pointed up to the sky. "Look. See the angel watching us?"

Cathy looked dreamily upward to the clouds in the sky. Maybe she did see some form in the clouds that could be wings. *Or, could it be an image of Helen in the clouds?* she wondered. It all seemed so surreal and peaceful to Cathy. It was the way she wished her life to be from now on.

"It is an angel," June chatted away. "See her face, long dress and wings."

She looked at her daughter's little cherub face, stroking it with a finger. "Yes, I see a wee angel with red hair right in front of me."

Exasperated by her mother's remark, June shook her head and encouraged her mother to look more carefully. "Look again, Mammy! No, not at me! At the sky. That's my angel. She follows us."

"Oh yes! Of course, I see her red hair. That must be why I thought it was you."

"Yes, you're right. Her hair is like mine," June said, smiling up to her mother, happy that she could see her angel, too.

"Do angels have a mammy?" June asked.

"They have Our Lady. She's the Blessed Mother to everyone," Cathy answered.

With a lighthearted feeling, Cathy stood up and offered an invitation. "I think it's going to be a hot day. Come on, let's get an ice cream."

It was such an unusual offering that June's rosebud mouth fell open in surprise. "In the morning?"

Her mother laughed gaily and said in a hushed voice, "Shhh. It'll be our wee secret, angel."

She took June's hand, leading her out of the magical garden and toward an enjoyment of one of life's simple pleasures: a cold ice cream sprinkled with brightly colored candy seeds on a warm spring day.

Chapter Eleven:
The Novena

THE SCENT OF pot roast and boiled potatoes filled the kitchen while constant chatter bubbled throughout dinner. Each of the older girls vied for a spot to showcase her achievements. Annie piped in first about her excellent grades in arithmetic. Then Maggie told how her artwork was chosen for display in the school hallway. Mary said she was the dodge ball champion.

"Good going, girls" replied their father, motioning to his wife to pass the salt.

June announced, "I saw Helen today."

Silence hit the room with a thud. At the end of the table her tired father perked up, "What did she say?"

Although Cathy knew that Jimmy really was trying to be patient with the girls, she still worried that his temper could flare at any time. She decided to take his attention elsewhere.

"Would you like some more meat?" she quickly asked him.

He grunted an answer as she hurried to the stove to fill the empty meat platter. With her back to the family, she tried to calm her growing fear. Her stomach began to tighten. She hoped desperately that June would stop talking about the day's events. She didn't.

"Me and my angel went to see Our Lady in the garden. She's a real angel! Huh, Mammy?" June insisted on telling her story.

"Mammy, did you take June to the garden today?" Annie asked.

"I told you. Just me and my angel went." June wanted to be thought of as a big girl.

Jimmy's silverware fell to his plate, which accentuated the interruption. "Stop fibbing. Finish your dinner—all of you," he yelled.

"Daddy, I'm not..." June tried to explain.

"That's enough. Take your plate to the sink," her father ordered.

June stood up, scowling, and scraped her chair across the linoleum, not caring whether it bothered her father. She passed in front of her mother without looking at her, and walked out of the kitchen.

∽ ∽ ∽

Cathy breathed easier as she watched her daughter leave the table. She knew that June wasn't lying. She just didn't want her daughter to tell the family that she had also gone missing earlier that day. If she did, then Jimmy would know that she wasn't always watching her, which was true at times. On some days, after the older girls left for school, Cathy would sit for hours, lost in memories, staring out the bay windows at Twin Peaks in the direction of the ocean.

Earlier that day June had wandered off, crossing busy Market and Castro Streets to reach the garden at the Holy Savior Church. And that's where Cathy found her.

As she stood staring out the windows, in the back of her mind she had heard June's voice, but not her words. When she finally turned to look, she realized the flat was quiet. June wasn't there. She peered down the backstairs to the yard, but she didn't see her. She checked the time and realized that her daughter might have been gone for up to two hours.

Quickly, Cathy walked down Castro Street and went from store to store to ask if anyone had seen her chatty little daughter. "Not today," they said. Feeling more frantic as the minutes ticked on, she felt tears burn behind her eyes. *Maybe she's waiting for her sisters outside the school,* she thought hopefully.

As she approached the school, Cathy looked to the church across the street. And there, behind the garden's fence, was a flash of red hair. She opened the gate and saw June kneeling on the prie-dieu talking to the statue of Our Lady. Her face lit up when she saw her mother. She cheerfully waved a tiny hand at Cathy, while the other was filled with daisies.

"Mammy! Angel and me got daisies for you. An' she wants you to be her mammy, too!"

Angry with her daughter for disappearing, Cathy jerked her up by the arm so hard that all the flowers fell to the ground. "Bad girl!" she yelled, smacking her daughter's bottom.

Immediately repenting her outburst, she dropped to her knees and pulled June into a tight hug. "You wee bugger!" she cried. "I've been sick with worry! Don't you ever do that again or I'll have Daddy *skelp*[23] you. Hear me?"

June pushed her mother away and said crossly, "I told you that me and my angel were going to find you flowers," and then marched away in a huff.

Cathy began to give a retort, then remembered that she had heard June's voice in the background as she mulled over her heartaches.

In protest, June kept at a distance all the way home and didn't say one word. Cathy looked at her daughter's red hair and thought of the old saying that redheads have hot tempers. She thought it must be true.

∾ ∾ ∾

"How's about a cup of tea?" Jimmy's voice snapped Cathy back into the present.

---

[23]   Skelp – Scottish for spank.

She picked up his cup and went to the stove for the teapot. The girls finished their dinners and left their parents alone in the kitchen. After serving him tea, she went back to her chores. The only sound in the kitchen was the clanking of dishes and silverware as Cathy washed them.

She turned from the sink and caught Jimmy looking at her. "What?" she asked, ready to hear that she'd forgotten something he needed.

"Nothing. Just looking at you."

She wiped a strand of hair from her eyes and picked up the pots from the stove.

"I wish I had a smoke," he said. He had given up smoking when they moved to America—a promise he made to Cathy.

Not wanting to talk about his nasty habit, she began a conversation about the girls' school. She told Jimmy that she volunteered to bake several items to help raise money for the school's sports program.

"You never had to do that at their school back home," he said.

"I'm trying to fit in," she said. "It makes things easier for the girls. Maggie says they get teased a lot about the way they speak. And, of course, then the girls get in fights."

"That's my girls," Jimmy remarked.

"We didn't want them to have to fight anymore. Anyway, it doesn't look good. The nuns will think they're troublemakers."

Cathy didn't mention that she, also, wanted to fit in. She was awfully lonely and she missed Granny B's presence and Patsy's good-natured friendship.

"Sandy gave me a book so we could start studying for our citizenship test," he said.

"Oh, yeah?"

Jimmy chuckled, his Glaswegian voice changing to an exaggerated American accent, "Yeah? You don't say? You sound *real* American, Mrs. MacDonald."

"Och, you!" She laughed lightly as she took off her apron, hung it over a chair, and brushed her blonde hair away from her face.

"You're still a good looking woman," Jimmy said softly.

She smiled, embarrassed by the compliment. The dripping of the faucet was the only sound in the kitchen.

Jimmy coughed, clearing his throat. "Oh, by the way, I met the couple from downstairs today. Seem nice enough. They were off to work. The woman's mother lives with them."

"The wife works? Hmm. Maybe I should get a job."

"You?" he snorted. "What'll you do? You've never worked before."

"I have too! I worked during the war."

"Och, during the war everybody had to help." Jimmy sounded annoyed with the idea.

"We'll see. I better get going. I'm starting a *Novena*[24] tonight."

"For Dad?" He was referring to Patsy's letter that arrived a week ago. In it she informed them that Granda B had stomach cancer. The letter said, "Don't bother coming home. I'll keep you posted. I'll send a telegram if need be." She then went on to talk about how Granny B was holding up. Patsy was the only one in the family who wrote regularly.

Placing the damp kitchen towel over a chair, Cathy said, "Of course I'll pray for him, too. I always keep my parents in my prayers."

Jimmy shared her quiet sadness for a moment. "Well, you know him, Cath. He'd be the first to say, 'It's my time.' It'll be Granny that'll need help."

She knew that he missed his father-in-law much more than he would ever let on.

"Are you asking Our Lady to help me get that promotion?" Jimmy's reminded her.

She took a long sip of tea before answering. "We need that to happen, don't we?"

---

[24] Novena – A Roman Catholic period of prayer lasting nine consecutive days.

Cathy looked up to the round kitchen clock high up on the wall. "I'll go get the girls out of the bath. I'll take June with me but will you see that the others do their homework and get to bed on time?"

"Okay," he answered readily, glad that June wouldn't be home to annoy him with her many questions.

As she turned to leave the kitchen, she heard a chair scrape backward. Jimmy stood close behind her. He kissed the nape of her head, asking softly, "Are you happier here?"

Stepping away from her husband, she said, "I am, Jimmy. Right, I better get going."

Guilt nagged at her for not returning her husband's affection. After all, he was, as her mother said, a good husband. He always had a job, sometimes two, and always provided for his family. Granny B had told Cathy that marrying Jimmy had been her best decision.

Cathy grabbed a few towels out of a hallway cupboard and entered the noisy bathroom. The girls were making so much noise that they didn't notice her at first. Annie stood away from the tub wrapped in a towel with her eyebrows drawn down. Maggie and Mary, with water dripping from their naked bodies, stood hugging and looking down into the tub. "Don't worry baby, he'll come back," Mary said in an exaggerated motherly manner. Puzzled, Cathy tipped forward to look over their shoulders and into the tub.

She jumped back in fright, panicked by what she saw. June was underwater with her eyes wide open, staring upward. Dropping the towels, she pushed the girls aside and fell to her knees. She grabbed her youngest out of the water and into her arms. "June, June," Cathy sobbed.

Sputtering, the little girl struggled to loosen her mother's hold and smiled dreamily up into her shocked face.

"My God, girl! What do you think you're doing?" Cathy shouted, shaken with fright. She turned to her eldest child. "Were you just going to stand there and let her drown?"

Maggie picked up a towel off the floor and covered herself. "We were acting," she said.

In irritation, Cathy grabbed the towel off her and wrapped it around June. "Pull the drain plug, Annie," she said as she stumbled back to sit on the toilet seat cover still holding June.

Annie did as ordered. With tears, she said defensively, "I told them it was a stupid game. I told them you'd be mad at us."

Mary jumped into the explanation. "It's a game, Mammy. June is the daddy. He drowns. And I'm the mammy crying for him."

Cathy sat quietly watching the bathwater slowly swirl down the drain. Condensation dripped down the bathroom walls as the room began to cool. The girls started to shiver.

"Whose idea was this?" she said finally.

The three older girls pointed fingers simultaneously. "June's!"

June sat silently on her mother's lap. Her eyes were downcast. Cathy touched her little girl's chin with the tips of her fingers, lifting up her face so they were looking at each other, faces only inches apart. "Why?" Cathy asked. Mother and daughter stared intensely at each other.

The last of the draining water broke the silence. Cathy sighed, "Alright girls, go get your pajamas on." They quickly filed out of the bathroom.

She put both her hands on June's shoulders to get her full attention. Through clenched teeth, she said, "You stop this. . . this story telling. I'm no kidding, June Elizabeth MacDonald."

"I'm sorry. I'll try to be a good girl for you." She leaned her wet hair against her mother and hugged her.

"Stop wiggling!" Cathy began to dry June roughly. "You're coming to the Novena with me tonight."

ᘐ ᘐ ᘐ

On the busy corner where Seventeenth Street crosses Castro and Market Streets, Cathy and June stood holding hands, waiting for the light to turn green. The wait seemed to take forever. June wanted to dance around a bit, but her mother held tightly to her hand and told her to stop fidgeting. Her mother had warned her that they must hurry so they wouldn't miss the opening prayers. When the light turned green, June felt her feet almost come out of her shoes as her mother pulled her across the street.

As the two rushed down the street Tony, the man from the delicatessen, called out a greeting. Although Cathy didn't seem to hear him, June attempted a wave, as she was hurried along. When they were in the deli the other day, June had heard Tony talking to another customer about her. He said, "What a quirky little kid. One day when the arthritis in my hand was killing me, the kid said that I should run it under warm water. She told me it would give my hand happy colors." The customer said, "Kids say the darnedest things, eh?" They both laughed. June felt good that she made people happy.

Cathy and June swept passed the donut shop and turned rapidly onto the next street. June had an important question to ask, if only her mother would slow down. She forged ahead anyway, holding up the rosary beads her mother had given her before leaving the house.

"Mammy, were these yours when you were a wee girl?" The white translucent beads dangled from her small hand.

"Aye. Granny gave them to me," Cathy said, not missing a step.

"If we do the whole Rosary, will Our Lady give us our wish?" the girl said breathlessly.

"We have to come nine times. Then we'll see if She grants us what we ask for."

"Maggie said that Sister St. Pius told her to pray to God when we want something. Why do you pray to Our Lady?" June squeezed her mother's hand, wishing she would stop to talk.

Cathy slowed her pace when they turned onto Diamond Street and could see the large granite church. The lights shining through the stained glass windows made the church look welcoming.

"Well, you know when you ask Daddy for something special and he's too busy? And I ask him for you? It's the same with God and Our Lady. She knows how to ask God because She's His mother."

"Is Our Lady the same as the Blessed Mother?" June was a bit confused with all the names for this person.

"Right," Cathy mumbled.

"Can I pray for something special, too?" June asked as she stuffed the beads into the pocket of her pedal pushers.

"Of course, that's why you're making a Novena." Cathy dipped her head slightly as they passed the small garden with the statue of Our Lady.

June copied her mother because, as Cathy had told her, it showed Our Lady that she respected Her. Finally, they reached the church steps. June piped up. "I'm going to pray that Daddy'll like me."

"Och, don't be silly, pet. Your Daddy loves you."

"Then I'm going to pray to Our Lady so I don't tell you any more stories to get you mad at me. Is that a good thing to pray for, Mammy?

The two could hear singing through the heavy, ornate wooden Church doors. Cathy let go of June's hand and started up the broad white marble steps. June's knees rose high with each steep step up to the doors.

She offered her mother advice, "Why don't you pray not to have bad dreams about . . ."

"Shhh. Quiet now," Cathy said, placing her palm on the door and giving it a hearty push.

The angelic hymn "Ave Maria," sung in Latin, echoed throughout the softly lit church and flooded June's senses as they quietly entered. With the few parishioners present singing loudly, the church seemed so very big and empty to the little girl. In awe, she gingerly stepped forward onto the burgundy aisle runner. The church took on a different appearance at night, with a mystical ambiance that wasn't present during the day. A few wall scones illuminated the area where the priest was singing. On the altar were a crystal vase with three long-stemmed white roses set on a crisp white cloth and two tall white tapered candles in brass holders. On opposite sides of the altar were countless candles that flickered in their red glass holders in front of pictures of Our Lady and St. Joseph. With eyes full of wonder, June realized that she was indeed in a sacred place.

Her mother dipped a finger into a small glass bowl attached to the wall by the door and traced the sign of the cross on her forehead. June followed suit. She then led June and tiptoed down the side aisle. They sat behind a row of elderly women and directly across from a middle-aged woman with two teen-aged girls.

June glanced around at the women, old and young. "Is this just for ladies and girls?" she whispered loudly. The elderly row turned in unison and frowned toward the source of the disruption. Upon eyeing the perky-faced little girl, they smiled and nodded a greeting, not missing a beat of the hymn.

When the hymn ended, the priest led the group in the prayers of the Rosary. Cathy sank onto her knees with her rosary beads looped around her hands. June copied her. She knelt next to her mother with her white beads between both hands and accurately recited her favorite prayer, the "Hail Mary."

She stared reverently at the life-size statue of a beautiful woman in a sky-blue and white robe. Pointing to the statue, she said, "Mammy, She's going to give you what you want." But her words were drowned out as the women began loudly praying in unison, "Hail Mary, full of grace. The Lord is with you. Blessed art thou amongst women. . ."

Chapter Twelve:
We Have A Friend!

THE BLACK-AND-WHITE TELEVISION set blared "I've Got a Secret" as Cathy ironed Jimmy's work shirts. Interrupting her private time, June ran down the hallway shouting, "Mammy, Mammy!"

"In here, pet," she called.

June burst into the room in a blur with her red hair flying behind.

"Call me *Mommy*. We're in America now. We don't say Mammy anymore," Cathy said reminding her daughter above the blare of the television. Taking a quick look at the game show, she said, "A private investigator! I bet you anything."

"Oh, I forgot, Mommy," said June, teetering back and forth excitedly from foot to foot. "I've got a surprise for you!"

Cathy looked back at the television as she heard one of the panelists give an answer. "I was right!" She turned down the volume and directed her attention to June. "What did you and your make-believe friend do this time?"

June was too excited to respond. Only the huge grin on her face could express the joy that she felt. Cathy added some starch to a shirt collar and began ironing again.

"I've found a real friend for us! Hurry up, Mommy."

"Now?" Cathy asked, putting the shirt on a hanger. "I've got to finish this so we can be on time when your sisters get out of school." She picked up a dress from the basket of clothes.

Grabbing her mother's hand, June pulled at her and Cathy chuckled at her daughter's excited insistence as she laid down the dress and turned off the television set.

They walked down the hallway and out the back door. Incense filled the air as they descended the steep wooden stairs to the second landing. The aroma was all around them when they reached their downstairs neighbor's porch. An old woman sat at a rusted metal table covered by a faded orange tablecloth with large green leaves. On the table was a brown teapot with the makings for a cup of tea, a crimson silk scarf wrapped around an object, a photo album, and incense burning in a tiny cast-iron pot.

The old woman's eyes were like bottomless black pools. Her salt and pepper hair was loosely piled up into a bun on the crown of her head. *Ah! This must be the old woman Jimmy mentioned,* Cathy thought.

June squeezed her mother's hand excitedly. "Mrs. Gorzalkowski's our new friend."

Cathy heard "new friend" followed by a garbled word. Shyly, she smiled and said, "Hello. Hope she's not been a bother."

The old woman chuckled and winked at June, who smiled broadly as she looked back and forth between the two women.

ᘒ   ᘒ   ᘒ

Earlier that day, Mrs. Gorzalkowski heard the delightful sound of a child's giggles. Curious to see who it was, she squinted through her kitchen window to the back porch. She saw a small silhouette sitting at the table with a doll on the opposite seat. The little girl was chatting away to her stuffed friend.

Before she could call out a greeting, June turned to face her neighbor and shouted a cheery "Hello!" Mrs. Gorzalkowski came out of her kitchen and the girl jumped up to stand in front of the old woman.

At that moment, their eyes locked. It seemed as if June saw her own image in Mrs. Gorzalkowski's fathomless dark eyes. A jolt of energy flooded the old woman's senses, pumping blood through her veins and quickening her heartbeat. In a sudden flash the old woman saw herself young, inspired and innocent, much like the little girl standing before her. For many years, she had a good life. Sadness filled her soul as she recalled what was to follow that happier time.

There had been a time for Lechsinska Gorzalkowski when it had been safe, not frightening, to see what others could not.

Her grandmothers had predestined Lechsinska's life from the second they saw the newborn's dark, inquisitive eyes staring back at them. They tenderly washed her plump body and coal-black hair and swaddled her in pure white cotton cloth on the frosty fall morning of her birth.

"An old soul. A magical child," the two old women agreed, shaking their gray heads in a way that only the wise can do.

They devoted their lives to teaching Lechsinska the age-old craft of herbal healing and the sacred art of visioning. In the years to come the girl grew in beauty as well as in psychic powers. Her reputation as a seer was respected far and wide. Farmers listened with deference as she directed them to avoid crop failure. People young and old, seeking successful unions, had success through her visions. The villagers agreed that Lechsinska was more accurate than the local matchmaker.

That was before the horrors of war had robbed her soul of her true identity. She was terrified into denying her sacred gift of prophecy.

It started with death.

When she heard that the invading German army had hung her husband and sons in the village square, Lechsinska violently tore at her clothes, ranting to God that never again would she serve Him. She fervently denied her life of mystical service. Still, her highly developed psychic mind, trained to hear and see beyond the physical world, heard the pitiful nightmarish cries of dying people begging her to guide them to peace. Fearing insanity, she forced herself to focus only on the survival of Tesia, her last remaining child. Lechsinska and her daughter hid in a damp cave-like room under the floorboards of a barn owned by a sympathetic farmer. There they survived the war.

Eventually, the voices stopped seeking her wisdom and Lechsinska had accepted a life without visions and spiritual guidance. That is, until she met her spirited young neighbor who stood before her, announcing, "I'm June."

Joyful memories of life before the cruel war flooded Lechsinska's soul. June's presence was the sun that penetrated the dark cloud of spiritual exile. Once again, Lechsinska heard the voices guiding her to share her sacred magical gifts. Like her grandmothers, she understood that she was to guide and encourage psychic abilities and her student stood before her.

∽ ∽ ∽

In a husky, accented voice, the old woman introduced herself to Cathy. "I'm Mrs. Gorzalkowski," she said. She extended her gnarled hand to Cathy, who stuttered over the pronunciation of the woman's name.

"It's okay. Nobody in America can say it right," she laughed. "Call me Mrs. G." She pushed a chair toward Cathy. "Sit."

A joyful feeling, like being welcomed by a loving grandmother, spread over Cathy, and she allowed herself a glimmer of hope. Taking in a whiff of the incense, she asked, "Isn't that frankincense?"

Mrs. G nodded "yes."

"I thought I recognized the scent. They use it at Benediction Mass," Cathy said.

"We're Catholics," declared June. She sensed her mother was comfortable with Mrs. G. *Maybe Mammy can be friends with her, too,* she wished privately, thinking of how many hours her mother would sit staring out the window toward the ocean.

Mrs. G said, "Your daughter, she. . . I say in my tongue, *wizjonerka*."

"What's that mean?" June asked, intertwining her tiny fingers around Mrs. G's weathered hand.

"Your mind sees many things different than most people," said Mrs. G, tenderly stroking June's pink cherub cheeks.

"Aye, right you are!" Cathy rolled her eyes at her young daughter. The women laughed.

Mrs. G poured black tea while Cathy opened the photo album on the table. On one page was the photo of a man, a woman and some children. Mrs. G pointed at it with a teaspoon.

"Husband, gone. These boys," Mrs. G waited for Cathy to get a good look at the photo, "my sons. Gone. All dead. The war."

She took the top off the sugar bowl and handed Cathy a spoon.

"It was a horrible time, wasn't it? Thank God it's over," Cathy said.

Mrs. G pointed her finger at her heart. "Not over here. You, too, family lost in the war?"

"A brother," she answered.

"Husband? Baby?"

Cathy busied herself arranging the teacup on the saucer. "No, not my husband. You're right about a baby. Two. Daughters. They died, but not in the war. After."

"But you have other daughters to love," Mrs. G said, her wise eyes piercing through the vapors of the steaming tea.

Wanting to be part of the conversation, June said, "I have three sisters. Annie, Maggie and Mary. They go to school. I'll go to school soon, too."

"Four girls. You are a lucky woman. You see in time. Your daughters bring you much happiness," said Mrs. G. She adjusted her arthritic body into the chair and took a long sip of tea. Slowly, her eyes came up from her cup. "You still sad like me."

"Aye, no wonder. After seeing so much," Cathy said. "Oh well. You know what I mean, don't you."

"Yes. This old lady know much of tears and death," said Mrs. G.

June broke the slight pause of conversation between the women. "My Mommy can play with us instead of watching television. We didn't have a TV before Daddy bought it so Mommy wouldn't be so sad."

"June! That's enough." Cathy shook her head. "Well, she's right. I do watch it too much. Couldn't afford one in Scotland. Like everyone else we knew."

"America. So much to have. In Poland we have not television. We have each other. Time for friends," said Mrs. G, handing Cathy the creamer.

With the ease of a gentle breeze on a spring day, Cathy and June settled in with their new friend as if it had always been that way.

They would have stories of their homelands to share.

಄ ಄ ಄

Every school morning after walking the older girls to school with her mother, June tromped happily down the old wooden backstairs to be with Mrs. G. Mostly, they talked and laughed. Their strong affection for each other surpassed the difference in their ages. Mrs. G kept the chatty girl busy with easy household tasks, or they would tend to the flowers in the small garden at the back of the building.

June's education in the realm of magic began with her wise old Polish friend and started in the small garden at the foot of the backstairs. Mrs. G said that the weather in San Francisco, mostly sunny days coupled with moist, cool fog, was perfect for the flowers, tomatoes and herbal plants that she grew. She sang in Polish as they gardened. Curious, June wanted to know what she was saying.

"I tell them," Mrs. G said spreading wide her arms to the plants and flowers, "how much happiness they bring. How they help us be healthy." She returned to pruning back a lavender bush. "This one help if you have headache. It also can heal sadness of the past."

June sniffed it. They moved on to a lemon tree. "She make your stomach good when sour," Mrs. G said.

"How'd you know it's a girl tree?" June asked.

"I talk to the garden angels."

"I've got an angel, too," June said proudly.

Mrs. G kept working, pulling off old dead leaves. "I know," she said.

"What do your garden angels look like?" June asked, squeezing a firm lemon.

"You can see them. But you must be still." Mrs. G put down her shears and motioned for June to stop touching the lemons. "Close your eyes," she instructed.

Being still was not easy for the rambunctious four year-old. But, wanting to please her friend, she squeezed her eyes closed, held her arms straight down with her fingertips pointing at the earth, and remained motionless. She breathed in the bountiful scents in the garden. The fragrance of the lilac bush relaxed her.

"Listen," Mrs. G said softly.

At first June only heard the rumbling of a plane overhead and faint sounds of distant hammering and sawing. After a moment she could she hear the buzzing of insects visiting flowers. Then the air around her moved with a light swishing noise. It gently disturbed a corkscrew curl that had escaped a bobby pin at the side of her head. The curl danced in the breeze, brushing across her cheek and tickling her nose. Yet, she continued to hold still. The grass moved under her feet, or so she thought. *Maybe it's ants going to work,* she giggled to herself, thinking of an army of tiny black ants with lunch pails like her father had. Then it seemed as though something touched her leg. It felt like a small warm hand. She jumped. *Something touched me,* she thought. The garden was full of life.

"They're here. Wee tiny green people," June whispered.

"The garden angels," Mrs. G whispered back.

It was there in the garden that June learned to communicate with nature's energies—both seen and unseen. She would stand in front of a plant, listen for a few minutes, and relate to Mrs. G what it needed, whether it was pruning, water, less water or a song. The old woman would consider what he said, and usually agree.

On colder days the two would stay in Mrs. G's living room with the gas-burning fireplace blazing. There they would drink tea made with heavy cream and spoonfuls of sugar. June asked if they could talk to the wee green garden angels inside the house. Mrs. G explained that they could enjoy the garden without even being there. She said the mind has great abilities to see places without being present physically. June knew about going other places in her dreams, but wasn't sure how she could go to the garden using only her mind. To help, her old friend suggested they play a fun game she learned as a child.

Mrs. G would imagine a place she had been to and June would attempt to describe it as though she were walking alongside her friend. As the description was given, Mrs. G would say, "Very good!" or "Close enough," or "Look again." But never once did she say "Wrong." June's confidence in her psychic abilities was bolstered with each game, and her mind's eye became keener. Visiting places inside her mind became easy to do.

Chapter Thirteen:
Remembering Helen

LIGHT FILTERED THROUGH the stained glass windows at Holy Savior Church. The pure voices of the many children singing hymns at Mass sounded heavenly to Cathy. She wished the singing could have continued as she watched the priest ascend to the pulpit. During the sermon, her mind drifted like the fog over Twin Peaks and out to the ocean waves. The priest began to read the names of the dearly departed souls. When he said, "Let us pray for Helen Marie MacDonald," the words pierced Cathy's heart like a dagger. As she bowed her head, her black scarf slipped forward, threatening to cover her eyes.

On the previous Saturday afternoon, when Cathy arrived home from confession, Jimmy told her that he had petitioned a Mass in memory of Helen. Cathy did not respond to his announcement, almost as if she hadn't heard. She still couldn't believe that it had been a year since her sweet, wee lassie had passed on. The grieving mother thought of how she could have saved her Helen. She felt responsible for not going straight to Dr. MacFadden as soon as Helen began having troubles, but as usual, she had listened to Jimmy. If she had been stronger and had taken control, then maybe her precious little girl would still be alive.

The move to America was supposed to relieve her grief. Instead it only caused a greater feeling of separation. She wiped away the tears that began to seep out from her closed eyes. *Did Jimmy feel guilty, too?* she wondered. She glanced in his direction. She saw that his face was downcast.

Consumed with guilt, she pulled her hand away when June's small fingers tried to engage her. Her thoughts were too dark and moody. She felt she didn't deserve her children. Helen's death was her penance for the wrongs she had done. Looking to the statue of Our Lady holding Baby Jesus, Cathy wondered if She had felt helpless and without hope at her son's death, as she had felt with Helen's death. The distraught mother prayed to Our Lady in hope of finding some absolution, but found none. God's mother had been a virgin without sin, and that is where their differences started. Cathy's lips moved as she silently prayed another "Hail Mary."

June sat in the pew, squeezed between her mother and Mary. She anxiously swung her legs back and forth as her eyes roamed around the church, looking for some sort of interaction—a smile at least. No one paid her any attention.

As she stared at the dancing light of the sun shimmering through the stained glass window, she saw her angel appear. The angel was raising her hand as though blessing a young woman. June was certain she was sending a message that she would see Helen at Mass that day.

She looked first at her father, but his eyes were closed and his hands were clenched tightly on his lap. She knew that he missed Helen a lot, too. She then turned to her mother. She could feel her sadness. In hopes of alleviating her sorrow, she lightly touched her mother's hand, only to have her push it away.

Her hurt at the rejection lasted only a second. A happy surprise made June gasp at the miracle appearing before her eyes. Standing alongside the statue of Our Lady was Helen—waving! She pulled on her mother's sleeve and pointed to her sister. "Mommy, wave at Helen," she said. But instead of making her happy, as June had hoped, Cathy began softly sobbing into a hankie.

Mary's voice was the next to interrupt the quietness of the Mass. "Mommy, why are you crying?" People in the pews nearby turned toward the MacDonald family.

"Mommy won't say hello to Helen," June said loudly.

"Be quiet," Annie hissed.

People shook their heads at the disruption.

Jimmy leaned across Mary and June and whispered, "Let's go, Cath." The girls followed him as he stepped outside the pew to give their mother room to pass. He motioned for everyone to follow and quickly whisked his family out of the church. Jimmy gave his arm to Cathy. She clung to it and leaned into him for support. Annie took tight hold of June's hand to keep her away from their mother. Outside the church she warned her sisters to say no more about Helen. She reminded them of the sadness of the day.

The walk home was a somber affair. The usual chattering and skipping was replaced with silence and trudging feet.

As they walked down the street, they passed Andy's Donut Shop with the scent of baking donuts permeating the air around the red-framed shop. Jimmy suddenly stopped and clapped his hands to get everyone's attention.

"How about donuts and hot chocolate this morning?" he asked.

The girls looked at him aghast. Mary questioned her father's odd offer, "Daddy, won't we be too full for Mommy's Sunday breakfast?"

Everyone was ravished, since they never ate on Sunday mornings until after they had taken Holy Communion at Mass. Once they got home Cathy would cook a big breakfast of eggs, sausages, potatoes and lots of buttered toast. They wouldn't eat again until Sunday dinner was served, which was another special event.

But the donuts looked good anyway. Jimmy raised a questioning eyebrow at his wife. Her small smile was an affirmative reply. The family walked happily into the sweet-smelling donut shop.

༄ ༄ ༄

As soon as they arrived home, Cathy told the girls to change out of their church clothes and she went to do the same. Jimmy entered their bedroom as she was changing. With her dress and slip laid out on the bed, he watched as she rolled down her stockings below her knees and removed her garter belt, exposing her waist. She was still slender after birthing so many children. She caught Jimmy's reflection watching her in the mirror. Modestly, she turned her back to him.

"I made plans with Sandy to take the kids to the beach today," he said.

She screwed up her face in a worried frown. "I really don't feel like going to the beach."

Quickly, he said, "No, of course not. Why don't you lie down and take it easy?"

He pulled the large brown bag that held their beach things out of the closet. "I'll let the girls have some rides at Playland, too," he said.

Cathy loved going to Playland as much as the girls did. The amusement park at the beach had some wonderful rides, although they were very costly.

"Can we afford that?" she asked.

"It's a special treat today."

She knew he was trying to make the day easier for her. She had cried that morning while they were still in bed. She had told him that she couldn't face the day. Jimmy had held her, stroking her hair, and told her not to worry. He said he would take care of the girls that day. But still she worried.

"What time will you be home for dinner?" she asked.

"Don't bother. I'll bring home fish and chips," he said readily.

She sighed deeply. "I don't know, Jimmy. The girls look forward to their Sunday dinners."

"Let's try to make this a good day. Please," he said.

Jimmy finished hanging up his Sunday suit and pulled a vest over his shirt.

She went up to him and, without words, pulled him into her arms. For a moment their grief mingled together.

A tiny rap on the door cut short their embrace. Jimmy warned the intruder not to enter. Cathy grabbed her Capri pants.

An overwhelming weakness engulfed Cathy's entire being. She collapsed onto the bed and curled into a fetal position.

Jimmy took the extra blanket from the closet, folded it across her, and tiptoed out of the room.

Mary and June stood behind the door.

"They're kissing," Mary whispered too quietly for June to hear.

"What are they doing?" June asked loudly.

The door opened abruptly. "Are you ready to go?" their father said.

Peeping past him, June saw her mother lying in bed. Her young, curious eyes stared up at him. "Were you kissing Mommy?"

Mary elbowed her sharply and said, "Let's go help make sandwiches!" and off they ran down the hallway to the kitchen.

Several pieces of white bread with jam and butter were spread across the kitchen table. Annie carefully assembled the sandwiches as Maggie put apples into brown lunch bags. Annie pointed to a big metal thermos on the shelf and told Mary to fill it with Kool-Aid.

"Mommy and Daddy were kissing," announced June.

"Big deal. That's what moms and dads do," Maggie said, taking the wax paper from a drawer.

The kitchen was already scattered with used silverware and breadcrumbs and when their father entered. Annie said, "I'm going to clean up, Daddy."

"Let me help," he said. "We've got to get going. Sandy will be here in minute."

❧   ❧   ❧

Sandy was parked at the curb, the radio blaring a baseball game when the MacDonalds spilled out of the building. He motioned for Jimmy to get in the front seat and the girls to sit in the back.

Annie opened the back door and hesitated, not wanting to get in. "Can't I sit in front, Uncle Sandy?" she asked.

"Kids in the back. Son, move over, please," he said cheerfully.

Sandy's son Mark, a plump boy Mary's age, didn't budge. June had to crawl over him to get in.

"I'm not going to sit with girls!" he said kicking his legs against the back of the front seat. His voice rose into a shrill scream, "Daddy!"

"No problem, wee man. Come sit with us men," Sandy said.

"Good riddance to bad rubbish," Maggie said under her breath about the seven year-old boy.

"He's a fat brat," June added. The girls nodded their heads in agreement as they drove off.

The fog lay thick in the direction of the beach as they drove up Market Street. It'll burn off, Sandy told them. The girls cheered at the prediction. With the good mood in the car, everyone began to sing funny Scottish songs. The children gleefully sang one of their favorites.

"*I love a sausage, a bonnie heilin'*[25] *sausage. I love a sausage for my tea. I went to the lobby to meet my Uncle Bobby, the sausage came aft'r me!*"

They laughingly sang more of their Scottish favorites. At the end of each song, Jimmy and Sandy would shout, "Up Dublin, down Belfast!" Annie told her sisters that it was a cheer for Catholic Dublin, and a put-down for Protestant Belfast. June didn't understand what that meant, and simply repeated what everyone else said.

When they arrived at the beach, the fog had lifted to reveal one of the rare warm San Francisco July days. Uncle Sandy asked the kids if they wanted to go first to the beach or to Playland. The kids squealed, "Playland!"

---

[25]   Bonnie – Pretty or charming. Heilin' – Glaswegian slang for Highland.

The day's fun started with Laughing Sal, a Playland favorite. The huge, mechanical, red-haired woman could be hilariously funny or a scary sight, depending upon the viewer. Her mad cackle bellowed out from the Playhouse. Maggie and Mary jumped back, feigning fright, then bent over in belly laughs. June held her fists to her mouth, wide eyed and giggling in awe of Sal. Annie laughed heartily over the large, preposterous face of the mechanical lady. It was a fun game to try not to laugh when Laughing Sal began her hysterical laugh.

The brat boy Mark didn't like Laughing Sal and ran away, yelling for his daddy. Mary pursed her lips and waved her hands, mimicking him running away. "Sissy boy," she said.

June saw that her father and Uncle Sandy hadn't seen them make fun of Mark. The men had turned away from the kids and were talking and laughing. June wished every day was like being at Playland.

Jimmy and Sandy strolled through the amusement park with beers in hand as their kids scattered with their coveted tickets to go on the rides. Jimmy decided to let the girls enjoy themselves for a few hours. But when he sounded the loud, piercing MacDonald whistle that the family knew so well, he expected his daughters to come running.

When none of the girls showed up, he went looking for them. He stopped first at the Playhouse. He cupped his eyes to peer inside, looking for the telltale sign of June's red hair. He looked over at the huge, human record player and watched the kids spinning off of it as the speed picked up. With no sign of them there, he continued the search, passing the Loop-by-Loop rocket planes and the Tilt-A-Whirl, the crazily spinning platform where riders sit in half-dome-shaped cars and try not to get sick.

After a while Jimmy spotted Mary, who was sitting on a bench wiping off her mouth as she hung her head down between her legs. It took only a few questions to find out the cause of her illness: mixing an It's It ice cream bar with a hot dog and the Tilt-A-Whirl.

When Mary was finally steady on her feet, they went to find the others. They first found Annie and June, who were just getting off the Big Dipper roller coaster. He told Annie to find Maggie and meet him by Laughing Sal so they could all leave and go to the beach together.

The search ended when Annie found Maggie behind the wheel of a red Dodge 'Em bumper car. She was forcing a teen boy's car into the corner so aggressively that it looked like his teeth chipped with each bump. The sound she made was reminiscent of Laughing Sal. With the bell announcing the end of the ride, Maggie got out and slid across the slippery metal floor toward the exit. Annie waited at the gate pinching her nostrils. She hated the strange smell of burnt electricity that came from the bumper cars.

With glistening cat eyes, Maggie asked, "Did you see I won?"

"Yeah, yeah. We gotta go," Annie said.

With the entire group now assembled, they walked across the street to the beach to watch the setting sun. The kids, mellowed by the busy, exciting day, sunk their tired feet into the cooling sand. The beach was mostly empty, except for a few lovers walking arm-in-arm, silhouetted by the orange glow of the sun dipping gracefully into the horizon. The kids ran ahead of the men toward the water's edge. June picked up a stick and handed it to Annie, asking her to write Helen's name in the wet sand. "So she knows that we still love her," she said.

Annie took the stick. "Help me smooth out the sand."

No sooner had an area been smoothed out than the waves would come. Annie couldn't write out the whole name before it was washed away. They decided to move back a little. As her big sister wrote, June suggested they add more and make it like a letter. By then the other girls wanted to be a part of the project. They all ran around collecting seashells. The message became a loving "Hello" with shells placed around Helen's name in the shape of a large heart.

As soon as they finished, the brat boy jumped into the middle of their message and erased their work by wildly kicking sand around with his feet. The girls yelled in disappointment and frustration and chased him along the beach with sticks. Mary yelled, "You stupid bugger!" He ran away and hid behind his father, pretending to be afraid, but poking out his fat face to smirk at the girls. June pleaded with her father to let them punish Mark for ruining their message to Helen. Jimmy ignored them and continued talking to Sandy about soccer.

June narrowed her eyes and pointed an index finger straight at the wicked boy. "I'll get you," she mouthed at him.

"Daddy, Helen will think we forgot her. Daddy," June whined, tugging on her father's trousers. Not wanting to think about the death anymore, Jimmy paid no attention to her, which made June fume with anger. She thought he must not care about Helen. Frustrated, she ran down the beach to sit on an old log and stare forlornly at the ebb and flow of the waves.

She searched the sky in hopes of catching a glimpse of Helen or her angel in the clouds. But the sky was completely empty of clouds. Disheartened, she closed her eyes and imagined the picture of her angel pinned above the altar at home. In her imagination, the angel flew out of the picture and across a hilltop full of yellow flowers and landed at a beach similar to where she now sat.

Pretending she was also flying, June opened her arms wide and wiggled her fingers. A seagull drifting in from the horizon caught her interest. It landed on the water not too far from where she sat. The bird bobbed up and down on the waves.

She pulled off her white sandals and walked to the water's edge to tippy-toe into the cold, Pacific Ocean. She loved the ocean—all of it. The sound of the waves, the smell of the salty water and the vastness of sea had a calming effect on her. The cold water helped to release her sadness. A picture of her mother's face came to her mind. In the image, Cathy was walking through waves, holding out her arms and crying. June moved towards her mother.

"June! Not so far in!" Her father's voice blended with the roar of the ocean. It seemed to her as though it was a voice from across the water, saying "June . . . in!" She splashed the water with her arms and stared up at the sky, lost in time.

Suddenly, someone grabbed her arm and pulled her out of the water. "Stop being so bad!" Annie said gruffly. "Daddy said to come back."

"I could swim back to Scotland and see Helen," June said with chattering teeth.

They started back down the beach toward the rest of the group. June saw the brat toss his daddy's beer bottle into the ocean. When he turned around, a big wave came up unexpectedly and washed over him, knocking him down. Everyone, including his father, laughed at the sight.

Suddenly, June was inspired. It occurred to her that she could send Helen a message in a bottle. She was positive the ocean would carry it to her, with help from her angel. Her little feet scampered along the beach so fast that sand flew up behind her.

Jimmy was shaking the last drops of beer from the bottle when he heard a little voice above the beating waves. "Daddy, can I have your bottle?" June asked.

"Can't give you beer. I'll give you a wee shandy tonight at home."

On special occasions, Jimmy would mix the half beer and half ginger ale drink for the girls. Cathy didn't like the idea of giving them alcohol, but Jimmy scoffed at her objections. He said that a wee bit of alcohol wouldn't cause the girls any problems.

"Just the bottle, to send Helen a letter. My angel will make sure she gets it," explained June.

Sandy laughed, "Well, there you go, Jimmy. She's not all that bad, eh? She may not be named after a saint, but at least she's got an angel on her side."

"My pagan baby. Aye, there you go." Jimmy handed it over to her.

June wondered why Sandy and her father had said what they did. She didn't know what it meant to be a pagan baby, and decided to ask her mother later. In the meantime, she had an important duty. Gathering her sisters together, she told them her plan.

Maggie looked in her small pink, patent-leather purse and handed Annie a piece of paper and pencil. Together, the MacDonald girls wrote a note to Helen.

"Dear Helen, Hello. How are you? We are fine. We miss you. We went to Playland today. Do you play in heaven with Baby Kit? June says to come to the altar tonight. We will wait. Love,"

The girls signed the letter and Annie stuck it into the bottle. She used a stick to press it down farther. She then shoved in a thicker stick to use as a stopper so that the letter would stay dry. It was decided that Mary, with her strong arm, would be the best person to toss the bottle into the ocean. The small group watched the bottle get caught up in the current and float out to sea. June felt content knowing that it would be watched over by her angel.

Chapter Fourteen:
The Secret World of Magic

THE COASTAL FOG drifted lightly over Twin Peaks. It descended into the Valley, rapidly cooling the October day. Cathy, June and Mrs. G sat on the back porch enjoying mid-morning tea. The scent of butter melting over Cathy's freshly baked scones accompanied it. Mrs. G put the quilted cozy on the teapot to keep it warm. June licked her fingers and brushed the crumbs off her mouth, and began telling a whimsical story about garden angels hiding in mist of the fog.

After a long description of the different angels she could see, June came to the story's ending. "They live in a place called the Misty World. It's a circle world with water all around it. Me and my angels dance all over a big hill with yellow flowers. Everybody is happy together." When she finished her story, Mrs. G clapped.

"That girl's imagination is going to get her in trouble some day," Cathy declared.

"It's real to her," the old woman said, wrapping her black shawl around her shoulders. "It's a little cold out here. Come inside. I make tea hot."

"I'm going to pick flowers with the garden angels," said June skipping down the stairs to the garden.

In the kitchen Mrs. G turned on the kettle and motioned for Cathy to sit at the table. Cupboard doors opened and shut as she prepared fresh cups of tea.

Hearing June singing outside, Cathy thought back to the days when she was a young girl playing in the backyard with her brothers and friends. She smiled slightly, recalling the days of her first love. She sighed, thinking how that seemed so long ago.

"Well, that day has come and gone for you," Mrs. G said casually, "It's the past now, my friend. Yes?"

She was always surprised when Mrs. G voiced her thoughts, but it also unnerved her, like when June told her stories about her angel.

The only reply to Mrs. G's inquiry came from the kettle whistling on the stove. The old woman slowly poured the steaming water into a teapot. She filled their cups and sat back on her chair as the vapors from the tea swirled around them.

"Maybe I'm just missing home," said Cathy at last. She didn't want to admit that her depression had gotten darker during the past few days.

"For you, it's not good to be so sad. You are young. Much to live for. I would like to see more for your happiness. Would you like that?"

Cathy gave a small laugh, uncertain of what she meant. Mrs. G reached for the object hidden under the crimson silk scarf.

"I think that you would not mind," she said, opening her scarf to reveal a stack of tarot cards. She placed a few on the table.

Tarot card readings were forbidden to Catholics, but Cathy had to admit that she was a bit curious about them, and also afraid. She wondered what the nuns would think. Enchanted by the cards' beautiful pictures and colors, she leaned in closer. *Perhaps it isn't a sin if I only listen and don't ask questions,* she thought.

"See that card," said Mrs. G pointing to a card with a red heart being pierced by three swords. "Your heart not open anymore. Must open." Mrs. G flipped over another card. Pictured in that card were three young women dancing and, in unison, raising goblets in celebration. "Must love again."

Impish laughter flooded the kitchen as June ran in to ask for a glass of water. "The angels are thirsty!" she said, and came to a sudden halt. Wide-eyed and mouth dropping open, June stared at the cards. She moved to the table and touched one.

"Don't touch." Cathy slapped her daughter's hand lightly.

"She likes. Yes?" Mrs. G said, raising an eyebrow to the awed girl.

Shyly, June slowly nodded her head, affirming that she did like the tarot. Cathy leaned close to her daughter. "We won't tell Daddy about this, okay?" she said putting a finger to her closed lips.

June mimicked her, nodding in agreement.

ᘐ ᘐ ᘐ

The tarot cards were easy and fun for June to understand. She enjoyed giving voice to the colorful pictures, which were different on each of the seventy-eight cards. One day Mrs. G fanned all the cards out across the table and told her to choose one and peer into it. June picked a card with a boy presenting a large goblet holding a white flower to a little girl. The children stood in a blooming garden. The card had bright and lively yellow and red colors. In the background was a large stone house, and in the foreground five more cups with a white flower in each one. Quickly, June described it as getting a present from someone who loves you. The old woman encouraged her student to go beyond her first thoughts and tell a story about it.

"Play this game. Look at the card," Mrs. G instructed her. "Now close eyes. Pretend you are in the card. Do what the person is doing in it."

June's story of the card, the Six of Cups, started hesitantly. "The boy and girl are good friends for a long time. The boy has a special present for the girl, but it's not a thing. I think the girl is me and the boy is a new friend. He believes in my angel." June saw a man in the background of the card, walking away. "When everybody is mad at me, the boy will still like me. Am I right?"

"Probably. Later you find the truth," said Mrs. G.

One of June's favorite cards was called The Sun. It pictured a young naked child waving a large red banner while riding a white horse. Behind the child were four colorful sunflowers in full bloom and a big bold sun with rays extended beyond the card's borders.

"That's me being happy in our magical garden. It means everybody should play, huh?"

"Yes, that's good," said Mrs. G, laughing heartily.

In a short time June understood the difference between the cards, how the images and colors looked, and how they *felt*. She also learned that not all the cards carried a happy message. One card had a picture of a devil and a man and woman chained to a cube. June thought the card looked very dark and gloomy. She said it made her feel "icky," and, in a very serious tone, said the card meant, "If you're not a good girl you'll go to the Devil."

Mrs. G shrugged her shoulders. "This card means people make a mess of life and that's why they're miserable. Soon they feel chained to unhappiness and blame it on somebody else. 'The Devil made me bad. Not my fault.' They say these things." Mrs. G then flipped to another card.

Soon June could lay out all the cards in perfect order. The cards became part of her and appeared in her thoughts and dreams.

Mrs. G was very pleased with her young student's quick understanding of the tarot. "You are like me, destined to serve others with your special gifts," she said.

Upon the advice of Mrs. G. and excited with her new knowledge, June offered readings to her sisters when they accompanied her downstairs to visit their elderly neighbor, who said the only way to really know the tarot is to read for others. Annie was the most reluctant to participate, saying that Daddy wouldn't like it. Maggie always asked about boys. And Mary wanted to know if she'd get better grades or win at basketball. At June's warning, all were sworn to secrecy.

The tarot cards, like all other things she enjoyed most in life, were best not talked about—especially to her father. Like the garden angels hiding in the mist, the little girl quickly understood that life was full of secrets.

Chapter Fifteen:
Hogmanay in San Francisco

THE MACDONALDS PLANNED to host their first party in America on New Year's Day, 1955. The family worked together to spruce up their flat in the weeks before the gathering.

Cathy busily washed the bay windows with June at her side, trying to be helpful. The soapy water dripped down her little arms and got into her rolled-up sleeves. Behind them they could hear Annie supervising the precocious Irish Twins, who were shrieking with laughter. Their job was to bring the newly waxed hardware floors to a bright sheen by skating back and forth across it with rags tied around their feet. Cathy suppressed a laugh as she glimpsed Maggie rushing to catch up with Mary who was whirling down the hallway with an unraveling rag wrapped around her foot. She decided to keep quiet about any pending disaster. The last thing she wanted was to upset Annie's position of authority over the mischievous girls.

"We have to make the house nice and clean for all the people coming. Is that right, Mommy?" June asked.

"That's right, my wee clootie dumpling," Cathy said.

She smiled at her daughter's newly adopted fashion of wrapping her hair in a headscarf, copied from Mrs. G who wore one when cleaning house. Bending over to squeeze out her cleaning rag, Cathy watched June's determined face as she carefully scrubbed at the glass, and thought back to when the idea of having a party on Hogmanay first arose.

ᘖ ᘖ ᘖ

Sandy and Nancy had invited the MacDonalds to celebrate Thanksgiving dinner with them—a new holiday for the immigrant family. Nancy was a fabulous cook and prepared an array of dishes that they had never before tasted. Besides the large, golden brown turkey, there were steaming bowls of food. Jimmy boasted that the cook had "laid a table fit for a king" as he filled his plate with the pasta, creamed corn, stuffing and cranberry sauce. But before he dug in, Cathy nudged him to wait.

Nancy halted Mark from scooping food into his mouth with an announcement that each person give thanks to God for something special in their life.

"*Before* we eat, darling," she reminded her son.

He quickly said, "Rub-a-dub-dub, thanks for the grub. Let's eat!" But only his parents laughed.

When it came to June, she prayed that Granda and Granny B would visit for Christmas. Her wish brought up a conversation during dinner about past holidays in Scotland. Jimmy said how much fun the Scottish New Year was. Annie, who was old enough to remember, reminded her father that in Scotland the New Year celebration was called Hogmanay.

"What a holiday it is! We had special things, traditions, like paying off debts before the first of January," Sandy told the children in seriousness.

"We won't have to worry about that tradition, eh, Jimmy?" Cathy said. Her husband didn't believe in accumulating debts, and lived frugally day-by-day. He prided himself in being able to send weekly payments to Granda B for the money he had lent them to help make their move to America possible.

"Mommy, what are the parties like in Scotland at Hogmanay?" June said crucifying the name the Scots called New Year's Day. It sounded as though the little girl had said, "Hug many."

The adults laughed so cheerfully that she joined in, thinking how happy everyone was with her question. She sat up in her chair, eager to hear about Scotland. Unlike Annie, who held on tightly to her remembrances of Scotland, June's memories of life there were fading.

The three adult Scots began to reminisce about Hogmanay. The descriptions of the holiday spilled out across the dining table as Jimmy, Sandy and Cathy related their stories about Scotland's most popular holiday, which was celebrated as though it was a religious event.

When Jimmy said the streets of Glasgow were busy with people going from house to house, visiting and bringing gifts, June gathered that Hogmanay was like Halloween night.

"What kind of gifts?" she asked.

Annie piped in. "Granny always baked special things like holiday oat cakes and black buns."

"Whiskey cake and her famous shortbread. Oh yum!" Cathy jumped in, winking at her daughters as she licked her lips and made a wide circle on her belly.

"Good whiskey," Jimmy added.

Sandy told a story about the time they went bathing in the Clyde River just to see who could endure the cold water the longest. "It was so bloody frigid. If it hadn't been for the whiskey keeping my blood moving and Cathy's brother, Peter, jumping in to pull me out . . ."

Nancy interrupted the story with a sharp, "Sandy! That's not a good example for the children."

"Right dear. We were silly boys then. It's a very dangerous thing to do," he said with a serious face.

Cathy covered her smiling lips with a napkin and made big eyes at her daughters.

"Tell us more, Mommy," June said, enjoying the cheery conversation.

Her mother clasped her hands and placed them on the table in front of her, her blue eyes glittering in the candlelight. Everyone sat still and listened as Cathy's soft Scottish voice told the story.

"The festivities of Hogmanay begin at midnight on New Year's Eve with a very special ritual acted out in the homes across Scotland. It's customary that the first guest, called the first foot, enters a home shortly after midnight. It's tradition that the first foot is a dark haired man who comes, bearing gifts, usually a lump of coal to keep the host's home warm through the long cold winter, and a bottle of Scotch to warm their souls."

Jimmy interrupted, "You hope it's a dark haired man who enters first, because then you'd have good luck throughout the upcoming year."

Cathy kept talking, "Girls, your Granda B was a most welcomed guest as the first foot because he was tall and had black hair." She was looking dreamily into the candle flame. "Until his hair turned white, that is." Although she said it lightly, June sensed sadness in her mother's voice.

"Aye, he was always the life of the party, getting everybody to sing and the ladies up for a dance. It's his favorite holiday," Jimmy said nostalgically.

The room quieted as the storytellers became lost in their own thoughts of the past.

Mark's demand for a piece of Nancy's delicious pumpkin pie made his mother jump up from the table to take orders. "With or without ice cream," she asked everyone.

June didn't want the enchanting Hogmanay tales to end. As the orders for pie were made, she asked, "Can we have a party?"

Her sisters cheered the idea loudly.

Jimmy and Cathy looked at each other across the table. She hesitated, fearful of letting down the girls if she took a spell of depression.

"No a bad idea," he said enthusiastically.

Looking at the girls' excited faces staring at her, it was hard not to give in to them. Cathy decided that celebrating Hogmanay in America would start a family tradition in their new county.

⚬⚬⚬ ⚬⚬⚬ ⚬⚬⚬

Cathy dunked her cloth into the bucket and stopped washing the bay windows as she meditated over the soapy bubbles and remembered past New Year's Eves in Scotland. The days before the event were always very busy with giving the house a thorough cleaning, as was the tradition. It was thought that starting the New Year with a tidy and neat house would bring good luck. Besides hauling the carpets downstairs to the backyard for a hard beating to clean them, all bedding and curtains were taken to the *steamie*, as laundromats are called in Scotland. On the family's last Hogmanay in Glasgow, it was decided that Annie was old enough to help out while Granny B watched the young bairns. Cathy and Annie pushed the baby *pram*[26] crammed full of curtains and linens along the streets, meeting other mothers and daughters on the same journey.

After waiting in line in the December chill they bought a ticket to enter the huge steamy room, smelling of wet clothes and soap. The steamie was full of women and girls, laughing and gossiping as they scrubbed their laundry on the washing board. Piece by piece they scrubbed up and down in big sinks filled with hot water, and then wrung it all out by hand. They hung the laundry on wall racks for drying, and placed larger items in big, hot cupboards that were pulled out of the wall. The gossiping and joking never stopped. The work was hard, but the excitement of the upcoming holiday created a festive atmosphere.

In reflection, Cathy realized how much she missed those times, especially the companionship of her mother and sisters-in-law at

---

[26]   Pram – Short for Perambulator; a large, ornate baby carriage.

the holidays. Still, she as was excited as the girls were about the party. With every wipe of the window, she assured herself that her family would be blessed anew.

A loud thump from her new Westinghouse washing machine on the back porch of the flat interrupted her daydream. *The sheets must all be on one side*, she thought as she tossed her washrag into the pail and went to deal with the problem.

∾ ∾ ∾

June proudly presented Mrs. G with an invitation to their party. "It's for your whole family," she exclaimed.

Mrs. G accepted the invite, saying that she, her daughter Tesia and her son-in-law would be most honored to attend. Later that day Mrs. G insisted to Cathy that she and Tesia would like to help with the preparations. Cathy gladly accepted, relieved to have the women's help as the things that still needed to be done overwhelmed her.

Jimmy and Sandy painted the living room and hallway a fresh coat of white paint with deep green on the wainscot and molding. Cathy used Mrs. G's sewing machine to make drapes and curtains for the bay windows. She chose a rich burgundy color for the drapes that went well with the green paint and lacey white curtains that would go beneath them.

When all was finished, Cathy and Jimmy watched their girls dance around with glee, exclaiming, "We have a house like a rich person." They indeed felt richly blessed with their new life.

The most welcomed gift of all was Mrs. G's offer to make new holiday dresses for the girls. At first Cathy declined the generous offer, having noticed how easily the old woman tired. But Mrs. G insisted. She worked at her kitchen table making the dresses. June helped by running around the table and tidying up unused material and pieces of thread.

Once the dresses were finished, the old woman invited Cathy down to look at them. "I make a party dress for you, too," Mrs. G said, pointing to a dress hanging on the back of a door.

What Cathy saw, took her breath away. She ran her fingers gingerly over the fine French stitching on the hem of a dove-gray satin dress that had an authentic store-bought look. In an unusual display of emotion, Cathy threw her arms around the surprised old woman.

As the day grew closer to Hogmanay, they shopped up and down Castro Street for the essential ingredients for the special Hogmanay foods that they would make.

Laughter and gossip erupted anytime the kitchen door opened as the women prepared the feast. When Cathy related funny tales of the steamie, the other women laughed heartily. The girls listened with merry curiosity as the adults reminisced about "home," each telling her own story about life in Poland or Scotland.

With the cooking underway, Mrs. G and Tesia agreed with Cathy when she said it was good that the girls would learn the proper preparation of the Scottish foods.

"We must not forget our customs," Mrs. G said adamantly. The other women nodded their heads affirmatively at her wisdom.

When it was time to bake the sweets June helped Annie roll out the dough for the cookies with a large rolling pin that Granny B had gifted Annie, before leaving Scotland.

The girls happily tested the freshly baked buttery shortbread, sugar cookies and the Dundee cake—a Hogmanay special. Mrs. G showed them how to decorate the cookies with sugar frosting by dipping a butter knife into hot water and carefully running it over the top of the frosting to give it a shinny glaze.

"Mommy, see how fancy," Maggie said, surveying the platter of cookies.

The women sipped glasses of sherry that would later be used for making the trifle pudding, which was a favorite holiday dessert made with cake, peaches soaked in wine and boiled custard poured all over it.

The baked goods were stored away and attention was turned to the main courses. Stewed meat with thick brown gravy was placed into deep pans. Annie used Granny B's rolling pin to make a thin crust for the top of the pans. She then brushed a raw egg across the top so it would bake to a perfect golden brown, just the way Granny would have wanted it.

By the day of the party, steak pies, a large ham, the delicate trifle pudding and other delicious holiday foods lined the shelves in the Frigidaire, ready to be heated up when needed.

With the kitchen work finished, the girls hung colorful streamers throughout the flat, and dangled fun paper party hats from them. Jimmy held Maggie up to hang a piece of mistletoe at the front door. This custom was not for kissing, like at Christmas, but to prevent illness in the household.

It was a fun time in the MacDonald house. Since many of the guests also had young children, the party would start in the early afternoon of New Year's Day. The girls were so excited they stayed up until midnight, giggling and talking before falling asleep. The next morning they hurried home from the special New Year's Day Mass to change into their party clothes, readying themselves for the guests arriving at noon.

Cathy brushed each of the girls' hair until it shined, or, in June's case, laid down and stayed in place with two pretty yellow barrettes on each side. She decorated her other daughters' hair with ribbons the same color as their dresses.

Annie wore a forest-green dress with gold threads running through it. Maggie wore a dress of plush cranberry velvet, and Mary donned a soft champagne lace dress that emphasized the gold in her brown eyes.

"Oh Mary, we must get a picture of you for Granda! You look lovely," Cathy said.

June's royal blue tunic and white blouse vividly accentuated her blue eyes and red hair.

"Heel, toe, heel, toe," June said gleefully as she tap danced into the living room to show her father her new outfit.

"You're beautiful, pet!" he gushed over her.

June's heart soared, and her face radiated with joy from the rare kind attention from her father.

Cathy, too, had on her new dress. The dove-gray satin dress had three large onyx buttons on the bodice that ended at her waist, cinched smaller by a wide black belt. The skirt puffed out with help from the petticoat borrowed from Tesia. The wide v-neck collar showed off a necklace of cut glass that sparkled like diamonds. The necklace was a surprise Christmas present from Jimmy, who usually gave her practical gifts.

"Cocktail, honey?" Jimmy called out from the kitchen. The girls, who were in the kitchen opening Coca-Colas, giggled at his use of the word *honey*, an American endearment.

With her satin dress swishing, Cathy entered the kitchen. Jimmy whistled, "My God, woman, you look smashing! You'll be the belle of the ball," he kissed her cheek, not wanting to mess up her red lipstick.

The girls stared at their mother in awe. Maggie said she looked like a movie star.

With the chime of the doorbell, everyone ran off to greet the first guest. They hurried into position, eager to view the first footer waiting downstairs at the door to the building. They were ready for a dark-haired man to walk through the door, signaling good luck in the New Year. What they saw was Sandy's thinning blonde hair as he stepped over the threshold and into the lobby of the building.

"Sandy! For God's sake, get out, man!" Jimmy yelled down to him.

The mistake was Mark's fault.

It had been pre-arranged by Jimmy that the first foot would be Ian, a Scottish friend who was a tall man with black hair. But before Ian could step into the building, Mark had pushed ahead of him. As Sandy reached past Ian to pull his son back, he had stumbled through the door when it opened. As fate would have it, light haired, balding Sandy was the first person with a foot in the MacDonald's building on Hogmanay.

The girls hung over the banister booing boisterously at Mark as his father backed out, dragging his son by the scruff of the neck. Ian bounded up the stairs. Hoping to smooth over the error, he adamantly protested that he did indeed have the first foot in the flat. He handed Jimmy the traditional Hogmanay gifts.

"Fattie brattie Marky," said Maggie mockingly when Mark dashed by.

Huffing and puffing, Nancy arrived at the top of the landing and, in her loud American voice, scolded the Scots on how silly they were to be so superstitious.

A stout Scottish woman coming up behind her said, "Wheesht, silly woman."

At first, guests were a bit sober from the unexpected event but it didn't last for long. The adults soon had a few glasses of cheer and the party began.

More guests arrived, singing out the traditional Hogmanay greeting, "A good year to you!" They brought gifts of food and spirits—whiskey, malt beer and gin. As the day went on, the story about the blonde first foot made its rounds and the celebrators kidded about what kind of bad luck might befall the MacDonalds in the coming year.

Inspired, June rushed down the hallway and came back into the living room with the picture of her angel and a roll of Scotch tape. She asked Uncle Sandy to put it up on the wall. When it was secure, Ian's wife exclaimed, "Look. Doesn't it remind you of back home in Skye? Especially around the Dunvegan area?"

"Aye, could be. Och, with those flowers, could be anywhere in Skye," Sandy answered, returning to his plate of food and glass of whiskey.

June looked at him curiously, wondering, *Flowers in the sky? Maybe Uncle Ian is like me. Maybe he can see things other people don't.* She reminded herself to ask Mrs. G if she ever saw flowers in the sky.

The mood lightened and the singing of Scottish songs became the main activity. Each person had a turn to entertain by singing a favorite tune. Before the party ended, and in keeping with another Hogmanay tradition, the adults and children stood in a circle crisscrossing hands, right over left, and sang the famous Scottish song, "Auld Lang Syne." June was bewildered as the adults' laughing voices changed to sad tones. Some of the women cried openly as they sang together, *"Should auld acquaintance be forgot, and never brought to mind? Should auld acquaintance be forgot, and the days of auld lang syne!"*

When June saw Annie's eyes mist over, she asked, "You going to cry?" Annie shook her head and bit her lower lip, and pulled her hands away from the chain. June thought she heard her say, "Granny."

It was dark by the time the guests gathered up their coats and children and said good-bye.

As the girls prepared for bed, June asked Annie why people were sad singing the last song. Her sister explained that they were sad to be so far away from their families. She said part of the song asked if people were suppose to forget their old friends and the times they shared together.

"I'll never, ever forget Granda and Granny B and how good they were to us," Annie said adamantly.

Maggie began to talk about the friends they left behind in Scotland. They agreed that Wee Gordie, their cousin, was like Mark—a spoiled brat. Auntie Patsy was their favorite aunt, and Uncle Peter always said the funniest things. Helen was remembered with sad sighs and a collective, "We love you."

"Will we ever go back to Scotland?" Mary asked, her voice quivering. They knew how much she missed Granda B.

June piped up that some day she would go back, and they could go with her. Excitedly she added, "Granda B was at our party today. He came in before Uncle Sandy did and kissed Mommy."

The sisters rolled their eyes simultaneously and groaned, "Oh, shut up."

Mary added, "You're going to get in trouble for making up big faker stories."

June huffed, hurt that her sisters thought she made up the story about seeing Granda B. Before she could argue, their mother popped her head in the door, telling them to go to sleep if they wanted to go to Playland the next day to celebrate Annie's tenth birthday. The light was switched off immediately.

"I LOVE A SAUSAGE," June sang out gaily as she scampered down the long staircase to where the mail slot banged moments earlier, announcing the daily delivery. She let out a dramatic gasp when she arrived back at the top of the polished wooden stairs. Her small hands thumbed through the mail searching for a blue airmail letter. Finding one, she ran to her mother and thrust the letter from Scotland into her hands. She was eager to enjoy the ritual of a cup of tea with milk and sugar and freshly baked goods as her mother read the news from home. June settled onto the kitchen chair and licked her lips in anticipation of that morning's baked oatmeal raisin cookies.

Her mother started to read the letter out loud. After reading "Dear Cathy, Jimmy and family," her eyes quickly scanned the letter and she cried out, "Oh no!"

Puzzled, June sat quietly waiting, but her mother didn't utter another word. Minutes ticked away on the clock before she ventured a query, "Are we going to have tea now?"

"What?" Cathy said, forgetting that June was there. "No," she said sternly, "Go downstairs. Ask Mrs. G if you can stay there until somebody comes to get you."

Cathy got up from the table and, with letter in hand, stoically strode down the hallway to the living room. Frightened by her mother's odd behavior, June followed, tiptoeing silently behind her.

"I can't believe they'd no tell me right away," Cathy babbled angrily.

Suddenly, Cathy started sobbing with abrupt gasps for breath. With each choking cry that escaped her mother's mouth, June's head spun with waves of dark colors. Her own breath shortened as she listened to her mother shouting, with fists waving upward, "It's too late, Daddy! Do you hear me? Too late!"

June stopped in her tracks, intuiting the aura of death. The frightened girl spun around and ran to the back stairs, away from her mother's madness, and toward the safety of Mrs. G's flat.

Mrs. G was folding clothes when June burst in. She looked up, smiling, expecting to see an excited, happy face and hear another colorful tale. Instead she saw June's frantic face, white as snow, with her blue eyes round like those of a wild cat.

"Oh, my little friend, you look like a ghost chase you!" Mrs. G exclaimed.

Paralyzed with confusion, June stood in the doorway, doorknob in hand and mouth agape, unable to answer. Mrs. G went across the kitchen to enfold the trembling girl into her ample bosom. Softly, she crooned a lullaby, but June pulled away from the maternal hug to look intensely at her trusted friend.

"Mammy's going away again," she whimpered. "You come and tell her not to do that."

June was always scared on the days when her mother sat for hours staring out the window, crying and talking to herself. She would find company with Mrs. G until her older sisters returned from school.

"She not well again?" asked Mrs. G.

June led her old friend upstairs to Cathy. With joints aching, Mrs. G groaned and grunted as she slowly hiked up the steep back stairs.

The January chill permeated throughout the large flat, with its high ceilings and long, drafty hallway, which made it appear gloomy. The old woman moved slowly down the hallway, and then stopped to catch her breath. June waited patiently behind her.

When Mrs. G placed a hand over her heaving chest, June worried that something bad would happen to her, also. A tremendous sense of sadness gripped the little girl's heart. She started to whimper.

"Ah, my little friend, I feel something very sad has happened to your family. But, I help," Mrs. G said as she continued down the hallway too painstakingly slow for June.

Cathy sat in front of an open window, staring into space, not moving an inch. She nervously rubbed the letter between her forefinger and thumb. Although she wore only a light cardigan over her dress, she seemed oblivious to the frosty winter air surrounding her.

Mrs. G shuffled into the living room and immediately shut the window. Wearily, she collapsed into the horsehair armchair.

In a strained voice, Cathy said, "My father died. He has been sick for a while with stomach cancer. Still, I didn't think he'd go this fast." She stopped covering her mouth. Her hand fell to her lap and her voice trembled.

"He died on Hogmanay. They buried him a fortnight ago. My family didn't want to let me know earlier. Didn't want to ruin my holidays, they said." She turned to Mrs. G and said, without looking directly at her, but past her, "We never had a chance to. . ." Her eyes roamed the room as though searching for something. She sighed deeply, and her shoulders sagged. "To forgive each other."

"Ah, the ghost of the past never lets go of our hearts," Mrs. G said so softly so that only June heard her.

Neither woman paid any attention to June's worried eyes peering from behind the door and into the room where she saw a small glowing aura of light forming behind her mother. It grew into a shape of a young girl. It wasn't Helen. The image looked almost like her angel, except that she wore a simple green dress. June started to point to the image when Mrs. G's voice broke the spell and the apparition vanished.

"You need your family. I go get the girls from school today. But first I phone your husband to come home."

"Oh, God. This'll kill Jimmy," Cathy said wringing her hands. Her blue eyes looked like a frightened child's. "I just want to sleep now. Please," she said in a tiny voice.

Mrs. G rose to help Cathy out of the chair and toward the comfort of the bed. When she came back to the living room, she held June's blue wool tartan coat and a matching cap.

"We must go," she said, cupping the girl's cheeks in her hands. "Don't share her pain so much, little one."

They left walking hand-in-hand through the cold winter drizzle to retrieve June's sisters.

At the school, Mother Superior patted the old woman's dry veined hand and told her that she "would offer up prayers for the deceased and the family." Mrs. G silenced further conversation with a small gesture of her hand when the MacDonald girls began trailing into the office.

On the walk home, Mrs. G lagged behind while the girls huddled together in front, whispering to each other and trying to guess what could have happened at home. Maggie thought that maybe their mother had lost another baby. Mary wanted to know how babies get lost. Annie changed the subject and said, confidently, "Maybe Granda and Granny came for a surprise visit from Scotland and nothing bad thing happened."

June bit her tongue, wanting to keep her promise to Mrs. G, who told her the news should wait until their father got home.

When the group came to the gas station on the corner of Market Street, the girls rifled through their pockets in hopes of coming up with fifteen cents for a soda pop. Their mother would often let them stop at the station to buy cold drinks from the machine. But Mrs. G kept them moving, not hesitating at their unhappy protests. As they approached their building they saw Uncle Sandy's car parked in front.

The girls rushed up the stairs and found their father sitting in the living room with tears pouring down his face. Only once before had they seen him cry, and that was at Helen's funeral, when he had shed silent tears.

Seeing his girls, he quickly held up a large white handkerchief to his mouth to muffle his sobs. Uncle Sandy came down the hallway from the kitchen holding two tall glasses of whiskey and said, "Girls, go to your room and be quiet."

The four sisters sat in their room without making a sound, eyeing each other to see who would be the first to speculate what the problem could be.

Maggie said, shivering, "I got the willies. Someone walked over my grave," which caused Mary to start wailing. She rushed to the bedroom door, threw it open, and ran down the hall screaming, "Mommy! Mommy!" Uncle Sandy caught her around the waist and carried her back to her bedroom. "Wheesht now, hen, your mother's sleeping."

The hysterical girl couldn't be calmed and demanded to see her mother.

"Is our mother okay?" Annie asked.

"Aye. Everything's just fine. Don't worry." Sandy's soothing manner seemed to reassure the frightened children.

The girls stayed silent after Sandy closed their bedroom door. Annie handed Mary a hankie to wipe her eyes.

"I think Mommy's really sick. Maybe it's something horrible," Maggie said shuddering dramatically.

Unable to keep her word any longer, June sputtered out that Granda B was now with Helen and Baby Kit.

"No!" Mary protested, her lip quivering.

"It's true. I heard Mommy tell Mrs. G," June said as she sat down in front of the altar.

Annie knelt next to her and beckoned the other sisters to join them. "Let's say a prayer to Our Lady," she said.

June held out both her hands, palms up. "Let's hold hands so we can talk to Granda B. Mrs. G and her daughter do it like that when they talk to their dead people."

Annie looked apprehensively at her little sister's eager face. "I don't know if that's okay for Catholics to do. Besides, I think it'd be too scary talking to dead people."

"No, it's not. It's fun," said June.

"Let's say prayers instead, okay?" Annie suggested.

"If it's for Granda, we should have a picture of him, like we have for our dead sisters," Maggie said.

"There's a picture of him in the living room on the mantle," Mary said before breaking into more tears. Maggie hugged her sister tightly. Annie sniffled back tears. And June came up with the idea of grabbing the photo from the living room.

The girls agreed they needed to do something special for Granda, although they also agreed that they didn't want to disobey for fear of getting a smacking.

A plan was hatched. Maggie was to lure their father and Uncle Sandy into the kitchen on the other end of the flat. Her pretext was that she and her sisters were hungry, which was true. When the three walked past the bedroom and were in the kitchen, June would sneak down to the living room and grab the photo. Mary offered to go along since June couldn't reach the photo on the fireplace mantle. Annie's job was to keep watch and, if necessary, detain the men if they returned too early to the front of the flat.

The deep rumble of the men's voices could be plainly heard down the hallway and through the small opening of the girls' bedroom door.

"Willie Buchanan was like a father to me," Jimmy said solemnly.

"Och, aye, Jimmy. There's no many like him," Sandy answered.

The men were standing right in front of the door. As their voices grew louder, the girls pulled back a bit and held their breaths.

"It's a sair fecht," Jimmy sighed.

"If it wasn't for Willie, I'd never have come to America. He said being a Catholic, it'd be a better life here," Sandy said.

"Wish I could go home to Scotland," Jimmy said.

"Me, too," Annie said gloomily as she leaned against the bedroom door. June wanted to say that she couldn't go to Scotland because the family needed her here.

The men's voices faded away into the kitchen. The last voice heard was Sandy's. "Nancy's on her way to help with the girls."

Maggie, who was following behind the men, gave the door a quick rap, signaling the coast was clear.

When Maggie closed the kitchen door, Mary and June slipped out and crept toward the front of the flat, trying hard to suppress their nervous giggles.

Although the early winter darkness had crept into the living room, they decided not to brighten it up by switching on a lamp, which would draw attention. Luckily, the streetlights suddenly snapped on, shining some light for them. The streetcar clanged past, and a horn blared. June walked to the bay windows and leaned her head against the frame to look down onto Market Street, which was now busy with people arriving home from work. Large raindrops rolled, one after another, down the windowpanes and onto the scurrying crowd below. Hypnotized by the scene, June became lost thinking about the ant colony in the yard.

"Neato, skeeto, I got it!" Mary hopped off of the big chair with a frame in her hand. She handed June the old grainy black-and-white photo of Granda and Granny B on their wedding day. Granda B, a handsome, tall, lean man with a full head of dark curly hair, reminded June of Maggie, with his slanted eyes and toothy grin. Granny B, holding a bouquet of roses, was dressed in an ankle-length wedding gown with her hair tucked up under a long laced veil. With her eyes wide and full lips closed, she seemed to be shyly looking out at the girls.

"Looks like mommy, huh?" Mary said.

"Take the other one, too." June pointed to the black-and-white photo of Cathy in her mid teens, linked arm-in-arm with Granda B in a summer garden. Both were smiling broadly.

A yellow cab stopping in front of the flat caught June's attention. She pressed her face against the cold glass to get a better view. A tall, heavy woman in a dark coat exited the cab.

"She's here!" June called out warningly.

"Let's scram!" Mary bolted down the hallway with June at her heels.

A moment later the doorbell's loud buzz was heard. Annie opened the bedroom door a slit, and June knelt beneath her to peek out just as Sandy trotted past. They heard him greet his wife cheerfully, and watched as she walked past with a full paper bag. Uncle Sandy, holding two more bags, stopped at the girls' door and tapped on it lightly. "Come say hello to your Auntie Nancy."

The girls disliked her as much as they disliked Mark. They wished they didn't have to call her auntie, as their parents had instructed them to do.

"Did she bring the brat?" Maggie asked in a low voice.

᪣ ᪣ ᪣

The pungent aroma of simmering garlic, spices and tomatoes filled the flat, creating an illusion of a warm home. Sandy breathed in the fragrances with hungry pleasure. He often boasted to Jimmy about his wife's delicious Italian cooking.

"I thank God every day that she married me," he said.

The girls were sprawled across the carpet watching "The Lone Ranger." Uncle Sandy had invited them out of their room to watch television while Aunt Nancy made dinner.

"Dinner!" Nancy's voice boomed down the hallway.

Sandy picked up Jimmy's empty glass and, trying to sound upbeat, said, "Let's get some food."

"Och, man, I can't eat." Jimmy's voice slurred as his head lolled onto the overstuffed chair.

His daughters eyed him cautiously. They knew his mood could quickly change when he was drunk. June sensed her father's mood growing darker and turned down the television just as Tonto galloped away from the bad guys.

"The girls, Jimmy. They need to eat and get to bed. For their sakes please," Sandy said kindly, trying to get Jimmy to come to the dinner table.

"You go. I'll see if Cathy wants anything." Jimmy stumbled off to their bedroom.

Dinner was solemn, even though Auntie Nancy made the girls her delicious spaghetti, the dish they always raved about when they ate dinner at her house. The pasta dish was something the girls had never experienced in their Scottish household.

Mary, who always ate heartily, sat with the others at the table with her head down, unable to eat.

Maggie whispered to Annie, "Good thing they didn't bring the brat." Her sister just stared at the wall with her thin lips closed tight. Only June, enjoying the buttery garlic bread, laughed at Maggie's remark.

When her sisters left the table, June stayed behind to have another piece of bread. Sandy and Nancy talked in hushed tones about Granda B's passing.

"I still feel guilty, though, you know. I brought them bad luck," Sandy said.

"Oh, honey. Don't be silly. It was his time. He was an old man." Nancy gave Sandy a peck on the cheek.

"The family told Cathy to not bother coming home. Oh well, perhaps it's for the best. She's needed here," Sandy said.

His wife remarked that Cathy was of no use to her family lying in bed with the curtains drawn and refusing food.

"And, that one. . ." Nancy nodded at June. "Making up stories about her grandfather coming to see them at the New Year's party. They ought to spank her for telling lies."

June munched away on her bread as she thought about how to get even with Nancy for speaking badly about her mother. Maybe she'd tell her that Mark called her a big mean monster.

Satisfied with her last bite, the grateful child thanked the cook and said, "Granda's with my dead sisters *and* my angel. I can talk to them. Want to learn how?" Auntie Nancy shushed her and warned her to stop saying naughty things.

Before going to bed, the girls decided to do what June had suggested. They lit the candles that were hidden under the bed with the matches Mary had snuck into the bedroom. Annie told her sisters to get their rosary beads. "We'll put them in the middle so Our Lady will help us talk with Granda," she said.

Maggie and Mary pulled the altar out into the middle of the room so they all could sit around it and hold each other's hands. With eyes closed, it was Annie who asked for Granda B to give them a message. Mary started to sniff back tears.

Just then June saw a white energy spark around the altar. "Granda is here!" she said excitedly.

Her sisters shivered. Although they couldn't feel him, they believed their little sister. They all said, "I love you, Granda."

Chapter Seventeen:
Hopes and Fears

EACH DAY FOLLOWING the sad news the girls knelt at the altar with their rosary beads and said ten "Hail Marys" for Granda B and their mother. Mary complained that it was too much, but Annie said it would help cure their mother more quickly.

Overtaken by grief, Cathy remained in bed for several days. Although the girls helped with the house cleaning and cooking, the majority of the work fell on Annie's shoulders. June felt sad for her and would try to be helpful.

On the second Sunday following the news, Jimmy and June were in the living room. He read the Sunday paper while she cut out paper dolls from store catalogs. They heard Cathy weakly call out "Jimmy" from the bedroom next door. He quickly went to her. June could hear only the deep rumble of his voice, followed by her mother's faint reply.

He returned to the living room and happily told June, "Your mother's hungry. That's a good sign. Let's go get her something."

June was relieved to see that her father didn't look as tense as he had been since learning of Granda's death. She quickly gathered up the scissors, paste and the paper cutouts and followed him to the kitchen.

The older girls, cleaning up after Sunday breakfast, began jabbering and giggling when Jimmy gave them the good news.

"Her face is rosy pink," he told them. "I think the fever broke. Annie, boil an egg. Maggie, toast two slices of bread, *lightly*. Mary, fill the kettle with water. And June, set the tray with one of the fancy cloth napkins. The kind your Mother only uses for special dinners."

Jimmy stretched up to the highest shelf in the cupboard where he kept his good Scotch and took down Cathy's favorite pink and gold teapot with matching cup and saucer—a wedding gift that the children were not allowed to touch. Whistling one of his favorite Scottish tunes, "I Belong to Glasgow," Jimmy began to spoon loose black tea into the teapot.

"Daddy, that's too many tea leaves," June said.

"Yeah?" Jimmy asked with sincerity.

She nodded very seriously, so he scooped some of the tea out and winked at her.

Ready to resume her art project, June wiped away the crumbs from the table to lay down her art supplies. She pulled out a faded yellow kitchen chair, climbed up on it, and resumed her project. She loved to create families from the models displayed in the catalogs. After cutting them out, she'd paste the pictures onto a white sheet of paper. Her fingers were too small for the big metal scissors, so she cut the figures slowly.

"Daddy, can we make a wee party for Mommy?" she asked without missing a snip.

Maggie echoed the request, "Can we Daddy? I'll draw her a picture of us at the beach. That'll cheer her up."

"I'll get flowers from the garden," Mary added enthusiastically as she put silverware on the tray.

"Don't be daft, you'll no find flowers in this cold," Jimmy said.

The January weather had been cold in spite of the winter sun, which tried to bring some warmth to the season.

"Me and Mrs. G kept some flowers alive," said Mary, gesturing to June to hand over the scissors.

Mary and June enjoyed working in the garden with Mrs. G, who always had time to teach them about gardening—no matter the weather. Like the garden, they thrived under her magical touch.

"Sounds like a party, girls!" Jimmy said as the toast popped up.

They all laughed with delight. The excitement of planning a surprise for their mother, in hopes of bringing her happiness, caught on. Each girl scurried around preparing her part of the celebration.

When it was time, Jimmy entered the bedroom to let Cathy know the girls would soon bring in her breakfast.

Hiding under thick blankets, Cathy moaned, wanting to escape her haunting dream.

෨ ෨ ෨

Her father drew away from her. She knew that he didn't want her touching him, not after what she'd done. It wasn't that she wanted to lean on him. It was the force of the bitter winds that blew her to him.

෨ ෨ ෨

Cathy propped up some pillows to help her sit up after Jimmy left the room. She didn't want to fall asleep again, and return to the disturbing dream.

Her throat tightened. She didn't want to cry anymore. If only she could dream of the loving times with her father, and not be stuck with the same image that played over and over again. Sadly, she could not remember the good times. She could only recall the last time she and her parents were alone together. All the other times before that were erased from her mind.

She slid down the pillows and brought one over her head, in hopes of hiding from the memory and from the words spoken that dismal night in the Highlands of Scotland so many years ago— words that sealed her fate wouldn't go away.

"I told your father we must come, for it may be the last chance to get you home before you worsen matters. Then he'd never let you home." Granny B said to Cathy.

Granda B stood at the front door of the cottage with his hands buried deep in the pockets of his Macintosh, waiting for his wife and daughter to finish packing Cathy's battered leather suitcase.

Granda B took the case from Granny and bitterly complained to her, "I can't believe I let you talk me into coming to this godforsaken place, let alone at Hogmanay."

Granny tutted, and turned to cover Cathy's head with a scarf, assuring her that he was just feeling a bit sorry for himself. He muttered how he was missing Hogmanay in Glasgow. By now the revelries would be in full swing. Instead, he was hours away in the Highlands of Scotland, and sworn to secrecy about their mission. He was a reluctant savior, and Cathy knew it.

"You'll see in time that I was right. It's the best for all. You're no leaving forever," said Granny. But Cathy pulled away at her mother's encouraging words.

The three huddled together trying to avoid being soaked by the pelting rain. A strong wind blew frantically around them. The winds sounded like the shriek of a witch's laugh.

The dim lights of the bus snaking down the dark winding road grew brighter, until they stopped in front of the three drenched people, saving them from any more punishment. Cathy balked as she climbed the steps into the bus. Her father pushed her onward. He said something to her, although she could not hear him over the sounds of the high-pitched storm winds surrounding them. The door closed, leaving the dead of winter behind them.

Cathy was certain that if she could have been stronger and never got on the bus, and never left the Highlands, then perhaps Granda B and she would have found a way to be as they once were—a loving father and daughter.

〇〇 〇〇 〇〇

The tea, brewed to perfection, stayed hot under the floral tea cozy. Jimmy placed it next to the teacup and a blue eggcup containing a soft-boiled egg and a plate of buttered toast.

"Ready, girls? Bring your presents," he said as he picked up the tray.

Annie proudly held a saucer with a few small butter cookies glazed with pink icing that Mrs. G had helped her bake the previous day. Jimmy remarked what a good girl Annie had been to take such good care of the house.

Mary had returned from the garden with a few decent looking snapdragons she put in a green plastic water glass.

Maggie had hurriedly drawn a picture of the family holding hands in front of a sign for Playland. She yanked at her father's arm and showed him the picture. "Look, see how happy we are?"

Jimmy saw the drawing and remarked on her talents. "Oh, aye, that looks like us! Right girls, let's get going."

The procession of well-wishers walked merrily down the long hallway to their mother. The room was dark with the curtains drawn tightly together, blocking out all sunlight. Cathy was lying deep within the layers of covers. Jimmy turned on a small lamp on the nightstand.

"You awake, hen?" he asked softly.

She mumbled something, but her head was buried in a pillow. The girls crowded around the doorway holding their gifts.

"Here's your tea and egg," Jimmy said as he put the tray on the nightstand. He motioned for the girls to come forward. "The girls got some gifts for you."

Annie stepped forward and laid the cookies beside the tray. Mary put the flowers on opposite nightstand. And Maggie leaned her picture against a tall water glass.

Their mother didn't lift her head. June sensed that she wasn't really asleep, but rather hiding away from them. The little girl felt miffed knowing this, so she stayed by the doorway and didn't go into the room. Her gift was a story told through the cut-outs she

had made from her many catalogs—Wards, Sears and Penny's—
and pasted on paper. It showed a hen with chickens. Pasted high
on the page was a pretty blonde lady, smiling and sitting in a
sailboat that seemed to be floating in the sky. June had prepared
a story to go along with the cut-outs. But now she didn't know if
she wanted to tell it to her mother. She let the picture drop to the
carpet.

Jimmy's shoulders slumped, hurt by his wife's rejection. "Let's
leave your mother to sleep. Maybe she'll be up a bit later," he said
wearily.

Watching her father and her sisters, June thought how her
mother's sadness made the whole family sad. They needed her to be
happy. She wanted to bring her mother back for everyone's sake.

The sisters filed out of the room and Jimmy quietly shut the door,
closing off Cathy from the family once again. Only the youngest girl
didn't follow the others back to the kitchen. June had decided to
visit her mother. She slowly opened the door and tiptoed into the
bedroom to stand by the side of the bed. Her mother stirred slightly.
To get into the bed without making a fuss, June pulled herself up tall
so as not to tug the blankets off and, like a cat, leaped lightly onto
the bed. She gingerly crawled over to her mother, almost crushing a
Life magazine under her knees.

With her warm palm against the back of Cathy's head, she
whispered, "Mommy. Here's my love." She laid her face against her
mother's hair and kissed it. "Now you'll be better."

Cathy rolled over onto her back and squinted at her pretty little
daughter with uncombed curls. Happy at being acknowledged,
June announced, "I'm going to tell you a story."

Her mother sighed and closed her eyes.

June opened up the magazine full of photographs. Flipping
through it, she found a picture she liked and began chatting away.
"Once upon a time. . ."

Her mother turned over, facing away from her. Nevertheless,
June continued on with her story, turning the large pages of the

magazine. At one page she stopped, keeping quiet, mesmerized by the black-and-white photo of a soldier kissing a woman in a train station. June had seen her mother and father kiss, and thought that maybe this was a picture of them doing it again.

June's voice suddenly became clearer. Cathy moved her head around and cocked her ear to see if she had heard right.

"Man says to the lady, 'What's your name?' Lady said, 'Cathy.' See. This is you." She held up the magazine, but her mother was still turned away from her. She patted her mother's shoulder, "Look Mommy! You and the big man kissing. 'Member?"

"What? What are you going on about?" Cathy answered.

Happy that her mother had finally responded, June went on with her story, the one she felt had been told to her by her angel. " 'Member? Before you were sad. You and the man laughed a bunch of times. Mommy, will you laugh like that again some day?"

Cathy propped up on an elbow so she could see the photo. Bolting up, she pulled the magazine from June's hands and threw it violently across the room.

"Damn you," she screamed. "You're always on at me with your lying stories. Stop it! Can't you keep that mouth of yours shut! Leave me alone you wee nyaft."

June slid off the bed, hurt that her mother called her a bad name, even though Mary had said nyaft was just the same as saying she was a brat.

"Get out. Get out! Jimmy! Jimmy!"

June ran wildly to the door to escape the wrath, and bumped into her father as he came through it.

"What in hell? Jesus, June! Didn't I tell you to leave your mother alone? Get out before I skelp you."

He started to take off his heavy leather belt to spank his daughter. But having felt the sting of his belt across the back of her legs before, June whizzed past him, screeching to Annie for help.

"It's okay. She won't bother you. Lie down." Jimmy sat on the bed next to Cathy, touching her hair.

She flopped back onto the pillow and rolled away from him. He moved further onto the bed and pulled the covers back away from her shoulders. She felt his warm calloused hands beneath her nightgown, massaging her neck and moving down her back.

"Oh hen, I've missed you so much," he said huskily. He leaned down and kissed her bare shoulders.

"It's been so hard not having you with me." He slid back the blankets to lie next to her.

She could feel his warm breath on her neck. Her first reaction was to shove him away. Then she sighed, thinking, *He needs comforting, too.* She turned to face him, tears wetting her face.

Chapter Eighteen:
The Spirit of Friendship

THE DELICATE BRASS bells hanging from Mrs. G's back door banged chaotically when June busted though it. Like a whirlwind, the girl ran through the kitchen and into the flat in search of her friend. Cathy tried unsuccessfully to hold her back by grabbing her daughter's oversized sweater.

Smoke from frankincense swirled around the living room as Mrs. G awoke, stretching from her position under a handmade afghan on the sofa. As she opened her eyes, she spied the mischievous grin on June's face as she pulled the crimson silk scarf and tarot cards from under a sleeve that was stretched down over her hand. Knowingly, Mrs. G smiled, moving her creaking body as she put out her hand.

Cathy entered the room wearing a pretty, light-colored suit with matching hat. "Good morning, Mrs. G," she called out in a singsong voice.

"Ah, you look so pretty. Just like this sunny spring day," Mrs. G said sincerely, noting the pink coloring that had returned to Cathy's cheeks.

The two women watched the little girl dance around the room. Cathy shook her head, always astonished at the energy of her youngest. "Sure it won't be too much for you to watch her?" she asked apologetically.

Mrs. G laughed, "Trouble? June?"

Cathy looked at her watch. "I better hurry. I don't want to keep Jimmy waiting. He's so tense these days with working two shifts. He's found the perfect house for us. I can't wait to see it. I don't want to be late."

"No problem," said Mrs. G.

Appreciatively, Cathy put her hand on the old woman's shoulder. "Thank you so much. And, please, would you no say a wee prayer for us that we get it?"

Mrs. G spread the tarot cards on top of a low brass table. Her arthritic fingers glided over them before pulling one out. "You have house before summer. I know."

"That's smashing news!" Cathy beamed.

Mrs. G gave a delighted chuckle that was followed by a rough cough. Spitting phlegm into a large hankie, she calmed her breathing and waved Cathy away. "Go. Hurry. I visit with my little friend. We have fun. You be happy now!"

Mrs. G looks so very frail lately, Cathy thought, feeling a rush of sadness. Impulsively, she gave her friend a quick hug, and then one for June.

"Be a good girl and don't bother Mrs. G with your wild stories," Cathy said to June. Leaning in closer, she added, "And, sssh, we won't tell Daddy about the cards, remember?"

June knew there would be a lot of trouble if her daddy found out about the cards. Annie had warned her about that many times. She put a finger against her tightly closed lips.

As soon as the tinkling bells announced her mother's departure, June scampered across to Mrs. G to sit snugly next to her. Mrs. G picked up the cards, shuffled them three times, and once again fanned them out across the table. June gingerly touched a few. She took a deep satisfying breath and became calm.

"You like, but Daddy no like," Mrs. G said. June's round eyes looked up at Mrs. G seriously, nodding in agreement.

"I know. My husband, he not like the cards either. Ahhh, men! So afraid of women's magic." The old lady laughed heartily. "Oh well," she said, tilting her head thoughtfully at June. "You, my little friend, you see much, eh? You are like me, *profetka.*"

The first time June heard the Polish word she liked the sound of it. When Mrs. G explained it meant "a visionary", she felt good that someone believed in her special ability. In time she became used to her friend saying Polish words. Without knowing why, she always understood what they meant. To June it was as though they had a secret language between them.

"Come, I show you how to see more," Mrs. G said as she lit a white candle. "Look at the flame."

The two sat quietly gazing at the flame, hand in hand. The wise old teacher taught her young student how to conjure up an image while keeping her eyes on the flame.

"Let the pictures come to you," she instructed. After a few minutes she asked June to tell her what she saw.

June began to see images take shape. Dreamily, she mumbled a few words about her Mommy and Daddy going up a very big hill. When another picture formed in her mind—a large white house with a dark trim—she said excitedly, "We have a big house! That's our new home, huh?"

The two seers looked knowingly at each other with wide eyes. June knew Mrs. G had the same vision.

The amber beads of Mrs. G's earrings jangled when she nodded her head with approval. "Good. You learning." She then cleared the vision away with a swoop of her hand over the flame.

"I saw my angel again," June said.

With a penetrating gaze, Mrs. G touched the girl's vibrant hair. "Your angel have hair like you. Yes?"

June nodded in agreement.

"She wants your mother to see her, too," said Mrs. G.

"Mommy says she's only my imagination. I'm not to talk about her anymore because Daddy will smack my bum if I tell any more stories."

June confided in Mrs. G about how angry her mother would get over her stories, especially the one about making daisy chains with her angel on the hill. She insisted it wasn't a dream, but a place she really went to be with her angel. Mrs. G explained that she shouldn't say anything at this time about her angel because her mother wasn't ready to remember certain days gone by.

Still, Mrs. G assured June that her angel was not her imagination. "You, she, good friends. Someday you be together. I see this. You and your angel are *duchy siostrzane*. Understand?"

Feeling a tingling throughout her body, June nodded. Once again as before, without knowing Polish, she had a good sense of what Mrs. G had said–– she and her angel were indeed spirit sisters.

"Always know this, June, you and I, friends forever. My spirit mingles with your spirit. Now we too are duchy siostrzane."

Her friend was so serious that June felt frightened, until the old woman smiled warmly and tenderly patted the little girl's cheek. Mrs. G picked up a family photo and said, "I miss my husband and sons."

They looked into each other's eyes in silence.

"They miss you, too. Before we go to our new home, you can go home to them," the little seer predicted, pointing at the photo.

Surrounded by tarot cards and swirling incense, the two sat quietly. Mrs. G took hold of her little friend's hand and closed her eyes, tears seeping through.

June knew she was remembering happier days before the war.

"Soon that pain there," June said, gently placing her small hands over her old friend's heart, "won't hurt anymore."

Chapter Nineteen:
The American Dream

June 1, 1955

THE BLACK FORD station wagon carried the MacDonald family up the hills of Castro Street, and toward their new home on Liberty Street. The girls sat in the backseat chatting with excitement. They counted out loud the numbered streets they drove by, starting with Seventeenth Street. Their car, filled with moving boxes and furniture piled on top, chugged up the steep hills past Twentieth Street. The next street was where their new home would be.

The station wagon, heavy with the load, weaved a bit. Jimmy over-compensated his left turn from Castro onto Liberty Street. The girls squealed and laughed loudly as they rolled against each other in the backseat.

Jimmy straightened out the car and then a loud bump alerted the family that the boxes on top of the car were loose.

Liberty Street greeted them with a variety of colorful homes ranging in style from Victorian to Edwardian. The large two-story Victorians had ornate carving around the frames of their long windows. The smaller Edwardians were almost cottage-like next to the larger Victorians. Most houses had lots of colorful flowers in full summer bloom. The street was not wide and busy like Market Street. It was quiet, with only a few cars parked outside the homes.

An elderly couple came out of one of the smaller houses, which had a garden of deep red, hot pink and yellow roses.

"Are we're almost there, Daddy?" Mary called out.

Unable to contain his pride, Jimmy pointed up the street towards the sudden rise of a short steep hill. "It's just up that hill— our new home."

He stopped the car and jumped out to tighten the cargo on top of the car.

The day the papers for the house were finalized, Cathy had told the girls what a big blessing it was for the MacDonald family. If they had stayed in Glasgow, it was likely that the family would never have been able to buy a house, and certainly not one like the one they had just purchased.

At the second house from the corner of Liberty Street, two women in their early thirties moved a frayed, heavy couch up the stairs of a Victorian. The woman pushing the couch was short with a trim body that moved nicely beneath her jeans and striped colored shirt. Her long, thick chestnut hair was pulled back into a low ponytail. She called out directions to the other woman to maneuver the couch past a curve in the stairs.

"For God's sake, Bernice, you're letting it slip back on me!"

"Okay, okay, Sadie," said the taller woman pulling the couch.

The tall woman reminded Cathy of Nurse Hamilton, the Highlander nurse who had the same wide-shouldered body. Cathy could tell from Sadie's dark glaring eyes that she was exasperated with their progress.

The various blue colors painted on their Victorian reminded June of the ocean, and she immediately felt akin to the two women. She wondered if these neighbors would become her friends.

Two children unloaded an old battered truck filled with boxes and furniture. The girl, about nine years old, had the same spirited look as Sadie, the shorter woman, although the girl was as skinny as a rail. She had light brown hair cut short with long bangs hanging over her eyes. The boy, who looked about June's age, had dark chestnut hair, also like Sadie's.

"Mom! Tell Brian to help me! He's so weak!" yelled the girl, struggling to get a small wooden table out of the truck.

"Hold your horses, Jeannie Callaghan! I'll be right there," Sadie called back.

Jimmy leaned his head into the station wagon and said, "Looks like move-in day for them, too. I'd say those women need my help."

The girls whispered to each other, wondering what he was going to do. As he walked toward the women, Annie rolled down the window to hear what would come next.

"Just moved in, eh?" he said, pushing up his sleeves as he crossed the street. The women looked at him briefly, but kept on with their task.

"Here ladies, I'll give you a hand," he said. "Why don't you call your men out, and we'll get this up in no time."

Sadie burst out laughing. "We are the men here. But, thanks anyway." She looked over to the MacDonald's car and said, "Looks like you've got a move-in job yourselves. We'll come over and help you when we're done."

"No. No. Couldn't ask you ladies to do that," Jimmy said, backing away from them. He quickly retreated to the car.

June had never seen the odd, perplexed look on her father's face before.

"Queer lot them," he mumbled, looking back at Brian who shyly ducked his head away from the staring girls. "Better keep the girls away from them," he added. "That poor wee fellow."

June wondered why her father said that about the boy. As the car started off up Liberty Street, Brian's eyes locked with June's. His face turned a crimson hue from embarrassment at seeing her looking at him, but he didn't turn away from her. Their friendship began on that day.

The family drove up the hill and stopped in front of one of the large two-story Victorian houses near the top of the street. It was newly painted white with dark rust trim. Alongside the house, in full bloom, were hydrangeas bushes in white, pale lavender and pink that accentuated the crisp cleanliness of the house.

The family got out of the car and stared up at it. It was a grand house.

June watched the colors around her father's body change from a murky brown to soft green. She knew how to read his emotion from the colors. Mrs. G had taught her how to match emotions with the colors from the aura energy surrounding people. She had explained that understanding a person's feelings would help her to know how to act toward that person. The green around her father was a good sign, the girl thought. It told her that her father was hopeful about their new home, and not worried as indicated by the darker color.

A tear rolled out of June's eye. She missed Mrs. G so much. Everyone in her family was too enthralled with the new house to mourn when Mrs. G had passed on in her sleep a month ago. Only June grieved openly for her old friend.

Tesia had asked Jimmy and Cathy to join her, her husband and a small group of Polish friends to say their final goodbyes at a gravesite ceremony. The girls stayed home with Annie. They had gone down to the garden and said a prayer for Mrs. G. June felt a bit of comfort being in the garden where the two had shared so many happy times together. After the funeral Tesia invited the MacDonald family downstairs for refreshments. When a guest remarked that Mrs. G's passing was for the best, since she was so sad, June yelled at him, "No! We were happy!" Jimmy quickly scooped her up in his muscular arms and apologized for the outburst by explaining that it was way past her bedtime.

June had been inconsolable for days, until Mrs. G appeared next to her bed one night.

"We're not apart," Mrs. G reminded her. "At your new house, go to the garden, out to the biggest tree. There I will be, smiling at you."

June had stopped crying, but she still missed her friend.

"Oh, Jimmy, the color is perfect. You've done good," Cathy said, admiring the new house and giving her husband a kiss on the cheek. He turned from her and hid a pleased smile.

"Holy mackerel! It's like the movies," Mary said as she looked up at the house.

"Gee, Daddy, this house is so big," Annie said, taking in the long broad stairs leading up to the two-storied house.

"Look, a garage," Maggie said, pointing.

"And, a big basement. That's where I'll put my new washing machine," said Cathy, merrily.

In a rare moment of Cathy being deeply fulfilled, June caught a glimpse of her mother's bright yellow aura like the rays of the sun.

The sisters all chattered about their beautiful new house. Only June stayed quiet. She was overwhelmed and couldn't say anything.

"Alright girls, everyone grab a box," their father said.

"I'll go on up and unlock the door," Cathy said, taking a suitcase with her.

June followed her mother carrying a small box that she had held onto in the car.

Maggie moved to pick up a little box, but Annie got to it first. She tucked it under one arm and took hold of a suitcase.

As a result, Maggie was stuck helping Mary with a larger heavy box. After some effort, the girls lifted it, and strained to keep it aloft between them. Then Maggie dropped her end.

"Jeez. Pick it up, sissy," Mary said laughing at her sister. They lifted the box again, and Maggie let out a whiny "huff" as she struggled with it.

"That's too heavy for you, hen," their father said to Maggie. "Annie, give that smaller box to Maggie then come and grab that end."

Maggie dropped her end sharply, and gave Mary a satisfied look. The box fell on Mary's toes. She stifled a yelp, swallowing her anger at her sister. Her father slapped her shoulder playfully.

"You're like a strong, wee laddie," Jimmy said to Mary, laughing as he headed up the stairs with the chairs in hand.

"I'm not a boy. I hate him," Mary said, glaring at her father's back as she and Annie picked up the heavy box.

"Mother Superior says 'hate' is a strong word. Don't say it. Come on, let's go," Annie said, taking steps toward the house. Mary scowled at her.

Near the top of the ten broad stairs leading up to the front door, June began to daydream about the room she'd be sharing with Mary. Neither the stairs nor the box she carried was on her mind. All she could see were pictures of her own bed and her altar floating through her head. Even though her box was small, it was large enough to keep her from seeing over the top of it. She stumbled when her toe got caught on a step. She regained her balance, and readjusted her grip on the box.

"Watch where you're going," Jimmy said coming up behind her. Her foot caught again on the last step causing her to drop the box. The contents of the box sprayed across the front porch as she fell onto her knees. Her mother turned around and what she saw stunned her.

Standing on the step behind her, Jimmy stared at a crimson silk scarf and tarot cards scattered across the porch—lying on the threshold of their new home, mocking him.

"What the bloody hell are those?" he asked glaring at his little girl.

His powerful arm swooped down and grabbed a few cards in his fist, holding them close to her face.

Her frightened eyes slowly looked up at him.

"Where'd you get these, you wee pagan?" he snarled at June.

"They're mine!" Annie and Mary called out in unison from behind.

"Lying wee bitches!" Jimmy shouted over his shoulder in their direction.

He turned around and found his wife standing frozen in the doorway. "You, Cathy, did you know about these—these bloody devil things?"

Cathy looked back and forth from the girls to him. She swallowed hard. "I think those were left behind when Mrs. G died. June must have . . . um . . . must have made a mistake. How's she to know what they are? She's only a wee girl."

"Aye, a wee girl that'll grow up a lying, thieving, bloody tinker! Get these things out of my sight. Here, you two take them out back to the bin," Jimmy said shoving the cards at Mary and Annie.

They hurriedly dropped their box on the porch and began to scoop up the cards.

It wasn't a mistake, June wanted to say to her parents, but her father was so angry she knew better than to speak. She had heard Tesia tell her mother that Mrs. G wanted June to have the tarot cards.

Nervously, Annie and Mary rushed to the backyard to find a metal drum. Their father stormed out behind them. According to Jimmy, it was June's destiny to burn in hell. He ranted on about the evil of his pagan daughter as he dragged her by the arm to the backyard.

"And any of you girls who go along with this will burn in hell, too," he said spitting out the words.

He threw June forward, forcing her to stumble onto her knees. Trembling, she didn't know if it was the beating or losing her cards that scared her most. Either way, she was filled with fear. She saw an angry, blood-red energy exploding around her father.

Cathy came to the back door, praying the situation wouldn't get worse. She could see Jimmy's face flush a deep red, and knew he was seething with anger. He would be blinded to any reason. Recently, when June had said that Mrs. G visited her in a dream the night of her death, Jimmy had demanded that June stop all the malarkey about seeing dead people and talking to angels. Cathy had reminded him that some people were fey. That was superstitious, he had told her.

"I'll have no disrespect against our Church. You're a disgrace. All of you," he ranted.

He rummaged through his jacket and found matches. June tried desperately to grab at the cards still on the ground. "No," she whimpered. Through her sobs, she looked up at him helplessly as he grabbed the few cards in her hands. She silently prayed to Our Lady for him to stop.

He struck a match and tossed it into the metal drum. The tarot cards easily caught fire, one by one. Devastated, the crying child watched the brilliant colors burst into flames. In a moment of final desperation, she reached out a hand toward the drum in hopes of saving some. Instead, her father caught her hand and pushed her to her knees, and held her down by the scruff of her neck.

"I'll no have you bring the Devil into my house," he told her. "Pray to God before the Devil takes you away to burn in hell!"

June cried louder, and hit at her father's hand. Cathy rushed down the back steps with Maggie hanging onto her waist to witness the vicious act. "Jimmy! JIMMY! Please. Oh Mother of God! Please. She's only a wean!"

"Yeah? Well, wait 'til the nuns get hold of her. She'll grow up right fast."

He thrust June down toward the ground and slapped her head fiercely before stomping back toward the house. At the edge of the steps he abruptly stopped and stared into his wife's face. "You're turning them against me, aren't you? You're teaching your girls how to keep secrets? Well, you're good at that, eh?"

He pushed past his wife into the house and yelled, "Doomed to hell, every last one of you!"

Stunned into silence, Cathy moved slowly toward June. Jimmy roared from inside the house, "CATHY!" In mid-stride toward

June, she stopped and turned to the house leaving her daughters in the backyard of their new home.

The sisters stood frozen in place around the bin, eyes glued to the blaze feeding upon itself. The fire burst into a sudden spark, crackling loudly, awaking everyone from the nightmare. Annie rushed over to June to put a protective arm around her.

Maggie found a stick in the yard. She flipped a couple of cards out of the bin. The smoldering cards cooled on the cement.

"Boy, oh boy, June. Daddy's right, wait 'til Sister St. Pius bangs your head with a ruler. You'll cry like a baby," said Mary, who now had the nun as her third grade teacher.

"Shut up," Annie ordered, holding June tighter. "She isn't as bad as you."

"They won't like me. Daddy said so," the youngest sister said between sobs.

Brushing off the salvaged, singed cards, Maggie advised June, "You'll have to learn to be quiet about certain things. Just smile at them like this." She demonstrated a coy smile. "That's all you have to do."

June pressed her head against Annie's chest, muttering, "I hate him."

"He's the big, bad wolf," said Maggie, her eyes flickering. She snarled at her sisters.

Mary glowered at the bin. "We could kill him. Then Mommy'll let us go to public school."

"Can we, Annie? Kill him?" said June, who trusted her eldest sister to have all the answers.

"We could. With my baseball bat," said Mary staring into the fire.

"Poison," said Maggie.

"Where'd we get poison?" asked Annie, shaking her head at her sisters' sinful suggestions.

"We have poison. DDT. I've put it on flowers," Mary said fiddling with her back pocket.

"Well then, we could put it in his tea," Annie contributed to the conspiracy.

The girls huddled in a circle while the last of the fire hissed behind them. Maggie held the cards up toward the sun, looking at each side carefully. "I can draw cards like this for you, June. Even better," she said with a sly smile.

June perked up at the solution to her loss. "You will?" she said, pushing herself away from Annie's tight hug. It was the first glimmer of hope the sad girl had after seeing her precious tarot cards go up in smoke. She wiped the last of her tears from her face.

Maggie looked at the five year-old tenderly holding a burnt card. "Happy Birthday, June."

"You'll need this, too," Mary said pulling the crimson silk scarf out from her back pocket.

"Oh, thank you." A smile returned to June's red-spotted face, her puffy eyes now crinkling from happy relief. Annie put out her arms to draw in close all of her sisters.

Chapter Twenty:
Wicked Behavior at Holy Savior

1959

SISTER ST. PIUS stood beneath a large, plain wooden cross. The elderly nun was a bit crotchety because her students took so long to settle down after the music teacher had left. As though to lengthen her small stature, the tiny wizard-like nun had a rigid backbone and a sharp chin that jutted out, which lifted her head up and back. From this vantage point, she scrutinized the preciseness of the rows of boys and girls seated at their desks. Finally, satisfied that the rows were aligned properly, she opened the religion book.

Adjusting her round wire-framed glasses, she began, "Praise be to the Lord. You are to love, honor and serve Him. It is your Catholic duty to always be good boys and girls. That is the only way you can enter into Heaven. Even when you are alone, God knows if you are *thinking* of being bad. God sees *everything* that you do. Now, let's open your religion books to page thirty-five." She suddenly stopped and snapped, "June MacDonald, what *are* you talking about?"

June immediately stopped whispering to the boy next to her and jerked up with a gasp. She looked up at the nun, guiltily. She tried to shrink deeply into her seat. Sister St. Pius, arms akimbo, moved from behind the podium to stand and stare ominously down the aisle at the frightened girl. June opened her mouth and a few incoherent words spilled out.

The nun's tight lips, barely opened, barked in a deep voice, "Stand up when you talk to me."

Bravely, June stood alongside her desk, hands folded in front of her as she was taught to do. She hesitated, embarrassed, and then answered quietly, "Yes, Sister St. Pius. I said that Mary is God's Mother and God has to do what His mother says because . . ."

"No one is more powerful than God!" The nun's voice was almost hysterical.

Afraid but angered at the nun's meanness, June said, "But, if Our Lady is His mother, didn't She teach Him everything He knows? Isn't She the boss?"

"Are you questioning the teaching of the Church?" The nun started to tap her hand with the pointer. A tilted, smile started to creep across her lips. The children were paralyzed, awaiting the nun's next move.

A loud bell suddenly jangled, announcing lunch. The abrupt noise caused everyone to jump in their seats. Hurriedly, the children put away their books, eager to leave the tense situation.

"Line up, everyone!" the nun said directing the students with her pointer. Relieved, June opened up the top of her desk and pushed in her book so she could join the other students in line. "Miss MacDonald, you stay. The rest of you may go. Quietly!"

The students cringed as they filed past Sister St. Pius. When the classroom was empty, the nun crooked her finger at the waiting girl. "Stand here," she ordered.

Trapped, June kept her eyes on Sister. She moved ever so slowly toward the nun while her fingers nervously bunched up her uniform skirt. She wished she could tell the nun how she really felt about her. And what she knew about her. The aura colors surrounding the old woman's head were darkish gray swirls with what looked like a blood red cap pressing downward over her forehead. June knew Sister St. Pius's crushing headaches would someday render the woman speechless. *She won't believe me, anyway,* June thought.

Recently, the old nun had ridiculed the girl's artwork to the class, saying that June should be sent back to kindergarten to learn how to color inside the lines. She would never understand how June saw color energy sprouting outside the physical boundaries of people.

"You are nothing but *trouble*, Miss MacDonald. I said, come here. Here!" Sister slapped the front of her long black skirt with the pointer.

June stood close in front of the nun breathing shallow breaths, waiting to wince when the pointer hit.

"Who do *you* think you are to question God?" Sister demanded.

Terrified, the girl took a gulp and said, "I didn't question . . ."

"Shut up! I've had it with your constant troublemaking and your sassy answers and blasphemous ideas. You know what happens to people like you who go against the Church's teachings? Do you?" June saw the pointer shaking in Sister's gnarled hand. "What kind of Catholic girl are you?"

"Am I a bad Catholic, Sister?" June asked nervously.

The small nun looked June up and down, and then grabbed the front of her white blouse, shaking her. "Yes, you are! With your heathen ways and heretic talk, you sound like a wicked witch."

From her unchecked anger, the old nun was sweating and trembling ferociously. Saliva spat out, hitting June's face as she yelled at her. June didn't dare back away or wipe it off, which would only infuriate Sister St. Pius even more.

With a mocking sweetness, Sister continued, "You know what happens to witches? They are burned. Oh yes, *burned*." Sister St. Pius sneered, her wild dark eyes searing into the young girl's frightened face.

"You . . ." she thumped June's chest hard, "will never get to heaven. No, you'll burn and go to . . ."

"Lunch, Sister?" said a pretty young nun who popped her head in the door. Her voice purred with a soft South African accent.

The old nun swirled around with June's blouse still in her fist. "Oh, Sister Noel! Good afternoon," she said releasing the girl. "Is the Mother Superior at lunch, or in her office?"

"Sister Wilma is at lunch. Why not come and join us?" Sister Noel offered.

Sister St. Pius screwed up her face at the young nun calling the Mother Superior "Sister Wilma." She thought that was disrespectful to the Mother Superior's position.

"I will. June, you go to Mother Superior's office right after school today," said Sister St. Pius.

She stepped out of the classroom without another word.

The room was dead silent. June didn't want to cry, but her lips trembled as she turned her face away in shame from Sister Noel. The young nun went to the sad girl. Taking hold of her hand, she said, gently, "Come on, June. Better get out to lunch."

The hard-held tears gushed forth. "She said that I'm a witch, and I'm going to be burned," she sobbed. The little girl wiped her sweater over her cheeks to dry her away the tears.

"No, dear. You won't be burned. It is true that a long time ago they burned a lot of people, a lot of innocent people that they said were witches."

"Are they burning witches again?" June asked.

Sister Noel put an arm around the girl's shoulder, cloaking her in the wings of her black robe. "Not that I heard of recently," she chuckled.

Silently, they started down the hallway toward the doors. Feeling the girl tremble beneath her arm, she said quickly, "June, I know that you do have a mind of your own about certain things. I've heard that you speak out quite a bit about them. What did you say to upset your teacher?"

"That Our Lady is as powerful as God. My Mom always prays to Her to fix things."

The nun exhaled lightly. "Oh, I see. Sister St. Pius is a little old to share those ideas with, so try to get along in her class. We can talk about your thoughts next year in my class."

"Why can't I say what I think is right?" June asked.

"Because we are teaching you what Catholics believe. You may not have enough information to give accurate opinions on your religion."

June stopped walking and looked up to the tall, slender, green-eyed nun. "But Sister Noel, I'm a good Catholic 'cuz I believe in God and Our Lady. I pray to my angel and I say the Rosary."

Sister Noel gave the eight year-old a big empathetic smile, making June's heart leap as she gazed at the beautiful nun. Impulsively, the little girl hugged her. Sister Noel returned the hug, thinking how June's fiery red hair matched her rebellious nature.

"I know you're a good girl. Now go to lunch," Sister said.

June pushed the hall door open into the large schoolyard. The radiance of the afternoon sun intermingled with the copper highlights in her hair. But even the warmth of the sun could not lift the girl's unhappiness.

Children sitting on aging wooden benches quickly ate their lunches as two nuns monitored the yard. They walked in a wide circle looking for any infractions.

Mary stood against the wall adjacent to the door tightly holding a brown paper bag. Her tapping foot gave evidence of her impatience. Spying her little sister emerging into the yard, she exhaled, "Gee whiz. Finally! What took you so long?"

June gave a huge sigh and rolled her eyes. "Boy, you weren't kidding about that old crabby St. Pius."

"Told you. She hit you in the head?" Mary giggled.

"Yeah. Worse, too," her gloomy sister answered.

"You're in trouble, huh?" Mary guffawed.

June's lips pouted.

Mary nudged her gently, and said, "Hey, it's all right."

They moved swiftly but quietly toward the back of the schoolyard so as not to be noticed by the monitoring nuns. June slowed her pace a bit. She wanted to tell her sister what had happened without anyone hearing.

"She said I'm a witch. That I'd burn in hell 'cuz I say bad things about Catholics."

"Must have been talking to Daddy. Here, want this part?" Mary said tugging off a generous piece of her sandwich.

The jelly oozed out the sides and June jumped a little so it wouldn't hit her white Oxford shoes. That's all she needed: to get in trouble for having dirty shoes. Since her stomach was still in knots, she took only a small bite to fend off her hunger.

They walked past the students dutifully remaining seated, ready to burst into play, but waiting for the nuns to ring the little brass bells announcing their freedom. When the bells rang, the schoolyard filled with rambunctious children.

A shadow walked up from June's right side. She was afraid to look at who it might be, just in case Sister St. Pius had followed her. The shadow became a presence behind her. Her hands trembled and her throat tightened, gluing the soggy bread to the roof of her mouth and blocking her breathing.

Then she heard Maggie say, "Okay kid, where's your cards?"

June coughed to dislodge the bread and catch a breath. Maggie's brilliant green eyes sparkled against her strawberry blonde hair that was held high up in a tightly pulled ponytail behind her, making her eyes even more cat-like. As she walked, she wiggled her head from side to side to swing the ponytail. Maggie and three of her friends surrounded June on all sides, shielding her from the prying eyes of the monitors.

"Keep smiling and the old bats won't bother us," Maggie said as she put one arm around each of her sister's shoulders. Maggie was orchestrating their secret mission.

Mary pulled out a deck of tarot cards from her lunch bag in a way that only the top card showed.

"Let's start soon. Sit over there," Maggie said impishly, motioning with her eyes to a bench where Mary's fellow six-graders sat eating lunch. The older girls, knowing what was to happen, moved apart to give June ample space to sit down between them.

June shoved the rest of Mary's sandwich into her mouth, and licked her sticky fingers. She now felt more focused on the task at hand. With her cards in hand, she sat patiently, enjoying the freshness of the outdoors, and waited for the cue from her sisters.

Maggie crossed her ankles and folded her hands across a small black purse on her lap. Settled on the bench, she nodded to Mary who then motioned for some of the girls to create a protective wall around June.

June felt safe inside the circle of girls. She was calm and happy, ready to attend to her purpose of sharing her insights. She patiently waited for the first person.

A honey-blonde beauty in the eighth grade stepped up to Maggie and carefully counted out some coins from her small leather coin purse. Maggie held out her open hand for the girl to drop them in. She counted a nickel and three pennies.

"Next time, Patti, make it a whole ten cents. Okay?" She called to Mary, "Patti's first."

The circle opened to let Patti sit next to June.

"What's your question?" June asked to begin the reading.

Before Patti revealed her private life, she surveyed the group to see who was listening. The circle of girls surrounding her was busy yakking away to each other.

"It's about a boy," Patti answered.

The girls stopped talking, and took a step closer to June and Patti.

"Golly you guys! Stop listening!" Patti complained. Afraid they wouldn't do as she asked, she cupped her mouth to June's ear. "Does Billy O'Hara love me?"

June closed her eyes for a moment, and then opened them to look up to the cloudless blue sky. Next she laid out some colorful cards on the bench. "Yes. But his brother Mickey loves you more," she said.

Patti's hands flew up to her mouth, which had completely dropped open. "Oh my God! He's in high school. Gee June! What should I do? Call him?"

June picked up the cards on the bench, shuffled the deck again, and held them out. "Pick three cards and lay them down," she instructed.

While the reading continued, more girls stood in front of Maggie, jiggling their coins and waiting as she dealt with another customer. One short Italian girl with tightly curled black hair reluctantly handed over a nickel.

"Come on, Loretta, don't be so cheap. It's ten cents," Maggie said.

"Gads, I can't believe you. That's my milk money. Come on. I'm your best friend."

With her solid Mediterranean build, Loretta stood squarely in front of Maggie, blocking anyone else from doing business.

Maggie shrugged, "I gotta share the money with my sisters. Come on. Don't you want to know if Frankie Cunningham is cheating on you with Patti?"

"Or you," Loretta challenged Maggie. Her long dark face was close to Maggie's. The other girls waiting backed away, concerned that this MacDonald would take offense. Maggie gave her friend a sweet smile and held up her palm, waiting for payment for the reading.

A commotion of shouts from several female voices interrupted the stare-down. Maggie leaned past Loretta to see a group of six boys headed by Eddie Gallagher, a boisterous, stocky boy of thirteen years with mischievous blue eyes. He bounced a basketball loudly on the asphalt as he jumped up and down, trying to peek over Mary. Like most of the kids at school, he knew what was going on but it was a wickedly fun time he was after. He loved to provoke the girls into screams.

"Hey June! Tell my fortune!" he yelled.

The other boys started to laugh and chanted, "Tell my fortune," over and over like a mantra.

Mary attempted to push Eddie back, but he didn't budge. He leaned against her body, teetering on his toes, trying to get close enough for June to hear him.

"Does he love me? Am I going to get rich?" he said mimicking a girl's voice.

The girls began to hit him. Soon the boys multiplied, coming from all over the yard. The group became a melee of pushing and yelling children. Mary began to feel panicky. She was afraid that the yard monitors would soon be looking to see which MacDonald was causing the trouble.

She spat out her words to Eddie, "Get out of here, you creep!"

A hard punch to his chest forced him to back off a bit. But he was full of mischief, and yelled loudly, "She's gonna put a spell on me! The witches are eating me! Eeww." He relentlessly kept his dialogue aimed at June, "What color is my underwear?!"

June stood up, collected her cards off the bench, and shouted at him, "Brown all around!"

The girls clapped and laughed at June's comeback. The boys started to boo. Eddie leaned far back into a pitching position, and with a mighty thrust, he came forward, throwing the basketball hard at June. Mary caught the ball midway with both hands and kept a firm hold of it. She would not let it loose, no matter how fierce the struggle between her and Eddie. The two careened crazily together in circles, eventually falling smack onto June, who scrambled to get out from beneath them, dropping her cards.

Eddie finally saw his opportunity to win the battle. He picked up some of the fallen cards and crushed them in his fist. "Whadda ya gonna do now?" he said taunting the sisters.

June's shrieks were frighteningly piercing. The kids backed away. Sobbing, she screamed, "No! No! My cards! I hate you!

I hate you!" She furiously flailed her fists, hitting him in the face and head.

Trying to get to her little sisters, Maggie pushed kids aside, punching them out of the way if need be. Mary had fallen down, pummeling a few boys and taking them down with her. Scared of Maggie's strength and anger, some of the boys scattered away as fast as they could.

Across the schoolyard, Annie sat with two girls, their books opened between them on the bench. She looked up at the ruckus and saw her sisters in the middle of it. One of the nuns on yard duty also saw the commotion and started across the yard in hot pursuit of the perpetrators. Out of the corner of her eye, Annie saw the nun as a flash of flying robes. She jumped up so quickly that her book banged to the ground. "My sisters need me," she told her schoolmates.

Dashing across the yard faster than a yearling colt in a summer green pasture, Annie reached June before the nun arrived. She slapped Eddie's face and took possession of the crumpled cards in his hands.

"Get out of here Gallagher, before I really hurt you," she warned him.

He didn't want to mess with this MacDonald. Annie may have been the quietest of the sisters, but she packed a mean full-fisted punch. He backed off, rubbing his face.

Annie shoved the remaining cards into Mary's lunch bag. "Shush now. Here, give me those," she said trying to calm the sobbing June.

Her little sister held forth the crumpled torn cards, but not before she attempted to smooth out the damage.

Annie saw the nun getting perilously close. Her heart started beating loudly, awaiting the confrontation. Just then she heard a cheery voice calling the nun, "Sister! Yoo-hoo! Could you help me over here?"

Then Sister Noel waved at the nun, indicating for her to come to the opposite side of the yard. The nun stopped and stood for a moment, with indecision about which problem had more importance. The group of children was dispersing and the scene appeared calmer, so she turned toward Sister Noel.

Maggie rushed up to Annie and June. She was breathless from punching and pinching anyone she thought may be guilty.

"Why did you let her do this? You know this will only bring her trouble, don't you?" Annie said, her cool blue eyes boring into Maggie's defiant face.

Chastised, Maggie pushed out a hip with her hand on it. A rising welt on June's face caught Maggie's eye. Guiltily, she said, "I'm just helping her be popular."

Mary swaggered over, feeling good that she fought so well. She was ready to brag, but Annie gave her a dirty look.

Puzzled, Mary asked, "What? What'd I do? They started it."

Annie turned her back on them. June kept sniffling, holding the bag with the cards. The school bell rang loudly to announce that lessons were to resume for the afternoon. Girls and boys began to line up.

"Don't bring those cards to school anymore," Annie said to June. "I won't be able to help you stay out of trouble after I graduate in a couple of months. You can't count on those two to keep you safe." She nodded backward at their sisters who were tagging along behind them.

"It doesn't matter what I do. They hate me here. I'm not like them," June muttered.

"Well, try to fit in better. You should pray to God and ask Him to help you be a better person. Okay?" Annie didn't see June shake her head "No."

Mary bounced the basketball she had won from Eddie. Each bounce was a taunt to his ego. She eyed him glaring at her as he stood in the boys' line, still smarting from his loss.

"You'll never get boys to like you if you act like that," said Maggie, tossing her ponytail around as three eighth-grade boys walked by smiling at her. She returned the gesture sweetly.

Mary rolled her eyes at her sister's flirtatious ways, and then asked, "Acting like what?"

"Like a boy," Maggie answered. She walked away with her friend Loretta.

Hearing what Maggie had said, June turned to look at Mary. From her look, June knew that her sister had been hurt by Maggie's insult. As she walked past the basketball hoop, Mary threw the ball at the hoop from a decent distance, making the basket. She looked to see if anyone had seen her successful accomplishment. Eddie was staring at her. June saw the interaction, and also saw a soft pink light travel between the dueling duo.

Chapter Twenty-One:
Kindred Souls

THE LONG LINE of children freed for the day from the containment of classrooms at Holy Savior snaked through the hallway, moving silently and slowly out of the building. The nuns herded them, and kept the lines orderly until each row reached the opposite ends of Diamond Street. As soon as the students reached their destinations, they broke free from their restricted lines. Happy voices ricocheted along the street.

June's woolen sweater was yanked back as she attempted to exit the classroom unnoticed. "You, Miss MacDonald, downstairs to the principal's office," Sister St. Pius snarled as she kept a tight hold of the sweater. "She's expecting you. And tell your mother to contact me."

"But, my sisters are waiting," June answered back.

"Now!" the little nun commanded before turning her attention to some unruly boys in the back of the line.

Heavy footed, June stomped all the way down the stone steps to the Mother Superior's office, fuming at the unfairness of the nun as well as the earlier incident with Eddie Gallagher. But worry replaced her anger. Ever since her mother had started a part time job at Cliff's Variety Store on Castro Street, she was supposed to walk home with her sisters. Each of the girls was to pitch in with the household chores and start dinner before their parents came home from work. And now her sisters would be mad at her, again.

Her only consoling thought was that her pal Brian would wait at the park next to Holy Savior to walk her home.

With most of the students gone for the day, the school's hallways were calm and quiet. June sat on a smooth wooden bench outside Mother Superior's office listening to the plinking of piano keys coming from the music room across the hall. The tune that was hesitantly repeated grated on her nerves. Trying to sooth the erratic fluttering of butterflies in her stomach, her fingers rose up and down on her lap as though it was she who was playing the piano.

She tried to not let her mind wander to her pending meeting with the principal. Mother Superior, who was stern enough, had lately become impatient with June's attitude and had insisted on bringing Cathy into the office for several meetings. Her mother always believed what the nuns said. She would take their side, agreeing that her daughter was wrong to interrupt with pesky questions during religious studies. Although June continued to take the punishment, she would not submit to the nuns' stance that she was wrong for not accepting certain religious practices without question. When she questioned her second grade teacher about why it was that only boys could serve with the priest at Mass, the nun gave her no meaningful answer. Instead, out of irritation, the nun gave June a hard poke on top of the head with a long sharp fingernail. Thinking of how mean the nuns were to her, she squeezed her eyes and small mouth shut, and imagined how she'd like to get even with them. She giggled, not caring if her thoughts were naughty.

Sister Noel, humming softly, walked past the office, her long black robe and brown rosary beads swaying with each step. June pretended she didn't notice her. With arms filled with books, Sister Noel sat next to the gloomy student. The sister playfully tapped June's foot with her shoe, hoping for a smile. The freckled face with vivid blue eyes looked at the nun, unsmiling.

She placed the books on the floor and patted June's clenched fists. The little girl stared down at the highly polished tiles on the floor. Slowly, the nun's gentle touch eased June's anger.

She opened her small hands and held them up in a questioning gesture, asking, "Why can't I be a good Catholic?" The nun had no ready answer. The girl spoke again in a quavering voice, "I don't want to burn in hell."

"Oh, June, please. Sister St. Pius really didn't mean that," Sister Noel answered.

"Sister, I've got a secret," the girl whispered. Sister Noel sat quietly, giving the girl time to reveal what was bothering her. June looked furtively around the hallway for prying ears. Seeing no movement or hearing anything other than the painful piano lesson, she surmised it was safe to reveal her secret.

"I know things about people. Even if they don't tell me, I just know. I can't stop the voices telling me things. Annie says that I'm not crazy. I'm just *unusual*. She says to keep it a secret from the grown-ups."

"I know how keeping secrets can become a heavy burden to bear," Sister Noel said. "Do you feel better, telling me your secret?"

June nodded "yes," thinking that this pretty young nun could be her friend. "I'm scared. Please, what will happen to me? Will I have to stop being a Catholic?"

"Would that be a terrible thing for you?" Sister asked.

Looking downhearted, June shrugged and revealed more of her dilemma. "Daddy wouldn't let me live at home anymore. He told me that only good girls could stay. Oh Sister, I really, really wish that I wasn't so bad."

Sister leaned closely to June as though they were having a clandestine meeting. "I understand. You're not a bad girl *or* a bad Catholic. You're just different in your thinking. And you speak your mind, too."

The woman's closeness, and the light, fresh scent of dusting powder encouraged June to relax. She took in a deep breath, and her eyelids dropped, partially closing.

"You're different like me, Sister. You get in trouble too, don't you?" June whispered.

In a surprisingly throaty laugh, Sister Noel said, "Oh yes, I do. And I did *a lot* when I was a little girl like you."

June leaned back to look up at the nun's gentle face. With eyes wide with wonderment at hearing Sister's secret, June exclaimed, "Bad girls can become nuns?"

Sister Noel laughed and encircled June with both arms, drawing her close. They stayed in the embrace, breathing softly in unison.

June's question was so quiet that Sister almost missed it, "Do you dream that you can fly?"

"I used to when I was a kid. I did fly over here from my home which is far, far away."

"Oh! Is that where you had Meise?" June asked.

The nun pulled back and looked down in amazement at the child's innocent face. "You can see that?" she asked.

June grinned, happy that she was free to show off her ability to know things about people. Matter-of-factly, the girl said, "You miss Meise, don't you?"

"I had a dog named Meise in Africa that I had to leave behind when I came here. Yes, I miss my Meise very much. But, tell me, how did you get that image?"

Excited to share her special gift, June explained as though she was teaching Sister about her abilities. "Well, I can see it in my head like a picture. I know more. You're going to fly back home again and have another Meise."

Sister Noel sat quietly, no longer smiling.

Not wanting to lose their connection, June took the nun's hand. "I wish I could fly with you," she said.

Neither heard the Mother Superior approach, but there she stood, frowning down at them. She pursed her colorless lips and said, crisply, "Sister Noel, aren't you in charge of dinner tonight?"

The young nun's eyes widened in surprise at being caught hugging a student—especially one waiting for reprimands. She regained her composure, and said, "Yes, Mother. I am, but June's upset and I..."

Mother Superior's long thin hand slashed the air, ceasing further conversation with her subordinate. "Miss MacDonald, come along. Quickly now." The principal turned swiftly on the heels of her black leather shoes and walked into her office.

The young nun laid a hand on top of June's mass of unruly curls. "Be brave. May *Mekatilili wa Menza*[27] bless you."

∾ ∾ ∾

The colorful buttons at Cliff's Variety store circled in front of Maggie when she turned on the conveyer belt that was used to display the huge assortment. Casually, she examined the buttons while waiting for her mother. The four large brick-red buttons coming toward her would be perfect for the black bandstand skirt her mother was making her for her upcoming thirteenth birthday. She wanted to wear it for her debut on "Dance Party," the popular new television show for teenagers in San Francisco. For a moment she became lost in the variety of colors and styles, until she caught her mother's disapproving look from across the room.

Cathy was annoyed that her daughter had come into the shop while she was working, not wanting her first job away from home to be a failure. She surprised Maggie by switching off the conveyer belt.

"Why aren't you at home getting dinner ready?" she asked in a hushed voice just as the shop owner, Ernie, walked by and merrily greeted Maggie. Nervous, Cathy started to apologize about her daughter being there but he walked on.

Maggie reassured her mother that everything at home was under control. She then said casually, "Call the principal right away. It's about June."

---

[27]   Mekatilili wa Menza – A female warrior and folk heroine who led the Giriama tribe in Kenya in a rebellion against British Christian missionaries in 1914.

"Oh, for the love of God. Not again! Now what?" Cathy hissed through her clenched teeth. She looked down, smoothed out some material, and grimaced as though she had an attack of indigestion.

Maggie had been unanimously voted the best one to present June's case to their mother. The girl's convincing smile and confident attitude seemed to intone that all problems had an answer.

"Take it easy, Mom. We thought you should know before Daddy. Anyway, it isn't June's fault. It's that old crabby nun." As an afterthought, she added, "Even I got in trouble with St. Pius."

"That's true," Cathy murmured.

Maggie was a very well liked girl, both with the nuns and the students. The problem between Sister St. Pius and Maggie had begun when the nun accused her of being indecent for putting on lipstick at lunchtime. The girl denied the allegations. The Mother Superior had to intervene to stop Sister's unfair punishment of Maggie.

"What'd she do now?" Cathy said, keeping her voice low and fidgeting with the lace doilies on the counter.

Making light of the situation, Maggie said, "Oh, Mom, St. Pius made it sound like it was a mortal sin. June was just saying that in our family we pray to God's Mother, too. Something simple like that. She's just an old nutty woman."

"Be respectful of the nuns, Maggie," Cathy said.

Yes, the nuns can be too strict at times, Cathy thought, although she still had an undying respect for the religious women. She shooed Maggie out of the store, promising to stop by to talk to the principal before coming home. She also promised to buy the big red buttons for Maggie's skirt.

After her daughter left, Cathy went back to work, distracting her mind from June's problems at school. She wished she had never let June play with the tarot cards, which she felt were the beginning of the problems. If she had been a better mother, as Jimmy reminded her, she would have squelched June's interest in the occult and demanded that she stop telling upsetting stories about her angel and dead people.

Nervously, Cathy rearranged a display while trying to work up enough confidence to ask to leave early to meet with the principal. Just then she looked up to see Mother Superior coming down the main aisle of the store with her hands folded inside her black robes. The nun's long thin face with its high cheekbones and deep-set steely gray eyes had a regal look. The patrons and salespeople greeted her warmly. Many of them had children at Holy Savior.

The Mother Superior paused to talk briefly with each person as she slowly made her way across the floor to Cathy.

"Good afternoon, Mrs. MacDonald. Do you have a moment?"

The two walked toward the back of the store as if seeking a particular item. When they reached an area out of earshot of everyone, the nun stopped and stood in front of several bolts of material. A rush of embarrassment spread across Cathy's cheeks as though she was the bad schoolgirl.

The nun spoke with a low, gentle voice. "I thought you'd rather that I didn't inconvenience you this evening. I am confident we can settle this matter about June without it escalating any further."

As was customary for conversations with Mother Superior, this meeting was short and to the point.

Mother told Cathy, "If June is to continue at Holy Savior, she must learn to not challenge her teachers on Catholicism any more, for it is disruptive and disrespectful. For her punishment, June is to stay after school every day for the next week to clean the blackboards. She is to offer an apology to Sister St. Pius. She will also spend her recess time with Sister Noel for an extra Catechism lesson."

The nun did not divulge that it was that Sister Noel who had presented a convincing plea for June, arguing that perhaps the third grader was a bit confused about the teachings of Catholicism.

At the conclusion of the conversation, Cathy gave her word that her daughter would behave properly and do whatever was necessary to remain in school.

Mother Superior cupped Cathy's hands and happily shared the good news that Annie had been accepted at Girls Convent High School with a full scholarship. The nun knew the cost of tuition at one the City's most prestigious Catholic high schools would have been an extra financial burden for the MacDonald family.

The rest of Cathy's afternoon breezed by. Her mind had been lightened due to the good resolution she had made for June, as well as the good news about her oldest daughter's achievement. Feeling that good fortune had come her way, she said a quick prayer of thanks to Our Lady.

∞ ∞ ∞

Stepping out of Cliff's Variety at five o'clock, Cathy breathed in the early evening air and prepared for the short jaunt up Castro Street. She checked her bag to make sure she had remembered Maggie's buttons, and saw them next to the candy bars she had bought for the girls. Falling into step with the others returning home from work, she noticed how warm and close the April air felt.

Removing her wool jacket, she thought, *It feels like earthquake weather.* The panicky sensation churning in her stomach recalled the 1957 earthquake. It was her first experience with one of San Francisco's infamous tremors. She hoped never to be in one again. She shuddered at her vivid recollection of that March day when their house shook so furiously that the refrigerator fell over and dishes, knickknacks and photographs crashed to the floor, shattering everything into pieces.

She had just set up the ironing board and was testing the iron's heat when a loud crackling sound whipped through the house. It sounded as though the house was coming apart at the seams. A split second later the kitchen floor rolled up and down like a ride at Playland. Panicked, she scrambled over the collapsed ironing board and ran from the house screaming, "Mother of God, help!"

With apron strings flying behind her, Cathy had rushed down the hill alongside other parents toward Holy Savior to check on the children. Mother Superior had the students lined up in a two rows in the schoolyard. The pupils were chattering loudly and some were crying. Even the nuns were talking amongst themselves and didn't try too hard to keep the students in line. They also didn't prohibit the parents from going to their kids.

Cathy was soon joined with her girls. They talked all at one time, telling her how their teachers had them get under their desks. Annie had said her nun had led the class in prayer until a bell sounded for them to leave the classroom. Maggie had run off to be with friends, while Mary wrapped her arms around Cathy's waist and hung on tightly. Only June laughed, saying with excitement how much fun it was to be "all shook-up." Mary had said, "You're nutty, June."

Mary's words seemed to give voice to Cathy's sentiments. She pondered the situation as she continued her walk home from Cliff's. *Maybe June isn't all there, with her constant insisting that she can see things that aren't there. It's caused a lot of problems.* Cathy knew she'd have to hide the latest episode from Jimmy.

Hearing an engine climbing the hill behind her, she turned to see a green and yellow 24 Divisadero bus chugging up Castro Street, leaving a trail of gray smoke trailing behind it. The bus shuddered to a stop at Twentieth Street, and a small group of people exited, including her neighbors Sadie Callaghan and Bernice Kirkpatrick.

Sadie called out a cheery hello as she came across the street with lightness in her step, even though her arms were laden down with books and a bulging briefcase. She was about the same height and dress size as Cathy, although the latter felt dowdy next to the fashionably dressed woman. Sadie wore a tailored dove-gray suit, not with a skirt but with straight-legged pants and a red silk scarf tied loosely around her neck. It wasn't common for women to wear trousers to work, but Sadie did, adding the brightly colored scarf for flair. She had recently cut her long chestnut brown hair into a pixie cut that made her dark eyes look even larger. Some of the neighborhood mothers spoke badly about her, saying Mrs. Callaghan was blunt and somewhat boyish. Cathy never contributed to the gossip. She thought her neighbors were only jealous, since she admired Jeannie and Brian's pretty, spunky mother. Besides, Sadie had an important job as a defense attorney, although Cathy was unsure of what that involved.

Cathy also liked the tall, soft-spoken Bernice who, like herself, wore simple neutral-colored clothing. She was a plain looking woman with striking violet-blue eyes hidden behind large horn-rimmed glasses. To Cathy, Bernice's most attractive quality was her kindness and her ability to listen attentively.

When the girls had first told their mother that Bernice was a doctor, Cathy naturally assumed that they had meant a physician. It wasn't until Cathy had asked for medical advise about June's recurring headaches that she had learned her neighbor was an anthropology professor at San Francisco State University. That was the first time she had ever heard the title doctor given to someone other than a medical doctor. Cathy held both women's educated positions in deep respect.

Seeing Bernice juggle two stuffed brown-paper grocery bags, Cathy insisted on helping and took a bag. The girls had said Bernice was a fabulous cook, better than Nancy. "She cooks Mexican and Chinese food the best ever," Mary had said. Annie tut-tutted and reminded Mary she couldn't say it was the best because they'd never had that kind of food before.

Cathy felt a bit guilty when the girls raved about the fine food. With her job, she didn't have time to make fancy dinners.

Bernice smiled, showing her gratitude at her neighbor's offer to help carry the bags, and asked how her job at Cliff's was working out. It was because of Bernice and Sadie's encouragement that Cathy had taken the risk of going in and asking for a job. Both women had become her friends, more than anyone else in San Francisco since Mrs. G.

"Good," she answered quickly, then added, "but it's hard on the girls. They have to take over for me with the cooking and cleaning. Jimmy's particular about that, you know."

"Hey, life's not easy," Sadie said decidedly. "My ex-husband was always nagging about the mess in the house. Our kids have to toe the line. They do house chores, too."

Bernice laughed. "You're dreaming," she said in her Southern drawl.

The words "our kids" caught Cathy's attention. She thought how nice it was that Bernice, who didn't have any children of her own that Cathy knew of, took such a caring role with her roommate's children. Still, although Jeannie and Brian were polite kids, they were a bit wild. Jimmy had said that it was because there was no husband to supervise them. Cathy wondered if life would be easier if she had a friend to help raise the girls instead of Jimmy.

The three women stopped on the corner of Liberty to chat for a bit about the kids. They agreed that June and Brian going to Eureka Valley Park after school was not a very good idea. The kids should be doing homework. Collectively they ruled: No park on weekdays. Before the women separated to go care for their families, Cathy asked Bernice for the recipe for her green chili enchilada casserole.

Chapter Twenty-Two:
Dancing with the Moon

May 31, 1959

THE CRISP NIGHT air and the bouquet of garden scents wafting through the open window of her small yellow bedroom beckoned June. Looking past the lace curtains to the night sky, she began to think of the next day, her ninth birthday, and what it would bring.

Last year just before her birthday, the family had received good news that they were now officially citizens of the United States of America. They had celebrated at Playland and afterwards with a walk on the beach. June hoped something special would happen for this birthday also.

Listening to Mary's soft snoring, she quietly slipped from beneath the quilted bedcover and slid open the wooden windowpane to step out onto the rooftop over the back porch. The window's pulleys squeaked with age, and for a moment her sister's snoring stopped. Crouched on the windowsill, she hesitated until her sister resumed her deep breathing. She had discussed with Mary her need to be alone to talk with her angel, and Mary had agreed to keep her sister's nocturnal excursions a secret. Even so, June didn't want to wake her up.

As the world slept, June stepped out and settled onto the sloped roof. Sitting alone, with her unruly, curly red hair freed from barrettes and springing up from her head, the solitary girl looked tiny. With her pink bathrobe wrapped tightly and her chin resting on her drawn-up knees, she enjoyed the magic of the dark night, and felt anything but alone.

The full moon was out and briefly showed its face before slipping behind a cloud. Hearing a faint rustle of leaves on the tall walnut tree whose boughs brushed against the rooftop, June smiled, knowing that the neighborhood cats were watching her. Soon, one or two would jump gracefully out of the tree to sit with her and take in the wonders of the nighttime.

Fully awake with excitement, June recalled how earlier that morning, when she and her sisters had hurried down the steep hills toward school, her sisters had divulged that they had a special plan for her birthday. Although no details were given, Mary did say it would be a big surprise celebration, something completely new for June's birthday. Their enthusiasm only fueled her anticipation. One thing she was certain of was that they would be going to the picture show. When Mary teased her little sister by saying, "You can't guess what we're doing for your birthday," the other two bumped her from either side and said, simultaneously, "Shut up! She will, too!" Although June was tempted to conjure up the image of what the surprise would be, she stopped herself as the images started forming in her mind. No, she'd wait, she decided. A surprise was too much fun to ruin!

The jittery butterflies of anticipation flew widely through June's arms. Imagining a party of them fluttering from her fingertips up into the night sky, she spread her delicate fingers toward the moon to release the pent-up energy. At that moment, the moon reappeared from behind a dark cloud, as though accepting her energy. Its powerful beams penetrated through the leaves of the trees, beaming a brilliant light onto the upturned face of the little girl. She trembled in awe, with her fingertips pulsating, feeling as though she and the moon were touching. In the fullness of the night, June felt her aura grow large. She began to dance with the moon. Slowly, she waved her arms back and then swept them outward and overhead, posing like a ballerina. Powerful energy surged through her as she pulled her arms across her heart and drew down the moon's bright light.

June thought of the past few months, and how much she enjoyed her new role as a "good girl." Having others happy with her was something that she hadn't remembered experiencing since her days with Mrs. G. Because of it, life at home had improved greatly. Her father hadn't once smacked her with his belt for being naughty. And her mother was more at ease because June didn't have to stay after school. Together with her sisters, she worked hard to have the housework completed and dinner on the table when her parents arrived home from work. June was so very thankful to Sister Noel for showing her how to fit in.

Her agreement to meet with Sister Noel was easy to keep. Each day at morning and afternoon recess they met in the principal's office, previously a room of contention, to discuss Catholic history. June found solace in her new education. She had backed down from her fierce stance on speaking out regardless of the punishment. Their meetings had helped settle June's feelings of persecution at school. And, more importantly, Sister had given June a most wonderful gift: She listened to her, without judgment.

Sister Noel answered June's questions about the life of Our Lady and also talked about other Catholic holy women. June's favorites were Teresa of Avila, Catherine of Siena and Hildegard of Bingen because of their ecstatic visions. June was anxious to learn more about Hildegard when she learned the Catholic nun began having visions at the age of three. Sister Noel borrowed a book from the convent's private library so they could read together about the holy mystic from the twelfth century. Hildegard was known to be a great visionary as well as an author who wrote about theology and medicinal plants. The holy woman held a position of great authority in the Church, and had the same influential power as a bishop, which was unheard of for a Catholic woman at any time throughout the history of the Church. Although, unlike June, the holy woman had kept her visions a secret for many years June was convinced of a connection. She prayed to Hildegard to help her become accepted by her family and church, just as Hildegard herself had finally been.

June felt Sister Noel taught her about the women saints to be supportive of her psychic abilities.

"If these ladies could be good Catholics, why do I get in trouble for saying what I see?" June had inquired of her mentor.

Sister didn't answer right away. When she did, she said, "I know how painful school life has been for you since you are so curious as well as a bit outspoken." She tipped her head sideways and smiled kindly.

June laughed, knowing the nun was right about her saying things that upset people.

"Perhaps people can't accept the possibility that they could be in the presence of a visionary," Sister Noel added.

At their last meeting of the school year, sadness overcame June. But Sister reminded her that they would be together in September when June would become her student in the fourth grade. Their time apart suddenly didn't seem so terrible to June.

Before they parted, June's mentor had given her a gift of a midnight-blue book with a small picture of the crescent moon on the cover. "This is your journal," she said. "Write your thoughts in it."

All in all, this was a very good time for the formerly troubled girl. As she sat on the rooftop, she again became lost in her imagination of what her sisters might have planned for her birthday. She absent-mindedly stroked a neighborhood cat nuzzling against her, purring. Maybe they would take her to Playland to see Laughing Sal. She erupted in giggles with the image of the wide-girthed, red-haired, freckled faced woman laughing hysterically.

Hearing her father mumble in the bedroom next to hers, she quickly covered her mouth with her hands to muffle her snickers. The startled cat objected to her sudden action and jumped back into the tree, causing the girl to laugh even harder behind her hands. Still, she kept her mirth quiet, not wanting to awaken the wrath of her father.

∽   ∽   ∽

What June didn't know was that her father was also part of the surprise, having given the girls permission to dine out—a rarity for the MacDonalds. Eating in a restaurant was a luxury Jimmy and Cathy couldn't afford. Annie had assured him that they would use their babysitting money to pay for June's special surprise gift. With a big smile, Annie had added they would also like to stay out until nine o'clock, three hours past their Saturday curfew. She knew that asking to be home after dark was the boldest part of their plan. She assured her father that at six o'clock, when the movie ended, they would go directly from the Castro Theater to a neighborhood restaurant, The Big Jive. They would come home right after that.

She had smiled sweetly at the end of her presentation, just as Maggie had instructed her to do. "Can we, Daddy? Please?" she asked.

Jimmy listened in silence, keeping his eyes on the boxing match on television. He kept his daughters on a tight schedule, without giving them hardly any free time to themselves.

Cathy sat across from him darning a pair of his woolen socks. She thought Annie's plan sounded reasonable enough, but would wait to see what Jimmy had to say first. The girls complied with his strict rules of coming home after school to clean, cook and do their homework, and always reserved Sunday for church and family activities. But Saturday was their day for fun, their mother had told them. She made this clear to her husband whenever he tried to pile on extra chores on Saturday.

"Your mother might need your help with dinner," he said, finally, turning his dark hazel eyes on Annie.

"You know Jimmy, that's not such a bad idea," Cathy spoke up. "You and me could do something special, too." She understood that her daughters wanted to be with their friends.

"You ever been to this—what's it called? Jive place?" Jimmy asked Cathy.

"Once. Met with some of the gals from the PTA. It's no a bad place," Cathy said, darning away and not mentioning that it was a popular hangout for the teens in the neighborhood to congregate after school as well as on Saturdays. *He probably thinks the girls and me are plotting against him again,* she thought.

Annie stood still, biting her lower lip. Cathy caught a slight movement from the living room's sliding wooden door. She knew that the other two conspirers, Maggie and Mary, were outside the room listening with bated breath for a reply.

The clang of a bell from the television set announced a boxing round was over.

"Let's go to the Edinburgh Castle for fish and chips and a wee drink with Sandy and Nancy," Cathy said. "We could try and be home by nine, at least."

She put down the sock and gave Jimmy a sly grin. She was confident that her husband would jump at a chance to see his Scottish friend for cocktails, as well as have time alone with his wife. Thus, the plan was set.

$\infty \quad \infty \quad \infty$

The chill of the late night finally permeated June's cotton robe and nipped at her bare feet. After blowing a kiss to the cat sitting on a tree branch, she raised her arms to the moon once more. An unexpected image flooded her mind. It was of steely blue ocean waters with waves lapping up over the feet of a beautiful young woman. The young woman had long, wild, flowing auburn hair. Her arms were outstretched.

June stretched out her hands a bit more, imagining she was touching the young woman. A sudden jolt like an electrical current zapped her. "I know it's you, angel," she whispered into the night air.

As she stepped into the house, the moon suddenly lit up her bedroom so that she saw the clock next to her bed read two minutes after midnight. Joyfully, June realized that she was already nine.

Chapter Twenty-Three:
The Castro Theater

WITH SATURDAY'S CHORES completed, the girls went upstairs to their bedrooms to get ready for the movies. Excited to get going, June grabbed a light green sweater off her bed and raced into Annie and Maggie's bedroom.

Her sisters were jabbering away about some boy Annie had a crush on. They were laughing about the time she had rushed away when he tried to talk to her as she and Jeannie walked past the Eureka Valley Park. June remembered him. He was a tall gangly guy with deep-brown hooded eyes, thick blonde hair that fell across his forehead in a curl, and greased-back sides, called fenders.

When they were a block away, Annie had said, "Don't you think he looks so handsome in his alpaca sweater?"

Their friend Jeannie sneered, "His pants are pegged so tight his legs look like sticks."

Annie's friends said he was a bad kid. It was true, he was. The rumor mill spread the story of how he had crashed a stolen motor scooter into a palm tree on Dolores Street and ran off before the police arrived. Jeannie had told her that he had been kicked out of Mission High School and was now a student at a trade school. In agreement with her girlfriends, Annie knew he was not a good match for a Catholic schoolgirl.

"You love him, huh?" Mary playfully elbowed her sister.

Annie blushed, squeezing her brush against her chest.

Pleased that somebody had finally tongue-tied their older sister, June listened as the others teased Annie unmercifully about the boy. Excited by the fun, she piped up, saying that Annie was "moonstruck."

Mary responded to June's comment by making a funny face like a person who was swooning and moaning. "I'm mooning over my lover boy," she kidded.

June liked seeing Annie moonstruck. It added a pink glow around her body.

"I sure hope that he's there today," Annie said longingly.

June had never heard her sister speak so pitifully.

Maggie assured her that she had heard he would be there. She then advised her sister on how to act when she saw him. "Give him a real quick look. Maybe a tiny smile. But then turn away fast. Flip your hair, like this." A demonstration was given. "Act like you don't care a thing about him. That'll get him real interested."

June covered her mouth and tried not to snicker.

Annie's eyes portrayed her dismay at her sister's advice. Maggie kept brushing Annie's straight blonde hair, trying to make it curve around her face a bit. Finally realizing that it was hopeless, she pulled it back into a high ponytail like her own.

"Mary, go get your black scarf," Maggie instructed. "We'll hide the rubber band and it'll look really neat."

Mary jumped at a chance to help Annie's transformation, and ran to her room.

"How can she flip her hair if it's tied up?" June inquired.

"Shhh. We're working here," Maggie said, turning up the small transistor radio sitting on the dressing table. She finished Annie's hair and held up a few lipsticks for Annie to choose from.

"Pink," Annie said

Maggie tossed the lipstick into a large handbag along with her black eyeliner pencil, rouge, mascara and a can of Aqua Net hairspray. "I'll do your make-up when we get to the Callaghans," she said.

"Daddy'll get mad if she paints her face," June reminded her sister.

"Well, only if big mouths squeal on us," Maggie told her. "Anyway, Annie's fourteen, and that means she's a woman. Not a little girl like some people we know."

Mary popped back into the room to announce, "It's almost noon, let's beat it."

The girls left for the movies together. But upon reaching the Callaghan's house, they separated. The two younger sisters were told to go on ahead and save a place in line. When Mary started to protest, Annie reassured her, "We'll be right down. We're just going to get Jeannie."

Mary hesitated as she watched her older sisters bouncing up the steps. Rebelling against her task, it was on the tip of her tongue to yell out, "Why am I always stuck with June?" Then she remembered it was her little sister's birthday, so she just turned away and started walking rapidly down Castro Street.

Brian Callaghan came out to join June. The youngsters followed behind Mary, happily talking to each other as best friends do. When the three arrived at the Castro Theater, the line of kids was already up to Market Street. There were lots of greetings and chatting with friends as they moved to rear of the line.

∽ ∽ ∽

June kept bobbing her head out of the line, looking for her two other sisters. Finally, she saw them racing up the street toward the theater. Annie trudged behind Maggie, Jeannie and Loretta, which June thought was weird because Annie usually was in the lead. When they arrived, June saw why her big sister was hiding.

Maggie had generously applied pale pink lipstick on Annie's thin lips. She then drew black lines along the upper lids of her big sister's gray-blue eyes and added black mascara on her blonde eyelashes. The make-up had an amazing affect on Annie's eyes. The blueness became magnified, giving them an alluring appearance.

The four older girls stopped where Mary, June and Brian waited in line.

"Va-va voom," Mary said to Annie, who rolled her eyes and blew out her pink lips.

"She looks boss, huh?" Loretta said.

"Move over, Brian," Jeannie ordered.

The kids behind them in line heckled the four girls when they cut in. But the disgruntled crowd clammed up when Eddie Gallagher and his sidekick, Larry Owens, showed up. Maggie flashed Eddie a Mona Lisa-like smile with her orange colored lips and black pencil-lined eyes. He looked adoringly at her. As he leaned in close to hand her something, his hand brushed against the front of her black sweater. June felt Mary's stocky body next to her tighten at the sight of them knitted together. Annie looked away disgustedly.

Maggie thanked Eddie and sent him on his way. "Hey, here's passes to get in," she said to her group. "Be cool. Just walk over to Mr. Newman," she instructed, jerking her head toward the pudgy balding man in a lumpy gray suit taking tickets at the door.

"I've got money for June and myself," Annie hissed to Maggie, who shrugged her shoulders and turned away from her older sister.

"It's wrong to use those tickets. It's like stealing," Annie said trying to reason with her. June knew, as did her sisters, that Annie thought it was her duty to teach her sisters not to sin.

In a hushed tone Annie reminded Maggie that it would be an insult to the kindness of Mr. Newman, the Castro Theater's owner. He gave Holy Savior School free movie passes to reward deserving students—such as the crossing guards—for their community service. Eddie Gallagher and his boys would sneak into the small hall closet by Mother Superior's office where the tickets were kept and take a few extra ones for themselves.

Maggie turned away from her big sister ignoring Annie's righteousness. She made a detour toward the back of the line to a classmate. Pulling out of the line she brought him to join her group. The kid hung back with uncertainty, as though not wanting to draw attention to himself. June felt sorry for Tim, the boy caught in Maggie's grasp. The young teen ducked his head in embarrassment. He was new at Holy Savior, and the only black student there. In fact, he was the first Negro student to ever attend the neighborhood parochial school. Maggie had become his first friend. Annie and Mary agreed with Maggie about how out of place he must feel, having experienced that position several years ago when they, themselves, first came to America. June couldn't remember that time, but she did know how difficult it was to be different from others. She always said a happy, "Hello!" to Tim, to help him feel liked.

Maggie, Loretta, Jeannie, Mary and Tim disappeared into the movie house. Annie pushed the little kids ahead and moved toward the cashier's box.

"Did Maggie commit a sin?" June inquired.

The youngest MacDonald wondered if Maggie was a bad Catholic as she had been accused of being. Although lately she had begun to feel released from her past sins, June still needed to learn more about how to be a good Catholic girl so as not to upset the nuns or her father. If anyone knew how to be a good Catholic, it was Annie. With her face furrowed in a worried frown, she waited the verdict on Maggie.

"Yes," her sister replied piously.

Anxiety continued to gnaw at June's thoughts. She wanted to know if it was a mortal sin—a sure fire ticket to hell.

"A mortal or venial sin?" June asked, wanting to understand the severity of Maggie's action. Annie didn't hear her. She had already stepped up to the cashier's box with her little white coin purse opened to pay the fifteen-cent entrance fee.

June hoped that Maggie's sin wasn't mortal. Sister St. Pius had warned the class that anyone who committed a mortal sin would go to hell after death, never to see God. It must be the lesser sin, June thought, like when your mother tells you to say she's not home when a salesman is at the door, that weren't really bad.

The whole group met in front of the candy counter inside the theater. As part of her birthday celebration, Annie handed June ten cents and told her to choose two candy bars. The birthday girl chose a Peppermint Patty that she would share with Mary, and a Big Hunk, from which she might give Maggie a bite.

The opening scene of the first movie, "The Diary of Anne Frank," had just started when they entered the darkened theater. An usher led them down the aisle with his flashlight and sat them two rows down from a row of older boys. June tightly held onto her candy bars as she stared at the screen, entranced by the face of the young actress playing Anne Frank.

A tremendous sadness overcame came her. Although she didn't know what the film would be about, she knew it would be painful to watch. She wished that the second movie, "Darby O'Gill and the Little People," would have been shown first, and then maybe they could leave for her big surprise.

Halfway through the film, popcorn started hitting Annie's hair. June was just about to ask her who was doing that bad thing when Jeannie's husky voice hissed, "It's gotta be Dave."

"Be quiet," Annie whispered, not turning her head around to see who it was.

"That's the boy that likes Annie," June informed Brian.

"Yeah, I heard Jeannie tell Sadie all about him," he whispered back.

June was still not used to hearing him call his mother by her first name. No other kids did that, but the Callaghans were different.

"Is he nice?" she asked. She wanted Annie to have a nice boyfriend.

"Dunno. Jeannie said that he hangs around the park. I saw him a lot there, smoking."

June knew that the park is where a bunch of big boys and girls hung around. Her father had warned the girls not to go near them. He said they were punks.

Brian cupped June's ear and whispered, "I heard he did a real bad thing."

June pulled away from him, wondering if Dave was a sinner, because that's what bad people are. Curiously, she stretched her neck and turned to look behind her at the row of boys, but it was too dark to see him.

The older boys behind them started making loud kissing sounds. A few others called out Maggie and Jeannie's names. Neither girl turned their heads to acknowledge them, although both giggled quietly.

"Let's go to the bathroom," Maggie whispered to Annie. Not wanting to be left behind, June joined the herd of girls who simultaneously got up and emptied the row of seats. Brian started to leave with them, but June said, "We're going to the Ladies Room." He sat back down. They scooted up the darkened aisle past the teen boys who watched their exodus.

∽ ∽ ∽

The dim lights in the Ladies Room made it difficult for June to clearly see the faces of the teenagers lounging on an old overstuffed couch and passing a couple of cigarettes between them. The teen girls, ranging from fourteen to sixteen years old, eyed the newcomers with a head nod. A few mumbled, "Hey." Although the girls didn't all attend the same schools, they were all Eureka Valley girls and therefore knew each other to some degree.

Annie ignored the teens and walked past them and into the other room where the toilet stalls were located. Maggie went to the long vanity counter with a large mirror that ran the length of it. She motioned for Loretta to join her. Jeannie leaned against the wall, hands in her jeans pockets, a small smile on her face, eyes diverted from anyone's face. June stood between the rooms looking shyly at the teens.

Mary squeezed onto the couch next to an older, tough looking girl. "Hey, what's happening?" she asked.

The older teen sucked deeply on her cigarette "Hi, kid," she said blowing out smoke rings. The other girls resumed their ruckus, laughing and gossiping about boys. The tough teen sat listening, not joining in the conversation.

Carmen O'Connell, the tough teen, had eyebrows penciled in a black arch and wavy black hair stacked around her long, thin face. She had a bad reputation with a lot of the older girls at Holy Savior. Behind her back they called her a skag, and said she hadn't run away from home the year before, but was at St. Elizabeth's home for girls who are pregnant and not married. But, to her face, they acted friendly, afraid to do anything else.

June didn't like the judgmental gossip. She liked Carmen's red lipsticked mouth with its full lips. She thought the teenager looked like a movie star, but when she looked at Carmen she saw a frightened and lonely person. *Maybe it's because she's from a broken home,* June thought, not truly understanding what that meant.

Her assumption was based on a conversation she had recently overheard her mother having over the backyard fence with a neighbor about the bad kids in the neighborhood. Carmen O'Connor's name had been mentioned. The neighbor, an amply built Irish woman, rolled her eyes to heaven, clucking her tongue.

"Oh sure, it must be hard for that girl, being a half breed and all," the neighbor had said. "They say her mother's some kind of Indian, and nobody has seen a father in the home. But he must be white because the girl's skin is as white as milk."

Both women had stopped their conversation long enough to dip down for a piece of laundry to hang on the line. "Pssst, Missus," the neighbor continued, nodding her large head at Cathy, motioning her closer to the fence, Cathy had shooed June away, not wanting her to hear the ugly gossip.

"Did you hear about that boy, Dave?" the neighbor asked and not waiting for Cathy to answer said, "I hear that the police are after him. He'll be off to the pokey in no time."

The women shook their heads in disgust at the bad youth. June had been annoyed at her mother's behavior, for was it not she who had told the girls that gossiping was unkind? June was not aware that Cathy's true purpose for participating in the conversation was to find out more about the boy her daughter was mooning over.

Based on the change in her daughter, Cathy had recognized that Annie was smitten and she soon figured out the boy's identity. One day after school Annie had met her so they could shop on Castro Street for groceries. When a tall boy had passed them and smiled at Annie, her daughter had become quite flustered. Cathy had decided to keep it a secret from Jimmy, since he had forbidden their daughters to have boyfriends until they were eighteen.

"It's a true shame for them kids, it tis." the neighbor continued. "What can you expect, them being from broken homes." She bent behind the fence with a "humph," picked up her empty laundry basket in one hand, and waved good-bye with the other. Cathy had begun to worry how she could help this boy fit in so that Jimmy would accept him.

Remembering that day, June watched Carmen hunched on the couch, sensing that the tough teen felt very unloved. The little girl wanted Carmen to feel happy, and projected onto her the color of a summer sun.

Suddenly, the sullen-faced teen shuddered. "Shit, this cigarette is stale, man!" Carmen said gruffly. She handed the cigarette to Mary, who had never smoked before. She took a drag and sputtered out a series of coughs. Almost everyone in the room, except Annie, laughed.

"Mary! Put that disgusting thing down! It's *bad* for you," Annie protested.

"Yeah, okay, Mother Superior. Always telling us what we can and can't do," Maggie smirked, crossing her legs.

Annie glowered at her sister for only a second before crossing the short length of the room to grab her arm. "Lets go," she ordered.

Maggie pushed her away. Annie grabbed her sister's arm again and jerked it. An intense tango of pushing and pulling began between the two. With faces only inches from each other, Annie shot forward with a hard punch to Maggie's shoulder. Maggie quickly regained her balance and rolled her hand into a fist and hit back. Their Scottish anger erupted into a volley of punches.

The room burst into a chaos of shrieking and pushing females. Some girls backed away from the dueling sisters, while others rushed into the melee. When Maggie lost her footing and fell against the counter, Loretta pushed her back up into Annie.

Mary stayed put on the couch, moving her feet out of the way when necessary, and babbled on to Carmen about how her big sisters were so stupid to fight all the time. The tough teen asked if their dad beat on them. "Yeah, kinda," Mary mumbled, to which the teen answered, "Well, there ya have it."

In an effort to quell the madness, Jeannie yelled out in a firm, calm voice, "Hey guys. Guys! Remember the surprise?"

Miraculously, she had interrupted the battle long enough for her to move through the group of girls to get between the sisters.

Red faced and panting heavily, both sisters dropped their arms and released the grip they had on each other. Jeannie gently nudged Annie toward the front door. Because of her anger, Annie missed her natural instinct to remove June from the bad influences. Instead, she stormed away from the scene in the bathroom.

June vacillated, not sure whether to follow her or hang on and wait for her other sisters to leave. Besides, she was very curious about what the other teens in the room would do next. June had seen the sisters fight before, although it wasn't as common as when they were younger. Annie always won anyway.

The room sat silent until the tough teen, searching her large baggy purse, brought out a bottle and held it up over her head. "What's the word?"

"Thunderbird!" the older teens answered, and then started singing loudly.

"You got a nickel. I got a dime. Let's get together and buy some Thunderbird wine!"

The bottle came around to Mary, who didn't take it at first. She hesitantly looked over to Maggie who bit her lower lip and shook her head "no." But Mary couldn't resist, and tipped the bottle up to her lips, letting the cheap wine tumble down her throat. June froze in place, shocked that her sister drank the alcohol. *Why would Mary drink that bad stuff,* she thought. The very thing that caused so much trouble in their home was when their father was "under the influence," as her mother would put it. Mary grinned foolishly before passing on the bottle, keeping an eye on it as it made its rounds.

Maggie turned to the mirror to brush her hair, letting the bottle pass by her.

June went to Mary's side. "Here, want some of my candy?" she offered.

"Go back to the movie," Mary said brushing her off.

June saw an image of a dark, low energy circle around Mary's head and cover her face. With a shake of her head, June dismissed the vision. She had already decided not to have those visions any longer because they caused her too much trouble. Unfortunately, the effort of trying to stop them gave June sharp headaches and nauseating jitters in her belly.

Once again the bottle was at her sister's lips. Not wanting to see any more, June left.

Chapter Twenty-Four:
The Surprise

A S DISAPPOINTED AS June was at having to leave half way through "Darby O' Gill and the Little People," she was also very excited to about her surprise. The other girls had already left before Annie, June and Brian emerged from the Castro Theater. Hands securely clasped together, they ran across the street, dodging a honking car. Annie stopped at the door of The Big Jive Coffee Shop and smiled at June. Awed by the prospect of hanging out with the big kids, she asked, "Is this my birthday surprise?"

"Yep! It'll be a lot of fun!" said Annie as she bent on one knee to smooth down her little sister's unruly curls.

Brian chimed in, "Neat surprise, huh?"

The birthday girl was very honored that her sisters were finally accepting her as a big kid. Maybe they'd stop bossing her around so much. But looking at Annie, she sighed and knew that wouldn't happen.

The Big Jive was jumping with teenagers from The Valley (as the neighborhood was called) and friends from nearby districts. June stood sandwiched between Annie and Brian at the entryway of the coffee shop, frozen in place. The sound of boisterous teens shouting above blaring music and the smell of fried foods assaulted June's senses. She put her hands up to her ears to stop the sharply deafening noise. Afraid she would look silly, she lowered them and tried to steady herself by mouthing the words of her favorite pop tune, "Venus," that was playing on the jukebox. Silently, she sang, *"Venus, Goddess of love that you are."*

Oblivious to her sister's situation, Annie stepped into the sea of teens. June saw her stop briefly at the counter to talk to Patti and Mickey. Brian bumped June as he moved past her to follow Annie. After that, bodies closed behind them, hiding them from her view.

Taking one step into the dense crowd, she faltered, acutely aware that she was so little amongst the tall teens. Determined to get to her sisters, she took a deep breath, lowered her head, and pushed against the crushing restraint of people.

"Angel, if you can hear me, please help!" she prayed. At that very moment, Jeannie's hand came between the bodies to clasp her wrist, jerking her along.

Before she knew it, she was in front of her gang's table. Everyone was so busy chattering that they took no notice of her. Suddenly, Maggie and Loretta jumped up from the booth. "Surprise, June!" they sang out in unison. Jeannie told June, "Scoot on down there." The birthday girl slid across the yellow vinyl booth to the far wall. Brian sat across from her. She was handed a large menu just as a waitress arrived to take their orders. It was a usual fare of cheeseburgers, fries and Cokes.

"That it, girls?" said the waitress as she scooped up the menus in one quick motion.

"I want a cheese sandwich and milk, please," a squeaky voice shouted out.

The waitress squinted over her jeweled winged eyeglasses to see a small girl squished in the corner. She cocked her ear to the side to hear past the deafening noise, "What'd ya say, doll?"

Annie, sitting on the outside of the booth, repeated the birthday girl's order. The waitress nodded wearily, confirming it, "Yeah okay, hon. Cheese on white. Milkshake."

June hadn't eaten fried food or meat for the past year. She had told her sisters that it was bad to eat dead animals. At first her mother fretted that her youngest wouldn't grow properly without meat. But she finally accepted that nothing would budge the girl's decision, especially after June had refused the family's favorite Friday dinner of fish and chips because it was cooked in lard made of animal fat. Besides her food dislikes, she had a list of noises, smells and other things that adversely affected her senses. Her sisters would just roll their eyes and call her a kook.

Settling down in the booth, June began to enjoy her birthday surprise. She took in the exciting fun around her. Their booth was a like a beehive, buzzing with laughter and talking. Teens in booths on either side leaned over the plump stuffed seats, adding to the hubbub. Maggie told everyone that it was her little sister's birthday party. Rounds of "Happy Birthday" were sung until the words swam in June's head. Loretta handed her some coins and told her what songs to play on the small jukebox attached to the wall next to their booth. When Loretta turned away, Brian and June read over the list and picked what they liked. The others really didn't notice because they knew all the songs on the jukebox and would sing a few lines from each.

Giddy from all the attention, June felt as though she was floating above the group. She thought that this had to be the best day of her life!

When Dave sauntered through the door, June immediately focused on him as though her eyes were beams beckoning to him. He looked directly at their booth with an expression of sheer joy that lasted only a moment. He quickly dropped his hooded eyes and slicked back the sides of his blonde hair. Casually, the tall youth slipped into the crowd. Although girls grabbed at him, he never let anyone stop him as he moved forward to their booth. June snuck a peek at Annie, who still hadn't noticed that he was only a few feet away from her.

Maggie was the first to begin singing when the Fleetwoods' song "Come Softly to Me" began to play. Their booth became quiet as she sang on with her beautiful voice rising above the ruckus of the restaurant. Annie joined in. She closed her eyes and sang, "*I've waited so long for your kisses. Come to me from up, from up above.*" The group of teen girls sang the chorus. At the end of the song, Annie opened her eyes to see Dave standing above her. She flushed a deep crimson and trembled.

Seeing Annie and Dave locked in a gaze, June experienced a sensation of lightness. Her breath became shallow, and her eyelids half closed. Suddenly, a sound like a shrill whistle pierced her ears. For a moment, she felt dizzy. A voice within her said, "Let your feelings show you a picture." She remembered how Mrs. G had taught her to let her feelings form an image. She closed her eyes and saw a picture of her mother looking up adoringly at the shadowy outline of a very tall man whose hair was red, like her own.

A sharp kick on her shin beneath the table broke her trance. Brian was frowning at her. She heard a deep voice saying, "Happy Birthday." She looked up to see Dave lean across the table and let go of a crumbled brown paper bag. His hips had rested briefly against Annie's shoulder. He slowly eased off her and drew back his six-foot-two frame. Then he lightly laid a hand on her shoulder and said "See ya later," before leaving their booth.

Perspiration popped out on Annie's upper lip. Her body flushed hot. Her heart thumped, her nipples hardened against her sweater, and her pelvis tingled. This unusual feeling invading her body frightened her. She couldn't say a word, and neither did anyone else. In stunned silence, everyone at the table stared at her until Maggie, with an eyebrow raised and tongue flickering across her full lips, inquired devilishly, "Did it feel good?"

June leaned an elbow into the center of the table to get a bird's eye view of the moonstruck Annie.

With eyes downcast and a small smile on her lips, Annie answered, "Really good," stretching out the last word before hiding her giggles in her hands.

Amazed at Annie's candor Loretta gasped in shock. "You felt *it*?" The older kids around the table erupted in peals of laughter.

"Let's see what Dave got you," Brian said enthusiastically, ignoring the girls' silliness.

Too busy jabbering about boys, the girls took no notice as June unfolded the bag and peaked inside. Shoving her hand inside, she pulled out a 45 record—her very first one! Excitedly, she announced the title, "Little Space Girl."

Seeing the record, the others quieted down. "What the heck is that song? I never heard of it," Mary said disparagingly.

Brian looked at her as though she was from Mars. "It's really funny. Like the Chipmunk song. You never heard it?" he asked, surprised.

"Kid stuff," Mary snorted.

"Yeah, like you're sooo cool. *What's the word?*" Maggie taunted her, remembering the Thunderbird song they had sung in the Ladies Room at the Castro Theater.

"Shut up," Mary snarled and tossed a straw at her.

Annie raised a hand to end the bantering. "June, that's really nice."

"Here's another one," Loretta said as she handed the birthday girl a small, neatly wrapped package. Carefully removing the wrapping, she found two white hankies with small yellow daisies embroidered on them.

"I heard they're your favorite flowers," Loretta said.

"They are. Thanks," June said shyly and kissed Loretta's cheek.

Over the mess of plates and tall malt glasses, Jeannie handed June a rolled scroll with a tartan ribbon tied around it.

"We made it for you. Happy Birthday," Brian said proudly.

June tugged off the ribbon and slowly rolled out the scroll. On the top of the page was a pen and ink drawing of a stately woman dressed in Roman clothing with a wreath of flowers around her head. A full moon was behind her. Beneath the drawing was the word "Juno" written in calligraphic writing. Below that read, "Optima Maxima—Great Mother. The best and greatest of the Goddesses."

Happily surprised with the Callaghans' gift, June exclaimed, "Wow! Is this about me?"

"It's where your name came from. I looked it up," Brian said, happy with his best friend's reaction. "Bernice has got plenty of books about goddesses." Bernice had a collection of books on many cultures and religions that the little kids had often poured through to giggle at the pictures of naked tribes people.

"Yeah, you're named after a really tough goddess. She's like the most powerful of the Roman goddesses," Jeannie said proudly.

"I know about goddesses," Loretta giggled between slurps of her Coke. "When I went to Italy to see my grandparents, I saw statues of them. A lot were naked. You saw everything."

"The Romans and Greeks had goddesses and gods to help them in life. Like you Catholics have saints," said Jeannie.

"They were superstitious," Annie said prissily.

Jeannie guffawed, "And you guys aren't? What about believing in a saint to watch over your travels, and another to help you find stuff you lose? Isn't that superstitious?"

"People prayed to the goddesses like you do to God's Mother," Brian told June.

"Maybe I'll pray to the goddess Juno too." June studied the scroll thoughtfully.

"Ooh, pagan stuff! Daddy was right, you are a pagan!" Mary kidded her sister.

"A pagan? How come she's at Catholic school?" Loretta asked looking bewildered.

"If it was up to St. Pius, she wouldn't be there. She said June's a witch," Maggie added.

"Yeah. Better be careful, Loretta. She'll put a spell on you," Mary said making a scary face at their puzzled friend.

"How'd that old nun know if you're a witch?" Loretta asked.

"Probably one herself," Jeannie said sneeringly.

"No, she's a bitch," Mary laughed loudly at her own comment. June looked at her sister puzzled why she seemed so giddy.

"Swearing again? Cut it out or I'll tell Daddy," Annie scolded her disobedient sister.

Mary folded her arms across her chest and slumped down. "I'll tell Daddy about Dave," she retorted.

Jeannie interrupted Annie's response. "No jiving? She really called you a witch?" she asked June.

Not wanting to ruin her birthday celebration with thoughts about the mean nun, the birthday girl kept her eyes on her scroll and ignored the question.

Jeannie didn't wait long for an answer. "Do you know that the Catholics took most of their major holidays from the pagans? Did you ever ask St. Pius what bunnies and eggs have to do with Easter?

Annie said testily, "You think you know so much about religious history, but you don't even go to church."

"Sadie and Bernice know all about that kind of stuff and about witches too," said Brian.

"Are witches as wicked as they say?" Loretta inquired, narrowing her dark Sicilian eyes.

"That's bullshit!" Jeannie said hotly. Then, in a calmer voice tone, she said, "Witches do a lot of good things. They can heal with plants and stuff. And they have special powers. Some can see things others can't."

June thought about Mrs. G and wondered if she had been a witch.

"June can be a good witch, huh, Jeannie?" Brian said.

"May as well. She's a bad Catholic," Mary suggested mischievously.

"And they dance like crazy people around a fire and cast spells," Annie added mockingly.

"Yep. They do spells. We read how to do one," Brian said, getting the full attention of the girls.

"Zip it." His sister pulled her finger across her lips.

June looked up from the scroll and asked Jeannie, "Can you do a spell?"

Aware that the other girls were waiting to hear more, Jeannie said, "I shouldn't say too much, with you guys being Catholics and all."

"We can keep a secret. Tell us, Jeannie," Maggie said in a hushed voice.

"Yeah, okay. When you cast a spell you have to be careful and follow a ritual."

"What's that mean?" Maggie's green eyes shone with excitement.

Jeannie pushed dishes aside and spread her arms across the table to pull the group closer. All heads, including Annie's, leaned into the center of the table.

"You know how you guys have rituals at your church?" Jeannie said. They nodded, eyes wide. "Well, they use candles and incense and stuff and say magical words, like the special things you say at Mass in that strange language."

"Latin," Annie said.

"Yeah, okay. Witches have special ceremonies at special times of the year. You know, like Halloween."

"It means holy eve. It's before All Saints Day," Annie said, giving her helpful input.

"What other holidays are pagan?" Maggie asked, playing with the cold fries on her plate.

"Tell her about the May one. I heard Sadie say they use a stag," Brian snickered.

Jeannie said, "Maybe I shouldn't say any more."

"Come on, tell us some more. Please," Loretta begged.

June knew why Jeannie wanted to keep the witch stuff secret. The Callaghans were judged in The Valley. The neighbors snickered about Sadie and Bernice being odd, and most kids in the neighborhood were not allowed to go to the Callaghan house. The MacDonald girls snuck over because they had been their best friends from the day both families moved to Liberty Street.

Jeannie continued. "Well, in the old religion for the pagan people, May Day was a big deal. The prettiest girl in the town was picked to be Mother Earth. She got all dressed up and wore a crown of flowers, and went all over the place with everyone throwing flowers at her feet. Then a bunch of people danced around a big pole called a Maypole in honor of Mother Earth. The pagans were always celebrating some goddess' special day. They all had some kind of special powers and influence over people's lives and were mostly beautiful women."

Some teens started to file past their booth on their way to the front door. One said, "Ya comin'?"

Maggie took a lipstick and a mirror from her purse. She asked, "So the coolest and prettiest girl gets to be the goddess on May Day?"

"Yep," answered Jeannie, as she exited the booth.

As Annie followed behind her, she reminded June not to forget her presents.

"Let's beat it," said Mary.

"Let's make like peanut butter and jam," Brian said. Only the two little kids laughed as they followed the others out of the booth and The Big Jive.

A pool of teens formed outside the coffee shop to make plans for the night. A boy with a crew cut and bug eyes stuck his head between Maggie and Loretta. "Hiya girls. See ya at the park?" he said.

Both girls put their noses up in the air and turned away.

"Hey, we're going to the park. Okay?" Maggie asked Annie with a big eager grin.

Annie harrumphed with an exaggeratedly surprised look. June tugged at her arm, gesturing for her sister to bend over. "If they go, we'll have more fun without them," she whispered.

"Yeah, okay. Make sure you're home before nine so we don't get in trouble," Annie warned her sisters as they headed toward Eureka Valley Park.

"Sure thing!" they answered.

"Swear to God and cross your hearts," Annie demanded. They did, grinning. Forlornly, Annie watched the gang of kids walk up Eighteenth Street toward the park.

"Is my surprise over?" June asked.

"Heck no! We'll stop at the comic book store," said Annie as she put on a big smile and reached into her pocketbook, pulling out a handful of loose change.

"Swell!" June and Brian shouted together and then skipped ahead of Annie.

On the warm San Francisco night, Castro Street was especially busy with couples and groups of young people strolling past Annie, the lone teen.

Eager to get to the comic book store, the little kids turned around and waved for her to hurry up. Concentrating on the kids, Annie didn't see Dave come up from behind. He fell into step with her.

Brian nudged June to look back at Annie. She saw her big sister and Dave strolling hand in hand. She and Brian giggled and ran into the comic book store. Her ninth birthday was more than she had imagined—it was magical!

Chapter Twenty-Five:
Sister Noel's Mystical Teachings

September 1959

THE FIRST DAY of school didn't come fast enough for the eldest or youngest MacDonald sisters, both were eager for fresh experiences. June missed saying good-bye to Annie, who had left at seven o'clock to begin high school across town. Impatient to start her own new adventure in the fourth grade, June decided not to wait for Maggie and Mary, who were reluctant to begin their first day. They lollygagged on the front porch, savoring their last minutes of vacation on the beautiful, sunny morning—typical September weather in San Francisco.

Skipping merrily down Liberty Street with her journal tucked under one arm and a lunch bag in the other, June missed seeing Brian waiting for her on the steps of his house. Catching a blur of red hair bouncing past him, he jumped up.

"Hey! Where's the fire?" he yelled, rushing to catch her.

"I look like I'm flying, huh?" she gleefully called back to him. With outstretched arms, she swept down the steep Castro Street hill.

"You always say that," Brain yelled to her. He'd never actually seen her fly.

As he jogged toward her, she saw that his clothing was askew. The zipper on his rumpled trousers was undone, and his shirt, with buttons in the wrong holes, hung lopsided.

"Gads, look at you!" she pointed giggling, "Your fly's open."

With his face blazing red with shame, he turned away to zip his pants and redo the buttons. Jeannie, who had always helped him prepare for school, now left earlier to walk over the Castro Street hills to James Lick Junior High School in another neighborhood called Noe Valley. Now Brian would have only June's company on their walk down the hill to Nineteenth and Diamond Streets, when he would turn toward the public school and she to Holy Savior.

Waiting for her pal to pull himself together, June opened her journal. "Look," she said showing him page after page filled with her careful writing. "I'm going to share it with Sister Noel, just like she told me to. It's all about what happened this summer."

Busy flipping through the journal, neither saw Mary sneak up behind them. Sarcastically, she sang, "June and Brian sitting in a tree, k-i-s-s-i-n-g."

June grasped his arm and ran away from her mean-spirited sister. Sadly, she and Mary hadn't gotten along all summer. Mary had cruelly belittled her younger sister's visions of her angel, and constantly made unkind remarks about June being a kook and an evil pagan. The unhappy little girl held her temper, even after finding the crimson silk scarf on her bed without the tarot cards. To June it was a sign that she must let the cards go. Before summer vacation, Sister Noel had advised her to "Put the cards away for now, and use your journal to express your visions."

The sisters' feud had begun with a misunderstanding. Mary had accused June of being disloyal and not keeping a secret between them. June had adamantly defended herself, "I swore to Our Lady I wouldn't tell!" Nevertheless, knowing that it was June who had spied her pouring a little water into their father's whiskey bottle, Mary was convinced June was the tattletale, and couldn't be told otherwise.

Jimmy's thunderous voice had boomed through the house, calling his daughters to the living room for interrogation about the evaporating whisky. He had immediately dismissed June. For once, he was not blaming her. She hated to abandon her sisters, but it would have infuriated him only more if she hadn't.

She slid the door closed and stayed rooted in the drafty hallway, plastering her ear against the door in an effort to hear. Her mother came to her side, wringing her hands on a dishrag, anxious about the punishment that the guilty one would suffer.

Jimmy's questioning was loud and harsh. "Do you know who drank my whiskey?"

June peeped through the slit of an opening in the door. Her father's back was to her, allowing a clear view of each sister.

Annie pulled herself tall to answer with a solid, "No."

Maggie swayed back and forth, nervously biting her full lips. Jimmy queried her with the same question. She blew out hard before answering. "I wouldn't do that, Daddy."

Another denial, Cathy thought. She knew how that would make Jimmy's temper boil. She could imagine how frightened the girls must be when he zeroed those narrow dark eyes on them. It made her nervous, too. A few weeks before, he mentioned that his whiskey had seemed awfully weak. Then, a few days later he had said he knew one of the girls was watering it down. Cathy had a good idea who it was. It wouldn't be Annie. She was piously responsible. Maggie was too vain to want to appear out of control. June was too young. It had to be Mary. *Silly girl would have no idea of the difference between good strong whiskey and weak watered brew,* Cathy had thought.

She heard his voice become dangerously low as he asked Mary about whether she knew anything about the whiskey. Cathy imagined Jimmy's eyes burning into Mary's face, causing her guilt to show. *I hope he remembers his own infractions,* she thought, remembering the many times she'd heard him laughingly tell Sandy about how he'd enjoyed his first taste of whiskey at twelve—Mary's age. She leaned against June's back to get a better view of the girls.

Inches from Mary's face, Jimmy growled, "Don't you dare tell me it wasn't you!"

Her head quivered a jerky "no" as she watched him cautiously.

"Bloody lying bitches," he snarled, his thin lips curled up. He began tugging off his thick brown belt.

Mary burst forth in tears as she screamed, "Mommy!"

Boldly, Annie came to her defense. "Daddy, it's not right to hit us. Look how you're scaring her!"

A fierce argument ensued between the strong-willed daughter and angry father. The sound of furniture scraped across the hardwood floor. June's stomach wretched in spasms as she held her hands tightly over her ears. Cathy squeezed her eyes shut, wishing it all to stop. She heard a swishing sound and knew it was Jimmy's belt whipping through the air. The loud slap meant the belt had found its mark.

"Jimmy! Stop it!" Cathy yelled as she swiftly rushed into the room, knocking June aside.

The ugly scene of the family discord terrorized June and she started to cry loudly, adding to the chaos. Mary flew past her, escaping upstairs as though the Devil himself was at her heels.

Firmly, Cathy took hold of her husband's upraised arm, catching it in mid-air, "Please. Don't hurt them anymore."

Jimmy's eyes, wild with rage, stared into her face. She could smell whiskey wafting from him. It made her heart leap in terror. He could get more dangerous when he drank.

Unexpectedly, Jimmy lowered his arm. The belt dangled from his calloused hand, which he placed over his heart. Slouching onto the couch, he spouted out, "Them girls will be the death of me yet."

Cathy patted his shoulder, saying, "I know. I know."

Annie stood next to her, breathing heavily and staring accusingly at her mother. Cathy lowered her eyes in shame for not stopping Jimmy sooner.

Maggie fled to safety without a moment's hesitation. Annie nudged June up the stairs. On the top landing, Annie popped her head into Mary's bedroom and told her, "Stop drinking Daddy's whiskey."

A couple of hours later, dinner was served at the usual time. It was a torturous affair for all. June ate around the meat, hoping her father wouldn't notice. She snuck a look and saw that he wasn't even looking at her. From under his bushy eyebrows, he kept his eyes trained on Mary.

∽ ∽ ∽

For June, school was a welcome relief from the summer. Sister Noel greeted each child with an enthusiastic smile and a kind pat on their heads, and joshed lightly with a few of the boys. The children looked adoringly at the nun. They were happy to be in her class.

It was in religious study that the innovative nun offered her students a new way of knowing God. She instructed her students to put away their catechism books.

"I have something very important to teach you that will help you be closer to God," Sister Noel said. She sat down and placed her hands on her desk, palms up. "Praying is talking to God. Learning to be very still quiets your mind to hear His answer."

Sister led the class in a time of contemplation, guiding them in a soothing, melodious voice to a joyful place. When some children fidgeted during the meditation, Sister encouraged them to focus on the picture hanging over her desk. The large poster showed billowy soft clouds crossing over an azure blue sky. June was drawn to the picture, having many times envisioned her angel in a sky similar to it.

Fourth grade became a peaceful enjoyment, filled with students enthusiastic to learn.

"Sister, can I show you something?" June asked, holding out the scroll she had received for her birthday.

She had hung back and waited for her classmates to leave, which they were more than happy to do on that hot Indian summer day. The windows in the classroom were wide open. Still, there was no breeze flowing through. Sister Noel continued to look fresh in spite of the heat, even though she was wrapped in a nun's black habit made up of a headdress and floor-length tunic dress with form fitting long sleeves.

The pretty nun put out her hand to receive the scroll. Unrolling it, she said, "The goddess Juno. Yes, she was considered a powerful goddess."

"You know about her?" June asked amazed with how much her teacher knew.

"Of course, she's part of ancient history. It must have been interesting to learn about the origin of your name." June moved closer to the nun. "Can you stay to talk a while?" Sister Noel asked.

"Yes. I can walk home by myself now. I'm nine," June said enthusiastically. Sister patted a chair next to her desk for June to sit down.

June studied how the nun's hair was completely hidden by a tight headdress and a stiff white headband shrouded by the black veil that flowed over her head and across her shoulders. It made June wonder what color her hair might be.

Curiously, she asked, "Aren't you really hot with all that stuff on?" Her own face was beet red with glistering sweat.

"No. I like the heat. I grew up in South Africa," Sister answered.

"Did you see lions an' stuff?"

"Oh yes! I saw many of God's wonderful beasts and beautiful skies, too."

"How come a white person lived in Africa?" the little girl asked innocently.

"There are many white people living there. I was there because my parents were missionaries. They went there to save the heathens' souls, not that souls needed to be saved."

Sister Noel began to weave a colorful story of life in Africa. June leaned forward on her elbows and cupped her face in her hands, keen to learn more about her favorite nun's life as a child in a far-away country. After sharing some adventurous stories about wild animals and the country she had lived in, Sister Noel stopped talking and stared into space.

"Did the black people like you?" June asked, breaking the silence.

"Yes, very much," Sister said. "I had many good friends. I think that growing up around them, I became like them— loving God's earth. They must have thought so, too. They were very kind to the little white Christian girl who had strange dreams."

"That's you, huh?" June asked.

Sister smiled and nodded "yes."

"That's why you believe me, 'cuz you and me are like each other," June said.

"You and I," Sister corrected her out of habit. "I was only four when we went to live in a village with the Swahilis. They are proud, handsome people who also have special powers to see what others cannot."

"Like I see Helen and my angel."

"Yes, somewhat like that. But, also, some of them could see into the future through their dreams," Sister said. She stopped, gathering her thoughts. Her dreamy ocean-green eyes captivated the little girl.

Sister Noel continued, "When I was six, I dreamt about a boy in the village being attacked by a lion at the river. I told my nanny, an old African woman. My parents were very busy teaching, so I spent a lot of time with her. The next day it happened as it did in my dream. From then on I had dreams about other people, like you have. Not all bad ones. The Africans enjoyed hearing about them and I enjoyed the attention. Finally, when I told my mother, she thought it was my imagination, or the heat, or the bad influence of the heathens, or something. 'Visions are only for holy people,' she told me. So I never again mentioned anything to her about it." Sister looked out the window and June felt her sadness.

Enthralled with Sister's private memories, June remained quiet, hoping the nun would tell her more.

"But my nanny understood. She told me that from the beginning of time her people, who were brave, fearless warriors, had great mental powers to communicate over long distances with not only humans, but animals, too. It helped the hunters. They called it dream walking. My nanny taught me how to use my gift of vision correctly." Sister Noel paused before going on. "Later, I read more about this ability. It is called telepathy, and the Swahilis had mastered it."

Sister told June how potent telepathic communication could be when learned and used properly. "To gain strength in it, you must still your mind to send or receive clear thoughts. Your intention must be good. That is most important."

June thought about how Mrs. G had already taught her about the importance of quieting the mind to hear and see beyond the physical world.

"Can I learn to talk with someone in my mind like regular talking?" she inquired.

"You already do with your angel and Helen."

"Not dead people and angels. Live ones. Like maybe my sister Mary." June then told her about their problem. She had been pining for her sister's lost friendship.

"You are a very gifted intuitive. When you knew about Meise, how did that information come to you?" the nun asked.

"I saw a picture in my mind of you playing with a dog," June said.

"Why did you say I would fly to Africa someday?"

"I think that my angel told me, and I just repeated it. Yes, that was it," June said.

Sister Noel looked for a moment at the girl, and said, "I think it is time to teach you more about your psychic talents. Seeing something when you don't have prior knowledge of it is called clairvoyance. That means clear sight. When you hear intuitive messages, it is called clairaudio, or clear hearing," Sister explained.

"Was the holy lady Hildegard a clear seeing and hearing person?" June asked.

"Yes, Hildegard would most likely have been clairvoyant as well as clairaudio. That is how she would have seen her visions, as well as heard her heavenly messages. After all, she did compose beautiful music. Let's talk about Mary and how you can intuitively send her a message. First, try to understand her thoughts and feelings, in order to send a stronger message. You will connect with her more easily when you have a sense of how she feels. In other words, put yourself in *her* place. If she is angry, send calming images. If she is sad, send a loving image. As best you can, don't send any sad or angry feelings or thoughts. Let's try. How do you think Mary feels?"

June thought of how Mary acted mean and tough. With her eyes squeezed closed, she envisioned red flames encircling her sister's mouth.

"She's angry because Daddy and Maggie make fun of her," June said. She paused, and then tapped into how deeply Mary was hurt when their father said mean things about her. "I see Granda B holding her. He liked her a lot. But he's dead." She stopped, her eyelids twitching, and then said sadly, "Now she feels all alone without him."

Tears spilled from June's eyes as she felt her sister's sadness. The warmth of Sister Noel's gentle touch wiping the tears from her cheeks comforted her.

"Don't become her. Only observe her," Sister said kindly. "Let's send Mary a happy picture of you, her and Granda B. I will tap into your picture and send it also. That will strengthen it."

"Like a novena when we pray together? It's stronger, huh?" June asked.

"Yes, like that. One clear picture, and don't sway from it."

June closed her eyes. "Okay."

"Now say a simple word or two to describe it," Sister said.

The girl's eyes opened. "Clairaudio. Sound," she said more to herself than to the nun. Her eyes roamed around the classroom searching through the numerous words written on large pieces of paper pinned on the walls. It was the picture of the blue sky above Sister's desk that brought the image of her angel.

"Happy together!" she exclaimed.

"Excellent. Now you shall use another intuitive skill, clairsentience, which means clear feelings. How does 'Happy together' feel in your body?"

Breathing deeply, June closed her eyes once again, turned her palms upward, and sat in quiet repose. Like when the sun breaks free of a dark could, she became clear with her feeling. Finally, she spoke, "My body feels good, like when Mommy hugs me."

"Good." A quiet moment passed before Sister continued. "See Mary being hugged by Granda B. As you mentally say your word message, feel your body being hugged."

Through Sister Noel's guidance, June developed a clearer understanding of her psychic abilities.

Off in the distance, the voices of children playing could be heard faintly through the open windows. June felt a light tap on her wrist.

"Go home now. All is well," Sister whispered.

After several days went by, June became disappointed that an immediate resolution didn't occur. But the determined girl repeated the exercise daily. On the seventh day, she found her tarot cards sitting on her bed.

Chapter Twenty Six :
May Day

THE WARM SPRING day of the first of May 1960, started badly for the MacDonalds. It would certainly prove to be an unforgettable day for the entire family, in one way or another.

The entire month of May, which is dedicated to honor Our Lady, the Blessed Mother of God, commences with a festive Mass on the first Sunday of the month. It is one of the most beautiful and joyful celebrations in Catholicism and was June's favorite religious event. As part of the Mass, an eighth grade girl, chosen by her peers, crowns the statue of Our Lady. The honor went to Maggie. Her sisters agreed that, after all her heavy campaigning, she deserved it.

৩৩ ৩৩ ৩৩

At first waking, Cathy assigned duties to her daughters before tackling her own. Her biggest project was starching the girls' dresses to smooth perfection. Satisfied with the outcome, she had only just laid down the iron when loud shrieks erupted upstairs. She was certain something terrible must have happened. She scampered from the kitchen to dash up the stairs, declaring loudly, "Mother of God!"

"Big, fat, lying sinner!" June screeched while pummeling Maggie's midriff with her balled fists. Screeching obscenities,

Maggie had her little sister's red curls wrapped tightly in her hands.

"Cut it out! We're going to be late," Annie demanded as she struggled to untangle the duo.

Mary only contributed to the bedlam by jumping up and down on the bed and frantically yelling, "Out of *my* room, Maggie!"

The bedroom door banged opened, announcing the arrival of their mother. The fighters broke apart and cried out their grievances against the other, each guilty before being judged. Surmising that a tragedy had not happened, Cathy hollered gruffly, "What's the bloody screaming all about?"

Blood from a red scratch on Maggie's cheek trickled onto her pure white slip.

"Oh no! Your slip is ruined," exclaimed Cathy.

A high-pitched shrill like a siren, diverted Cathy's focus.

"Maggie's a sinner!" June choked out. "She says she's a better goddess than Our Lady 'cuz she's *more* beautiful. That's a sin for her to say that, huh?"

More concerned about Maggie's injury than the moral issue at hand, her mother ignored June, which didn't stop the agitated girl.

"She committed a sin of vanity and Mommy, tell her it's true that Our Lady *is* the goddess of Scotland," June demanded.

"Och, all this talk about sinners! Stop going on about that damn pagan stuff," Cathy stormed at her youngest as she grabbed her arm and shook her roughly. "Look at your sister's slip. See what your bad temper did? You're just like your father."

The girls knew their mother was very angry because her Scottish accent was stronger when she was upset. They shut their mouths. Annie tried to creep away.

"Annie! Bring the dresses from the kitchen up here," Cathy ordered. She spit on a finger and started to rub at the bloodstain on the slip just above the girl's slightly budding breast. Caught off guard, she observed that her tall, skinny daughter was becoming a young woman.

"Go get ready, hen, or you'll miss your cue," Cathy said as she tenderly brushed back Maggie's strawberry blonde hair.

She then turned her attention to Mary, dressed only in a t-shirt, panties and a wreath of tiny purple flowers wrapped around her head. "Mary, put on that trainer brassiere. You're too big there for only a t-shirt."

The twelve year-old gasped and covered her chest with both hands, and cussed under her breath at having to wear a bra.

To June, she barked, "And you, Miss Know-it-All, the great goddess of Scotland is Calleach.[28] Downstairs. Ten minutes." She closed the door sharply.

Cathy stood in the hallway with her hand still on the doorknob, shaking from her altercation with June. She hated reprimanding June so unsympathetically. The effort over the years to squash her daughter's curiosity had become nerve wracking. She felt a sickening uncertainty, and doubted that she was a good mother. A sorrowful fear that any of her daughters would think that she rejected them gripped her heart. *Do they know how much I fight Jimmy for their privileges?* she wondered sadly. Because of her, they were sometimes allowed night visits to the library and hamburgers after the movies on Saturdays.

A throbbing headache began in her temples. In an effort to soothe the growing pain, she pushed aside her whitening hair to rub her forehead. Indecisive about whether she did the right thing by telling June about Calleach, her thoughts swam back and forth. *She doesn't understand what she's saying,* she decided before her thoughts changed. *Jimmy's right. I've got to make her stop this pagan malarkey for her own good.*

---

[28]   Calleach – The Scottish winter goddess Calleach Bheur dies of old age and is reborn over and over again into a young body. The goddess of death and rebirth, Calleach was said to frequent parts of the Scottish Highlands. She is associated with winter, and can stir up great storms.

When June was a little girl, the stories about her angel and Helen and Baby Kit looking down from the clouds had comforted Cathy's heart. At times she would play along with June and watch the clouds forming images in the sky. June had told her that if she watched the clouds and pretended to see Helen and Baby Kit looking down at her from Heaven, then she could believe they were still with her.

But it was the eerily clear details in June's dreams and visions of Cathy that upset her. *Why can't I tell her the truth?* Cathy thought guiltily. She knew why.

Her troubled thoughts were jarred by Jimmy's forceful shout from downstairs that he was going to start the car. Wearily, she went on to the tasks at hand.

෪ ෪ ෪

Lost in deep thought, June finished interlacing the yellow daisies on her wreath. She wondered why her mother had never mentioned her knowledge of goddesses, especially a Scottish one. On more than one occasion June had enthusiastically shared with Cathy what she had learned about them from Sister Noel. Her mother would mostly say, "That's nice," except for the time when June had told her about how people used to pray to the gods and goddesses. Her mother had said gruffly, "What about math? That's what that nun needs to be teaching you." Afraid that Sister Noel would get in trouble for teaching pagan history, June said no more about school. Now she wondered why her mother hadn't told her what she knew about this Scottish goddess. Rolling Calleach around on her tongue, saying it with a Scottish emphasis as her mother had, June decided to ask Sister Noel about it. But that chance never came.

෪ ෪ ෪

In the early dawn of May Day, Sister Noel awoke to the silence in the Holy Savior's convent. She had struggled to escape a nightmare, enfolding herself in her twisted bedding. Perspiration soaked her white cotton nightgown. Her dream was of a terrified gazelle encircled by a pride of hungry lions, licking their lips, ready to enjoy their prey. The gazelle, exhausted from running, gracefully lowered herself onto the soft grass, accepting her fate. A spray of hot blood enveloped the young nun's mental screen.

She moaned as she came out of her dream state. *The day would be long*, she thought as she untangled the sheets from around her slender body.

ᛰ ᛰ ᛰ

Two long honks of the car horn blasted through the otherwise quiet morning on Liberty Street, alerting the MacDonald females that Jimmy was ready to leave for church.

"Hurry up. Don't keep him waiting," said Cathy shooing all the girls but Maggie out the front door.

Stepping into three-inch heels so she could stand face-to-face with her tall fourteen year-old, she began to pat make-up onto Maggie's scratch in hopes of diminishing the redness.

"I look so ugly!" Maggie whined pitifully. Cathy pressed down lightly to smooth out the make-up as Maggie winced. "Ouch! Watch out for the scar!" she cried out.

Fed up with the dramatics, Cathy suggested that the injured girl do what their religion taught her to do: When suffering, offer up the pain for the poor souls in purgatory.

Maggie looked in the hall mirror and pouted out her lips. "Doesn't matter how much powder you put on, she ruined me."

June poked her head in the door and warned them to hurry up. "Daddy said come now or walk to church." She then stuck out her tongue at her vain sister.

Seething with anger, Maggie bared her teeth and hissed at June.

Cathy didn't like the look on Maggie's face. *I hope she doesn't spoil the day,* she worried.

൭ ൭ ൭

The church was transformed into a heavenly garden filled abundantly with fresh, colorful spring flowers emitting sweet scents. After the congregation settled into the pews, the procession started with the Monsignor walking down the main aisle sprinkling holy water over the parishioners. Behind him came both of the parish priests in pristine white and gold vestments flanked by several altar boys. Once they were all assembled in the sanctuary, the organist heralded in the children. Boys and girls in their respective lines came through the front doors to parade around the church on opposite sides. The girls were dressed in a rainbow of pastel dresses with wreaths of garden flowers adorning their hair. The boys had their hair neatly slicked down and wore crisp white shirts and dark pants.

As the lines snaked around the pews, the children sang in harmony praises to God's mother. *"Oh, Mary, we crown you with blossoms today. Queen of the angels, Queen of May."*

When the children finally settled into the first rows of pews, the eighth-grade girl chosen to crown Our Lady would enter the church. As the organist began to play "Ave Maria," heads craned backward to watch the chosen one walk down the aisle.

Beautiful as a spring goddess, Maggie, poised between the church's heavy wooden doors, waited to allow time for the parishioners to view her. A murmur of appreciation spread throughout the church. In a periwinkle-blue gown, holding a wreath of delicate white roses cut from the MacDonald's garden, she gracefully glided down the burgundy-carpeted aisle toward a life-size statue of Our Lady waiting to be crowned by the maiden. So lovely was the honored maiden that no one would have guessed that only an hour earlier she had been involved in a fight with her sister.

After the ceremony, parishioners spilled out of the church into the warming May Day, eager to get to breakfast. Jimmy emerged gripping his Kodak Brownie camera and squinting into the sunlight. He looked out into the group of people. "Do you see her?" he asked Cathy.

Cathy spied Maggie with Mother Superior and Monsignor. The rotund priest had his arm loosely around her shoulders, leaning down into her face, smiling and talking.

Jimmy saw her at the same time. "There she is!" he said as he rushed down the church steps.

Cathy spotted Annie and Mary amongst the crowd and beckoned them over. Jimmy and the Monsignor were vigorously shaking hands when Cathy and the girls joined them.

"You must be so proud of Margaret being the chosen one to crown the Blessed Virgin. Maybe someday Margaret will become a real bride of Christ," Monsignor gushed, his fat red cheeks shaking as he pumped Jimmy's hand up and down. Cathy thought how Monsignor reminded her of a fat rooster crowing for praises.

Out of the corner of her eye, she saw Mary jab Annie with her elbow and giggle. She had a good idea what Mary was communicating to her sister. She, too, was amused at the idea of her boy-crazy daughter becoming a nun.

Jimmy proudly winked at Maggie. "She's a good girl, alright."

An exaggerated moan escaped Mary's lips. The group stared at her, puzzled by her utterance. Quickly, Annie said, "She's just hungry." The attention turned back to Maggie.

"I understand that Margaret will follow Anne to the Girls Convent High School. What a reward!" Mother Superior beamed a proud grin at the parents.

"We have no choice but to send them all to Catholic higher learning. That's where our girls belong, right mother?" Jimmy said, his grin broader with each compliment.

Cathy nodded her head "yes," giving a half smile. For weeks she had fretted over the cost of the high school's tuition. Maggie had not won a scholarship, like Annie had.

Loud voices of children squealing and singing interrupted the conversation. They looked over to the schoolyard to see a group of young girls dancing around a basketball pole, holding the various colors of streaming ribbons attached to it. Cathy's attention went to the bright red hair flying around the circle. Her heart sank. *It has to be June,* she thought. Mary mumbled, "Oh-oh."

Monsignor inquired, hesitatingly, "Mother Superior, what's going on over there?"

"I don't know," she sputtered nervously, licking her lips, uncertain if she, the Mother Superior of Holy Savior School, was guilty of some sin.

"I know what they're doing," a sugary sweet voice sang out.

Everyone looked at Maggie.

"Sister Noel has been teaching her students about the old pagan celebration of May Day. She said it's the story of Mother Earth giving birth. The pole is the Father Sun." She hesitated, giving the group a pleasant smile. She continued in a singsong way. "The ribbons are like him showering down his love over all the young maidens. Whatever that means." Maggie's bright green eyes, wide with innocence, looked directly at the Monsignor.

The adults stood frozen in place.

Monsignor finally gasped out, "Mother. . ."

"I'll take care of it, Monsignor," Mother Superior said, regaining her poise. With arms swinging as though to propel her faster, she marched over to the happy, cheering children.

Cathy fumed at Maggie. *I knew she had a plan up her sleeve to get June in trouble,* she said to herself.

"Bloody troublemaker," Jimmy swore under his breath looking toward the playground, his temper starting to brew.

With hands folded within her habit sleeves, Sister Noel stood facing the children, quietly watching them. Although her back was to Mother Superior, she did not jump with surprise when a voice gruffly asked, "What is the meaning of this, Sister?"

The pretty young nun slowly turned to her. With eyelashes lowered, she hid her eyes. "It's a celebration of May Day, Mother," she answered with quiet dignity.

"We just did that in church, Sister Noel, in a lovely *Catholic* celebration," Mother Superior said.

"Well, Mother, this kind of celebration for May Day is still done throughout many countries. I thought the children would like to learn about how other countries celebrate. . ."

"We do not celebrate pagan holidays, Sister. Was this June MacDonald's idea?" the older nun asked, glaring at the dancing girl.

Sister Noel had had a premonition that she should cancel the pagan celebration. When she had told June, the girl begged her not to cancel it. She said they must honor the renewal of spring in the old ways, as Sister had taught the class. Sister decided that she must support June's interests, and ignore her intuition. The two continued their plan to surprise the fourth graders with ribbons to dance around the basketball pole as though it was a maypole. The young nun had not asked for Mother Superior's permission.

"It was my idea. I take full responsibility," Sister Noel said as she turned to squarely face her superior.

Grimfaced, the Mother Superior said, "I am shocked by your decision to so blatantly desecrate one of our Holy Days, Sister. Dismiss the children immediately, then come to my office."

Chapter Twenty-Seven:
Aftermath

U P UNTIL THE May Day fiasco, the girls had often visited the altar in June and Mary's bedroom to pray or merely to share stories about life in The Valley. At times even Cathy would sit before it to recite the rosary.

After the maypole event Jimmy had became suspicious about the altar. He said that June couldn't be trusted to behave like a good Catholic girl. He questioned her about what she did at the altar.

"I believe you use it for your sinful pagan practices," he had blared.

When they reached home after the catastrophe at church, he stormed up the stairs to destroy the altar, while June and the rest of the family stayed frozen at the foot of the staircase, listening to the violent crashing of glass and ripping of paper.

He then yelled, "June, get up here!"

With her wreath of flowers still clutched in her hand, the little girl hesitantly trudged up to her father. Everything; the candles, the incense holder, the small sacred objects, were tossed into a pile. Even the angel picture Maggie had drawn when they lived on Market Street was pulled off the wall and torn up. Luckily, June's tarot cards were hidden in a drawer.

As she stood enduring his wrath, she noticed a broken piece of a small object roll under the bed. Quickly, June snuck a glance at it. It was a very small statue of Our Lady, a special gift Sister

Noel had given to her. When she first put it on the altar, her sisters had laughed because the statue was of a black Our Lady. Her sisters said God's mother was a white person. June didn't care what they thought, and placed her prized gift in the center of a circle of small pebbles. Now all that was left of it was the head and shoulders.

"I'll teach you yet how to faithfully follow our religion," he panted breathlessly from the destruction as he unbuckled his thick belt. June braced herself, determined not to cry too loudly.

After a few loud slaps and only one yelp from June, Jimmy stomped down the stairs buckling his belt. He mumbled something about meeting Sandy and banged out the door. Grim face, Cathy didn't acknowledge him. Instead, she told Maggie to set the table for breakfast.

"Should've poisoned him years ago," Annie muttered under her breath as soon as he closed the door.

Only Mary had heard her, and she quietly agreed. She then followed Annie upstairs to help tidy up the mess. Silently, the two girls tossed the broken objects into a small trash pail.

In opposition to their father's overbearing rules, Annie showed loyalty to her sister by recommending that a new altar be hidden in the laundry room in the basement. He never went in there, she assured June.

Later that evening, as their father and mother watched "The Ed Sullivan Show," Annie recruited Mary's help to empty the trash. They took the trash to a large garbage bin beneath the front porch. In privacy, they went through the bag from the bedroom and rescued anything that hadn't been destroyed beyond further use. Annie decided that the sky-blue candle, chosen to celebrate May Day, could still burn, and tugged up the wick in an attempt to fix it. The white candle was too smashed to be repaired.

"We'll just buy another one," Annie said smugly.

She was sure that she could sew the ripped scarf that had covered the altar. She also saw that one of the glass candleholders had only a nick, and two of the seashells collected at Ocean Beach were still intact.

Mary stuck her hand in the bin and brought out the bottom half of the black statue, and said, "Maybe we'll find the top part, and I'll glue it together."

Task completed, they snuck into the basement through a side door. It was there that they stashed the booty in a trunk filled with old toys and household things.

Before the week ended, Annie's plan to setup the ironing board in the laundry room to give the girls easy access to the new altar had been put into motion. As Cathy watched the three girls carry the board, iron and basket of wrinkled clothes downstairs, she wondered aloud what was going on.

"It only makes sense, Mom," Annie said nonchalantly. "The basement is only steps away from the clothesline. Plus, the dining room will be free of cluttered laundry."

"Is that right?" Cathy murmured, and went back to sweeping the kitchen floor.

As Annie predicted, Jimmy never noticed that the altar was set up in the laundry room. She also decreed that June was to cease talking about her visions and angel for the sake of peace in the family.

Grateful for her sister's help, June readily agreed, although it was difficult to reject her angel's messages. "No! Away!" she would say sharply. Dismissing her visions was not as easy. She'd squeeze her eyes shut and shake her head to free her mind of them. Unfortunately, a headache always followed the dismissal.

Maggie was under threat to keep her mouth shut, or suffer the penalty of their father finding out about her make-out sessions with Eddie at the Castro Theater. When Maggie retaliated by saying she'd tell their father about Dave, her sisters banded together, and said they'd all deny any knowledge of Annie having a boyfriend.

On Monday morning when June returned to school, the elderly music teacher, and not Sister Noel, greeted her. The substitute teacher announced to the class that Sister Noel had been called away unexpectedly, and that she would be teaching the fourth grade for the remaining weeks until summer break. The old nun was kind, although rather dotty and yet, June was still too fearful of creating more trouble to venture an inquiry into Sister Noel's whereabouts. Numbly, she did as told, finishing schoolwork and housework without question or joy. In time, her father resumed ignoring her, and the nuns ceased causing her grief.

On the eve of her tenth birthday, and already depressed over the events that month, June opted to snuggle in bed rather than pop outside onto the rooftop. The weather had been miserably wet with low-lying fog, making the MacDonald's big Victorian house feel cold and damp. That night she dreamt of Sister Noel for the first time. In the dream, June was standing close to a blazing bonfire when her Catholic school uniform caught fire. Quickly, Sister Noel came to her rescue, beating out the flames and comforting the hysterical girl by cuddling her close. June awoke, her pillow wet with tears and her heart aching for her friend.

∽ ∽ ∽

In the fifth grade, June made no effort to be friendly with her schoolmates and she soon went unnoticed.

The sixth grade at Holy Savior marked a big change for June. Mary's recent graduation from grammar to high school left June alone without a sister to talk with or protect her. In silence, her unhappiness grew.

Unwilling to forget or forgive Maggie's betrayal of the secret the sisters had held, a silent feud continued to brew hotly in June's thoughts. The two sisters basically avoided each other. June blamed Maggie for bringing an end to one of the happiest times in her life. Soured over the loss of Sister Noel, she no longer found pleasure in sharing her psychic powers. With bitterness, she held onto her misery and the memory of it all ate at her.

Her resentment spilled over to Brian. Their walks home from school were no longer full of jokes, or the hatching of plans for the weekends. Instead, June repeatedly drug up the miseries of the past and complained about her present dull life.

Sick of hearing his friend's constant complaints, they had their first argument.

"Man, shut up! I can't stand you anymore, June," he grumbled between clenched teeth. "Get off your cross about everybody being mean to you."

"Not everybody," she said defensively.

They argued back and forth about June's pitiful "poor, poor-me attitude," as Brian called her behavior. He mimicked a sad expression and pulled his face downward with his hands, which didn't humor her. She smacked his hands and started to cry. He put his arm around her shoulders and drew her close.

"You're acting like a quiet little mouse. Going unnoticed isn't your personality, June. Show them you're still a spitfire witch," he advised jokingly.

In time she did ease off the complaining. Soon, the two returned to kidding around and talking about the movies they saw at the Castro on Saturdays. Although June continued to be quiet, she began to participate a bit more in class, especially with art projects. Her art became an expression of the words she no longer spoke, and her enthusiasm to share her drawings with Brian gave a lift to their conversations.

But Brian didn't tell her about the darkness he saw in her artwork, with its downcast faces amidst dark clouds and turbulent waters. The drawings made him think of June's description of how her mother would hide away from the family at times. He thought June must have been suffering from the same inner turmoil.

By the seventh grade, she no longer cared to keep her views on Catholicism quiet. She parroted the nun's teachings during religious study.

"Jesus left the building of his church to Peter. Men were therefore the leaders, and only they can be priests. They are the head of the Church and women are the heart," she said before sassily questioning the teacher. "Where does that leave the women of the Church? Are we just to be good little girls and follow without questioning? Why can't we lead, too?"

Her salty attitude continued throughout the school year. Her report card had checks for "improvement greatly needed" in the conduct section. Cathy hid it from Jimmy, hurriedly signed and returned it to June.

By the time June entered eighth grade, her sisters had become so absorbed with friends and boyfriends that she rarely saw them. She found solace in her clandestine trips to the Callaghans. Unlike the MacDonald home, the Callaghan house was open to Jeannie and Brian's friends, and kids stopped by often, usually when Sadie and Bernice were at work. Any free time she had to spend away from home was with Brian, hanging out in his room reading comic books, playing records and talking about magical things.

While searching for a soda in the Callaghans' refrigerator one day, June overhead Jeannie talking to Mary about how there was going to be a worldwide revolution.

"Everything's changing real fast. Haven't you noticed even here in The Valley a different kind of people are moving in? There's a revolution coming," Jeannie said. Her fingers plucked at the strings of her guitar as she sang a few lines from "If I Had a Hammer."

Mary took a long drag from her cigarette. "Yeah?" she said, blowing perfect smoke rings.

"Sure is. You can always tell the political climate from contemporary art," Jeannie explained. "Just listen to how the music is changing. People are getting fed up with the oppression of the government. It's up to us, the younger people, to change society. The 1960s will go down in history as a time of revolution. It'll be a fight." She stroked her guitar strings.

"Are you taking June's place with making predictions?" Mary kidded as she opened her large handbag and pulled out a 45 record. She put it on the portable record player, and the song "Louie, Louie" was soon blasting.

Jeannie's right about how quickly things are changing, June thought, dwelling on how much her family life had changed. The house felt empty. Jimmy spent more time at Twin Peaks, a bar down on Castro and Market Streets, which would have been fine if he was not so quick to anger when he got home. Urged by Annie, her mother attended secretarial courses at night. Even Annie was now busy day and night. She had taken a job after graduating from high school, and after work would secretly meet Dave. She wasn't ready for him and her father to meet in fear that Jimmy would disapprove of her boyfriend. Popular Maggie, more focused on her busy love life than school, helped only minimally with housework, and spent every free moment gossiping on the telephone. Mary, whose busy life was kept mostly secret, only caught up with The Valley's gossip with June while they lay in bed at night.

June popped off the cap from the 7-Up bottle she had taken from the refrigerator and poured two tall glasses of the soda. She didn't understand what kind of changes Jeannie meant, but it sounded exciting to become part of a fight for a cause.

∾ ∾ ∾

In the summer of June's thirteenth year, her menstrual flow started. When Mary learned of it, she immediately took charge of educating her.

"You're a woman now, so I've got to tell you some things," she told her. She then set up June with a box of Kotex and a belt to attach a pad to, and told her about sex.

"Be careful because you could get knocked up," she warned her sister, before describing the sexual act necessary to conceive a baby.

June listened wide-eyed, and then declared, "That's sick! I'm never going to do that."

They never discussed what June later experienced with the onslaught of her monthly bleeding—intense mood swings that could rapidly change from high to low. And each month, two days before her cycle started, a recurring dream occurred. In it she stood in front of a full-length mirror talking to her own image, except that the reflection was of her at an older age. The red hair and blue eyes with small nose and cupid lips matched her own features, but the reflection was of an older female in her early twenties. Each time the older female repeated the same message to her: "Someday you and I will know why we see each other." Though puzzled by it, June was also relieved that she would someday gain an understanding of her visions.

༄ ༄ ༄

During one especially gloomy mood in the eighth grade, June disturbed her class by spewing forth her utter disbelief that Our Lady had a virgin birth. Loudly, she scoffed at the "Catholic miracle."

"It's not possible for a woman to get pregnant without having sex," she ranted to the class before getting cut short by the nun.

Fueled by June's rebellious stance, her teacher's pencil-thin lips quivered in anger, and her fat face, encased in the tight headdress, become redder. She calmed herself, and said to June, "I know of your reputation of criticizing the Church and our religion. I will not tolerate your impertinence in my class, Miss MacDonald."

Her sacrilegious opinions flourished with her newfound audience. Some of her classmates also began to voice their doubts about their religion.

An especially quiet student inquired about Jesus. "In the Ten Commandments, it says kids are supposed to honor their parents. Jesus disobeyed His stepfather Joseph by wandering off to be with the rabbis instead of going home. And because He didn't follow the Jewish religious leaders or the laws of the country, He was crucified. Even though it sounds like He caused a lot of trouble, He became one of the world's most important religious leaders. Sister, should we follow what God tells us, or do as the Church says?"

Then the girl voted to crown Our Lady that coming May Day also had a question. "When Jesus was crucified, why do you think it was His women followers who were there for Him, and not His men apostles?"

Sister replied by saying how dangerous it would have been for the apostles to show support. They were slated to be the builders of Jesus' Church, and had to stay safe. She reminded the class that Jesus had one faithful male supporter at His crucifixion.

June interrupted before she could continue. "Would you say that the women were braver and more loyal than the apostles, Sister?"

Her rebellious uprising was squashed with a command from her teacher to see Mother Superior.

June walked confidently to the school office and handed Mother Superior her teacher's note. She stood still in front of the principal's desk with her arms at ease at her sides and a shadow of a smirk on her face. The November rain tinkled in a gutter outside.

Mother Superior watched June with stern reproach. "You are trying our patience, Miss MacDonald. If you continue to do so, there will be grave consequences," she warned.

The student's defiant stare did not waver. The principal was all too familiar with such attitude from trouble-rousing students throughout the years.

She pondered the girl's Achilles heel. "Perhaps a meeting with your father is in order. Is that what you want?" Mother Superior coolly asked.

"No, Mother," June said shrinking away from the threatening words and her fear of her father's rage.

Suddenly, the school secretary barged into the office, crying loudly, "Oh my God, the president's been shot!"

Mother Superior sprang up from her chair and gasped, "Mother of God!" She fingered her rosary beads hanging at her side.

"You are dismissed. Go back to your classroom," she said curtly. She waved June out of the office and closed the door behind her.

The tragic assassination of President John F. Kennedy in November of 1963 was mourned worldwide, although not as greatly as it was by the citizens of the United States. Even Jimmy sniffled tears, while Cathy wept openly.

June had liked the handsome president and his popular wife, Jackie. Watching the funeral on television, she was brought to tears when the president's young son, John John, bid farewell to his father with a salute. She confided to Brian that if only someone, like the holy woman Hildegard of Bingen, had a vision that predicted the impending danger, perhaps Kennedy would have been saved and the visionary would have been seen as a hero.

Her comment gave Brian an idea on how June could redeem herself.

"I bet if you had a vision and saved someone, your dad and the nuns would see you like one of those holy women you talk about," he said.

"That's kinda stupid, Brian," she said. "Besides, I don't get visions anymore."

Her friend's suggestion stayed in her thoughts, though, and she gingerly opened her mind. Praying to Hildegard as well as to the goddess Juno, she asked for a worthwhile vision to tell her if she was to become a savior.

Her petition for a vision was answered later that week.

❧ ❧ ❧

June slouched low in her chair at the kitchen table. She covered an ear in hopes of keeping out the sound of her father reading aloud from the Sunday newspaper, The San Francisco Examiner. She then began the process of sending a telepathic message, just as Sister Noel had taught her to do. First she imaged her father's lips shut tight, reading the paper silently. Seeing that clearly, she next sent the clairaudio message of "quiet." The last part of the process, to send a feeling, which she decided would be "calm," was opposite to the jumpy gurgles in her stomach.

Jimmy snapped back the newspaper and folded it, then meticulously creased it into a quarter section. He adjusted his eyeglasses, cleared his throat, and continued the front-page article about the assault and battery of two men at Dolores Park the previous Friday.

"The police arrested three boys and one girl. There's a warrant out for another young man. Oh, oh! Two of the boys are the O'Hara brothers from Eureka Valley. Isn't the youngest one an altar boy at Holy Savior?" Jimmy inquired to Cathy's back.

Cathy cracked an egg into the frying pan and shrugged an indifferent answer, knowing quite well that Billy O'Hara had been an altar boy in their parish before joining his older brother, Mickey, at a Catholic boy's high school. Recalling the mayhem her own brothers had caused while altar boys in Glasgow, she held her tongue and refrained from telling Jimmy that being an altar boy was not a guarantee that a lad would be good.

"He was, Daddy. Now he goes to Sacred Heart," Maggie answered him as she picked up a sausage to nibble.

"Use your fork, young lady," Cathy said flipping the egg onto to a plate. "Jimmy, this isn't a very nice conversation at breakfast, especially right after Mass."

He continued, "It says that the oldest O'Hara repeatedly hit Dwayne Smith with a baseball bat while the other brother and another kid knocked Cedric Nottingham to the ground. They also kicked him unconscious. Sounds like a right dandy name. It says both men, that were attacked, are residents of Church Street."

Reading from the paper, he continued, "Let's see, it also says, 'They were taken to San Francisco General Hospital where Mr. Smith remains in a coma. He's on the critical list. If he dies that'll be a murder charge. Carmen O'Connell drove the get away car.' A woman driver. Ha! No wonder they didn't get away."

In disgust at Jimmy's personal views, Cathy tsk-tsked while dodging the flying oil spitting from the sizzling bacon.

Paraphrasing the long article, he said, "O'Hara said that it was an older boy who came up with the idea to 'bash some queers.' They drove around drinking beers that the older boy bought. And when they saw these two men near Dolores Park, they followed them, asking if they were queers. It says Nottingham shouted back, 'What if we are, you punks.' Sounds like these men challenged the boys. No wonder they were upset."

Jimmy flicked the page and pulled it straight. He slurped his tea and continued, "That's when an argument ensued. The boys got out of the car with two baseball bats, demanding an apology. When Mr. Nottingham tried to grab a bat, a fight broke out. I'd say them fags..."

"Please. That word." Cathy tut-tutted reproachfully as she slid a fried egg onto Mary's plate alongside three sausages. "Still, it's a shame those two men were hurt."

"They're homosexuals. That's a sin against God," he declared.

"What's a homo..." June interrupted him, pushing away her plate with remnants of scrambled eggs.

"Ho, ho it gets worse," Jimmy spoke over her. "It says, 'A warrant has been issued for Douglas (Mad Dog) Dougherty, the man responsible for buying the beer.' Seems he's already got a criminal record for violence."

Annie gasped loudly when she heard that Dave's brother Douglas—Mad Dog—was involved. He had just gotten out of prison, and Dave was trying to help him stay straight, though he had said that Mad Dog had been bad news since they were kids. He had said he suspected more trouble in the future.

Jimmy peered at Annie over the top of his bifocals and the newspaper. Her sisters ducked their heads, not wanting to get involved.

"Please, dear. Let's not talk anymore about it. It's upsetting for the girls, especially since they know the O'Hara brothers," Cathy said refreshing his tea and laying a hand on his shoulder.

"Now you girls see why I said to keep away from those hoodlums hanging around that park. I know what them boys are up to," Jimmy admonished his daughters.

Aye, that's for sure, he knows what goes on, Cathy thought, knowing of her husband's past reputation as a cad with the girls as well as a hotheaded rebel rouser.

"Mom, can I wash the dishes later? I need to get some laundry done." Annie looked pleadingly at her mother.

He droned on, "Bloody Valley's becoming a haven for queers and killers and God knows what else."

A sudden loud jangling from the telephone stationed in the hallway stopped Jimmy's rant. Maggie made a mad dash to it. "Hello, MacDonald's resident," she answered sweetly. A second later her toned changed to rudeness. "Oh, you. June, it's for you."

"Can I go, Daddy?" June asked tentatively. The girls weren't supposed to leave the table at mealtime to talk on the phone.

Cathy answered, "Yes, go. You look like you've had enough." She sat down next to Jimmy to eat breakfast.

"Hello," June said, questionably, uncertain as to who would be calling her.

"It's me," Brian said in his crackling voice, which was changing from the high of boyhood to a deeper tone.

She could hear voices behind him. One was shouting loudly and another wailing.

"Guess you can hear Sadie yelling. And the crying one is Jeannie. Two of Sadie's friends got beat up bad last Friday night," Brian told her.

"Is that why Jeannie's crying?"

"Nope. It's 'cuz Bernice said we gotta move outta here." Brian waited for June to respond. She didn't.

"Did you hear what I said? Move, like far away. She said to San Jose. I don't even know where that is. Do you? Bernice said we'll be safer there. Sadie's pissed about some of Jeannie's friends getting arrested. She wants to make sure the guys get prosecuted. And stuff like that."

"Jeez, that's not fair. I mean, you guys can't leave. Why would anybody bother you guys?"

Mary came out of the kitchen and closed the door behind her. "What's wrong?" she mouthed.

June cupped the phone. "Callaghans are moving," she told her sister. To Brian she said, "Mary says, why?"

"You know, because Sadie and Bernice are, like, married. You know what I mean." His voice became lower so that she could hardly hear him.

June knew the women were very close and slept in the same room, but so did she and Mary. Although the way Brian said it gave her a new idea about the situation at the Callaghans.

"Brian, you can't leave me. You're my best friend. What'll we do?" June whined pitifully.

"Can you come down here and bring your tarot cards?" he asked. "Sadie and Bernice really believe in you. They said so. Especially after you had that dream where your angel saved them."

June thought about the vision she had shared with the Callaghans just last week. It was about Sadie and Bernice. She had clearly seen them walking arm-in-arm along Market Street near Castro Street. Suddenly, they were caught in a brutal downpour. The lights of the 8 Castro Street bus that would take them closer to home slowly drove toward them. As the women moved to flag the bus, several men emerged from the shadow of a building. They charged toward the women with bats raised high. The frightened women ran toward the slow-moving bus, screaming for it to stop.

When the bus doors opened, June's angel appeared in the doorway. She shot a blinding white light from her fingertips at the gang of men. They fell back and the women jumped on the bus. The last thing June had seen was Sadie's face peering out of the bus window that was being pelted with heavy raindrops.

When June shared the vision, she had warned the women that something bad would happen to them if they went out when the weather became rainy. Sadie had laughed, and said that Bernice's new hairdo would probably flop. Bernice scolded her for laughing and assured June that they would pay attention. Then, on Friday night it started to rain. They agreed that, because the rain was coming down so heavily, they would stay home instead of meeting friends at the Castro Theater. That night, two of their men friends had been beaten walking home from the movies.

"Sadie's been calling you Saint June, the Catholic goddess to odd fellows and social misfits," Brian said laughing half-heartedly.

June giggled.

"If you come down and do a reading, maybe they'll stay in The Valley. You can sneak out, right?" Brian was pleading not asking.

June thought of the two women who had trusted in her psychic abilities. She also considered the importance of her friendship with the Callaghans.

"I'll be there soon," she whispered into the phone.

Chapter Twenty-Eight:
The Devil Passed Through

1964

THE COLD SIDEWALK chilled June and Mary's bums as they sat on the curb waiting for the 33 Ashbury bus to go home. The day had been pleasantly warm for late March, until the sun dipped behind the trees in Golden Gate Park and the ocean fog spread a chill through the Panhandle and up to Haight Street.

Mary tucked the extra material from her bellbottom pants around her legs to keep the wind from shooting up them. June sat on her large black leather purse that held her schoolbooks. The short skirt of her Catholic school uniform (which, in the opinion of the nuns, was too short) did not protect her shivering white legs from the cold.

No matter how nippy the days could become, the two never let the capricious San Francisco weather discourage their trips to the Haight. It was a fun time there. They met up with the young, hip people moving into the area who were bringing a whole new scene to the city. The mood of the Haight-Ashbury was rebellious with young men with long hair playing harmonicas and writing poetry, and the tough Harley-Davidson motorcyclists cruising the street, some with Hell's Angels emblazed across the back of their leather jackets. The scene was a much-needed relief from the girls' restricted life. At home the sisters didn't talk openly about their jaunts, knowing the problems they would produce.

"Stop moving," June said impatiently. Her fingers were getting colder by the minute. She wanted to finish painting a dark-blue crescent moon in the middle of Mary's forehead. She had recently read that witches wore the symbol to stimulate clear visions during certain rituals.

The yellow daisies Mary had painted on each of June's cheeks were only inches from her eyes. She wanted to make them precisely as June had instructed her, including the large brown-gold centers.

Laughingly, Mary said, "I'd love to hear what St. Pius would say about you now, you evil witch. Too bad it wasn't her that got thrown out instead of Noel."

June wanted to lash out and condemn those she deemed culpable in Sister Noel's transfer. But fear of exposing her own guilt for her role in the matter kept her silent. She reminisced how things would have been different: If only she hadn't pleaded with Sister Noel to let her class dance around the maypole. If only she hadn't been so driven by self-righteousness and accused Maggie of vanity. If only she hadn't been responsible for these things, then she'd still have her loving mentor's guidance. Ironically, in her moody anger, she silently relived the disappointment over and over again. Bile erupted from her stomach as she fought back words so bitter that they scorched her mouth and her jaw muscles twitched. Still, she said nothing.

"You know you weren't to blame. Right, sis?" Mary asked, concerned with the suddenness of her sister's ashen pallor.

June shrugged hopelessly and then recovered. "Aye, right you are," she said in her best Glaswegian burr, wanting to keep things light as Scots will often do in times of adversity.

They fell against each other, laughing and bantering such things as "och, the cheek of you!" and "wee bugger." The Scottish saying that had Mary rolling in laughter was a request for a kiss. June puckered up her lips and said, "Gie's a wee kiss, will you no?" They leaned onto each other shoulder-to-shoulder until their laughter ebbed away and quietness settled between them.

A misty pale-gray fog drizzled around them, lightly wetting their faces. June began humming, ever so softly, "Over the Sea to Skye," a favorite Scottish song that her mother would sing to herself. Slowly, the humming drifted away and she felt as melancholy as the tune. She looked to the skies. There was no angel to be seen.

"Dig those two," Mary said nodding to the young couple bundled in matching Navy pea coats approaching them. Both had the latest hairstyle. They wore long bangs that almost entirely covered their eyes, a style they copied from the popular British group The Beatles, who had made their American debut on "The Ed Sullivan Show" the previous January. Although dress and skirt hems were growing shorter each month, the girl's dress was the shortest June had seen yet. Her white lacey leggings on her slender legs ended in stylish ankle boots. Tall and wafer thin, and with an air of confidence, she strode over to sit next to Mary.

"What's happenin'?" the girl greeted her.

"Whadda ya want to be happenin'?" Mary asked.

"What's up with her goodie, goodie Catholic girl uniform?" the girl snorted like a horse, tossing her long iron-straightened blonde hair at June.

"Whadda ya want? I don't have all day," Mary said roughly, knowing what they wanted. She was not one of Mary's favorite customers. The girl complained too much about the quality of her products.

"Got some bennies?" the gangly guy asked.

The girl said quickly, "Weed, too."

Mary opened her big suede handbag and delved deeply into it as she joked with the guy about his tattered jeans being so dirty that they'd stand up by themselves. Finally, she handed him what he wanted with one hand, and took his money with the other.

"Cool. Thanks. Hey Mar, I swear, ya shoulda come with us last night. Bob Dylan is so slick!" the guy exclaimed.

The girl rose from the pavement. "Shit. All this talk! It's cold. Come on. Let's go get high. Bring your friend, too."

"Naw. I'm high already," Mary said. Her dilated pupils conveyed the truth of her statement. "Besides, my little sister don't do drugs. It interferes with her visions. She's on a natural high," she said proudly, putting her arm around June's shoulders.

"Yeah, right! Like whadda ya vision about me?" the snooty girl said challengingly.

"It's not real good when people are on drugs," June said rejecting the request. She was not about to share her precious energy with this haughty person.

"She can read your aura," Mary said twirling her hair around her finger.

June knew her sister was leading the girl along, trying to get her to part with some more money.

"That's bull!" the girl retorted putting her hands on her hips.

"You don't even know what an aura is," Mary taunted, keeping the girl's interest.

The girl stood directly over June. "Yeah, do it then," she said as the wind blew her short skirt even higher.

A flash of hot anger hit June's stomach, stirring up the familiar feelings she had when she was ridiculed for her abilities. In the past she had been comforted with what Mrs. G and Sister Noel had told her. "People who scoff at your psychic gifts are actually afraid of them."

Good, be afraid of me, she thought. She also surmised that the girl shared Maggie's egotistical belief that her beauty allowed her privileged behavior. Slyly, June scrutinized her up and down, and felt assured that she could put the arrogant girl in her place.

In a sweet voice, June said, "Okay, I'll tell you this. . . maybe you should go to the clinic."

The couple looked at each other astounded. "Shit!" they said in unison.

"Man, we just got tested for the clap," the guy said.

Mary guffawed loudly. It was on the tip of her tongue to interest them in a reading, but the seer was not finished. She had another prediction, and knew this one would hurt.

"When she gets pregnant," June tossed her chin at the girl, "it won't be his. It'll be. . ." Her eyes drifted beyond the couple and upward to a gray sky. A fierce gush of wind ripped down the street, temporarily clearing away the fog.

". . . Roger. You know him, right?" Her eyes focused on the gaunt face of the guy.

"You bitch!" he yelled to the snooty girl. He walked briskly away down Ashbury Street, with the girl chasing after him.

"Man, you blow my mind! That's his best friend's name. What a trip. Showed that skag, huh?" Mary laughed, enjoying her sister's uncanny abilities.

It wasn't showing off that brought a sense of satisfaction for June, but more of a need to be accepted for her abilities. Since she was a small child, her parents and the nuns had punished her for being unusual. Enduring this only made her cling to her visionary gifts.

Like a freight train coming through a tunnel, the deafening boom of a Harley startled the girls. The biker roared to a halt in front of the sisters. His thick brown hair laid straight back from riding against the wind. The jet-black sunglasses hiding his eyes reminded June of a fly. His Levi jeans, extended to the front pegs on the bike, tapered off at his sturdy, black steeled-toe boots, giving the illusion that he was taller than he actually was. And with his black-leather jacket, he was the perfect image of the bad boy rebel, especially for a former Catholic school kid.

Eddie Gallagher sat on the rumbling black motorcycle, grinning widely as he stared down at the sisters.

"He's hoping to impress us," Mary giggled.

He does impress her, June thought, eyeing the two. She was reluctant to warm up to Eddie, whom she never really forgave for crumbling her tarot cards. More importantly, she blamed him for Mary's drug addiction. At first her sister took the bennies to help her lose weight, only she never stopped taking them. Although June repeatedly praised her sister's beauty, Mary's self image was stuck in their father's taunts about her being "a sturdy boy."

Switching off the engine, he pushed up his glasses over his hair, revealing his Mediterranean blue eyes fringed with black lashes. He curved his full lips into a lopsided half smile at Mary.

"Hey babe, how's it goin'?" he said.

Grimacing, June thought how, even at eighteen years old, he hadn't changed much from that boastful boy at Holy Savior School. June had heard that he got kicked out of the boys' Catholic high school in his junior year and never did get a diploma.

Mary's tawny waist-length hair blew across her face as she looked up at him. Tipping her head to the side, she answered with a half-smile, "Copasetic. Dig your new pan head," she said referring to the type of Harley-Davidson that Eddie was riding.

Now who's trying to impress? June thought.

"Yeah, ain't it boss, man," Eddie said swinging his long legs over the seat to squat on his haunches in front of Mary.

Flustered at his closeness, she immediately ducked her head and dug into her handbag, rummaging through it. June watched Eddie lick his lips nervously while resting his eyes on the swell of Mary's full breasts rising and falling beneath her tight brown-leather jacket. He readjusted his position, causing him to tip forward, almost as though he were collapsing into her. His arousal from being so near to her was apparent.

Her hand shook as she pulled out a bunch of greenbacks. Like a bank teller she smoothed out the rumpled bills, and carefully turned them all in the same direction as she tallied up a balance. Satisfied with the count, she glanced up and down the street before handing him the bills, keeping her eyes diverted from his face.

Accepting the wad of cash, his fingers lingered on her hand longer than necessary. "Good deal, Lucille," he said in his rich baritone voice.

Their private dance of desire left June feeling like an interloper. Eddie was Mary's connection for drugs to sell and indulge in, but the younger sister knew it was more than just that. Mary needed his attention, as meager as it was. June's distaste for Eddie spilled beyond the boundaries of her mind. The young man's eyes twitched as he sensed her searing blue eyes boring into him. He pulled his sunglasses back down and stood up. Casually, he leaned against the seat of his bike, lit up a cigarette, and blew a couple of smoke rings.

"Saw Maggie singing at some joint with that guy Jerry Garcia," he said. "Man, can she fuckin' groove." His last comment was drawled out as long as his wide grin.

The very mention of Maggie's name produced an ill effect. June watched Mary scrunch down, scowling. She knew her sister felt inadequate to Maggie's female prowess. But it wasn't jealous insecurity that grinded at June's gut. For her, it was pure dislike. Maggie never apologized for her grievous betrayal of June's secret.

Eyeing a beat cop walking their way, Eddie ground out his cigarette and swung a leg over the Harley. He nodded his head toward the cop, and said "Later," as he roared away.

It took only a few strides for the big cop to come up to June and Mary. He tipped his cap with his nightstick, and asked, "Shouldn't you girls be home?"

"Waiting for the bus to get home, Officer," Mary answered politely.

He smiled and continued his beat, his nightstick swinging alongside his leg.

When the cop was a block away, Mary ordered June to "Go get me some Zig Zags." She waved several bills in front of her face and nodded toward East Meets West, a head shop[29] on the opposite side of the street.

Although she really didn't want to support her sister getting high, June understood that Mary was hurting from Eddie's comments about Maggie.

---

[29]   Head shop – Boutiques that catered to hippies and young people. Head shops sold beads, clothing, candles, jewelry, incense, drug paraphernalia and psychedelic merchandise. Some sold occult merchandise.

"More," June said, gesturing for more money.

Her big sister's mouth dropped in mock surprise.

June wasn't put off. "For my stuff, too. You promised."

"How come I gotta buy *your* stuff?" Mary said cheekily, knowing full well that she had agreed beforehand to buy incense and candles for her sister's hidden altar.

A dark sullen look crossed June's face.

"You owe me," she answered strongly. "Because of me, you didn't get your butt kicked by Daddy for cutting school—again." June knew that Mary understood how influential she had been in helping her stay clear of their father's wrath.

Ever since Mary had been warned about expulsion from Girls Convent if she was truant again, her father had become ruthless, trying to catch her doing anything out of order. When he did, the punishment was usually a solid beating with the belt, which Mary endured. She hated going to the Catholic high school, and planned to join Jeannie at Mission High, a public school, by flunking out of her present situation. June pleaded with her to finish her junior year which was only months away. "Mommy's getting sick again from all the fighting," she had told Mary.

The need to protect her sister and mother drew forth June's strong telepathic psychic ability, which had become increasingly effortless over the years. She employed it often, and chose to ignore Sister Noel's sage advice never use it for selfish purposes. With great concentration, she would scramble her father's thoughts by bombarding him with images of unfinished work projects so that he would forget about Mary. As stubborn a man as Jimmy was, June was equally so. Her telepathic thoughts won out.

Mary didn't offer more money, so June didn't budge from the sidewalk. The sisters continued to stare across to the head shop's large window display of pot pipes, candles, incense and hippy adornments. Also, there was occult paraphernalia like tarot cards and talismans. Religious statues of Our Lady sat next to idols of the Santeria and Voodoo religions.

"The same stuff we use at Mass. Incense, candles, statues, flowers. All that stuff. Occult and Catholics, it's like a big old magical mystery trip, man," Mary laughed ironically.

"The mystical part of Catholicism is what I've always liked about it. It's the other stuff that got to me," June said seriously.

"Yeah, like don't question anything," Mary added.

A self-proclaimed atheist, Mary would still pray a "Hail Mary" when feeling needy. June had often reminded her that praying to Our Lady and having faith that She would help was the mystical part of Catholicism. Still, she understood why Mary didn't want to be a Catholic any longer. Like her sister, June was also irked by the memories of the Sister St. Pius, as well as Jimmy's warnings whenever she committed some infraction. He would say things like, "God doesn't like bad girls" or "Good Catholic girls don't behave like that." Still she yearned for ritual in a spiritual practice to support her psychic gifts in a positive way. As little as she knew about it, witchcraft was fulfilling that need.

"Yeah, I guess it's true. Catholic girls can make good witches," June admitted.

"Of course you'd think that way, you heathen pagan," Mary snickered teasingly, knowing it annoyed June to be called the name their father called her. Before June could retaliate, Mary jumped up and threw her bag over her shoulder just as the bus rolled to a stop in front of them. June hurried on after her.

The girls sat down in the warm bus, happy to be out of the cold. Twilight was beginning to fall. Unsure if they'd make their curfew, the girls agreed to say they had been studying at the library, which was the only excuse their father was likely to accept to pardon their tardiness. With their fib settled upon, they sat quietly watching the lights from the cars and street lamps moving past them.

"Hey! Let's go up to Twin Peaks and trip out on the city lights," Mary said dreamily.

June slumped into the seat, depleted of energy and sick of Mary's stupid jabbering. She yanked off the ribbon that held her wild curls in place. Tears sprang to her eyes. Fear for Mary's growing substance abuse interfered more and more with her psychic ability to keep her sister out of trouble. She looked down at the bright orange ribbon and twirled it around her fingers. She felt utterly alone.

"Hey, cool, there's Jeannie," Mary said pointing to the front of the bus.

June turned her attention to Jeannie Callaghan coming down the aisle of the bus with an armful of books and her head bobbing to the music blasting through the headphones of her transistor radio. Her heavy black Cleopatra eye make-up dramatized her bleached blonde bouffant hair.

Not only was June glad to see Jeannie but also that the Callaghans didn't move away after all. Sadie and Bernice had decided not to move away from San Francisco after Jeannie and Brian had agreed to come straight home after school and stay there until the women returned from work. Also, June gave a tarot reading that revealed a positive financial raise for Sadie and predicted that The Valley would soon become a safer place for the women.

"Cowabunga!" Jeannie greeted the sisters as she plopped down on the seat across from them. Her recent interest in the surfer crowd at Kelly's Cove, a popular area of San Francisco's beach for surfing added new spice to her vocabulary, and fodder for her wild stories. The colorful tales had enticed June to start spending time at the ocean. It wasn't since she was very young that she had spent much time at the beach. The family had often gone there together. June recalled the first time she and her sisters put a message into a bottle and sent it off to sea to Helen. They were always eager to return to the beach to send more messages to their departed sister. And June had always sent one to her angel, too. The last time she had done that was during the summer of her ninth birthday, when the MacDonalds had stopped going to the beach as a family. For her upcoming fourteenth birthday, June thought she'd send another one.

"Guys, don't forget to wipe off your face paint," Jeannie said and handed them a package of Kleenex from her pocket. "Oh, and here. Brian got this for you from Bernice's library." Jeannie handed June a heavy black book.

On the cover of the book was a picture of a woman standing on top of a mountain with her arms outstretched over a gray churning sea. A sense of familiarity pestered June's mind. Then it dawned on her. The picture reminded her of a recent vision, one she hadn't enjoyed receiving.

Lately her visions had become disturbing. When she was a young girl, they had generally been fun visions, like the one of her dancing on a hilltop with her sisters and a red-haired teen, or traveling with her angel to a grassy meadow full of golden-yellow daisies. But now they were foreboding. The week before she had dreamt of Sister Noel being hunted by snarling lions. Sister Noel had been cornered on the edge of a cliff. The nun's panicked breathing had caused June to jerk awake with her heart beating wildly. Shortly after the dream she had an urgent feeling to flee. She didn't know exactly what she was to escape, although the fear that *something bad is brewing* troubled her thoughts. The disturbing feeling grew stronger each day, and she became disoriented in its wave of fright.

One day after school, as she plowed up the hills toward home, she discovered that she had strayed from her usual route. She had been distracted by an image of her mother wailing and collapsing on a hillcrest. She had covered her ears to stop the sound of the piteous cries, causing her books to clamor to the pavement, and dispelling the vision. Standing breathlessly at the top of Diamond Street, she had stared down the hill toward Holy Savior and cried a plea to Our Lady to help her get away, far away, from the school and her father.

Feeling desperate to hide, she began to walk aimlessly in the opposite direction of home. Her oxford-clad feet carried her out of The Valley and on a hike up to Twin Peaks. She arrived red-cheeked, and quickly settled onto a grassy patch in the bosom of the Peaks' twin hills. There, away from the world, she rested and soon became lost in the panoramic view of San Francisco. The late winter's darkness had come swiftly and the lights of the City twinkled brighter than the stars as June raced up Liberty Street. The family was finishing dinner by the time she had arrived home.

"Sorry I'm late, but Sister asked me to do a special report on Mary Magdalene," she lied.

ᘒ ᘒ ᘒ

"Man, check this out," Jeannie said flipping open the black book to a photo of a naked woman kneeling in front of an altar and waving a wand across three candles. "It says that she's doing a spell sky-clad. It makes her energy more powerful."

They looked at the aging woman with sagging breasts and rounded belly.

"Sky-clad. Must mean naked," Jeannie said shrugging.

"Mmm. Brian would love to see June sky-clad," Mary joked.

Jeannie and June ignored her smart aleck comment.

"Banishing? What's that?" June pointed to the heading above the spell.

"Get rid of. Blow away," Jeannie said.

"I'll start with Maggie," June said with an impish grin.

"Amen," Mary piped in.

"Hey, dig this. You're supposed to do this spell nine nights in a row," Jeannie said.

"Oh yeah! Sounds like making a novena, huh? Another Catholic-like witch thing," June said. She read aloud from the page.

"The secret to a successful spell is to keep your thoughts clean and simple and always create spells with harm to none. So mote it be." She remembered how Mrs. G and Sister Noel both had spoken about simple, direct thoughts.

"Look up what mote means," Jeannie said.

The girls huddled together, excitedly pouring over the book.

Chapter Twenty-Nine:
Banished

A SMALL WHITE STATUE of the Our Lady with Baby Jesus in her arms graced Mother Superior's large oak desk. The image reminded Cathy of a mother's duty to protect her child. She chastised herself for not always successfully doing that. With her hands clasped on her lap, she said a silent "Hail Mary," and prayed that the issue at hand wouldn't be too serious. She peeped up at the large round clock on the wall, hoping that Mother Superior would come soon and bring an end to her torturous wait.

Jimmy, perched stiffly on a wooden chair, sat next to Cathy. She could tell he was stewing with anger. Not only did he miss work to deal with June's misbehavior at school, but now he was left waiting. Several times he blew out long hot breaths, gritting his teeth with each inhalation.

He sounds like a like a steam engine idling at the station, Cathy thought, irritated by the noise. Warily, she glanced his way. She reflected on how he had always been a controlling man, and lately his temper often flared out of control. For the sake of peace, she had kept their daughters' mishaps from him, not wanting to see them cruelly punished for every little action he deemed inexcusable. With great sadness, she watched as Jimmy destroyed the power of their daughters. Little by little, each girl waned and ebbed, until, in exhaustion, they became their father's prophecy. Cathy thought of Annie, and wondered if she would ever stretch beyond her father's constraints that had ended her dreams of going to college.

Rapid footsteps on the highly polished marble flooring grew louder, announcing the arrival of the principal. Jimmy stood up when the Mother Superior entered the office. The tall nun sat behind her wide desk and gestured for him to sit.

"Mr. and Mrs. MacDonald, thank you for coming," she pleasantly greeted June's parents. "Sorry to keep you waiting. Monsignor asked me to meet with him first."

Cathy noted that the nun's face, never an attractive one, had become thinner and sharper with age, giving her a rather severe look.

Mother continued speaking. "First of all, I want to congratulate you. I hear that Anne was offered a scholarship at a prestigious Catholic university. She'll make a fine doctor. But I understand that she has taken a full-time position at Hibernia Bank?"

Jimmy squirmed in his seat, sensing that Mother Superior was questioning his decision about their oldest daughter.

"Well, she'll need money if she's to go away to school. I told her to work for a year first," he replied defensively.

The Mother Superior dropped her hooded eyes. "I see," she said tapping the desk every so slightly with her long fingers.

The prolonged silence that followed became awkward enough to make Cathy flustered.

"She wanted to go to work, Mother. Annie's like that, always doing the right thing for the family," Cathy lied, recalling how Annie had cried when her father decided that college had to wait.

"You must be very proud of her. And of Margaret, too, receiving the lead in the school play!" Mother clapped her hands with glee and smiled broadly.

Jimmy returned her grin. Cathy's lips twitched nervously. She wrung her hands and waited for the purpose of the summons. After years of meetings with the principal, Cathy knew that the nun was usually fair, in spite of her strict discipline. She especially supported female students to excel beyond their expectations.

"Alas, all this good news makes it difficult to tell you why I asked you here. What I must say is not good," Mother Superior said dropping an octave on the last word.

Her pause was followed by a deep sigh. The nun slumped her shoulders before resuming her straight-back position. It was as though it were she that was about to face the music. It would have been comical if her deep-hooded eyes were not filled with such concern.

The principal pushed a book across the desk to the MacDonalds and said, "This was found in June's desk."

They leaned forward. Jimmy pulled it closer to read the title aloud, "'Holy Witchcraft: The Path to a Woman's Power.' Jesus, Mary and Joseph!"

Cathy put a hand on his arm to quiet him.

"No, Mother, this isn't June's," she said, pushing the book toward the principal. She swiftly recoiled her hand as though the book burned her skin.

Mother's eagle-like eyes fixed on her. "Yes, I'm sorry, it is."

Cathy opened her mouth to argue that a mistake had been made, but bit her tongue because of the nun's intense stare. Her woman's intuition told her that a message was being sent. She felt she was being warned to keep quiet in order to not bring attention to June's other violations at Holy Savior.

Sunrays coming through the window behind the Mother Superior created a halo around her. Mother's face was a shadow hidden in the beam of light. It only added to her aura of omnipotence. She sat back and folded her hands inside the bodice of her habit.

"June has had a troubled history here, and, quite frankly, I've had my concerns about her beliefs in Catholicism for quite some time," Mother said.

Jimmy squinted into the light, his thin lips tightening as his face flushed hotly. In a voice too loud for the small office he sputtered, "What do you mean by that?"

"I truly have my doubts whether June is committed to her faith. As you know, her confirmation is only a week away. That's an important time for a Catholic child to become a true advocate, a soldier of Christ, Our Lord, and become a perfect Christian by accepting the Holy Ghost into her life. From my observation, your daughter is not a good candidate for this holy sacrament."

In defense of her daughter, Cathy spoke up strongly, "She's too young to really know what she thinks about religion. June's got a very active imagination. Besides, you know young girls. Even Mary had a few hard years." She didn't share that June already believed that she had ghosts in her life.

Mother waved her hand, interrupting further comments.

"No, no," Mother replied. "It's not the same. Mary was just, well, hadn't grown out of her tomboy stage. I understand how difficult this news is for you."

Returning to the severity of the situation, she spoke with authority. "June refuses to adhere to the school's religious policies. We have had much trouble with her. Surely you two have discussed her problems outside of school when I, or one of the nuns, notified you?"

"Are you saying that June is a bad girl?" Cathy asked, annoyed by the nun's evaluation.

"Wait a minute. When did we get notified about June misbehaving?" Jimmy asked incredulously.

Cathy ducked her head, knowing she should not have tried to defend her daughter against the Mother Superior. She was uncertain about what to say now that the secret about June's troubles at school had been exposed to her father.

"The bottom line is June is difficult to manage," said Mother. "We at Holy Savior have decided she must leave the school immediately."

"Sister Noel managed her well enough. Besides, June has a mind of her own," Cathy said volleying a quick response back to Mother.

Mother said sternly, "Sister Noel is no longer with us, is she? The other nuns do not have time for June's special needs. She will not be graduating from Holy Savior."

"Please be reasonable, Mother. It's only a month to graduation. Then she'll be off to Girls Convent with her sister Mary," Cathy pleaded.

The principal responded with a cool finality. "Have you not received a letter from Girls Convent? I spoke with them recently. June was not accepted. I doubt any Catholic school will have her."

Cathy speculated as to which of her daughters would hide the mail from her. She offered no suggestions about who the culprit might be.

Jimmy's beady eyes widened and he glared at Mother Superior as though ready to pounce on her authority. Instead, he blew out a loud sharp breath, shook his head, and stood up. He then picked up the book, and, in a surprisingly patient voice, said, "You tell me one of my girls is no good enough to be in a Catholic school? It's no right. I worked hard for that. I'll take the matter to the Monsignor. We'll see then."

The Mother Superior rose sharply from her seat. She informed them that she and the Monsignor had already discussed the matter and agreed upon on the solution. June must leave Holy Savior at once. With a curt nod and a short "Thank you for coming in," they were dismissed.

The couple, stunned into silence, obeyed Mother Superior and shuffled out of the office and into the bright spring sunlight. Before they were scarcely through the front doors, Jimmy spun to face his wife.

"You happy now?" he said angrily. "See the trouble you've caused, letting her mind run wild with that damn imaginary friend shit? Well there's your wee pagan baby grown up to be a bloody heathen witch excommunicated from the Church! It's all your fault, Cathy."

He walked briskly away from the school with his wife scurrying behind him.

Riled by what she thought were unfair accusations about her daughter, she said, "Och, for God's sakes Jimmy! She's not excommunicated, just expelled."

Jimmy got into the driver's seat of the car and slammed the door closed. For a minute Cathy thought he'd drive away without her. Finally, he unlocked the passenger door and she got in.

Violently, he threw the book onto the dashboard and yelled at her as he fired up the engine. "Oh, aye. Poor wee June. Nobody understands her. Isn't that right?"

Cathy trembled as his rage escalated. His Scottish burr thickened as he continued ranting. "And you tell Annie, scholarship or not, she's going to no bloody university. I need her to keep that job and help out at home. College for a woman! What a stupid idea! What she'll be doing is getting married and having weans. That's that."

A fire leapt up from the pit of Cathy's stomach as she spat out angrily, "Jimmy, you can't force them to live as you want. And, those people," she said pointing back toward the school, "can't tell me that any of my girls are bad. I won't have it. I won't!"

"Woman! Be quiet!" He put a fist close to her face. "You're a lousy mother. You're lucky I took you as you came."

Shrinking away, Cathy silently prayed to Our Lady to protect June.

The old black station wagon careened up Castro Street as Jimmy continued raging about the evils of his daughter's heathen ways. Cathy couldn't wait to escape from him. The tires squealed with a fast and furious turn onto Liberty Street, causing the car to fishtail and forcing him to slow down. The air was heavy with tension.

Jimmy spotted a girl leaning into a '55 Chevy parked in the middle of the street a few doors from their house. Her rear end was pointed up in the air and swayed side-to-side, causing her short skirt to swish around her hips. Cathy saw her, too, and from the long skinny legs she knew which daughter it was. Jimmy slowed down the car and they sat watching her.

"She's up to no good," Jimmy sneered.

Maggie flipped her hair and threw back her head laughing. Engrossed in her flirting, she did not see the station wagon park and her father leaping out from it.

"Margaret!" Jimmy bellowed as he stormed up to the car.

He pushed Maggie aside and leaned into the car filled with a gang of pimply-faced young men staring back at him. In fright, they paled at Mr. MacDonald's furious face.

"You punks get out of here before I kick your bloody arses," he screamed at them.

The car squealed away. With his fist up in the air, Jimmy yelled after them to leave his daughter alone.

"Look at her face all done up. There's one of your good Catholic girls, *mother*," Jimmy spat.

Cathy was shocked. Maggie didn't look like the same girl who had left home that morning in a crisp, clean school uniform. Instead of her clunky oxford shoes, she now wore white vinyl go-go boots with her uniform skirt rolled up short, showing off her boney knees. Her hair was backcombed high on top of her head, and her pale pink lipstick accentuated the blackness of the eyeliner around her striking green eyes.

Jimmy made a quick thrust and grabbed his daughter's neck, but she sidestepped him. Cathy nudged Maggie behind her. They stared at him like animals facing a hunter.

"You look like a bloody whore!" Jimmy shouted.

"I do not. And I'm not a whore. I am a virgin," Maggie said defiantly.

"That's enough cheek from you," her father sputtered. Regaining his wits he shouted, "Where's June?"

Self-consciously, Maggie wiped at her eye make-up with the cuff of her sweater as tears began to well up in her eyes.

"I don't know. Maybe at the Callaghans," she answered meekly.

"The Callaghans? She better not be! Cathy, didn't I tell you not to let them go to that den of iniquity? Those two women, a bunch of man-haters."

"Jimmy, please, not so loud," Cathy said, fearing the neighbors might hear him.

"Shut your mouth, woman." To Maggie he yelled, "Go get your sister!"

Hesitating, Maggie stared at him, and then quietly said to her mother, "I don't want to bring June back here."

"Now!" Jimmy ordered, his voice booming.

"Better do as he says," Cathy said, her face peaked.

As commanded, Maggie took off running down the street. Cathy thought of the many times when the girls were young when she had stood on the front porch and enjoyed watching Maggie and June skip down Liberty Street, hand-in-hand. The memory would have been sweet had it not been darkened by the present situation. Cathy's heart thumped in anticipation of the scene yet to unfold.

A figure turning the corner at the bottom of the street caught her eye. It was Annie coming home from work. Cathy felt a leap of gratitude knowing that her eldest would be there to help, if need be, against Jimmy's anger. But then she shuddered recalling that the week before Annie had told her that she was fed up with the worsening MacDonald dramas. She said that she might want to find a place of her own for just a little peace of mind.

෮ ෮ ෮

Sun filtered through the curtains into the spacious Callaghan living room. Five teenagers lounged around on the floor on a pile of large, multi-colored pillows. Like bookends, June and Brian leaned against the large doorway to the room. The older teens didn't really encourage the younger ones to hang out with them, but they didn't exclude them either.

Music blared from a hi-fi. An empty bottle of wine and several glasses were scattered around a dark lacquered coffee table. The room swarmed with spiraling smoke as a joint was passed among the teens. Jeannie sat on the floor next to Tim, a handsome black teenager who had been good friends with both Jeannie and Maggie since his first difficult days at Holy Savior. He sucked the joint deeply and blew out smoke.

"Look, I just came to get stoned, not for a religion class," he said jokingly.

"Tim, this is about freedom, man. Something your people have been fighting for," Jeannie said energetically. "We women are also oppressed by religion and society. It'll be you and I who will change the existing social and political environment. Can you dig it?"

"Yeah, yeah. God's really black. No, wait! God's a woman," he chortled as he stretched over to crank up the volume of the music. In his baritone voice, he began to sing along with the song playing, "She's Not There," by the English band, The Zombies.

"Hey man, 'member that you're getting high on a woman's pot," Mary quipped, snapping her fingers for him to pass the joint.

Several rapid knocks at the front door interrupted the party. Loretta, who was snuggled on her boyfriend's lap, jumped up as though she had been sitting on hot coals. A month ago she had asked June to put a spell on her parents to help free her from their control. They had forbidden her to see "those hoodlums," referring to the MacDonalds and Callaghans. Plus, she was tired of hiding her relationship with Alejandro, a Puerto Rican kid from the lower Mission District. Like the others in the room, except for Mary and the two younger ones, she would be graduating from high school in a few weeks, and her parents were planning her marriage to a newly immigrated Italian man. Loretta had said she was sure they had imported him for that very purpose. "He's so ancient, twenty-eight years old," she had cried. Jeannie had suggested that she run away, since she wasn't strong enough to tell her parents no. June had said she hadn't yet found the right spell to help her.

"Somebody open a window. Hurry," Loretta begged.

The teens started to giggle nervously. Tim turned off the music. Soon they were spilling over each other, dashing around and fanning the smoke with their hands. Mary yanked open a window. June lit a stick of incense.

"Thought Sadie and Bernice were out for the night?" Jeannie whispered hoarsely to her brother.

Brian shrugged, and hid the glasses under the coffee table after taking a gulp from each one.

"Maybe it's the fuzz," someone said.

After another impatient knock sounded, June peered through the peephole.

"Guess who?" she said as she backed up, retreating deeply into the shadow of the hallway.

Jeannie took her place at the peephole. "Hell! You scared the shit out of us!" she said as she pulled opened the door widely.

Maggie pushed past her and stormed into the living room. Everybody stared at the black make-up smeared in big circles around her eyes. She looked like a raccoon. They all burst out laughing.

"What?" she spat out breathlessly.

Their laughter ebbed away.

Mary sucked on the joint. It sparked. She handed it to Maggie as she blew out smoke. "Hey sis, mellow out," she croaked out.

"Jesus, Mary!" she said knocking it away.

"And Joseph," Mary teased.

Her sister narrowed her eyes. "I'm not kiddin' around. Something's come down at home."

Mary sat back down on a lime-green cushion. "Why? Is the big bad wolf pissed at us again?"

"Heck yeah, it's bad. Mom looked really bummed out. Get June," Maggie told Brian.

June had heard the conversation and could tell from Maggie's quivering voice that the news was very bad. She walked into the room with a small scythe in her hand.

"Omigod! Who you gonna use that on?" Maggie asked, her voice nearly hysterical.

"Relax, I just cast a spell. You should be squealing soon," June said snootily.

"Unless you can do a spell for disappearing, you better get your butt home," Maggie shot back.

June stood very still and studied Maggie. Pictures of her father and his emotions from the day's events appeared in June's mind. She quivered.

Guilty at being so sharp-tongued, Maggie added in a kinder tone, "It'll be okay, Annie's there."

"He knows," June said quietly, but loud enough for all to hear.

Solemnly, she moved to Brian and passed him the scythe, as if in a ritual. No one spoke as June walked out the front door.

Chapter Thirty:
The Consequences

JUNE PLODDED UP the hill toward her home. She was leery as to what lay ahead. She wanted to make the short distance between the Callaghan's and her house last longer.

Maggie and Mary walked behind her. Not wanting to disturb her thoughts, they whispered cautiously, and caught only a fleeting glance of their sister as they passed her on the hill. She ignored them, not wanting to build her anxiety by speculating with them about her father's anger. She didn't want to be part of any fearful discussion about the consequences. Instead, she softly sang a few lines from her favorite hymn, "Bring Flowers of the Rarest."

"Sweet Mother... In danger defend us, in sorrow befriend us..."

As her sisters scooted up the stairs, June lingered at the bottom staring at the dark, thick fog hovering over Twin Peaks. Soon it would drift down to mist The Valley. Taking a deep breath, she went up the stairs. She hesitated at the threshold before entering the house. She saw her mother and sisters down the hallway, standing at the kitchen doorway. Annie grimly held the old wooden rolling pin brought from Scotland.

Before June could take another step, an arm rocketed out, grabbed her hair and pulled her inside the living room. Without a word, her father started to smack her head and face with the book. She fought back in a panic, screaming in pain with each hard hit. Jimmy shoved her further into the room and pulled the door closed. In a second, Annie yanked it back open and barreled in with the others like a wailing horde of banshees descending upon an ill-fated soul. They surrounded him, shrieking.

Alarmed by the unexpected onslaught, Jimmy dropped his hold on June and backed away until he was pressed up against the fireplace mantel. Annie madly swung the old rolling pin around in the air overhead.

"Never again!" she screamed over and over.

Her father lunged at her and grabbed the weapon. Mary joined the struggle of tugging and pulling. The three spun wildly around the room, grunting and cursing, wrestling for control of the weapon.

"Stop! Or I'll call the police!" Cathy yelled. The chaos ceased abruptly.

An intervention by law enforcement was never before threatened when the MacDonald household erupted in pandemonium. It would have been an embarrassment if the police were called to the house. The police, whose authority would overshadow Jimmy's, might not be sympathetic to his predicament. Not with all the hysterical females telling tales of woe, he rued.

"Och, you crazy bitches," he snarled. He pushed through the panting group to grab his frayed work jacket from a peg by the front door and stormed out of the house.

Cathy nursed June's swelling eye with an icepack and gave soothing words of sympathy. To each daughter she gave a gentle kiss, and then fell exhausted into bed. She hoped for sleep to take her away from what she knew lay ahead. Jimmy would come home later, drunk. She feigned sleep when Annie popped her head in the bedroom, asking if she was awake. Cathy didn't need to be questioned again from her eldest about her plan to stop the abusive behavior. She, too, was sickened with the escalating family conflicts, but knew of no solutions.

Eventually, by ten o'clock that night, all the females were in their bedrooms and the house was quiet. Soon after that, the sound of the front door banging woke Cathy up.

By eleven-thirty, she had had enough of the noise downstairs. After all, tomorrow was a workday. Padding barefooted down the carpeted stairs, she mumbled, "Damn foolish bugger."

Sharply, she jerked open the kitchen door, ready to face the problem. Jimmy sat in his usual chair facing her. The Formica table was littered with scraps of half eaten fish and chips laying in newspaper, malt vinegar, the salt container spilled over on its side, and a bottle of Johnnie Walker Red. The glass in his hand was now empty.

He raised his head to squint at his wife and then lowered it again. He continued his loud drunken singing of his favorite Glaswegian tune.

"I belong to Glasgow. Dear old Glasgow town. There's something the matter with Glasgow, for it's going round and round. I'm only a common old working chap . . ."

In her long-faded flannel nightgown, arms folded across her chest, Cathy stood watching him. With his bleary eyes, thinning gray hair in disarray and dark-blue shirt opened to show a stained t-shirt beneath, she realized how old he had become. Calmly, she said, "That's enough, Jimmy. Come to bed."

He stopped singing and looked at his wife, trying to focus his eyes.

"You've turned them all against me," he said, dejected.

"You're doing that on your own," his wife answered brusquely,

"I'm no good enough for you. Right? I'm no some brave soldier going off to war for his lovely lady. Aye, I'm only a common old working chap."

He moved his hand toward the whiskey bottle. In one swift motion, Cathy reached out and grabbed it away. Surprised by her action, his mouth opened to order her to give it back. But her scowling face challenged him. He decided against it.

"No more of your silly talk. Come on," she said, putting the bottle in a cabinet over the kitchen sink.

"Your father and mother thought I was a good man for you. Wasn't I a good enough husband for you, Cathy?" he whined.

"It's no that," she said gently.

"Then what is it, *Mrs.* MacDonald?"

He stood up. The two faced each other. Only the ticking clock could be heard. The scent of fried fish and strong vinegar mingling with his alcoholic sweat repulsed Cathy. With tears forming in her tired eyes, she was the first to look away.

"Couldn't you have just accepted her?" she asked in a barely audible voice.

He backed away from her and shook his head "no."

Stretching out her hand as though to touch him, she pleaded with him, "Before it's too late. Take some time to know your girls." She stopped, dropping her hand to her side.

He turned his face from her, mumbling, "I just don't know any more. I love my girls, Cathy, but I'm afraid." He cupped his head in his hands and he sobbed quietly, his shoulders shaking.

Confused by his display of emotions, she hesitated before taking his arm. "Come on, let's go to bed," she said, hoping to quiet him.

In bedrooms across the hall from each other, the girls stood— two to a room—with their ears glued to their doors. They listened with bated breaths for the signal that their parents were asleep. After ten minutes of escalating snores signaling it was now safe, Annie carefully eased open her door. At the exact same time, as though on cue, Mary popped her head out of the other bedroom and flicked on a flashlight. She playfully placed it under her face, rounding her eyes wide. Annie stifled a laugh and put her finger to her lips, mouthing "Shhh." Maggie's head appeared above Annie's. She went into a fit of silent giggles when she saw Mary's funny face. June was in no mood to join the mirth. She hurriedly snuck downstairs. The other three followed suit.

At the bottom of the landing Annie gestured that they shouldn't use the hallway's creaking basement door. Stealthily, they moved through the kitchen and out the backdoor. The fog had settled, nourishing the flowers and wetting everything else. The new moon, void of any light, gave them no guidance. The black night sky accentuated the whiteness of the damp sheets hanging on the clothesline. The four stopped to watch the sight.

"Looks like ghosts," June whispered for all to hear.

She was surprised that Annie, ever the responsible one, didn't stop to grab them off the line or remind Mary of her unfinished housework.

In possession behind the flashlight, Annie ushered the group across the yard and down into the basement. Maggie grabbed a tight hold of her older sister's checkered cotton bathrobe, afraid that she'd slip on a slug slithering in the yard. Hand in hand came the younger ones. June looked up to the tall walnut tree and sensed the eyes of the cats watching them. She breathed in deeply the cool night air, and fought back the dread of the unknown.

Arriving at the laundry room, Mary went to the trunk and took out the shoebox she had turned upside down and covered with a pale blue scarf embroidered with tiny red roses. Maggie took out two half-burnt white candles and the small brass candleholders. She lit the candles and placed them on the altar.

"Let's see your face, June," Annie said, gently taking the younger one's face in her hand. She used the flashlight to get a clearer view.

June's left eye was puffed up and almost shut. It had a deep purple bruise running from her temple down the side of her swollen cheek. She winced when Annie touched it.

"Mother of God! I can't believe he hit you with that book," Annie exclaimed. To Mary she said, "Go upstairs. Get some ice and the aspirin in the kitchen cupboard." Mary was the most light-footed amongst them.

Soothingly, Maggie stroked June's hair, while telling her, "My beautiful little sister. I'm so sorry for everything."

June shivered. Her lower lip trembled. She was overcome with the uncommon sympathy.

"Cold?" Maggie cooed. "Here, put my robe on. There's a clean hanky in the pocket."

Anticipating tears, June pulled out the hankie and a square white package toppled out of its folds. Annie picked it up and held it in the beam of the flashlight.

"Maggie! What are you doing with these? Catholics can't use birth control," Annie scolded.

"You and your Protestant boyfriend better be careful then," she answered snidely.

"You're disgusting. We don't do it," Annie said curtly.

"Oh, well then, poor Dave. Anne, you're such a big bummer," Maggie smirked.

Annie tsked. "*You* better be careful. Someday you'll be sorry."

No one heard Mary coming back into the room. In her hands she had a kitchen towel, a bowl of ice, a bottle of aspirin and something hidden under her arm.

"Oh Junie, poor wee soul," Annie wrapped the ice in the towel and carefully put it on June's face. Her father's cruelty made her temper boil.

"Mom may put up with his bull, but I won't," Annie said. "How could Our Lady let this happen? I pray for Her help all the time."

"It's not Her, it's *him*. The Big Bad Wolf. I told you long ago we should have gotten rid of him," Mary chimed in her two cents worth.

"So, what's the plan? Poison or bat?" Maggie inquired wickedly.

"Something better. We're going to cast a banishing spell. Ouch." June said as Annie held the cold compress against her eye.

"A spell? Is that what you learned from that book? Don't we have enough trouble?" Annie asked sternly.

"THE book," Mary said holding it up.

Annie tried to grab it from her, but Mary pulled it back.

"Hey, Bossy!" Mary said loudly.

Her sisters hissed, "Shhh." All eyes rolled to the upstairs. Everyone held her breath, listening. But no sound came from the house.

"Witchcraft!" Annie said fiercely, crossing herself. "That's a sin! We're Catholics, for God's sake! That's what caused all this trouble—this pagan stuff."

"You're getting more like Daddy every day. I guess you think we're all going to hell in a handbasket, too, eh? Well, may as well make it a party," Mary said, grinning devilishly.

"It's not the book that caused this. Mary's right. It's him. He's afraid of anything that's different from *his* beliefs," June said.

"Yeah. To him it's all evil if it isn't his way." Maggie agreed with the others.

"Our religion hasn't made us happy, or Daddy either. You don't want to be like him, do you? " June asked Annie.

Annie cringed. "How could you ask that? I've always protected you! Besides that, I am happy with my religion," she said piously.

"Maybe you don't understand. Why don't we just listen to June's ideas about witchcraft?" Maggie smiled, wanting to appease her older sister.

Hoping to make Annie understand, June said, "I guess Daddy was right from the beginning. I am a pagan. Maybe Mommy knew that in some way, and that's why she didn't name me after a saint. I did try to be a good Catholic. I always liked the magical part."

"Don't you realize that witchcraft is evil? It controls people's minds," Annie said firmly.

"Oh, and we're not told what to think or how to act like good Catholic girls so we can get to heaven?" Mary said, ever the smarty-pants.

"If a Catholic girl can become a witch, maybe a witch can be a good Catholic. So, there's hope for June yet," said Maggie philosophically.

"If you have to change religions, at least pick a Christian one. Like how about Episcopalian?" Annie suggested, looking hopefully at June.

"Is that what your Proddy boyfriend is? Oh, Daddy will love that!" Mary teased.

June answered Annie by shaking her head back and forth with a strong "no." Resolvedly, she said, "Only witchcraft lets me use my special powers and feel like I have a religion, too."

"I don't want any part of this witchcraft stuff. Something bad is going to happen," Annie warned them, wagging a finger at her sisters.

"I'll do a white magic spell. I'll block him from hurting us. I won't hurt him," June declared.

"It'll be you that I worry about," said Annie, putting out a hand to rest on June's shoulder.

Mary took out incense and a red and black candle from the trunk. "Come on, join the party," she said placing the items on the altar.

Annie shrunk back away from the three, saying, "I never would have helped you with this altar if I thought you'd be involved with this. . .wickedness. Don't you know that you're opening the door for the Devil to come in?"

They just stared at her.

Miffed at her sisters, she continued, "Then I'll leave you to your own devices." With those words she departed, stealing back upstairs through the darkness.

June fought back tears. She felt how deeply Annie was hurt by her choice of witchcraft over the family's religion. The two of them used to sit at the altar, praying the Rosary and talking about the lives of the saints. Annie had always trusted June, and shared her feelings of being unloved by their mother. Annie said that Granny B was the only one who ever really cared for her. That was, until she met Dave.

When Uncle Peter had telephoned with the news about Granny B's death, it was just days before Annie's graduation. She had run to her bedroom grief-stricken, sobbing sorely. June had found her in bed, rosary beads clutched in her hands, crying "Granny" over and over. In vain, June had tried to comfort her big sister. Cathy didn't try to console her or the other girls. Instead, she went quietly upstairs to bed and remained there for two long days.

"Let's get on with it," June said.

The sisters sat in a circle around the small altar. Maggie lit the incense sitting in an ashtray, while June lit the two colored candles she had placed between the white ones. Mary reached into the pocket of her red flannel bathrobe for her comb and put it next to the altar. June picked up the ashtray with smoldering incense and walked around the four corners of the room. Starting with the east and then going south, west and north, she called in the energies from each direction. Next, she placed the incense back on the altar and circled once again, pointing with her finger.

"The circle is cast. The spell is made fast. Only good can enter herein," she chanted softly.

The spiraling smoke and scent from the frankincense gave off a mystical aura that surrounded the room. Solemnly, June prayed, "We invoke the Goddess Juno, Warrior Woman and Protector of Females. We ask for her protection from Jimmy MacDonald. Bind his power and banish the seed of his rage. So mote it be."

Her sisters repeated the phrase "So mote it be," an old pagan expression meaning, "So may it be." It declared that the truth be known, or so be it and was similar to saying amen after a prayer.

June picked up the comb and untangled a couple of strands of hair that she tossed into the ashtray and set on fire with the red candle. Smoke smoldered up. The smell of burnt hair mingled with the incense. She slowly picked up the black candle and circled it around the altar. She then placed it down and began to sway back and forth, her arms stretched over the candle flames.

In a dreamlike state, she began to speak. "I sense his fear... he's afraid... can't control. No control. He's so afraid. Afraid of *me*." With her voice escalating, she said, "I banish you, Jimmy MacDonald."

In the magical swirls of incense and glow of candle flames, June envisioned a raven flying around and around a snarling wolf that was cowering low, trying to get away from it. The flame of the red candle expanded, leaping high. Suddenly, the sleeves of June's robe burst into flames and rushed swiftly up her arms. Mary knocked over the altar as she jumped up to beat at the flames. Maggie, screaming for help, tried to rip the robe from her sister's small body.

Chaos erupted once again in the MacDonald household.

Chapter Thirty-One:
Shrinking June

CATHY FELT CROWDED in the stuffy office filled with heavily packed bookcases lining the walls. In front of her was a large desk cluttered with files, stacked one on top of the other. She fidgeted on an uncomfortable white plastic chair.

Next to her sat Jimmy, his head hanging low staring at his calloused hands clenched on his lap. His worn, lined face, mottled with broken veins and haggard from lack of sleep, gave him the look of a man much older than fifty-four. Her heart had not softened, though. *He's not so bloody angry this time,* she thought. She noticed his jagged breathing was different from the time they had met with Mother Superior. Then he had been full of irritation and sounded like an impatient steam engine.

Cathy was furious with him for agreeing to have June transferred from the burn center to the psychiatric ward for a mental evaluation, without first speaking with her about it. But most of all Cathy was angry with herself. She exhaled loudly, settling as best she could on the chair. She mused over the many times June had attempted to engage her in conversation about memories that she felt were too heartbreaking to discuss. If she hadn't been so stuck in the miseries of the past, perhaps she could have helped June understand her visions. Guilt gnawed at her like a hungry rat in a garbage heap.

But now I will speak my wee darling, if it's not too late, Cathy thought. Her lips moved as she mutely repeated the vow she had made to herself during the ambulance ride that fateful night of the fire.

෨෨ ෨෨ ෨෨

None of the girls spoke to her about the night of the accident. Annie became more distant than ever, and often didn't come home until after dinner. Maggie remained in her room and played loud music, and Mary only came home to sleep. Jimmy listened, but said nothing when Mary and Maggie claimed they had been in the basement praying for the family after the big fight. But Cathy knew better. She knew her girls had been cooking up something when Annie first announced they were going to do the ironing in the basement. Mother's intuition had told Cathy that, when revealed, something would happen that would impact them all.

When she took the girls to visit June in the hospital, they showed no shock at the sight of her burned face and hands. Instead, like Scots do during times of adversity, the girls showed strength, and cheerfully chatted about what they'd do when June returned home. Annie pulled out the many get-well cards the neighbors had sent. Maggie pinned blue barrettes on either side of June's hair. And Mary teased her about how her burnt skin matched her red hair, what was left of it, anyway.

However, Cathy shuddered with sickness whenever she recalled that night. She had woken from her light sleep disoriented and feeling as though she were on a distant shore. Thinking she had heard *Mommy* being screamed over and over, she elbowed Jimmy to try to get him to stop his loud snoring. Without success, she sat up in bed, cocking an ear to the stillness of the house. Something seemed eerie to her, and dread coursed through her body. Her intuition told her that one of her girls was in trouble. Slipping out of the bedroom, she met Annie on the top landing.

"They're in the basement," her daughter whispered.

The smell of burnt clothing permeated the air in the basement. There was wretched sobbing and incoherent mumbling. In the dark room Cathy couldn't see who it was. She stumbled to find the light switch. She saw what appeared to be a heap of smoldering rags between Mary and Maggie.

"Don't die, please," Mary cried as she patted the rags.

Maggie fanned her hand across the red hair that spread across her lap.

Realizing the pile of rags was actually June, Cathy became an efficient machine, springing into motion and taking full control of the emergency. Later she would wonder how she was able to do it.

Liberty Street was alive in the midnight hour with small knots of gathered neighbors speculating on what might have happened in the MacDonald house. The headlights from the rescue vehicles illuminated the street as though it was a movie set. The Irish woman next door wrapped a tartan wool blanket around Cathy and another around Mary and Maggie, who shivered more from shock than the cold. Jimmy talked with two of the four police officers. Annie stayed next to him, listening carefully to what her father might say about the accident. He said nothing more than that he was asleep and had no idea why his daughters were in the basement.

An old weathered-faced police officer informed Jimmy and Cathy that one parent could ride in the front of the ambulance, and the other could ride with him to the hospital. When Jimmy stepped up to the door of the ambulance, Cathy pushed him aside roughly, saying, "June's going to want me with her."

Jimmy stood stunned, dwarfed between two burly cops. That was the last image Cathy had of her husband before the ambulance sped off with sirens screaming.

Unlike what she had seen in movies, Cathy wasn't allowed to hover over her daughter in the back of the ambulance. Instead, she rode in the front with the driver as he sped down the hills of Noe Street toward St. Luke's Hospital. Although the hospital was only ten minutes away, to Cathy, it was too far.

As the siren screeched the urgency, Cathy searched her soul. She trembled as she imagined the pain her daughter must be experiencing. This was her baby, her youngest.

Wistfully, Cathy thought of the night June was born, when she had pulled down the energy of the moon in hopes of reconnecting to a wish made long before on the Isle of Skye. It was a young woman's wish to have a life full of passionate love and many healthy children. Her days on Skye had been a magical time. Unfortunately, the goodness of that time had retreated deep into the dense fog of her psyche. Nonetheless, she realized, no matter how futile her attempts to banish her memories of Skye, and to make a new life with Jimmy, those memories had found a way into June's spirit. How could she tell June that her natural attraction to witchcraft was inherited? Would her daughter still love her if she confessed that June's angel was a vision of a special someone she had left behind in the Highlands?

Her throat tightened as she held back tears and recalled the time she yelled at June when she had shown her a picture in a magazine of two lovers kissing at a train station. She should have said, "Yes, that could have been me," rather than rejecting her young daughter's vision. She chastised herself for not accepting June's psychic gift without judgment. There was the gypsy who had predicted that the eight-month June was fey. Her mother, Granny B, had put aside her religious beliefs and also recognized how June's special touch had calmed Helen when she was sick. *But I couldn't see it even when Sister Noel told me her thoughts about it after the May Day fiasco that June was a visionary. I've been denying it too long,* Cathy thought.

Mrs. G's dark, knowing eyes flashed into her mind as the ambulance sped past a red stop sign. She wondered if the old Polish woman would have reminded her that it was she, Cathy, who set June's fate by choosing not to give her child an acceptable Catholic name. *Could it be that a child inherits a parents' past sins, just as they inherit eye color? If so, then June became heir to my pagan ways,* she concluded.

Shamefully, she acknowledged to herself that she had not protected June or her other children. She wanted to profess her sin and be absolved, so life could start over.

As the ambulance swerved to avoid a slow moving car, Cathy's determination to keep the secrets of the past crumbled like the stone walls of a Highland castle that were pounded down by too many battles. She knew that there was only one way to help her daughters.

The ambulance jerked to a stop at the emergency entrance of St. Luke's Hospital, and June was whisked into surgery. Jimmy joined Cathy and the two sat together in the stark white waiting room until dawn. Neither said a word about the accident.

A young doctor with a no-nonsense attitude gave the MacDonalds the news about June's burns. Although some small areas on June's arms and hand were third degree, other areas were less serious second-degree burns, thanks to the quick actions of her sisters. He said, because of her age, she would heal quickly and without too much scarring. It was her state of mind that concerned him the most.

"Your daughter told me that she held her arms over candle flames until she caught fire," the doctor said. "Has she tried to hurt herself before, Mrs. MacDonald?"

Cathy quickly corrected the doctor by saying the girls were getting ready to pray by first lighting a candle. June must have said that because she was delirious with pain, the anguished mother told him. The doctor didn't believe the explanation, and said it seemed that there was more to the story. He felt strongly that June had hurt herself on purpose—a statement that would result in her admittance to the hospital's well-respected psychiatric ward.

❧ ❧ ❧

A pretty woman in her early forties with dark brown hair bobbed below her ears, entered the office carrying a briefcase. She was dressed in a stylish striped gray suit with a pearl pink blouse. Her blue eyes were large and round, and made her appear surprised. She flashed the MacDonalds a friendly smile that produced dimples on each cheek, which helped to soften her square face.

The woman greeted them in a bland voice. "Glad you could make it with such short notice. My schedule is very busy, and this is the only time I have available to talk with you." She introduced herself as Dr. Schmidt.

The MacDonalds knew Dr. Schmidt was the head of the psychiatry department, but had no idea that the doctor would be a woman. Cathy watched her move across the room with short, solid footsteps as though marching to her post. It wasn't just woman's intuition that caused Cathy to be on guard, it was the doctor's whole demeanor.

The warm room became clammier. *She'll appear to be helpful, but she'll be a force to be reckoned with,* an inner voice whispered to Cathy.

Dr. Schmidt dropped heavily onto her burgundy leather chair, causing the air to wheeze out from it. She bent over to her briefcase, snapped it open, took out a folder and began silently reading the top sheet of paper. Her thin lips moved rapidly as she read to herself.

The MacDonalds waited patiently for word of June's prognosis. At last Dr. Schmidt sat back and touched her fingertips together as though in prayer. Her large eyes stared at them. *Like a tiger watching her prey,* Cathy thought, recoiling.

Jimmy moved around uncomfortably in his chair. "We've had a lot of problems with our daughter," he said.

"So I understand, Mr. MacDonald. What do you think the problem is?" Dr. Schmidt inquired, her lips pursed.

"I'm afraid, Doctor. . . I. . . I just can't control June anymore," he gushed.

Cathy thought he'd start bawling right there if the doctor hadn't then asked him how he felt about having no control. *Same as you would,* Cathy thought.

"Feel? I, well, I think the girl's not all there, in some ways, I mean," he answered.

"Let's get down to the brass tacks here, Mr. and Mrs. MacDonald. We must face the truth. After evaluating June, I have diagnosed her condition. Your daughter is a very sick girl."

The parents gasped. Dr. Schmidt relaxed back in her chair. "I assure you that we have the right drugs to counteract her problems with her hallucinations."

"It's her imagination. Her age. She's almost fourteen, and girls her age, well, I remember how I was," Cathy interjected hoping to change the doctor's mind. She wanted only to bring June home where she could make everything better.

A minuscule smile appeared on the doctor's lips, but her eyes stayed intensely wide. "It's true that girls her age are sometimes irrational. But no, Mrs. MacDonald, this is not simply an overactive teen imagination. Clearly, she is withdrawing. Hearing voices and seeing things no one else does. Thinking she has certain powers. These are delusions of the mind. June is out of touch with reality. According to you, Mr. MacDonald, she blames you and a nun for persecuting her."

"You said those things about June?" Cathy said accusingly as she turned to face her husband.

Jimmy slouched lower and mumbled, "She always fights me like I'm the bad guy."

"Mrs. MacDonald, I am an expert in the field of mental illness. Your daughter has the classic symptoms of schizophrenia." The doctor looked squarely at Cathy.

Furious with her husband's betrayal and baited to anger by the doctor's arrogance, Cathy said testily, "Have you ever been wrong with a diagnosis, Doctor?"

Dr. Schmidt's eyes flickered and her mouth tightened before widening into a controlled smile. "Mrs. MacDonald, I know how hard this must be to accept. But judging from your daughter's behavior, no, I am not wrong in my diagnosis."

"Accept it, Cathy. The doctor knows better than you. June's no all there. My God, woman, she set herself on fire," said Jimmy, his voice rising.

"She didn't set herself on fire! It was an accident," Cathy yelled back.

"You sound very angry, Mrs. MacDonald," Dr. Schmidt said calmly.

Cathy's anger grew as fast as Dr. Schmidt's condescending smile. She looked squarely at her and said, "June is very different. She really does see things, things that others can't. Not just crazy things. She can tell when someone is not well before others know it. When one of my daughters was very ill, June. . ."

"She told me that she's a witch, did you know about that?" the doctor said leaning back in her chair and bringing her fingertips together again, tapping them.

"So? There are those who practice witchcraft in our country." Cathy sat back on her stiff chair and folded her arms across her chest.

"Och, that's bloody stupid," Jimmy said.

"I happen to know witches in Scotland," Cathy said ignoring him, as she kept her eyes on the doctor.

"What are you talking about?" Jimmy was looking at his wife as though she were nuts, too.

"Mrs. MacDonald," the doctor interrupted, "let's just wait and see how well she does under my supervision. That would be best for all." She looked at her watch. "I think that's all we need to talk about at this time. Please see my receptionist for the information on visitation and to schedule another appointment in, shall we say, a week?" She rose, taking some folders from the desk and tucking them under her arm.

"Thank you, Doctor. We'll do that." Jimmy said, jumping out of his seat and standing aside to let the doctor pass.

You'd think his arse was on fire, Cathy mused to herself. She did not rise from her seat.

Dr. Schmidt passed by so close that her broad hip bumped against Cathy. She paid no attention to the departing doctor. Her thoughts focused on bringing June home before the week ended.

Chapter Thirty-Two:
Swimming with the Mystics

Flames licked hotter at June's back as she was forced closer to the pyre of wood by a snarling wolf. Baring its fangs, the yellowed-eyed wolf leapt closer, snapping at her hands. She twisted sharply to one side, stepping on a burning log and screaming in pain. The heavy smoke and the rank odor of the wolf's matted black fur sickened and frightened her. The sleeves of her dress burst into flames. She beat at them, screaming out for help. An image of a woman manifested behind the wolf. It was her mother, stretching out her hands in a futile attempt to connect with her. The figure of a man appeared. June gasped, seeing it was her father brandishing a burning tree branch at her mother. Terrified, June shrieked, "No, Daddy. Mommy, help!" Her mother retreated, evaporating into shadows.

June became aware of a presence to her right. Quickly, she braved a glance and saw a young woman with waist-length red hair dressed in a dark green and yellow tartan cloak. On her shoulder perched a raven. June's father dropped the burning branch and disappeared from sight. The wolf cowered low and slunk away when the woman waved a hand high in the air. She lowered her hand and extended it to June, who grasped it. The woman led her to a path hidden between thick fir trees.

The pathway narrowed and descended gradually as June and the woman walked deeper into the woods and moved through the thick foliage. Neither spoke. June felt her energy revitalized as she soaked in the earthly smells and cool air of the forest. The woman's hands brushed over various plants as though searching for a special one. She stopped at a plant with waxy leaves. In the center of each three-leafed stem was a milky blossom. She chose one with a flower that had begun to bloom. Carefully, she plucked it, inhaled its aroma, and then tucked it into the tan leather pouch hanging from her waist. June watched quietly.

After a short time, they emerged out of the woods and into an expansive field with golden-yellow daisies scattered amongst the emerald green grass. The woman's cloak dragged across the daises as she carefully moved across the meadow and down the sloping hill toward a cove. Upon reaching the inlet, they walked to the edge of the deep gray ocean waters. Small waves rolled and curled, unraveling frothy foam at their feet.

A light dewy fog swirled around them. June sank to her knees onto the cool sand, and rested in the tranquility of the cove. The woman tossed the robe from her shoulders and lifted her dress, anchoring it in a sash at her waist. Stepping into the water, she bent down and swished her hands back and forth. June watched her. The woman treaded back to the beach, carrying a handful of dripping seaweed. Slowly, she wrapped it around the burns on June's arm, humming as she worked. The tune was familiar to June. Her mind was too jumbled to recall the title, but she knew that her mother used to sing it.

A part of the seaweed fell around the woman's wrist, linking her together with June. The woman looked at her with gray-blue eyes. The blackness of her pupils was like a mirror in which June saw her own image reflected back. Sleepiness overcame her. Her eyes closed slowly and she fell into a light sleep. Soon she awakened and heard the woman softly say, "The old way of healing is what you need. It's best for our kind." Another voice spoke, "I'll take care of her, Calleach." The Scottish goddess, June thought in awe.

❧ ❧ ❧

"Give me that," a nasal voice commanded.

June thrashed her body from side to side, trying to get away from the tight gripping around her wrists. She recognized the voice of Dr. Schmidt.

"Stop! Evil person!" June spat out.

"That's quite enough, Miss MacDonald." The doctor ordered.

June felt a sharp burning jab in her arm, followed by a sickening sensation of liquid flowing through her veins.

"I told you, Nurse Morales. When she won't cooperate and take her medicine, you *must* give it intravenously," the doctor said. "Good, now she's quieting down."

"No more. Please." June's protest was pitifully weak.

Nurse Carla Morales took June's wrist to feel her pulse. Shaking her head with worry, she felt the young patient's forehead. Burning heat radiated from it.

"You know she keeps getting fevers with this new medication, Doctor," the nurse said gravely.

"It can't be helped. My goal is to stop her hallucinations. If you're worried about a fever, ice her down," Dr. Schmidt answered.

The nurse caught June watching her through half-open, watery blue eyes. She tenderly patted the mess of tangled red curls.

"She's so frightened," she said, more to herself than the doctor.

Scribbling furiously on June's chart, Dr. Schmidt said, "I've readjusted the dosage again. And this time the voices should stop entirely. That's what's scaring this girl. It's those voices. To her they seem real—the angel, her dead sister, the nun and God only knows what other annoying characters."

June babbled a garbled retort in her drug-fogged state. The drugs, flowing through her body made her sick and intensified her visions and dreams. They had become frightening scenarios, ones that she had never seen until she had been in the hospital. Although some visions, like the one she had just experienced, gave her hope that she'd be rescued and in the safety of her mother and sisters. She longed for the company of sisters, but in the four months she had been hospitalized, they rarely came to visit.

The doctor checked her gold watch. "Oh shi... Oops... no potty words," she said snorting a laugh. Regrouping, she said, "Let's hurry up here. I've got a whole ward to finish, and I have a meeting to get to. Chop, chop, Morales. Let's move it."

"Water," croaked June. Her mouth was as dry as though it was stuffed full of cotton balls. A terrible thirst was one of the unfortunate side effects of the medication meant to control her hallucinations.

Nurse Morales poured a glass of water and raised June's head, clucking, "Here you go, sweetie. We must brush your hair. Your mother's bringing a special visitor today."

Gently, she caressed June's puffy cheeks that came with her weight gain, another side effect of the drugs.

"I don't recall seeing Mrs. MacDonald's name on the visitor's list for today. I certainly did not give permission for a new visitor," Dr. Schmidt said.

"Well, she's coming in, whether you saw it or not," the nurse answered her. "I talked with her an hour ago. And she's bringing June's favorite teacher."

Schmidt's eyebrows rose as she exclaimed, "Aha! Sister Noel! Another one who encouraged the girl's hallucinations."

"We won't have to worry about hallucinations, not with the new dosage. Shall I say that you don't want the sister to visit the patient?" Morales asked testily.

"Tell Mrs. MacDonald to schedule something for later. Oh yes. Her hair is a mess. It irritates me. Cut it, Nurse," the doctor commanded before she whipped out of the room.

"Don't worry, my little friend, I'll get them in here." Nurse Morales began to loosen the straps around the girl's swollen wrists. "Let's use your blue barrette. It'll look nice with your eyes," she told June merrily.

A hint of a smile crossed June's dry cracked lips. She knew that Dr. Schmidt's authority did not intimidate Nurse Carla Morales.

∾ ∾ ∾

On a morning after a strong dose of medicine, June vomited her breakfast. Nurse Morales and an orderly bathed her. They chatted over her as they worked. June delighted in listening to the hospital gossip. It reminded her of the fun times talking with her sisters.

Feisty Morales spouted her distaste for Dr. Schmidt. "In my twenty-odd years in this ward, I've never met such a pompous psychiatrist, and I've met some doosies. It's disgusting how she's drugging this kid."

"She don't take kindly to opposition. I'd keep my opinions to myself, if I were you," the orderly warned.

After that conversation, June trusted Nurse Morales and began to share her visions about the woman in the green cloak. The nurse listened good-naturedly, but didn't comment.

One day June grabbed Morales' wrist. "You shouldn't worry so much about your daughter's baby. It can't be stopped. He's coming soon, but he'll be okay even when the doctors say he won't be. My angel is telling me this. Please believe me. I'm not crazy," she said before lapsing into a light sleep.

A month later, Nurse Morales confided in June that her youngest daughter had gone into early labor. Thankfully, all turned out well. Although puny, the baby boy was a real fighter.

"He's being watched over by a tiny old witch-like lady who's like an angel to you. You've never met her, but you know her," June said.

Immediately, Carla Morales knew whom June was referring to. It was surely her great-grandmother.

༄ ༄ ༄

Since the age of three, Carla Morales knew she had a healing touch. She readily shared her gift with the ill or injured animals living on the family's farm. After laying her hands on a sick beast, she would tell her father what to do to help get it better. The animal usually was cured.

Her first human patient was her father, who suffered from searing headaches that caused him to lie in bed for hours. He couldn't work the family's small farm, and the chores mounted up as fast as the bills. With seven children under the age of eight, her mother could only ring her hands in despair. One morning when her father writhed in pain in a darkened bedroom, Carla had a miraculous encounter.

While playing in the barn with a litter of newborn kittens, a brilliant light appeared in front of her. Being an adventurous, strong-willed child, she was not afraid. She put her tiny brown hands into the ray's warmth. A voice of a woman spoke and told Carla to lay her hands on her father's head. She did as she was told, and laid her warm hands on either side of his head. He fell into a deep sleep that lasted for a full day. When he awoke, the headache was gone and never returned. Everyone was glad that Papi, as they called him, laughed and joked once again. His wife was happy for his renewed vigor for work. He said it was Carla's touch that had cured him.

The praise Carla received for curing her father ended when she recounted that it was a woman's voice that had guided her. Her mother reprimanded Carla, telling her to beware, for the voice might be the Devil trying to steal her soul. Frightened by the thought of evil working through her, she pushed the voice away when it came again.

Years later when she was studying to be a nurse, her mother revealed that Carla's gift of healing was connected to her Mexican heritage. Her mother's grandmother had been a well-respected healer, known as a *curandera* in Mexico. She had a wide knowledge of herbs and other natural remedies to cure illnesses. She also was a mystic healer, who could cast out evil spirits invading the bodies of the sick to restore good health to a person's mind and heart. That was the true healing force, her mother had said.

Carla had always sensed the voice who spoke to her had been her great-grandmother and she questioned her mother to why she was warned off accepting the voice. Her mother had said that when they arrived in the States for a new life, Papi decided it would best for the family to forget the old ways.

Relieved that her healing powers were not evil, Carla prayed to the curandera for guidance. Soon her enthusiasm for the study of the human psyche was ignited. She gravitated toward nursing in the psychiatry ward where she, too, could help heal the spirits of those with mental pain.

Over the years she had experienced a few uncanny incidents with schizophrenic patients. One patient vividly related a dream that Carla had the previous night, while another described Carla's home in exact detail—room by room. And then there was June's prediction that Carla would travel to another country, where she would meet a woman who would teach her about the healing power of plants and herbs. She listened to June's prediction, but she was too emotional to speak, and didn't confirm or deny her young patient's psychic information. What Carla didn't reveal was that she had often dreamt that she would travel to Mexico to search for a curandera. But she always woke up before finding her.

Carla's interest in psychiatry led her to continue her education in the field. Her doubts about Dr. Schmidt's diagnosis of June's problem were supported by Joseph Campbell's book "Hero with a Thousand Faces," which toppled out of a bookshelf right into her hands as she researched information on mental patients in her library of medical books. Since she was a person who respected the magic of life's unplanned events, Carla thought is was not a coincidence that this book had come to her.

Many years ago when studying psychiatry, she had a favorite passage in Campbell's book: "The schizophrenic is drowning in the same waters in which the mystic swims with delight." Carla meditated on the passage. She now had a clearer understanding of what Campbell had written, and began to believe her intuitive thoughts that June was not mentally ill.

She observed June closely, and listened to her delusions carefully. She began to realize the girl truly seemed to have the ability of visions. The stout, dark-haired nurse became a staunch advocate for her young patient's freedom.

Chapter Thirty-Three:
The Circle Widens

THE EARLY OCTOBER morning threatened rain with its gloom. It matched Cathy's mood. She sat on the edge of her bed, exhausted after another fitful night with dreams of June calling to her for help.

The past five months had felt as though she were in a never-ending nightmare from which she couldn't wake up. Cathy would always remember 1964 as a hellish year. June had turned fourteen while in the hospital. She missed her Confirmation and graduation from Holy Savior, and didn't have the chance to start high school. Those special times in her daughter's life could never be experienced again. She needed to bring her daughter home, and prayed for it to be soon.

Cathy's resolve to fight for her daughter's release had been bogged down within the first months of June's admittance to the psych ward, and she received no support from Jimmy. He was completely happy to leave his daughter's fate in Dr. Schmidt's hands, whereas Cathy was not confident in the doctor's diagnosis. When she sought solace from Holy Savior's Monsignor, he had offered no empathy for June's situation. He had told Cathy that the girl was being punished for her sacrilegious ways. After that, over Jimmy's loud protests, Cathy had stopped going to Mass. Eventually their differences alienated them, and she moved into June's bedroom. With no one to turn to, she felt at her wit's end.

She rolled over and took her rosary beads from the bedstand. Closing her eyes, she began to pray a "Hail Mary," and suddenly remembered that she had promised to meet with Nurse Morales. She tugged off the patchwork quilt blanket and dragged her tired body out of bed.

June's nurse, who had always been kindly and helpful, had approached Cathy in the visitor's lounge the week before. In hushed tones, she asked that they meet outside the hospital. The nurse said she might have useful information that would help move along June's recovery. The conversation abruptly ended when Dr. Schmidt appeared and demanded the nurse's assistance. As Nurse Morales turned to follow her, she gave Cathy a conspirator's wink.

~ ~ ~

Cathy met Carla Morales at a small donut shop on Mission Street a few blocks from the hospital. They squeezed past two tall police officers who nodded a friendly greeting to the women. Ignoring the seductive scents of freshly baked donuts, they ordered just coffee, black for the nurse and heavily creamed with a few spoonfuls of sugar for Cathy. They picked up their cups and moved to the farthest corner to sit at a small, round table.

Carla immediately got to the point. The drugs being given to June, which were actually quite helpful in treating schizophrenia, were causing the young girl serious side effects, physically and emotionally.

"If some intervention doesn't occur soon, I'm afraid of the long-term damage. I encourage you to seek a second opinion." She laid a slip of paper on the table. "Here's the number of a friend of mine, Dr. Weissman, the best psychiatrist I've ever worked with. He's retired, but still very influential in his field, and he's not afraid of Dr. Schmidt. I've already talked with him."

Gingerly, Cathy picked up the paper and murmured, "Thank you for your help."

"You might find him a tad bit. . . umm. . . he's a character," the nurse confided.

"If you mean he's different from the others, then I think June will do well with him." Cathy attempted a weak laugh.

"Your daughter's been my inspiration. Because of her I've had to be honest with myself. More than you'll ever know."

Carla's parting words, "The time has come to encircle June with our protection," coincided with Cathy's thoughts. She decided that now was time to move forward.

୧୨ ୧୨ ୧୨

Sitting on the bus going home, Cathy felt euphoric. Hope filled her heart that June would come home soon. Two young teens got on the bus, one with very wide flowered bellbottoms and the other with fishnet hosiery and a shamefully short skirt. *Everything is changing so fast nowadays. Me too,* she thought.

Her focus changed to her next task—to win over Jimmy to the plan.

Getting off the bus at Castro Street, Cathy stopped by the butcher shop to buy Jimmy's favorite cut of meat, T-bone steak, and a few cheaper steaks for the rest of the family. She hesitated as she walked past the liquor store. She counted her household allowance to decide if she should buy a bottle of whiskey for Jimmy. Deciding against adding fuel to his already hot temper, she opted instead to buy a chocolate cake for dessert. After all, Annie was bringing Dave as a guest.

Jimmy hadn't really warmed up to Annie's boyfriend, although he no longer forbade him to come to the house. The two men had even had a brief discussion about how well the Giants' baseball team was doing. Cathy and Annie had discussed that it was time that Jimmy accepted Dave, so they agreed on a plan for a dinner where the two could get to know each other better.

The morning of the dinner, Annie had cornered her father on his way out the door to work, to ask if Dave could come to dinner to celebrate his acceptance into the Police Academy. Jimmy had said it was okay.

Dinner was ready at exactly six o'clock. Jimmy liked having his meal served the minute he arrived home. However, on this night, he wasn't home at six.

Cathy's cheerful mood started to fade as she fretted over keeping his steak warm. The silly bantering between Dave and Mary began to annoy her.

"Mom, do you think Daddy forgot?" Annie inquired, nervously biting her lower lip.

"Yeah, sure he forgot. Let's just start without him," Mary said, picking up her plate.

Cathy's face was tight with displeasure. She took Mary's plate and began to spoon mashed potatoes and peas onto it. "No use waiting," she said irritably.

"Not too much. I'm dieting," Mary said.

Dave was stroking Annie's arm, telling her, "Don't worry, hon. He'll be here."

Just then the front door banged loudly.

"His Majesty's here," Mary muttered, under her breath.

At first sight they knew Jimmy had had more than a few drinks. The lopsided grin on his red face and his bloodshot bleary eyes were dead giveaways.

"Ahhh, dinner's ready. What a good wife you are," he said slurring the last two words together.

Cathy abruptly slammed down a plate on the table, sending the peas and potatoes flying up in the air.

"What the bloody hell!" Jimmy exclaimed.

"Daddy, please," Annie said calmly as she rose to pull out her father's chair at the head of the table, so he could sit down.

He stumbled over and plunked down heavily, rocking the water glasses on the table. Dave immediately started a conversation with him about baseball. The topic helped to lighten the tension while dinner was eaten.

Cathy sat in silence, her face as white as her best tablecloth that was spread across the dining room table. With her head hanging low, she pushed her food around her plate. *Why can't I believe I'd be better off without him?* she said to herself, as she pondered dark thoughts about her marriage.

She raised her head to the sounds of clinking spoons and requests to pass the milk or sugar. A cup of steaming black tea appeared in front of her. Annie smiled down at her mother as she placed a slice of cake next to her tea. Cathy saw Annie nudge Dave with her elbow as she sat back down next to him.

Dave smoothed back his hair, cleared his throat and sputtered forth, "Umm, Mr. MacDonald. Annie and me, we. . . umm, would like to get married, sir. If that's okay with you, sir."

Somewhat sobered by the food, Jimmy carefully placed his cup down onto the saucer before speaking. "You seem like a good enough young man. It's just that you two are too young. You're no ready for marriage."

Cathy saw her daughter's jaw clench, grinding her teeth. "We are ready, Daddy," Annie said, her hands balled into tight fists.

Dave placed a hand over hers, but spoke to Jimmy. "Mr. MacDonald, I've been accepted into the Police Academy. I'm going to make decent money."

"Will you become a Catholic?" Jimmy asked.

Dave raised his eyebrows. "I'm not really a religious kind of person, Mr. MacDonald. So, why lie. But I've already agreed that our children will be baptized Catholic, if that helps."

"We're getting married, and that's that," Annie said wrapping her arms around her midriff and looking sternly at her father.

"Over my dead body will I give you permission to marry," Jimmy blared.

Annie's response was sharp. "You've got no control over this. I'm nineteen, I don't need your permission."

"I'll no bless this marriage," said Jimmy, fiercely.

"Since when did you ever thank me for anything I've done for this family? I don't need your blessing!" Annie said furiously.

Abruptly, father and daughter stood up, squaring off. Annie's face had become as red as her father's. Dave stood next to her. Mary silently sneaked out of the room.

"Out of my house!" Jimmy demanded, pointing towards the direction of the front door.

"You'll not throw out another one, Jimmy MacDonald! I'll not have it," Cathy spoke up. To the young couple she said, "You have *my* blessing."

Jimmy's beady eyes peered into his wife's face. He threw his hands up in the air. "I wash my hands of all of you. Get married and have a load of wee bastards."

Dave tugged Annie's hand to pull her from the room. Before budging, Annie said, "Mom?"

Cathy told them to leave.

When the room was cleared, she spoke. "I've had it. You're killing me."

"Me? It's your whore daughters," Jimmy said defensively.

Ignoring his insult, Cathy said, "First, it's my baby locked up for months in that nut house! Then my Maggie, and now Annie. Who do you think you are, throwing them out? It's *my* house, too!" she said hotly.

❦ ❦ ❦

Maggie had come to her mother in late September to confess that she was four months pregnant, and that Tim was the father. After the shock, Cathy assured her eighteen-year-old daughter that they'd work something out. Finding the courage to tell Jimmy, her worst fears were realized.

Jimmy ranted and raved about how sex before marriage was a sin, and about the horrible shame of having a baby with a colored boy. When he insisted on speaking with Tim's father, Maggie reluctantly gave him the telephone number. After a curt introduction, he got to the purpose of the call, only to learn that Tim's father was equally upset. He told Jimmy that his son would be attending the University of California at Berkeley, and that marriage was out of the question, especially to a white girl. After Jimmy slammed down the phone, he turned on Maggie and threw her out of the house by the scruff of her neck. When Cathy objected, he yelled, "You condone her having a bastard child?"

Cathy's answer was to grab a coat off a peg in the hallway and join her daughter outside. Together they went to the Callaghans where Sadie and Bernice welcomed Maggie into their home, and later helped her find an apartment.

ᕲ ᕲ ᕲ

Jimmy slurped his tea as Cathy gathered dishes off the table. She could not calm her fuming thoughts. Her voice echoed in the spacious room. "What kind of father are you to abandon your daughters when they need you the most?"

Her comment startled him. "What a joke, coming from you. Going to bed every time there's a problem and leaving me to manage the girls."

She jabbed a finger up to his face. "Don't you dare judge me. You, get out of the house."

With his face menacingly close to hers, he said with measured words, "I worked for this house. It's mine. All of it, mine!"

"I'm not yours. No, never was I yours," Cathy answered him through clenched teeth.

"I married you, even knowing I was getting a whore," Jimmy said cruelly.

"That's what drove June to madness—always denying her the truth. She sees things we can't. She's fey. I know it," Cathy screamed, her voice becoming hysterical. "I'm going to bring her home," she said in a trembling voice.

"Women! Bah! Crazy lot. Burn them at birth!" Jimmy yelled as he banged out of the room and up the stairs.

Cathy finished picking up the dishes and moved toward the kitchen. The light of the moon caught her attention. She placed the dishes on the kitchen counter and walked through the back porch and out under the October sky.

The night air was brisk and refreshing. The illuminated moon was more than a half circle. In a couple of days it would be swollen to its fullness. The scent of a neighbor's burning wood fireplace drifted through the air. The branches of the large tree in their yard moved as a cat jumped onto the roof of the porch. She thought of the time when she had stood on a hilltop making a wish for the future. If there was ever a time to fortify that desire, it was now.

Cathy carefully unhooked her nylons from the garter belt and folded them inside her slippers. She unbuttoned her blouse and let it slip to the ground. She tugged at her skirt and let it fall, too. Her bra and panties swiftly joined the other pieces on the ground. Naked to the celestial skies, she stood with her arms outstretched to the pale orb above her. With the grit of a warrioress going to battle, she cast her spell.

"Mother Moon, goddess of wisdom, insight and love. Great Calleach and Juno, goddesses of power. I call upon you to stand by my side as I manifest a loving healing within my family. Blessed be, so mote it be."

Chapter Thirty-Four:
The Wise Man

THE BUS RIDE from Eureka Valley to Russian Hill was an anxious journey for Cathy. She was worried about her meeting with Dr. Weissman. Would he really understand June, or would he scoff at her as so many others had?

The nippy Fall morning reminded her of the many times June had rushed into the house after school, with cheeks rosy from the crisp weather, red hair sprouting in every direction, blue eyes dancing with life, and full of tales about school. As quickly as she had entered, she would run off to play with Brian. That now seemed so long ago.

Catching a reflection of herself in the window, she patted down the baby-blue pillbox hat to secure it on her head, and noted how wornout she looked for her forty-four years. Even with her best woolen jacket and a new hat, she was uncertain if she was presentable enough to visit Pacific Heights, one of San Francisco's upper-class neighborhoods.

"Jesus, Mary and Joseph," Cathy gasped for breath as she reached the front door of Dr. Weissman's apartment building, perched on top of Hyde and Lombard Streets. Afraid of being late, she had opted to doggedly climb the steep hills instead of waiting for the cable car, all the time cursing her decision to wear high heels.

Finding Dr. J. Weissman's name on the list of occupants on the callbox outside his building, she pressed the button to ring his apartment. A moment later, a loud buzz indicated that the door had been unlocked and she could enter. The elevator ride was a quick, smooth ride up to the doctor's fourth-floor home office. On his door was a large brass bull's head knocker. Cathy laughed, lifted its nose ring and banged down sharply. Before her hand came to rest, the door was flung open. An elderly man with a face decorated with many deeply grooved lines stood before her. Thick-lensed horn-rimmed glasses magnified his lively brown eyes. A pleasant smile framed by a pencil thin mustache and a sparse gray goatee gave him a positively impish appearance. She could see that Dr. Jacob Weissman, a small man stooped with age, was full of robust life.

She would have laughed at this delightfully cheerful-looking old man if she hadn't known of his importance. Nurse Morales had said Dr. Weissman was an esteemed psychiatrist, whose long career had included being chief of psychiatry at Langley Porter at the University of California, San Francisco. He had also written a book on schizophrenia, and sat on several prestigious boards of directors for organizations dealing with the advancement of treatment for mental disorders.

"Mrs. MacDonald, I assume?" he said with a lilt of laughter.

She smiled broadly and nodded slightly, not wanting to upset her hat.

"Please come in," he said stepping aside.

Cathy entered a long hallway, painted a deep red. The walls were covered with colorful artwork. She wanted to stop and enjoy them, but was shy about taking up the doctor's time. He motioned her in the direction of a soft light shining at the end of the hallway, which led to a spacious living room. Her high heels sank into a luxurious Oriental carpet with brilliant yellow flowers woven throughout. A sleek Siamese cat curled in the center of a red velvet ottoman opened a lazy eye, then faded back to sleep in the warmth of the sun. The beautiful room was an uplifting delight for Cathy.

The doctor took a pile of magazines off a dark-tan leather chair. "I'll be right with you," he said, as he scurried out of the room.

Cathy stood facing a floor-to-ceiling picture window. She stepped over to it, and was awestruck by the spectacular panoramic view that spread out beneath her. The late October dew clung to the buildings, glistening in the sunlight. The sapphire blue sky, patched with billowy clouds, matched the blue of the shimmering Bay waters. Above the water, towered the majestic Golden Gate Bridge. The orange paint on the bridge reminded Cathy of the day her family had first crossed the bridge ten years ago. She remembered being surprised to find out that it wasn't gold. She thought back to the day the gypsy had predicted that she'd cross a bridge of gold to live in a faraway place. The gypsy had been right, although she didn't pay heed. At the time, she was still a young woman full of romantic notions of living with a handsome, loving husband in a wee cottage in the Highlands.

A flock of birds flew by. One straggled behind, before disappearing into a fluffy cloud. The others flew on, across the bridge and toward the Marin Headlands. Cathy felt sad for the slower bird. She wanted to call out to the flock to wait. The birds and the clouds brought to her an image of Helen. She pined for her dead child. *Didn't I fly away from her in search of some peace of mind?* She reproached herself. Tears glistened in her eyes. Her breath became ragged as she struggled to hold back the tears.

"Here we go." Dr. Weissman's voice startled her.

Embarrassed that he'd see her teary eyes, she spoke to him over her shoulder. "This view is so very beautiful."

After a few moments, she turned to find a silver tray sitting on the oval coffee table. It held a white teapot decorated with pale pink roses and two matching cups.

"Tea?" he asked.

"Please," she said eyeing the platter of assorted cookies and feeling hunger pangs. She nodded "yes" to some cream, and settled into a chair, eager to enjoy a cup of hot tea.

Dr. Weissman first poured a thick cream into a cup and then added the steaming black tea, blending the liquids into a perfect light brown.

Picking up silver tongs, he asked, "Sugar?"

Cathy enjoyed the familiar ritual. "Two, please," she said, relaxing her tightly crossed ankles and hands.

He delicately dropped the lumps of sugar into the teacup. Cathy gratefully accepted the tea and nestled comfortably into the chair. She slipped out of the tight heels (an unusual thing for her to do in public) and dug her toes into the thick carpet.

"When we lived in Ireland we learned to appreciate a good cup of tea," said the doctor, holding out the plate of cookies. She chose a butter cream. He poured himself a cup, and settled back on a long couch and faced her.

"Shouldn't I be on the couch?" Cathy joked.

"Freud would agree with you," the doctor said in good humor.

"Was your wife Irish?" she asked.

"Yes, but born in America. In the '50s we moved to Ireland so she could find her roots, as she put it. A most adventurous, spirited woman!" Dr. Weissman exclaimed. His eyes drifted over to an end table full of framed photographs.

Cathy focused on a black-and-white photo of a woman with dark wavy hair, smoldering eyes and full lips in a pouting half smile. It was hard not to notice the photo. The woman looked like the sultry movie star, Rita Hayward.

"That's Peggy, my wife. It was my charm, not my looks, that got her," he chuckled.

Silently, Cathy agreed. "How long were you married?"

"Forty-four years before cancer took her life," the doctor answered.

"I'm sorry," Cathy said.

"Actually, our many happy years are what we focused on during her illness. She made me promise to always think of her in that way," Dr. Weissman explained.

"At least you have happy memories. Losing love is awfully tragic," Cathy said pensively.

"Love is never lost though, not if your love is true. Isn't that so?" He smiled nostalgically.

She looked at him, uncertain of where to start her story, and skittish about admitting there was truth in June's vision about the redheaded angel and hilltop with daisies. Would he think she was also delusional as Dr. Schmidt thought of June?

"Do you have children, doctor?" she inquired.

"Two," he said.

Cocking her head at a photo of two young men with their arms around each other's shoulders, she asked, "Are those them?"

He pointed to the wavy dark-haired man. "Sam is, and Mike's his boyfriend."

Cathy's mouth fell open at his calm candor that his son was a homosexual. She wasn't naive about people of the same sex having relationships. There had been gossip up and down Castro Street for years that Sadie and Bernice were lesbians. It hadn't influenced her friendship with them, but it wasn't a subject discussed openly. She now knew that Jacob Weissman was not a man to follow the mainstream of society. Perhaps he would accept June's independent thinking.

"Most parents would be mortified if a son or daughter admitted that," he said. "All I know is my son is happily in love, and that's good enough for me. In my field I've seen and heard a lot. One of the most damaging things I hear is how hurtful it can be to deny one's true self, and live a life of lies just to appease others."

Is he that good that he can read me so well? Cathy wondered guiltily.

She shifted in her seat. Watching the old man sipping tea in the sunny living room as calmly as the sleeping cat, she pondered, *Who am I to judge another person's children when one of my own is locked up for thinking she's a witch? And another is having an illegitimate baby with a colored boy. Then there's Annie, my most practical daughter,*

*rushing to marry at City Hall and not marry in the Church. I suspect
she's pregnant, too. At least Mary isn't a problem.*

"Your other child?" she asked politely, hoping not to appear too
shocked at the doctor's information.

"My daughter is as adventurous as her mother. She lives in
Brazil," he said.

"What's she doing there?" Cathy asked, very curious about this
most unusual family.

"She's an anthropologist, studying the indigenous people's
witch doctors and their power to heal."

"Witch doctor? Do you believe that kind of person really
exists?" she asked cautiously.

Chuckling, he answered, "Not by that name, but yes. Brazilian
Indians have a *xamã*, a man of great knowledge of healing herbs and
plants. He's also a sorcerer who can use spells involving the forces
of nature to create a magical energy to heal. For instance, to heal a
sickness, the xamã passes incense over the body while praying to rid
the person of the evil spirits causing the illness. People believe, thus
a healing usually occurs."

"Do you believe in magic, Dr. Weissman?" Cathy asked,
cautiously.

"I think our minds have a greater influence over our health and
life conditions than we admit. If that is seen as magic, then yes, I do
believe in it. And you, Mrs. MacDonald?"

Cathy shrugged her shoulders. "I'm not sure I have faith in
anything anymore. But if it's magic that will bring my daughter
home, then tell me the spell to cast."

"Tell me about June," Dr. Weissman said sitting back with his
hands folded on his rounded belly.

From what the doctor had told her, Cathy trusted that he
would understand the difficulties of being a parent to a child that
was a social outcast. She told him her problem had started when she
gave June her name, a name that Jimmy had adamantly objected
to. Going against her husband had caused much trouble for the

family. Jimmy blamed her when June started telling stories about her conversations with an angel, and when she started seeing dead people, and when she got in trouble with her tarot cards. Cathy thought that maybe it was her fault. She recited all her failings as a mother, and admitted feeling sick over her guilt of not being a good enough mother. She told the doctor that she would go to bed hoping to sleep away her problems, which left many of the household responsibilities to her children. She wiped away a tear as she confessed that Jimmy's temper frightened her, which was why she didn't defend her daughters when he disciplined them harshly. Her unhappy marriage felt like a thankless job.

"You didn't marry the man you loved?" Dr. Weissman asked quietly.

To Cathy it sounded more as a statement and she was stunned by his observation. She was unable to answer immediately. "No, I didn't, Doctor," she finally admitted.

Cathy wondered if it would help if Dr. Weissman knew about her role in June's difficulties. The entire family had suffered because of the secrets and lies she had insisted on keeping. Freely, she told the story from the beginning.

It started with the lover she had before her marriage to Jimmy.

"It was 1940. The German bombs were devastating England, especially London. I wanted to help. So, off I went to London to fight the war. I was a young, naive girl who believed I knew everything. I was just like June, only a bit older at nineteen."

"Your parents agreed to your leaving?" he asked.

"My father forbade it. It wasn't like nowadays where young people leave home without their parents' permission. And certainly no decent a woman my age would move out alone, unless she was to be married. My father told me, 'You're just a lassie and you're no going off alone.' " Cathy spoke her father's words with a Glaswegian accent.

Her Scottish burr grew more distinct as she continued the story. "He was overly protective of me since the death of my brother,

Francis. Besides, I was his wee darling, being the youngest and the only girl with five brothers."

"And your mother?" the doctor asked.

"She and I were very close, and had always got along as thick as thieves when it came to getting my father to agree to our plans. She talked my father into letting me go. She told him that Stevie, my oldest brother who was in the war office in London, would take care of me. I remember the day I left Glasgow. It was an unusually clear, dry day for March. My mother came with me to the train station."

༄ ༄ ༄

Glasgow's central train station was bustling with the early morning activity of passengers arriving and departing from the many train platforms. Dropping a sturdy brown suitcase in the station's café, Cathy's mother scurried off to buy two cups of tea.

Upon returning, she immediately repeated her orders to Cathy, "Now, hen, when Stevie meets you at the train station, you telegraph me right away."

"I know, Mammy," Cathy said, and then, "What about Daddy?"

"Don't you worry about him. Now listen to me, lassie. There's lots of men roaming around in London. You be careful. Your Daddy's hoping that you and Jimmy MacDonald will get married when you get back."

"For God's sake, Mammy! I can't stand him with those beady eyes an' all. Besides, he's ancient!" Cathy wailed.

"Och lassie! He's only thirty-one. The same age as Stevie," Granny reasoned with her daughter.

"Mammy, I'm no even twenty yet."

"Don't remind me that we'll no be together next month for your birthday. The first time ever. I wished you waited until afterwards, don't you?"

Cathy pursed her lips and scowled, ignoring her mother and watching a middle-aged gypsy woman in a long colored skirt make her way around the crowd. She stopped to talk to a very tall red-haired man. He laughed heartily and handed the woman his teacup. Cathy was keen on the handsome muscular young man in the naval uniform. As though sensing her scrutiny, he looked straight over at her. Her stomach lurched and her face reddened at being caught spying.

"Maybe I'll fall in love in London," she said dreamily.

"Don't you dare bring home a Sassenach," her mother said strongly, referring to name the Scots called the English.

"Maybe an American, like Clark Gable," Cathy said jokingly.

"You'd no leave your mammy for Hollywood, would you?" her mother chided.

They sipped their tea and talked about handsome movie stars until her mother announced that she better be getting home.

"Don't go yet. Wait 'til my train comes," Cathy said realizing they were truly parting for the first time in her life.

"Sorry, pet, your daddy will be wanting his supper. Cheerio, my wee darling. May the Blessed Mother protect you." She cupped her daughter's face in her gloved hands. "Come home to me, you hear?"

"I promise." Cathy moved closer to her mother. An awkward silence hung between them. After a quick kiss on Cathy's cheek, her mother hurried away.

"Mammy!" Cathy called after her, raising a hand to wave. But her mother was already lost in the crowd.

Nervously, she chewed her lips as she peered toward the trains. A sudden chill went through her and she pulled her red coat snuggly around her. Feeling a hand on her arm, she spun around to look into the dark face of the gypsy.

"I can see your future. Love beckons to you," the woman said, motioning to Cathy's empty teacup. The gypsy lifted the cup close to her face and circled it around from the left to the right. Her dark eyes peered at the leaves clinging inside it. The loud sounds of people and trains caused them to huddle close. Cathy heard her say something about crossing a gold bridge and love.

After a moment of listening, she gave the gypsy a few coins and sent her on her way. She then hoisted her heavily packed handbag on her shoulder and bent down to pick up the suitcase. A hand reached it before she did.

"Let me help you with that," the red-haired man in the Navy uniform said in the soft voice of a Scot from the Highlands.

"Oh! Thank you," Cathy said, pleased at his attention.

"I'm Malcolm Macleod. And you are?" he asked.

The loud noise of trains pulling into the station drowned out her answer.

∾ ∾ ∾

Cathy smiled sadly as she continued her the story to Dr. Weissman. "Malcolm Macleod was the name of my handsome lover from the Isle of Skye. That's in the Highlands of Scotland. We took the train together to London. He was returning back to duty. I was on my way to my new job to help children find safe homes in the countryside, outside of London and away from the bombing."

"My brother Stevie met me at the train station when I arrived there. He was pleasant to Malcolm, seeing that he was also in the military. Stevie had secured me a room in a boarding house for young women. That way my morals wouldn't be in question. Before I left the station, I snuck Malcolm the address. On my second night in London, he was waiting for me in front of the boarding house. We went for fish and chips, but before we could even eat our meal, the sirens sounded. Oh, doctor, if you've ever heard those loud sirens screaming, you know how your heart stops. And you don't even think of death. You can only think of getting away from the noise. We dropped our food and ran."

"The whole of London went into darkness as we ran along the streets trying to find a bomb shelter. Buildings were exploding. People were screaming and yelling. It was bedlam. We clung to each other and waited out the bombing in the corridor of a building. That was our first date," Cathy said with a weak laugh.

"Later on, after he and I knew we were truly in love, we decided to hurry and marry because he was shipping out. In my weekly letter home, I arranged a day and time to telephone my parents from my boarding house. Our parish priest was good about letting people use the telephone in the rectory for important business. In those days most people in Glasgow couldn't afford to have phones in their homes. I was very nervous, but full of hope that my love for Malcolm would win over my parents about us marrying."

"I called the rectory where my parents were waiting for my call. When I told my mother I wanted to marry Malcolm, she handed the phone to my father. He asked if he was Catholic, which many Highlanders are. Malcolm was not. My father threatened that I could be excommunicated from the Catholic Church if I married him. As you probably know, Catholics were not expected to marry outside of their religion without grave consequences, such as being ostracized from their family and religion."

"Were your excommunicated?"

"No. That would have been up to our parish monsignor and with Glasgow also being heavily bombed, I don't think he was too interested in my sins. I knew it was just my father's way of trying to get me to do what he thought was best."

Dr. Weissman shook the pot of tea and then refreshed her cup. "At least he wasn't a Sassenach. Your mother must have been glad for that."

"She didn't want me to marry a man from such a faraway place. I think she was afraid I'd leave her. But my father said that I'd no longer be welcome at home if I went through with it. I was as stubborn as him and said that I'd do what I wanted with or without his permission," Cathy explained.

"How did you feel about that?" he asked.

"Devastated," she said bitterly and then, sadly, "So horribly alone, separated from my family for the first time in my life. That was my first mortal sin. I loved a man without the sanction of the Holy Church."

She told him about the gripping heartache of saying good-bye to her lover, who departed for the war only a couple of weeks after the phone conversation. Alone and angry with her father and saddened by her job of separating children from their parents, she went to live in Skye with Malcolm's mother, who welcomed her. When Malcolm died fighting in the war, her parents came to bring her home to Glasgow. She hung her head and began to cry.

Dr. Weissman handed Cathy a large cotton hankie as she sobbed. After a moment he asked, "Does Jimmy know about your lover?"

"Oh, yes. He was part of my mother's scheme to redeem me and make an honest woman of me. I went back to Glasgow and married him, and life went on," she said reflectively.

"But the past shadowed your life, has it not, Mrs. MacDonald?"

Dabbing her eyes dry, Cathy said, "Enough of me. What about June?"

"Does she know about Malcolm?"

"Strangely, I think she does. It seems to be part of her visions ever since she was a little girl. One time she showed me a picture in a magazine of a tall man kissing a woman at a train station. It frightened me so much to think that my children might know about my secret past that I, well, I hate to admit, I yelled at her to stop with her story. I buried any memories I had of Malcolm and my life in Skye a long time ago. How can she know?"

"Somehow, you are sharing your past memories with her through your thoughts. It can be called thought transference or telepathy. We can explore that with June," he said.

"I'd like to know more about it because June has said some uncanny things ever since she was just a wee thing. Like seeing an angel in the sky watching us. I used to pray to an angel to watch over Malcolm when he was at sea. And the yellow daisies June always loved. They're like the kind I used to pick on the Isle to make daisy chains. It's almost as though June's been in Skye."

"Or, that Skye is in June," the doctor said.

Cathy's spirit had lifted with the confession of her secret past. But still, most important to her, she wanted to know when the doctor thought June could come home.

"Before I can talk to you about releasing your daughter, I'll first meet with June and get to know her. I'll also have to run tests and find out what medication she is taking. This is the only way I can truly evaluate the situation fairly."

"I think I should warn you that Dr. Schmidt is a very controlling person, who doesn't like her power challenged." Cathy said, while slipping into her high heels.

Dr. Weissman removed his glasses and wiped them clean with a napkin. "Oh yes, Deborah Schmidt. She was once a student of mine. Such an ambitious young woman," he said with a delightful chuckle.

Her heart sunk. Had she said the wrong thing? Would he now dismiss her as a neurotic mother who didn't understand the purpose of psychiatry?

"Deborah and I will have a little chat," Dr. Weissman said reassuringly.

Cathy laughed out loud, which surprised the cat rubbing against her leg. She petted his black face and thought that she'd take time to enjoy the art in the hallway on her way out.

Chapter Thirty-Five:
Cleansing June's Energy

THE FRIDAY BEFORE Thanksgiving, Cathy met Dr. Weissman for their weekly meeting to discuss June's situation. He told her that June wouldn't be released for that holiday. Cathy complained to him that her daughter had been in the hospital for six months, and that she wanted her home for Christmas at the latest.

"It's a greater challenge than I initially thought," he told her, and added an explanation of his position. He said that traditional psychological practice would have declared June to be mentally ill. However, he was confident with his judgment that June's case was different. He closely observed how some mentally ill patients, like June, displayed their psychic impressions. He felt that such unusual cases allowed him to be more objective.

There were also a few serious problems that he wanted to deal with before allowing June to go home. In good faith, he agreed with Dr. Schmidt that the process of purging the medications from their young patient's system by cutting back the dosage would continue to produce unpleasant mental reactions, and some unexpected physical ones as well. Also, June's conversations with unseen characters had become more frequent. Dr. Schmidt, who had no belief in psychic phenomena, voiced her concern that her patient's psychosis was only worsening.

Dr. Weissman was very curious about one of June's visions that seemed to match some of the details Cathy had given about Malcolm's death. He told Cathy what he had heard.

The foghorn sounded louder as June and the red-haired woman moved closer to the beach. The mist was especially dense that morning. June felt mysterious changes in the air. With the red-haired woman she had named Angel, June began picking purple blossoms from a large leafy plant in the forest. The woman said it was time to heal the poison that the enemy had given to her.

When their hands were full, they went to the cove. The rhythm of the surging waves soothed June's spirit. They moved further down the incline and onto the beach. Between two large rocks they spotted a long shape laying half on the sand and half in the water. They rushed over and discovered it to be a young man dressed in a dark woolen jacket with brass buttons and dark pants covering heavy laced-up boots. His face was waxy white and his mouth slack. Two ringlets of his hair dripped down on his forehead, giving him a boyish appearance. He lay in sad repose, his eyes closed to the light of day. Even in death, he looked peaceful and handsome. Seaweed entwined his arms close to his body.

June looked out to the ocean to see if perhaps a boat had capsized and tossed him into the water. But there was nothing. Angel said that his body came as an offering from the ocean deep to lie there on this isle in his final sleep.

Two shadowy figures came down the beach toward them. One was a tiny woman dressed in black with a shawl wrapped around her head. With her wrinkled face, June thought she looked like an old crone. The other was a younger woman in a flowing dress and cardigan buttoned up to her throat to protect her from the cold wet air. She wore a flowered scarf that had slipped low on her forehead, somewhat obscuring her face. She carried a yellow daisy chain that was so long it trailed behind her.

June was taken by surprise when Angel called out to the women, "He's come home to us."

The women walked over to June and Angel. The older woman immediately fell to her knees before the corpse. The younger woman cried "Malcolm!" as she pushed back her headscarf. Her long blonde hair cascaded down her shoulders. She started to wail.

June's mouth fell open in shock when she recognized the blonde woman. It was her mother, even though her face was much younger.

"Bidh sàmhach," the old crone said sharply.

By the way the word had been said, June could tell that her mother was being told to be quiet.

Cathy paid heed to the crone, and her wailing became a soft crying. She knelt down next to the body and stroked Malcolm's cold cheeks. Her fingers twirled around his red curls as her salty tears dripped onto his face.

Angel joined them. She placed her hand on his heart.

June watched the three—the crone, her mother and Angel—pull the body from the water and up onto the sand. They gently unraveled the long ropes of seaweed from his body. When Malcolm was free, they encircled his body with the daisy chain. Seeing the women work in quiet unison, she felt a deep bond between them, and she desired to be part of it.

The crone crossed Malcolm's arms on his chest and began to speak in a language strange to June.

Angel said to June, "She's saying a prayer for his eternal rest in his new home, the after-world."

In a voice barely audible against the frigid Artic winds, Cathy said, "She's speaking Gaelic, the true tongue of the Highlanders before the Sassenach forbade them to speak it."

The crone spoke to June. Cathy translated, "Our journey is not over. You will be the one to reunite us in peace when the truth is known. Until then, your visions will not cease to trouble you."

June was puzzled by how her mother knew Gaelic. Cathy handed June the end of the daisy chain to complete the circle around Malcolm.

∽ ∽ ∽

"Oh Mother of God!" Cathy gasped when she heard Dr. Weissman's retelling of June's vision. "It's true Malcolm was found by another—a fisherman found his body in the water. His mother and I ran down to the beach when we heard. But all the rest, the angel helping to heal June, I don't know. If I could just bring her home I could help her understand more," she said pleadingly.

"Please trust us. We're doing the best for your daughter," the old doctor assured her.

She didn't tell him that Nurse Morales had confided in her that he had thought of a way to secure cooperation from Dr. Schmidt to release June to his care. He had charmed Dr. Schmidt with a promise to co-author a book on the treatment of schizoid personalities.

Cathy had no recourse but to trust him and Carla. She planned a Thanksgiving dinner without June.

∽ ∽ ∽

The four months it took to wean June off the drugs had been tough going for the slight fourteen-year-old. On a good day, June was again her natural self—optimistic and funny. But most days she was agitated and restless. Her swollen body had thinned down, and was now returning to her normal weight as the drugs drained out of her. Her hair, shorn in the hospital on Dr. Schmidt's orders, had come back a stronger Titian-red. The once wild curls had softened to loose waves that framed her face.

At her release from the hospital, Dr. Schmidt prescribed sleeping pills to help combat her insomnia. But June wanted better control of her psychic visions, and didn't ask for a refill when the prescription was finished. Still, her jangled nervous system fought to balance the energy rushing chaotically through her slight body, causing uncontrollable facial and body twitches. She would curse loudly at the pains of drug withdrawal when her fingers curled in uncontrollable spasms.

June was given certain conditions as part of her release from the hospital. As stipulated by her parents, especially by her father and approved by the two psychiatrists, she put aside her stubbornness and agreed that she'd no longer have an altar, practice witchcraft, or talk about her visions to anyone but Dr. Weissman. She would have said yes to almost anything in order to be released from the hospital.

Christmas in the MacDonald household was barely acknowledged. Cathy's nervous twittering about things being much better now that June was home went ignored.

Home life, as June had known it, had changed drastically. The house was very quiet. Maggie had been exiled from the house. Annie, married to Dave, came home only for Sunday dinner. Jimmy was quietly docile. June noticed that her mother rarely spoke to him.

Mary, a senior at Mission High School, was like a ghost drifting in and out the house. She kept her odd hours as a carhop at Mel's Drive-in restaurant on South Van Ness at Mission Avenue. When home, she stayed in her bedroom, while June now shared her pink bedroom with her mother. The only time the two remaining sisters talked was when Mary shared Eddie's letters. He had enlisted in the Marines, and recently wrote that he was being shipped to somewhere called Vietnam, where he'd finally see some action.

The days when Maggie visited were fun for June. The MacDonald females had once again united in secrecy to keep quiet about Maggie's visits home while Jimmy was at work. Even as her thin body enlarged with pregnancy, she remained typical Maggie, full of dramatic life. Sitting around the kitchen table with tea and Cathy's homemade sweets, she told them all about The Nomads, a popular band living across the hall from her and her assortment of flatmates. Tim, who was now in college, supported Maggie the best he could with the meager pay from his part-time job. June admired her sister's brave stance to have her baby without the sanction of marriage, and against society's rules. But June was sad to hear that Loretta hadn't been so bold. She married the man her parents had chosen for her and moved to the small coastal town of Pacifica. No one had heard from her since.

Difficult as it was to accept the changes at home, June found solace in her secret study of the pagan religion and witchcraft. Although she had agreed to leave all of that alone, a greater need to clear her psychic visions won over her promise.

She felt out of balance with her psychic energy. In reading the book, "The Triple Goddess of Time"—a gift from Sadie and Bernice—she found the right ritual. It was part of the celebration of Imbolc[30], February's holy day. Paganism, like other religions, had holy days and times. The message of Imbolc was to purify, retreat from the outer world, and quietly reconnect with one's creative magic. Part of the ritual was to choose an item to stimulate a flow of new ideas. Flipping through magazines, June found a picture of a castle that sat on a lake and was connected to the mainland by a stone bridge. The caption under it read, "Eilean Donan is a well-known castle in the Highlands of Scotland."

"I could be happy there alone," she had told Brian when she showed him the picture and explained the ritual.

Since Mary had shied away from helping her make a hidden altar at home, Brian was the only one she trusted to practice her witchcraft in secret. The two friends met clandestinely in Brian's bedroom to practice witchcraft because it was only in his room that she could safely perform her spiritual rituals. The fearful images of Dr. Schmidt force-feeding her drugs were a constant reminder to keep playing it safe. Like the witches of the past who had to hide their practice, she, too, must keep silent.

∾ ∾ ∾

---

[30] Imbolc – Known in Scotland as Là Fhèill Brìghde, Imbolc is a festival dedicated to the goddess Brigid; adopted by Christians as St. Brigid's Day. Imbolc is a time of weather predictions, and its tradition of watching to see if serpents or badgers come from their winter dens is thought to be the precursor to Groundhog Day. Fire and purification are an important aspect of Imbolc. Brigid is the goddess of poetry, healing and smithcraft. As both goddess and saint, she is also associated with holy wells, sacred flames and healing.

Irritated with her inability to light a match, June tossed the matchbook onto the smooth oak table that held four candles: white, black, red and green. The candles set up for their ritual to celebrate Imbolc were arranged around a small group of seashells and the picture of a castle that was propped up against the red candle.

"Shouldn't be playing with matches anyway. I could burn," she said crossly as she threw her scantily clad body onto Brian's bed to lie amongst the jumbled covers.

Brian struck a match and bent over the altar to light the white candle, as June had taught him to do. The white candle symbolized purity of heart and mental clarity of intention.

"Do I light the black one next?" he asked.

"What's the book say?" she said leaning up on an elbow. "Ugh, your crack is showing," she huffed, cupping a hand over her eyes.

Brian tugged up his white briefs and squinted at the open book. "The crone's first." He lit the black candle.

It had been her suggestion to do the ritual sky-clad, saying that it was the best way for making strong magic. It symbolized that they came pure and clean. Brian hadn't opposed, although he wasn't thrilled with the idea. He didn't like showing his naked body to anyone, even to his best friend. He argued that it wasn't cool to be caught together undressed.

June reminded him that at least they didn't have to worry about Jeannie's ridicule if she found them semi-naked. Jeannie had moved away from home when she was accepted to a prestigious woman's college back east.

They had agreed to compromise, and kept on their underwear.

"Let me light the next ones," she said as she shimmied off the bed.

Brian struck another match and handed it to her. As she lit the green candle, she said, "Welcome mother goddess. The fiery maiden is welcomed, too."

She pivoted over the altar and the red candle's wick burst into flame.

With the jasmine incense floating around them, they retreated to the comfort of the bed to enjoy the flickering glow of the candles that created dancing shadows on the walls.

The pitter-patter of the February rain on the window enhanced the magic moment in the candle-lit room. A dreamy sensation filled June's body, mind and spirit.

"Let us begin," she said softly to Brian.

They stood.

Dutifully, Brian circled the four corners of the room, from east, south, west and then north. As he circled the room, he lit the different-colored candles placed in each corner to invite the energy of each direction to give power to their magic.

When he was finished, June picked up the anthame, the ceremonial knife. Holding it breast high with the blade pointed outward, she moved it around the room to cast a circle while she said, "The circle is cast. The spell made fast. Only good can enter herein." Standing in front of the altar, she opened her arms wide and said, "I invoke the powers of the crone, mother and maiden into our circle to guide me to the truth and wisdom of the visions presented me so I can fulfill my destiny. So mote it be."

Chapter Thirty-Six:
Jagged Edges

JUNE FOUND COMFORT in her weekly counseling sessions with Dr. Weissman. Because her experiences with Dr. Schmidt had made her mistrustful, she was still very reluctant to share her feelings or psychic experiences with him, although she developed an immediate bond with Simon, his Siamese cat. As soon as Dr. Weissman would open the door, Simon would rush up to greet her, entwining himself around her bellbottom-clad legs. Simon would lead the way to the living room, and together they would sit on the ottoman. The hour-long session would slowly tick by as June cuddled Simon and enjoyed the refreshments Dr. Weissman offered. She gave very little information about her feelings. Instead, she would say a bit about how she was doing without the medicine and give updates on her sisters' lives.

One day Simon didn't greet her when she arrived for her session. When she asked about him, the doctor assured her that Simon would appear shortly. She settled into the ottoman and graciously accepted a chocolate from the See's candy box on the coffee table. She nibbled the candy as her eyes drifted over to the large picture window. Unconsciously, her hand moved down to stroke Simon. She bolted up when she realized that Simon wasn't there. She needed him as a buffer, as she always had in past sessions. She preferred to focus on the cat while mostly ignoring Dr. Weissman. So she chose her second line of defense, and rose from the ottoman to look out the window to avoid the doctor's gaze. Looking out over the Bay, she became mesmerized by the sailboats gliding past, and the sturdy, slow moving tugboats hauling barges behind them. Her mind was traveling to a distant cove wrapped in misty swirls when she heard the muffled voice of the old psychiatrist. She listened closer and realized that he was asking if she was ready for school. Her head shook lazily from side to side, still imagining seaweed lapping on a cold rocky shore.

"June," Dr. Weissman said in a voice louder than normal, jolting her out of her daydream.

Although he was kind and polite, she always kept a small part of herself safe from him or anyone else who might come too close to hurting her again. But more than anything else, she didn't want to go back to Dr. Schmidt and the hospital, so she tried to participate in small ways at her sessions with Dr. Weissman.

"Hmm," she said, turning toward him.

"I asked if it was better at home with your father," he said.

"Yeah. Well, basically we ignore each other." She held back volunteering any further information.

"How are you doing without your medication?" the doctor asked.

"Fine. Better." She didn't divulge that she was still having lucid visions of traveling with her angel across the sea to a distant shore. She looked out the window and imagined being back at the cove and feeling the seaweed wrapped around her body.

"Have you been out to sea much, Doctor?"

"Let's talk about you," he answered with his usual response when June asked him a question. She didn't like to talk about herself. It made her feel vulnerable, and, besides, her mother had said it's impolite to talk about yourself.

June turned back to the room and spotted the artwork above the red couch. She had always been passionately drawn to this particular painting, and once again she found it intriguing. There was a prolonged silence as her eyes examined it.

"It's a Pablo Picasso print called 'Girl with Red Beret.' Do you like it?" he asked.

"Yes," she said, without elaborating as to why. The picture of the girl with two faces sharing one head crowned with a red beret was like her and her angel. Brian had said that perhaps her angel was her own subconscious mind, and not a separate entity. June didn't agree with him. She remembered when her first teacher of magic, Mrs. G, had predicted that she and her angel would be together someday.

"Where's Simon?" June asked, unable to retain her curiosity.

"My housekeeper took him to the vet. He hasn't been well lately."

"He's not sick," she blurted out, adding, "I mean, not in his body."

Dr. Weissman peered at her, tapping his finger to his chin. "Hmm," he said under his breath.

She knew he was analyzing her. She became more agitated, sensing that the doctor was staring at her with his coke bottle glasses. Perturbed that the he might think he was in control, she decided to show him her powers.

"Simon's sad. He misses his girlfriend." She sat down on the ottoman. "Was he crying a lot?" Her eyes were closed and she stroked her arm as though she was holding the cat.

Dr. Weissman affirmed that Simon had been meowing more than usual, but it was the cat's lack of interest in eating that worried him. He chuckled at June's comment, and said that with all Simon's meowing, he hadn't mention that he was lonely.

Her eyes popped open. "Sassy," she said suddenly.

"No, June. I'm only telling you why Simon went to the vet."

She sighed and questioned him further. "Simon's girlfriend was Sassy, right?"

"Oh! Classy Cat! That was her name."

June cringed. She didn't like being wrong with her psychic information, especially now. She wanted to impress the doctor.

"She died just about a year ago today. How did you know that?" he asked, his face showing a surprised interest.

"Simon told me telepathically a while ago. Do you think I'm nuts?" she said, testing him.

Dr. Weissman leaned forward, put both hands on the coffee table, and pushed aside the half eaten box of candy. "I think you are a most interesting young lady with true psychic abilities," he said intently.

Intuiting his energy, she felt pleased by his genuine interest and his acceptance of her extrasensory abilities. Without further hesitation, she shared her history. She vividly recounted the life of reproof and ridicule firmly imprinted in her memory bank. Her words, like a monsoon, scattered across the table and pelted the doctor. Her earliest memory was at the age of three when she had a great fear that her ill sister would die. She was still haunted over Helen death. "Was it my fault?" June wailed.

Without stopping for a breath, she told him about the years of anguish she endured for being labeled a misfit by her father and her religious instructors. They had unleashed in her an inner fury that she knew was destroying her spirit. How could she heal? She wanted the doctor's answer, but bitterness over being betrayed kept her from asking. She recalled how Sister St. Pius had cruelly humiliated her and threatened her with burning in hell. The nun had frightened her so very much. She still feared that maybe she truly was a bad girl, as her father and the nuns had declared her to be.

Dr. Weisman sat still and listened.

June railed on. At home, her father mocked her name, which made her sad and mad. But she still sought his acceptance, and didn't discuss the things that would upset him—like learning the tarot from Mrs. G and talking to the spirits of dead people. She desperately wanted him to love her. "But he doesn't," she cried. Secrets had become a way of life. When do I speak the truth? she wondered.

Hollow from purging her grievances, she paused to gulp in air like a drowning person fighting for life. Her breathing soon settled to a natural rhythm, and a small happy smile touched her lips.

"I've always got my sisters to help me," she said. "They like my tarot readings, except for Annie. They usually don't make a big deal about my angel messages either. Besides them, there's my best friends, the Callaghans. We all stick together."

She pulled up her legs to sit Indian style on the ottoman, and continued chatting, "My real first friend was Mrs. G. She saw me for who I really am." As she talked, her voice became lighter with happiness. "Mrs. G was like a genie granting my wish to understand how magic works. She taught me that it was okay to see and hear what others didn't. Our souls were connected. We were spirit sisters."

She touched her heart as she recalled her memories of life on Market Street. Some stories she weaved into a colorful rainbow of images, which brought forth laughter that ricocheted around the doctor's living room. Dr. Weissman joined in, clapping his hands at the fairy stories. She then recounted the death of her old friend. It was a time filled with such wretched loneliness.

"I kept inside how sad I was because no one seemed to care as much as I did that she died," June said sadly. Then a sly smile spread across her face. "Mrs. G would speak to me after she died, especially at night outside." She left the story at that.

Finally, June said, her angel sent another understanding person, Sister Noel, who helped make Catholic school bearable while encouraging June's psychic abilities. She felt Sister was a kindred soul because she had also suffered parents who disbelieved her powers. But then June and Sister Noel were separated.

"I lost her, too, for a long time, 'til she came to help me in the nut house. We still talk sometimes. She can't phone too often since it's a long distance call."

She explained to Dr. Weissman that it was those two women who had the most positive influence on her psychic path. Nonetheless, she still felt odd and outside the normal.

The doctor didn't think June was odd. He was intrigued with the girl's extrasensory talents. "The vision about the young man who drowned, tell me when it first came to you."

"It was when we lived on Market Street. My sisters and I were in the bathtub, and I had an image of a man floating in the ocean. So I made up a game. I would be the drowned man and Mary would be his wife. Maggie was their baby, and Annie was supposed to be the fisherman who pulled the body out of the water. Only she wouldn't play the part. It was strange because when I was under the water in the tub, I felt like I was really dead. It was so peaceful. Then my mother came into the bathroom and got angry at our game. I think it scared her because she thought I was dead and my sisters didn't try to help me."

She paused to see if the doctor had anything to ask. He didn't.

"I had a fight with my mother this morning because I said I didn't want to be a Catholic anymore," she said.

The years of spiritual loneliness, the death of Mrs. G, and the terrible separation from Sister Noel had led to the decision. At fourteen, June had become blazingly angry, and wanted to separate from the offending parties. She saw her mother as a main culprit.

"She doesn't care if I'm happy," June complained. "She let me talk about my angel, then she told me to stop lying about it. She wouldn't protect me from the nuns or my father. My father always said I was a pagan baby. I always felt like an outsider in my family. It was my mother's fault for giving me a heathen's name." She stopped, and said more softly, "I loved her so much. But she always turned away and hid in bed, pretending to be sick."

Even though she hadn't expected to reveal her fears and hopes so candidly, Dr. Weissman's calm presence allowed for her to do so safely. *It's part of my cleansing*, she assured herself when she collected her pocketbook and jacket.

Since Dr. Weissman didn't judge her, she felt safe and free to be herself.

As she was leaving, the doctor suggested that her mother come to the next session to resolve their differences. June readily agreed, trusting it would be beneficial for both of them.

∽ ∽ ∽

June sat on the ottoman and gently stroked Simon. She didn't look at her mother. As the session went on, no matter how much she ran her fingers through the cat's fur, she couldn't rid herself of the anger she felt toward her mother. June wasn't so upset by her mother's complaints about Jimmy's harsh strictness with her sisters. She was disturbed by the details of her romantic first encounter with Malcolm at the train station.

Cathy's eyes and voice softened dreamily as she described how he had to bend low to kiss her. She was short, and he was so tall. "His kisses were very soft and sweet. It was the beginning of our love affair, as short as it was to be." Cathy's voice dipped low, and unhappily.

In utter shock at what she had just heard, June stared with anger at her mother. Cathy saw June's expression and stopped talking, and looked away.

A silent space enveloped the room.

June's fiery rage made her want to strike out at her mother. Her body catapulted from the ottoman, causing Simon to yowl in protest at being flung from her lap. She clenched her hands into tight fists and her face flushed as red as her hair. With a strangled yelp, she stormed to the picture window and focused on the vastness of the view.

A gusty March wind agitated the Bay, churning the water steely gray. A flurry of erratic waves tossed around on the water. It was devoid of any boats. Only the seagulls circled, flying low. Her mood was as turbulent as the small waves tossing around. She tried to calm her stormy mood.

"June, what are you feeling?" Dr. Weissman asked the sulking teen.

She glanced back toward the doctor when he called her name, and saw Cathy huddled in her chair like a naughty child. Puffing out hot breaths, June decided to prolong her response, deriving pleasure from her mother's uneasiness. *Let her simmer in her guilt,* she decided.

Cathy squirmed in the chair. The leather protested and sucked at her dress as she shifted, separating the material from her sweating body. She cast her eyes down and away from June's scorching look that bored into her. She had prayed that telling June her story about Malcolm would make her daughter understand her visions. Instead, her fear of being rejected seemed to be coming true.

Dr. Weissman had warned Cathy that healing such a painful past would be a messy affair. He explained that healing one's psyche is like a pot burnt from overcooking that must be scrubbed cleaned. The grimy guck that floats to the top is the shame, guilt and hurt that would have to be released. He assured her that no matter how difficult and unpleasant it is at first, clear water will eventually appear. The clear water represents freedom from mental and emotional pain. It is part of the healing process that's necessary if the subconscious mind is to become whole and healthy again.

Cathy's nervous fingers kneaded the small tin frame she held partially hidden in her hands. She sneaked furtive glances at June, and awaited the clearing.

∽ ∽ ∽

A bleating foghorn broke June's single-minded thought of hoping that her mother was as miserable as she was. Finally, she said, "She was having sex with him without being married."

"June!" Cathy exclaimed.

"My vision was right! It did happen. Why did you have Daddy smack me? Remember when I showed you that picture from the magazine that showed a man and woman kissing? Why did you deny it? Why?" June demanded stamping her foot.

Cathy answered slowly, "I was afraid. I. . . I wanted to leave the past alone, like Granny B said was best to do."

She looked at her mother mutinously. "So, I had to suffer? I had to take all the punishment because you wanted everyone to see you as a holy Catholic and not a fallen woman?" She used a term that Jimmy had flung at Maggie.

She plopped back down on the ottoman. "You brought this on me. All of it," she accused her mother.

"I *was* married to Malcolm," Cathy's said defensively, her lips quivering.

"Would you like to say more about that?" Dr. Weissman said encouragingly.

"Before Malcolm left London we had a hand-fasting ceremony. We took wedding vows holding hands. We laced a red ribbon around our hands to bind us to our vows."

"Bet you made that up so you could live in sin," June said, hissing the last word. Without waiting for an answer, she told her mother, "You haven't been in a state of grace with the Church for years. You shouldn't have taken communion."

June knew that receiving Holy Communion was only for Catholics who had been to confession and were absolved of sin. This meant they were in a state of grace and ready to receive the communion host.

With a frown, Cathy dismissed June's accusation. "It's a real marriage contract. From the old ways. That's what couples did."

"Old ways? Like pagan religion? You did pagan things?" June asked accusingly.

"Not at first. But I knew that my choice to be with Malcolm meant I could no longer practice my own religion. So I learned his family's ways and rituals from his mother, Eilidh, when I lived with her in Skye. I needed some form of religion in my life."

"*You* made me a pagan! It's all your fault. First giving me a heathen pagan name that Daddy always hated, then sending me telepathic pagan thoughts. You're a wicked witch!" June denounced her mother cruelly.

In vain, Cathy attempted to defend herself. She said, "We didn't call ourselves witches." Eilidth had warned her about the consequences of using the word witch when practicing the old ways, even in Skye. She explained, "We just practiced the old ways—the pagan ways. After all, pagan only means people of earth . . ."

A fierce wind banged against the large window startling them. They looked over and saw a lone black bird perilously close. It flew away.

"You sound angry with your mother," Dr. Weissman said calmly.

June hated when the doctor said this. Of course she was angry. But, like the lone bird, she felt frightened and unable to control the turbulence of her stormy moods.

"Mom, you ruined my life," June said in frustration. She covered her eyes and her small shoulders heaved with her sobs.

"What do you need from your mother?" he asked gently.

June said severely, "She's got to stop lying to me. No more secrets."

Dr. Weissman looked at Cathy.

Looking abashed, Cathy agreed, "No more secrets." Holding forth the small picture frame, she asked meekly, "Can I show her this now?"

Dr. Weissman asked June if she wanted to know more about her mother's life with Malcolm.

Without looking at her mother, June held out a hand to accept the frame. In it was a black-and-white photo of her mother as a young woman and a handsome man with classic features and a full head of curly hair. He had on a Naval uniform.

"That's him!" she said triumphantly as she wiped away tears on the sleeve of her sweater. She quickly described the vision she had in the hospital of the man who drowned.

Cathy had confirmed June's vision. As unbelievable as it was, Malcolm's body had indeed washed ashore back home in Skye.

Hoping that the muck would soon disappear, Cathy tried to explain. "Malcolm was finally coming home for a visit when his ship was torpedoed. Many of the sailors drowned in the Irish Sea. That's where the German U-boats hid to attack our ships. Lots of bodies washed up on the other isles further south of Skye. But I believe my strong love for Malcolm brought him home to me on the Isle of Skye. I think his spirit heard me calling him. You see I used sit on top of a hilltop overlooking the sea, waiting for his return. When the weather became nicer, especially in late May and June, I'd make daisy chains. You always liked those kinds of flowers, remember?"

"You lived on Skye? Oh, what's the use asking," June said. "I can't get the truth from you." She paused for a moment before declaring, "I'm really a visionary, not a bad person. Not a loony. Only that's how I'm seen, like a crazy witch. A bad Catholic—like her." She pointed an accusatory finger at her mother and tossed the picture frame onto the coffee table.

"Do you think your mother decided your fate or can your fate be thought of as your destiny?" Dr. Weissman asked.

"What's the difference? Look how bad my life's been because of all the lies and secrets," June said, turning sour again.

"To me, they are like two sides of a coin," the doctor explained. "One side is destiny, which I see as optimistic. The other side of the coin is fate, which I think of as pessimistic. It's like a prophetic declaration of what must be, and what cannot be changed. My theory is that when we are born we have a predetermined path of where our life is going, which is destiny. But it's up to you to decide how to get there. You decide when to stay on your path, or when to leave it in your own way and time. Fate, on the other hand, is when you think there's no control over what happens and you have no free will. Which is it for you, June? Are you ready to have control of your life?"

"Dunno," she replied patting her lap to Simon.

"It sounds like you feel you're connected to your mother's life in a subconscious way. Would you like to learn how to separate from her past?" the doctor asked.

"Doctor, are you saying that children might be linked to their parents through more than just inheriting their genes—like eye coloring?" Cathy asked. "Do you think they can inherit our past experiences, too?"

"That's an interesting hypothesis. A psychiatrist named Carl Jung had a theory on how the collective unconsciousness is the great circle that links all living things. And Albert Einstein talked about parallel worlds. The longer I live the more I learn that there's more than what meets the eye. But let's discuss this next week. In the meantime, the rule is, no more blaming or accusing if you talk further about what you have learned here today. Agreed?" Dr. Weissman asked to the two.

Cathy agreed easily, June reluctantly. They gathered up their coats and purses. Neither spoke as they left.

ᏝᏝ ᏝᏝ ᏝᏝ

Not a word passed between mother and daughter during the short elevator ride downstairs. As the door rolled open, June dashed outside and away from her mother.

The ground rumbled and a bell clanged loudly, announcing the cable car. They watched it through the misty light rain appearing over the top of the hill. It shuddered to a stop, shaking from its effort to climb the steep San Francisco hills. They climbed aboard. Cathy tightened her scarf to protect her hair against the increasing rainfall. She was wary of how they would fare on the ride home.

Cathy glanced at her daughter slouching on the wooden bench. Her red beret, tipped to one side of her head, was perfectly angled.

Her daughter's profile, with its small, straight nose and full pouting lips, reminded Cathy of herself many years ago when she, too, had spunk. She shivered as a gust of wind raced up her skirt. She wished they had sat inside the cable car, but June had chosen the outside seat. Cathy said nothing, not wanting to add more tension to the situation.

A strong wind blew open June's unbuttoned pea coat. She pulled it tightly around her chest. She looked down at the passing road and saw raindrops dribbling down her mother's nylon-clad legs, while her own legs were kept dry by her pants. A stab of guilt pricked at her for choosing to sit outside.

Cathy scooted closer to her. She tried to say something, but between the noise of the cable car and the blowing wind, June couldn't hear the words. She leaned closer to speak directly into June's ear, "I'm sorry for all the times I hurt you. Please forgive me."

This time June heard her. She tightened her lips, not wanting to accept the apology. Casting her eyes upward, she blinked away her tears. She noticed the rain had finally lessened and patches of blue sky shone through.

The grinding noise of the cable car's brakes as it slowed to their stop was ear piercing. June stood and took hold of the metal pole. She swayed outward as she readied herself to jump from the platform when they reached the intersection of Powell at Market Streets. The thrill of hanging out of the cable car and the feel of the brisk wind against her face had charged her energy. She felt a sense of freedom.

As they lurched to a stop, she hopped off and hollered to her mother, "Did you get a transfer?"

Cathy nodded a "yes," and gingerly stretched out a foot to get down from the cable car. June took hold of her arm.

When Cathy was steady on the sidewalk, June threw her arms around her mother in a tight bear hug. "I love you, Mommy," the teen said, to Cathy's surprise.

She returned the hug, clinging a bit longer than normal before letting go and remarking, "You're taller than me now."

Arm in arm, they walked over to the Woolworth's department store on Market Street to look at the items for sale in the window.

"We could get that for Maggie's baby," June said pointing to a pale-pink baby jacket and hat.

"I've already crocheted a yellow and white set," Cathy said.

"Bet it's a girl," June said.

"Making a prediction?" Cathy's eyes twinkled in mirth.

June smiled and shrugged a shoulder. "Maybe. I think you're a good witch like me. You can join my coven. Only Brian is in it. That'll make three of us." She smiled slyly at her mother.

"Okay. I could show you a thing or two, Missy Witchy," Cathy laughed bumping her shoulder against her daughter.

"Do you have psychic powers, too?" June asked, curiosity sharpening her eyes.

"No, nothing more than the usual mother's intuition. I was always interested in people like you who do."

June was happy to hear that her mother believed in her. "I thought all witches would have them," she said.

"I said I was a pagan, not a witch. Eilidh warned me to never use that word because of the bad connotations associated with it. It's true that pagans are often highly sensitive to the changes in nature and how it influences their lives. Some pagans have the ability of second sight. We call them fey in Scotland. Others have different gifts. Eilidh was a well-known herbalist. She used the local plants and flowers to heal her family and neighbors. Her sister was a storyteller who kept alive the Highlanders' legends in the Gaelic language that the English had banned."

"Is *bidh sàmhach* a Gaelic word?" June asked, saying the words to sound more like, bee savax.

Her mother laughed loudly in surprise. "Yes! It means to be quiet. How'd you know? Oh, never mind. I know. Your angel told you."

Cathy's usual pallor now glowed with a pretty soft pink coloring in her cheeks.

"You were happy there, huh?" June was eager for more information about her mother's past.

"Very. Skye is a beautiful and magical place. And Eilidth was so kind to me. Never once did she tell me what I *had* to do to fit in. Did you know her name translates to Helen? I think I was trying to bring that happiness of being with Eilidth back to my life when I named your dear sister after her. But I couldn't talk about my life in Skye to my family in Glasgow. I had to keep it secret. Always the damn secrets."

June didn't want Cathy to sink back into unhappy thoughts. "Let's celebrate. We'll call Mary and have her walk down to meet us at South China for dinner," she said referring to the popular Chinese restaurant in The Valley. June and her sisters had often sat in the wooden booths designed for privacy and dined with Dave and the Callaghans on several plates filled with a variety of good food.

"Annie will be just getting off work. She can meet us there, too," June said.

She wanted to include her eldest sister, who worked at Hibernia Bank on the corner of Castro and Eighteenth Streets. Since her marriage to Dave, Annie had lived in a studio apartment on Hancock Street. It was an easy walk from Liberty Street to visit her and keep her company while Dave worked at night and went to the Police Academy through the day. June could tell that Annie was lonely for her family's company.

"Can't. I've got to get your Daddy's din. . ." Cathy suddenly halted. She thought briefly about it, and then said enthusiastically, "That's a grand idea, pet!"

At their bus stop in front of Woolworth's, June dropped a dime into a pay telephone. It rang a half-dozen times before she started to hang up, disappointed. Then she heard a snappish, "Yeah?"

"Hey Mary, it's me. I'm with Mommy and . . ."

"Let me talk to her," Mary said brusquely.

June handed over the phone scowling at Mary's rude tone.

Cathy's listened with wide eyes. "Right. Where? Leave a note for your Dad."

She hung up the phone and filled June in. "Annie was outside when you called. She was in the car waiting for Mary. They're on their way to drive Maggie to the hospital. She's in labor. Now, which bus takes us to St. Mary's Hospital?"

They started to reconnoiter a route to their new destination.

Chapter Thirty-Seven:
Blessed Be!

S T. MARY'S HOSPITAL sat across from Golden Gate Park. Three nuns glided past Cathy and June in single file. They wore large white-winged headdresses and soft dove-gray habits with white collars that dipped down their chests. Reverently, Cathy lowered her eyes and greeted them softly, "Good evening, Sisters." The three gave a slight nod and smiled benevolently.

They spotted Annie sitting uncomfortably on a sagging dark-brown couch in the visitor's lounge. In her seventh month of pregnancy, her stomach was so big that she looked like a butterball.

Mary sat splayed out across one of the twin couches across from her.

"Thank God, you're here, Mom," Annie said as she struggled to get up, her belly challenging an easy rise from the low couch. Her mother went to help.

"We've got to get the story straight," Annie said bossily.

"Let's go to Maggie," said June.

"In a minute," Annie answered impatiently.

Under her breath, June whispered to Mary, "Man, you're stoned. Why now?"

Mary tapped her chest. "Mea culpa."

Annie gestured for the family to form a huddle. She explained the importance of coming up with a story about the whereabouts of Maggie's husband.

Usually, young women in Maggie's predicament were sent to San Francisco's St. Elizabeth's Home for Unwed Mothers. Or they left town and returned without a baby. Either option was better than bringing shame to their families.

"Why did she have to pick a Catholic hospital?" Annie complained. "She could have gone to San Francisco General Hospital, and we wouldn't have to fake her being married. I hope we don't have to lie to one of the nuns." She was worried because many of the hospital's nurses were nuns.

No one had a ready answer to the unacceptable situation.

Finally Mary offered as a solution. "Say her husband is a soldier stationed at Camp Pendleton." That was the Marine Corps based in Southern California where Eddie had trained.

"Tell them her husband went to war in Vietnam. They'll feel sorry for her," June said, keeping her voice low and enjoying the intrigue.

"I tried to put my wedding band on her, but her finger's too fat." Annie ignored her sisters' ideas and kept focused on her issue of her unwed sister.

"Oh goody, Maggie's fat," Mary said gleefully.

"I'll put my ring on her. Let's go. She'll be needing me," Cathy said.

"Wait. That's only part of it. What'll we say if the baby comes out black?" Annie fretted.

The four looked at each other, puzzled and unsure of what might happen if their milky-white, strawberry-blonde relative produced a black baby. No one had an answer to that one.

The hallway was becoming busy with visitors arriving and milling around them.

Their silence lengthened.

At last, June spoke. "How about saying the baby is a Black Scot. You know, like the Black Irish?"

Mary guffawed loudly.

"It's no joke!" Annie hissed.

Cathy said sternly, "Girls, that enough. The only important thing we should worry about is that the baby be healthy." She then abruptly broke away from the huddle and hurried off toward the elevators. The sound of her heels clicked rapidly behind her.

"Let's skedaddle," Mary said.

The sisters followed their mother to the elevators and into the maternity ward where a nurse directed them to Maggie's room. Writhing beneath a white sheet was a very pregnant Maggie, looking quite woebegone. With her face scrunched up with pain, she stretched out her hand to her mother to plead for help.

"Now, now, pet. Don't make it worse for yourself. You've got to relax," Cathy said, trying to ease her daughter's grasp. "Go with the contractions. Breathe deep, in and out." Cathy breathed deeply to show how it was done.

A seasoned nurse, stern of face and round of girth, came bustling into the room. Her mouth set tartly when she saw the group gathered around her patient. "Visitors are not allowed in the patient's room. You may wait in the lounge on the first floor."

The family began to shuffle away from the bed.

The nurse's wide body knocked June out of the way as she tried to squeeze past. She took hold of Maggie's wrist and checked her watch. After returning her patient's hand to the bed, she turned, and with one hand on each hip, announced, "You'll be notified when the situation changes."

Pleadingly, Cathy said, "Please, this is her first, and she's frightened to be alone. I'm her mother and these girls are . . ."

"Where's the husband?" the nurse queried, her lips tightened into a tight line. Her narrow eyes roved around each family member.

In no coherent order, the three sisters burst forth with the tale of Maggie's husband's whereabouts.

"He joined the army?" Maggie asked faintly.

Cathy shushed her. "You know how they are at this stage." She smiled hopefully at the nurse.

Annoyed by her mother's kowtowing to the nurse, June intervened. In her mind's eye she conjured up an imaginary wand that she could wave to dismiss the irritating nurse.

The nurse ignored Cathy's comment and turned to Maggie. "You haven't signed the necessary forms to receive a saddle block. That's what you asked for, right Mrs.?"

No one offered up a last name.

Maggie gurgled some response between gritted teeth.

"Well, I better get that going," the nurse said pulling the blanket tight over Maggie's protruding belly. "She's got hours to go. There's coffee in the cafeteria, second floor," she informed the others. She then bustled out of the room, leaving the door wide open as a reminder that the family must leave.

Scooting back to Maggie's side, Cathy tried unsuccessfully to force her wedding band onto her daughter's swollen finger. "This baby will be born within an hour," she predicted.

"Mom, I think the nurse knows better about these things," Annie said crisply. She wanted to become a nurse. Dave promised that she could go to nursing school as soon as he completed one year with the police force.

"I think I know the signs after seven babies," Cathy responded. She gave up on the wedding ring and dropped it into her coat pocket.

Perplexed by what her mother had said, June corrected her. "Six babies," she said.

A riveting scream followed by wretched groaning took the attention from June. Mother and sisters quickly clustered around Maggie to offer soothing and helpful advice. "Breathe." "Be brave." Cathy brushed back her hair, and Annie wiped perspiration from her forehead.

Another contraction brought forth horrific screams, accompanied by a string of cussing.

The scene disturbed June. She felt helpless to stop her sister's pain. Moving away from the bed, she pressed her back into the wall and tucked her head down low between her shoulders.

The nurse swept into the room and gruffly reprimanded Maggie for being so loud. Following her was a nun.

"Hello Mrs. MacDonald," the nun sang cheerfully. "I'm Sister Mary Dorothea."

June's head popped up at the sound of the gentle, accented voice to find an angelic ebony face enshrouded in a winged headdress and round glasses framing her bright black eyes.

"Sister," Cathy bowed her head slightly.

"Mom, she's talking to Maggie," Annie whispered.

"Now, let's see how Baby MacDonald is doing," the nun said to the whimpering patient.

In one quick motion, the nurse pulled off the sheet and pushed up the hospital gown, exposing Maggie's nakedness to everyone in the room. The family turned their heads away in embarrassment.

The nun's gloved hand examined her patient.

"Oh my! The little head has dropped. Baby is raring to get here," the nun said joyfully. "By the time your husband arrives, he'll get to hold his baby right away."

"She's not married," Cathy spoke out boldly, and then reverently added, "Sister."

Both nun and nurse stared at her with mouths opened in a silent O.

The old nurse dropped the sheet and tsked-tsked loudly.

"If that is the way it is, so be it," the young nun said with a kind smile. "Margaret, you are blessed to have your women folk here with you." She pulled up the side rail on the bed and said, "Off we go to the delivery room."

The nurse yanked up the other railing and helped the nun to wheel Maggie out of the room.

"Visitor's lounge," the nurse said dramatically as she clicked off the light.

"Meanie," June said, wondering why her telepathic of "Be nice to us" hadn't worked. *Must be too much going on,* she concluded.

"Yeah, the old bat," Mary said supportively.

"We should go to the waiting room," said Annie standing at the opened door.

Cathy moved to the window and parted a slat in the blinds to peek outside. "I think we'll wait here."

June noticed how pale and tired Annie looked against the harsh light of the hallway. She called to her, motioning to the lone chair in the room. Annie happily plunked down and sighed loudly.

Milling around the room looking for a place of comfort, Mary finally chose to slide slowly down a wall to sit Indian style on the floor. She delved into her big leather handbag and fished around in it. She pulled out a half-eaten bologna sandwich wrapped in wax paper and offered it to Annie, who gratefully accepted it.

Leaning against a wall, June watched Mary nervously tap her foot. She knew her sister was in need of a nicotine fix. She was curious about what else Mary had in that big bag.

Mary delved back into her bag and took out a pack of Wrigley's chewing gum. She popped a fresh stick into her mouth and vigorously chomped it, blowing small bubbles.

Cathy tugged up the blinds and stood looking out the window. Dusk was slowly turning into nightfall. Across the street in Golden Gate Park, she could see tiny pink flowers beginning to bloom on the tree branches. Soon, spring flowers would adorn the park and the days would be longer. A crescent moon drifted onto the night horizon, casting a mere slit of light across the darkened room.

"Look, it's waxing." She beckoned the girls to the window.

Before joining her mother, June closed the door to give her family privacy. Mary scrambled up from the floor to stand at the window by her mother.

Grunting, Annie rose from the chair and waddled over. Tucking her hair behind her ears, she squinted out the window and asked, "What's does that mean?"

June noted how luxuriously healthy Annie's hair had looked since her pregnancy. *Finally, she's happy,* June thought. Aloud, she said, "That's the time when the moon gets rounder until its full. Now is the best time to think of things you want to grow—like getting a bigger place before the baby comes."

"For the love of God, not now, June," Annie objected, rubbing her eyes and yawning.

"The crescent moon is a female symbol," Cathy said.

"Maggie's going to have a girl," June announced. They looked at her, and then gazed back trace-like at the silver-white moon shining in the heavens.

"Fortune-teller," Mary said with a hint of laughter. She knew her sister hated that name, and instead preferred to think of herself as being "aware of the unseen world around her."

"Let's make a wish for our new baby. Hold hands," Cathy said. She held up her palms, and June and Mary each took one.

"Falling under June's pagan influences?" Annie questioned her mother.

"It's a wish for your sister and her baby. Is that a bad thing to do?" Cathy asked.

Annie lowered her eyes and gave her mother a mini-smile to show she was willing to be part of their ritual.

"Long ago, the first time I called down the power of the moon, I stood on a hilltop in Scotland. I wished for a life full of happiness with many children, and with a man I loved deeply. At least half of my wish came true." Cathy looked at each daughter.

"Is this like a story where we learn a lesson?" Mary asked.

"I hope so. I learned a very important lesson today," Cathy said. "Keeping secrets in a family doesn't necessarily mean we will be happier. Girls, I need to talk." Her eyes glistened with tears.

Haltingly, at first, she retold her secret story, starting with her journey from the Glasgow train station where she had met Malcolm, the love of her life. She ended by confessing her pagan practices on the Isle of Skye.

Annie slumped back into the chair with her mouth agape. "You're kidding, right?"

Mary kept repeating, "damn" over and over.

Annie was too shocked to reprimand her swearing, and Cathy was too focused on telling her story.

Then she came to the part of her story when her words became bitter. "Granny and Granda B said I could only return home to Glasgow if I agreed to marry your father. They didn't care how I felt. They were only worried about how I'd look in the eyes of the Church."

Protesting their mother's criticism of their beloved grandparents, Annie and Mary reminded of her how well Granny B had taken care of them all, especially with the cooking and cleaning. And Granda B had been great fun, especially at Hogmanay.

Cathy thought of what they had said. "I know Granny thought she was helping me. She wanted me to have a good marriage. To her, cooking a good meal and going to Mass together on Sundays was a good life. My daddy, your Granda, fought hard to keep his family safe. He wanted me to stay his wee pet forever. He couldn't accept that I had grown up and become a woman. And besides, I did a terrible thing. I ruined his Hogmanay that year when he came to Skye. Granny had told me it was a time of hope for him, that life would be better in the New Year. We all knew how badly he needed that hope, especially after the deaths of my two brothers. He hardly spoke to me after that. Aye, they did the best they could, considering the alternative—to leave me in Skye half crazed with grief, with an old woman."

The revelation of their mother's rift with her parents seemed to stun the girls, for they said no more after seeing the great pain that showed on her face.

"You've been angry at them all these years because of that. Is that why you didn't answer Granny's letters?" Annie asked gently.

Cathy nodded "yes," and tears formed in her tired eyes. "I wasn't very forgiving. I was unhappy, and I wanted to punish her. I realize now how much she must have missed me when I left Scotland for America. Not a day goes by that I don't pray that my parents forgave me." She looked sadly at June. "I only wish that I had Dr. Weissman to help me a long time ago. I now understand that I've been suffering from depression for all these years."

June put an arm around her mother's shoulders, and said, "Granda and Granny loved you. They forgave you a long time ago."

Cathy smiled at her shyly. She still felt guilty for her years of emotional separation from her daughter.

"Did you know that Granny B believed you had special powers with Helen?" Cathy asked June. "When your sister was sick, it was *you* who helped her rest. Maybe it was your angel guiding you."

"My angel didn't speak to me in Scotland," June told her. "Finally I remember the very first time I heard her. It was when we were on the plane to America. Daddy was reading me a book that had a picture of a big boat. I heard a girl's voice saying that we had fallen off of it, and we were in the water. I asked Daddy if I fell off a boat. He said no and kept reading to me."

June didn't mention that Jimmy had slapped her leg hard for asking too many questions. She pretended to fall asleep so he wouldn't do it again.

"Man, you give me the heebie jebbies when you say you hear voices. It's kinda spooky, huh?" Mary said looking to Annie for an agreement.

"I thought you believed in my psychic abilities," June said, surprised by her comment.

"Thought it was the tarot cards," Mary shrugged.

"Gee, thanks a lot," June said.

Annie interrupted their bantering with her sniffles. "I couldn't imagine Dave dying and not having you to comfort me, Mom. Or, worse, having to marry somebody I didn't love. Then losing two children. I'm so sad for you. You're braver than I thought." She gave her mother a woeful stare.

"Annie, I'm so grateful to you for all the years you took care of the family," Cathy said sorrowfully. "I'm sorry for all the years I wasn't the kind of mother you needed. Maybe I can make it up to you when you have your baby."

"No one's perfect. Let's leave the past behind us," Annie said wanly as she rubbed her belly.

"Do you feel okay?" June walked over to Annie and gently put an arm around her sister's shoulder and a hand on her belly.

"The baby is kicking up a storm. Hey, it just stopped. Guess you do have the magic touch." Annie breathed deeply. "Yes, Mom, I'll need your help."

"Thank you. It's going to be nice to have babies around again. I'm going to buy a stroller and walk all over The Valley," Cathy said happily. She then returned her gaze to the moon. "Three weans I lost," she said sorrowfully, squeezing her eyes shut to keep back the tears.

"We know about Kit and Helen. Who was the other kid?" Mary asked.

Cathy bit her lower lip under the scrutinizing eyes of her daughters. There was no going back. She longed for the blessing of absolution and to be free of the shame that burdened her for so many years. Her parents were dead. Her marriage to Jimmy did not redeem her sins. She suddenly realized that no one could punish or condemn her anymore—not even the Church.

"June knows her, I think," Cathy said forging on with her commitment to stop the secrecy.

All eyes went to the youngest sister.

June closed her eyes, and her lids twitched a bit. When she opened them, she looked wide-eyed at her mother. "My angel is your and Malcolm's daughter?"

A dual gasp came from her sisters.

"Did she die, too?" June asked.

Chatting and laughing voices from the hallway filled the void as the girls waited for her answer.

"Hear the visitors coming to see the new wee babies?" Cathy said merrily, postponing an answer. "It reminds me of when I was in St. Andrew's Infirmary. That's the hospital you girls were all born in. Annie, you probably remember Dr. MacFadden, don't you?" Not waiting for an answer, she chatted on, "He's the doctor that helped bring all my weans into the world. He was so gentle. He saw me through all my difficult births. And when my girls died, he was there, too."

June saw a warm orange glow spreading around her mother as she talked about the kindness of the handsome Highland doctor.

"He knew more about my true feelings than anyone ever had. Aye, the good doctor was my trusted friend."

Other than Malcolm, June had never heard her mother speak so lovingly about anyone from her past. She sensed there was more to the story about how Dr. MacFadden had gained Cathy's trust.

"When did you two first meet, Mom?" she inquired.

"Actually, I got to know him through the letters he sent Malcolm when we were living in London. He had been Malcolm's childhood friend, and they stayed pals even after he had left for medical school in Edinburgh. Then he went into the army and Malcolm to the navy. I met him in Skye . . . in a rather awkward position." Her sudden laughter startled the girls. They looked at her curiously.

Still smiling, she continued, "It was late spring. Malcolm was still away at war, and I was in labor with her. Callie was her name. There I was, a young woman like Maggie, only I wasn't in a hospital. I had her in a small cottage by the sea. I was having terrible labor pains with a baby that wouldn't come easy into the world. She was breach. That's when the wean's bum comes out first. It's not a good thing for the baby or mother. The midwife was busy, miles away, with no car to get to me. Eilidth and her sister, older than the hills she was, were doing their best to help me. After a long night, morning finally came. There was a knock and in poked a head. It was Harry MacFadden, home for a visit from his war assignment. That's when I met the good Dr. MacFadden, at Callie's birthing. Don't know if I could have made it without him. He was able to move Callie around and help her out and into my arms."

"Holy moly! What a story. Do you have a picture of him and Malcolm?" Mary asked.

"Aye, I have some hidden away." She winked at the girls.

"And the baby? Our sister?" June asked with great interest.

Cathy decided not to answer, and instead told them about Malcolm's ship being torpedoed and his body washing ashore near his home.

"I saw him lying there on the beach so peacefully, as though he were asleep. Only he was dead. I went mad with grief. After that I couldn't nurse Callie anymore. I didn't even want to hold her. You see, girls, I was no good as a mother to her either. Eilidh finally wrote to my parents that I needed their help. My wee Callie was only six months old when I left Skye. Granny B promised me that I could bring her home later, after your father and I married. She thought he was a kind man and would accept Callie." She shook her head sadly. "But Granda forbade me to tell him. He said that no man wants to take in a bastard child. That's what they used to call a baby borne out of wedlock. I felt so ashamed of what others would say, so I wallowed in my misery. Och, aye, it's a sair fecht."

"It is," Annie said, her voice cracking. She searched through her pockets for a hanky and came out with rosary beads. Mary offered her a Kleenex from her handbag.

Their mother continued, "So when I left Skye, I kept a secret from my parents. Eilidh would send me an occasional letter through Harry, who by then had set up a practice in Glasgow. She would write me all about Callie's life. But when Helen died . . ." she stopped and sighed deeply before continuing, "well, I no longer wanted any more news about Callie. I couldn't take any more pain of being without my lassies. Like I did with Kit and Helen, I buried her, too."

"For me, it wasn't buried deep enough," June said sadly.

Putting her arm around June's shoulder, Cathy said kindly, "I think we've learned that you can't really bury the past. When you were just a baby in my arms, a gypsy came to the door and said it would be you that would bring my love back. I thought only of Malcolm as my love, but really it's our child, Callie, that is the lost love of my life. That gypsy also predicted we'd move far way from Glasgow, and we did come to San Francisco."

"June's always attracted strange people," Mary said sardonically.

"Is Callie like me?" June asked.

"You both have that flaming red hair, just like Malcolm. When I found out that I was pregnant with you, and that you'd be born in early May, I rubbed my belly and asked you to please wait until June the first. That's Callie's birthday, too. I imagined that if I had another baby on that day, then somehow it would be like she was back in my life."

"You can ask an unborn baby to wait?" Annie said incredulously.

"I did and June must have heard me," Cathy said. A wide smile spread across her face and her eyes shone with tears. "That night when I stood under the moon before entering the hospital, I felt Callie so strongly in my heart that I knew she and I were connecting once again."

June saw an aura of pale-yellow and dark green manifesting in front of Cathy. She was enthralled to see the spirit images held within it. She saw Malcolm, Helen, Baby Kit, Granda and Granny B, and the old crone from her vision of the beach that she now knew was Eilidth. June's hands fluttered in the air in front of her as though trying to reach for someone.

"The grief of the past is waning, and the power for us is now," June said dreamily.

She continued to move her hands around as though wanting to embrace the unseen forces. The group of spirits parted, and a young woman came forward. She had an abundant head of red hair that swirled around her shoulders, and blue eyes nearly as dark as her irises. She held out her arms in a welcoming gesture to Cathy, who couldn't see her.

In the background, June could hear her mother saying, "Malcolm's body was found on November first, the day honoring the goddess Calleach. On that day the goddess sends a banshee—that's a woman spirit—to unite the living and dead. I've had little faith in ever seeing Callie again. For all I know she's dead."

June shuddered remembering what Mrs. G had told her many years ago. "You and your angel are duchy siostrzane."

"She's alive! Callie's waiting for me," June said excitingly.

"Creepy," Mary said as she stepped away from her sister.

"We gotta find her! She's our sister, part of our clan," June stated boldly.

"Oh, I can hear Daddy now," Mary said, giving a wry grin.

"He can't do anything," Annie said, her square jaw jutting out.

"She's still my angel you know. I'll send her a telepathic message wherever she is," said June assuredly.

"Eilean a' Cheò ," Cathy whispered.

"Is that her full name?" June was giddy with a feeling of divine connection between her and the angel.

"No. That's Gaelic for the Isle of Skye. It means the Isle of Mist. That's where Calleach, that's Callie's full name, might be, or not. It was a long time ago."

"The goddess is calling me into the mist," June whispered very softly.

She had so many more questions for her mother. Still, the ones that had been answered had cleansed away much of the angry hurt that had divided mother and daughter for so long. June felt a surge of confidence. It was just as the gypsy had predicted: She and Callie would find each other. June was satisfied for now.

"I remember the last words Eilidth whispered in my ear on the night I left Skye. She said, 'Pray to the goddess and all will set itself right in time.' Now you say the goddess is calling you. It seems as though this is the time for setting wrongs right," Cathy said hopefully.

Just then the door swung open and Sister Mary Dorothea came in holding a small bundle swaddled in a white blanket.

"Aha," she exclaimed. "I thought I'd find you here. Margaret is doing well."

A sound of relief vibrated throughout the room.

The nun held out the baby. "A new MacDonald girl to play with," she said grinning from ear to ear.

Without hesitation, Cathy's arms opened wide to accept her first grandchild. The girls crowded around. June folded back the blanket to a see a chubby-faced infant with a small, flat nose, plump pink lips and long slanted eyes. June thought how the baby's light brown face looked so pretty against the white blanket

"Look, her hair's got a reddish tinge," she exclaimed touching the strands of frizzed hair.

"She'll be a strawberry blonde like her mother. Can we keep her here for just a bit?" Cathy asked.

The nun hesitated. "I'm suppose to take her to the nursery."

Annie held her hands wrapped in her rosary beads in a gesture of prayer. "Sister, we want to pray to Our Lady in gratitude for this blessing," she said innocently.

The young nun's eyes shined with reverence at the idea. Cathy hoped she wouldn't offer to join them.

"Blessed is she amongst her kin women. Yes, most sacred. I'll be back in a few minutes." Sister Mary Dorothea left humming "Ave Maria."

Mother and daughters formed a circle next to the window where the crescent moon nestled between two soft gray clouds. Cathy glowed. June felt sheer joy at seeing her mother and sisters poised under the moon, ready to consecrate the newest family addition to the goddess. She thanked Our Lady for the years of guidance. *Catholic girls can make good witches,* she thought.

June raised her arms to the moon. "We declare our new MacDonald girl to be a child of the goddesses, blessed with much love. So mote it be!"

The End.

Dear Reader;

I hope you enjoyed the story. Would you please leave a comment at Amazon.com and/or Goodreads.com—even one sentence?

Thank you,

June Ahern

Made in the USA